THE CAMBRIDGE THEOREM

TONY CAPE

The Cambridge Theorem

A NOVEL

DOUBLEDAY

New York   London   Toronto   Sydney   Auckland

PUBLISHED BY DOUBLEDAY
a division of Bantam Doubleday Dell Publishing Group, Inc.
666 Fifth Avenue, New York, New York 10103

DOUBLEDAY and the portrayal of an anchor with a dolphin are trademarks of
Doubleday, a division of Bantam Doubleday Dell Publishing Group, Inc.

Library of Congress Cataloging-in-Publication Data

Cape, Tony.
    The Cambridge theorem : a novel/Tony Cape.—1st ed.
in the United States of America.
    p.   cm.
    I.   Title.
PR6053.A65C63   1989
823'.914—dc20   89-37607
CIP

ISBN 0-385-26490-9
Printed in the United States of America
March 1990
First Edition in the United States of America
BG

For My Parents

ACKNOWLEDGMENTS

The author wishes to thank Police Constable Alec Garty of Muswell Hill Police, London, for his contribution to the composition of this book.

THE CAMBRIDGE THEOREM

Prologue

THE OLD SPY sat at his study window and watched the dusk gather. It had stopped snowing, and the streetsweepers had left. Below him a streetlamp blinked on and began humming.

Determinedly, an aging matron made her way down the corridor of cleared pavement, her shoulder bowed beneath the weight of a grocery bag. With her other arm she held firm a wriggling child, who jabbed at the embankment of snow and ice with a short stick.

He raised his eyes past the featureless rooftops that were Stalin's architectural legacy to the city. By craning his neck he could just see the illuminated onion domes of St. Basil's in the failing light. After so many years, the sight still cheered him faintly.

The matron, no doubt housekeeper to some dignitary such as himself, was turning into the building like a frigate re-

1

turning to port. The boy hurled his stick into the air as a Chaika limousine drew up and disgorged two passengers before slithering away down Mira Prospekt like a dark fish. At this hour the deskmen from Dzerzhinsky Square returned steadily, always in pairs.

He reached for the glass of whiskey at his elbow and contemplated again the crossword he had clipped from *The Times* that morning. As he had done every day for almost twenty years, he had laboriously ironed the dense cylinder flat before beginning his unhurried review of its contents. He had often reflected that if the KGB were to choose between a mole in the British cabinet and a subscription to *The Times,* he would recommend the latter. Arriving every morning at his post office box, the newspaper had been indispensable to the arc of his career. As a member of the British Establishment himself, he saw through the veiled code of its news reporting like glass, and it had been the simple source of the mordant analyses that had fueled his career in the First Chief Directorate. Now, in restive retirement, he continued quietly to steer his reports to the chairman's office, where he knew they were appreciated. He had usually completed the crossword by midafternoon, but today a final clue eluded him. "Put it with the stars and it flies," two blanks *r*, three blanks *s*, a singular clue with a plural ending. He pushed the clipping aside in annoyance and lit another cigarette, then took a drink of whiskey. The smoky taste was familiar and comforting, and he felt the ache across his skull ease. Since his doctor's warning that his liver would not much longer withstand his habitual half-liter-a-day intake, he now limited himself to two glasses, most nights.

The two Chekists below stamped their feet on the swept flagstones before walking briskly into the building, their breath a white fog against dark coats and hats. He could see clearly where the zone of privilege ended at the street corner, where the government building's swept walkways gave way to the corrugated ice of Moscow's public streets. It was early

2

April 1981, and even for Moscow the frigid weather was lingering. He turned to the other document on his desk, the case officer's report clipped to Conrad's decrypted message, and the polite, handwritten request for his comments from Veleshin. Since his forced retirement he still received the occasional request for commentary on European and particularly British affairs, but he suspected it was only the chairman's patronage that overrode objections to the practice from his enemies in First. Here was corroboration. Veleshin, head of the Third Directorate, was rumored to have become one of the chairman's senior advisers, and the expensive writing paper confirmed that the inquiry came via the chairman's suite itself, not from Veleshin's office at First. He and the chairman were two of the handful of people still alive who knew Conrad's identity, so the invitation was not perhaps surprising. Blunt had known, of course, but although Blunt was blown he would never, ever reveal his knowledge. He had personally assured the chairman of this conviction.

He read again the decrypt of Conrad's puzzling appeal for assistance. A student, of all people? Such a request would have to be met, obviously, uncharacteristic though it seemed. He was being asked to respond to the case officer's opinion, who was predictably recommending that heavy equipment be rolled out of Department Five. But the old spy knew Cambridge, and knew such an approach was unwise. It was then an idea occurred to him.

He thought with sudden nostalgia of his old friend Conrad, a man who was his superior in every way. Conrad was undoubtedly the most successful deep-penetration agent in Soviet history, a solitary, an agent so trusted and skilled no controller had ever run him from Britain. His cover and fieldcraft had always been impeccable, and his commitment unwavering. That he now perceived a threat from such an unlikely source seemed odd, suggesting even the infirmity of age. Certainly, his retirement had been richly earned, but given crucial developments in Britain and America, the reac-

3

tivation had been essential. He wondered if Conrad felt resentment at the unsung nature of his work, but dismissed the
idea immediately. He had never sought reward.

The canaries began their customary evening song. He
glanced at them through the jungle of hanging plants and
ferns, the legacy of Eleanor, his third wife.

From the bedroom, he heard Rufa's low voice, crooning a
lullaby to their youngest boy. The voice rose sharply into an
angry, scolding tone. He knew what had happened. The boy,
wide-eyed and enraptured, had put his finger to his nose and
then to his mouth, a reflexive habit that enraged his mother.
She had a quick temper, this central registry clerk turned
watcher turned devoted wife. She was his fifth and, he presumed, his last.

He let his mind scan the implications of responding to
Conrad's request by playing the new agent, Painter. He had
seen the chairman's hand once more in the decision to circu-
late the recruitment memo to him. The chairman knew his
personal file intimately, and would have been amused by the
coincidence, the strange personal connection from so long
ago. He had been impressed by the simple but ingenious recruitment, the combination of dogged research and initiative
that it displayed. But the head of the Mosque field office was
one of the new breed that the chairman had cultivated: subtle,
intelligent and daring. Painter was untried and relatively un-
trained, but an unorthodox response was perhaps what was
needed. Maybe it was his mood of nostalgia. He remembered
cutting his teeth in the sewers of Vienna during the Dollfuss
pogrom and wanted to offer this unknown scion of former
flesh a like opportunity. He would need to convince the chairman to waive the normal repercussions that followed the discovery of Conrad's identity. It had been a ruthless and expensive rule over the years, and was a potentially awkward issue.
He knew also if he held sway, his enemies at First would
exult, willing the mission to fail. But if it succeeded?

The ailing peasant who nominally occupied the general

secretary's chair could only have a year or two to live, and the chairman was now poised to move. The renewed intelligence from Conrad would only burnish his star, and his files on potential rivals were sedulously groomed, as they all knew. When the move came, the senior offices of the *nomenklatura* would be shaken up, and perhaps even head of the First Chief Directorate would be in the offing. He had not chosen to retire. If the threat to Conrad were removed through his recommendation? It was probably only a policing action after all.

He stared out into the thickening night and thought again of Conrad's extraordinary career, and his seamed face broke into a slow grin. Stripes, of course. Put it with the stars, and it flies. The Stars and Stripes. Quite appropriate. He reached for a pencil and carefully completed the crossword puzzle, then slowly inserted two sheets of paper, with carbon, into the old Cyrillic typewriter. He finished the whiskey, which would be his last that evening. This memo must be meticulously composed, and would take him the rest of the night.

The Prime Minister of Great Britain closed the file and placed it carefully on the rosewood desk, adjusting it so its corner aligned perfectly with the leather writing panel. She understood now why Sir Keith Bowman, her science adviser, had insisted she read it before that afternoon's meeting of the Economic Policy Committee. She reached for the button below her desk to summon her private secretary, but checked herself and adjusted her coiffure, an involuntary gesture.

As she often did in times of reflection, she turned her chair to look across the Downing Street lawn to the sky above Westminster. Heavy metallic clouds were looming in from Stockwell, presaging another autumn storm. October had already been one of the wettest on record.

If the report was not exaggerated, British science was on the threshold of the biggest military breakthrough since the Manhattan Project. The implications were extraordinary.

A movement on the lawn distracted her. A stooped figure dressed like a cricket umpire in a white smock and black trilby was pushing a wheeled contraption across the manicured surface, dispensing pellets across a spiked drum. She really should ask the cabinet secretary where he found such a gallery of eccentrics to tend the grounds. But then she supposed they must all have special clearance, and she ought not interfere.

The brilliance of British scientists was really most reassuring. At least they weren't all lured away to America by huge research fellowships. The President of the United States had already confided to her at their private meeting in Ottawa the previous year the importance he attached to the research. This third generation of nuclear weapons had the potential to render all other nuclear forces obsolete. They could practically emasculate the Soviet threat.

"The shortness of the wavelength, my dear. That's the key to the destructive power, as my science people explain it. We really must get there first—between us," he had told her.

The gardener had moved away from his machine toward a group of pigeons that blocked his path, flapping his hands at them as if signaling a boundary. They fluttered away and settled a few yards to his right. He resumed his mechanical grooming hesitantly after a glance at the sky. Large spots of rain hit the window with surprising force.

She was pleased the breakthrough had been made in British laboratories. The Americans would not like it, but the Americans would have no choice. It would mean millions in defense contracts and inestimable prestige for her government. The Wets would be silenced, once and for all. Wimps, the President had called them, she thought with a smile. For all their vulgarity, the Americans could occasionally turn the right phrase. Let them all defect to the Wine and Cheese Party. Her Conservatives, the real Conservatives, would be swept into a second term.

6

She would be sure to give Sir Keith's request for an additional research appropriation her full endorsement.

The student bar of St. Margaret's College was crowded and full of smoke and din. In a corner booth sat a young man and a woman, somewhat similar in appearance, arguing. Across the littered bar table from them sat a second young man, listening distractedly to their discussion and nursing an almost empty glass of beer in his lap. Occasionally he removed a hand from the glass to push the heavy-lensed spectacles up on the bridge of his nose with a forefinger. He sat hunched on a low barstool.

The woman wore a white shirt, dark jeans and a long, old-fashioned coat that hung open, and leaned accusingly toward her opponent, propping a foot against the table. He slouched backward in the booth, his hand resting absently on her knee. He had luxuriant black hair which reached the collar of an old blazer, and a strong, handsome face. He wore a red T-shirt and white painter's overalls. He kept glancing over to their companion as if for support. The woman shook a crown of unruly curls at him in exasperation.

The woman wheeled around to the hunched figure and said something he obviously did not hear. She repeated the question and he answered hesitantly, chewing at the corner of his thumb. She gave him a sudden dazzling smile, her eyes widening behind the round-rimmed glasses. Then she turned again to her combat.

The young man made no response. Unlike his friends, he seemed awkward and tense and downtrodden, his light hair unkempt and unwashed, his complexion pitted, a striped jersey that was too big for him, corduroy jeans that sagged at the crotch. He looked down into the remains of his beer and then toward the exit, making no effort to listen for the thread of their argument.

Two other young men suddenly pushed through the crowd toward them with noisy greetings, and the couple in the

7

booth began to make room for them. The nonparticipant seemed to take this as a cue, gulping the dregs of his beer and standing. He leaned forward and pressed the woman on the shoulder, held up his hand to the man, and edged away from the table, picking up an ancient sports jacket from the floor. One of the newcomers immediately took the vacant stool. The couple in the booth looked at each other, then exchanged a theatrical shrug. Their friend had already left.

The young man stopped and caught his breath in the sudden silence of night, then began skirting the west side of Great Court, passing in and out of the pools of light at the foot of each staircase. He paused and looked across the lawn to the brightly lit porters' lodge, as if weighing a decision, then continued, quickening his step. The illuminated clockface above the lodge read ten fifteen.

In the passageway to Second Court a group of singers poured out from the chapel, still rehearsing Easter madrigals, and forced him to step aside. As they passed, an inner urgency seemed to take him over, and he covered the last twenty yards to his staircase at an awkward trot. He took the stairs to the first landing two at a time, wheeled left and entered his room. The corridor, lit by a single bulb, was silent, except for the sound of a labored breathing and the muffled fall of a bolt into its metal pouch as the door was locked from the inside.

Inside his room the young man had taken his seat at a desk just inside the door. The room was dark except for a narrow disk of light from a small adjustable lamp above the electric typewriter. He removed a manila file from the desk drawer, placed it beside the typewriter, and then, reaching further in, withdrew a sheet of typing paper. His hands shook slightly as he rolled the paper into the machine, and more noticeably as he straightened the sheet and then hesitated, his right index finger poised over the power switch. He dropped his hand and then carefully placed both elbows on the desk in front of the machine, slowly taking his head in his hands, then run-

8

ning his hands backward through the limp hair into a clasp at the back of the neck. Then he made a guttural sound, which might have been a sigh, or a grunt of determination.

Nigel Hawken caught his telephone on the third ring. He had been deeply asleep but reacted instinctively. Phone calls after midnight were never good news.

He snapped on the bedside light and stiffened when he heard the voice on the end of the line. "What the hell are you doing calling me here?" he hissed.

"Simon Bowles is dead. He's hanged. I just found him."

Hawken was horrified. He demanded to know how he had discovered the body, what he was doing visiting a student after one in the morning. The answer almost caused him to panic.

"You wretched man! Are you telling me you have been in the habit of visiting this person for weeks, even months? Why have you never told me?"

"Well, Nigel, I knew it wasn't allowed, that you would be angry."

"You fool. You bloody fool. What else did you find?"

"Nothing. I panicked and ran back here to the lodge and called you. What am I going to do?"

"Nothing. No one saw you, did they?"

"No."

"And, Alan, no one in the lodge knows of our association, do they?"

"No."

"All right. Say nothing. Take a day off if you need to. I will pretend this phone call never happened. We'll let the bedder find him."

"So what should I do?"

"Nothing. You didn't touch anything in the room, did you?"

"No, of course not."

"Go home. Understand? And, Alan?"

9

"Yes?"

"Never call me at home again. Never. Understand?"

"Yes. I'm sorry. I'm just . . . I'm very upset."

He and his wife had slept in separate rooms for years, but he was concerned the call had woken her. He stepped out onto the landing and walked toward the bathroom.

"Who was that, Nigel?" she called.

"That was Sir Felix, my dear, of all people. Completely in his cups. Had no idea what the time was. He wanted to give me the latest gossip about the general election, of all things."

"He gets worse."

"He does indeed. Go back to sleep, Gwen."

One

DETECTIVE SERGEANT DEREK SMAILES threw the statements down on his blotter in disgust and tilted his chair back to stare at the ceiling. Last year's water leak had left brown stains on the stippled concrete of its surface. The one above his head looked like the map of Australia.

He already knew what would happen to the two juvenile miscreants he and Swedenbank had interviewed the previous week. A judicious call from Chief Superintendent George Dearnley to the head of the bus company, and the charges would be dropped. The two teenagers would be hauled in for a tongue-lashing and warned to stay on the right side of the law in future. Although they probably would, he still felt angry.

Acting Detective Constable Swedenbank had not done a bad job with the statements, considering it was a first effort, but Smailes always wondered why police statements had to be written in a foreign language. Policespeak had always irritated him, because no one actually talked like that, except perhaps his father. He often wondered whether his father, if he had lived, would have derived any satisfaction from his modest success with Cambridge CID. He doubted it. That would have been completely out of character.

Swedenbank came noisily into the office and thrust a lunch box into his filing cabinet. He was a clumsy man with untidy manners and an overeagerness that he tried to contain around Smailes. He was also one of the hairiest people Smailes had ever met, barely hacking a clearing for his features from the bush that enveloped him. There were dark patches of hair under his eyes that his razor did not reach. Though three years his junior, he looked older than Smailes, with the haggardness of married men in debt. His new tweed sports jacket made him look conspicuously out of uniform. He saw the statements on Smailes's desk.

"Are they okay, Sergeant?" he asked casually.

"They're fine, Ted. I don't think you left anything out. Not that they're ever likely to see the light of day in court."

"Yes, I guessed that," said Swedenbank, trying to sound rueful. "Pretty upper-crust pair, really. No TICs, no juvenile record. Probably just a lark, really."

When they had been called to the headmaster's study at the Crowe School the previous week to interview the two terrified suspects, Smailes had immediately recognized the older boy as the son of one of the big-time desk jockeys at County Hall. The two boys, day students at Cambridge's minor public school, had been caught by a vigilant conductor using forged bus passes on the trip to school. It had been a minor but potentially damaging fraud, but Smailes was satisfied only the two dud cards had been made. The pair were hardly hardened criminals, and had confessed the whole scheme with little prodding. Smailes had let Swedenbank take them into the secretary's office for statements while the headmaster, an old-timer with academic gown and half-moon glasses,

12

had asked Smailes whom he could call at the Cambridge police station to keep the matter out of the courts. The boys were from good families and had bright academic futures. They were probably unaware of the criminal nature of their actions. Like hell, Smailes thought, but gave him George Dearnley's name anyway.

If Swedenbank had any sense, he would recognize the surname of the older boy and realize the matter would probably be dropped. But he couldn't also know that the County Hall official, whose son had been caught red-handed in a petty crime, was also one of the chief super's regular tennis partners, which would settle the matter beyond doubt. Smailes had known George Dearnley all his life, and had played tennis with him regularly as a teenager. The chief super had been one of the top amateurs in the county.

Smailes did not tell the headmaster of the Crowe School that he could save his breath. There ought to be some consequences, no matter how minor.

What bothered him as he rocked his chair back onto all fours and gathered the statements was the feeling that the score might have been different had the offenders been ordinary lads from the Comprehensive, as he had been. A kid from a council estate in Cottenham or Histon would no doubt have found himself hauled before the juvenile magistrate, fined, probation, criminal record, the lot. He felt irritated by these thoughts, and turned sharply to Swedenbank, who had the knack of making him feel off balance.

"Yeah, just a stupid lark, I guess," he agreed. "They were scared shitless enough they'll stay clean. Take these up to Gloria, will you, Ted?"

Smailes handed Swedenbank the statements for Dearnley's secretary and saw him stiffen at the insignificance of the task, and probably also at the mid-Atlantic swagger in his voice. He tried to keep the American patter out of his dealings with his fellow officers, because he knew it sounded affected, which it wasn't. It was just the way he talked.

13

Smailes got up as the ADC left the room and walked to the window. It was midmorning and he hadn't had a cigarette yet, which pleased him. He could see across Parker's Piece to the green copper towers and featureless modern façade of the Cambridge Arms Hotel. A few loners were out with dogs and a long-haired pedestrian made slow progress toward the hotel, the collar of his donkey jacket turned up against the late March wind. It was Wednesday of the week before Easter, always a bleak time of the year. Over by the central lamppost a Labrador lowered its snout in a charge at a group of sea gulls. They wheeled into the air, shrieking. Below him a bread van honked its horn at a bicyclist who was approaching the roundabout too wide.

The sky hung low like a dirty washcloth. He heard a trace of melody in his mind and smiled. Willie Nelson's version of "Blue Skies." He loved that man's music. He could almost smell the mescal and sagebrush in his songs, which spoke to him of oil derricks and old trucks, an idyll of masculinity where the cowboys wore their heartbreak as proudly as their Stetsons. His proudest possessions were his collection of Western shirts, and in particular his hand-tooled lizard-skin cowboy boots that had cost him almost a week's pay at a fancy London boutique. Sometimes he fantasized showing up for morning briefing in a pigtail and bandanna, seeing the chief super's face. He smiled sadly at the ordinariness of the morning.

Derek Smailes was a big man with big hands and feet and sandy hair that he combed forward in short waves. This was probably a mistake, as he looked baby-faced already, but he'd never worked out what else to do with it. He had always looked younger than he was, but he didn't mind that, now that he was almost thirty. Thirty, divorced and broke, he reminded himself. He had too much weight on his big frame, which didn't bother him much, although his mother nagged him about the beer and cigarettes. His father had been dead of a heart attack on this side of sixty, she reminded him. He

wore the nondescript civilian clothes of policemen everywhere, and expensive shoes. He always bought expensive
shoes. They lasted longer.

He felt annoyed by Swedenbank's simple enthusiasm, a
quality he had never mastered. It would probably make Swedenbank a better detective than he would ever be, because
Derek Smailes acknowledged that, for all his ability, he never
quite had the gas for the extra mile. Although he was the son
of a policeman, he remained an outsider who had never quite
learned the policeman's lore, and he was sure his senior officers knew it, including his Uncle George.

The phone rang. It was Paula in the Operations Room, and
her voice still wore the injured edge it had had since he had
stopped seeing her around Christmastime.

"Smailes."

"Derek, we've got a sudden death at St. Margaret's College
in Trinity Street. Apparent suicide. Whiskey Michael Three
has responded."

"On my way," said Smailes as Swedenbank came back into
the room, still wearing his subordinate's scowl.

"Let's go, Ted," said Smailes, reaching for his raincoat
from the back of the door. "Topper at St. Meg's. Get the PRs
from the desk. I'll bring the car round front."

"Own goal, is it?" said Swedenbank, brightening. Smailes
snorted at the notion that a student terrorist might have
blown himself up with a bomb.

Outside the Gothic portal of St. Margaret's College, one of
Cambridge University's oldest, a small crowd had gathered to
gawk at the police car and ambulance parked on the apron of
cobblestones. The panda car had left its light flashing, an unnecessary ostentation that irritated Smailes. He drew his car
alongside as Swedenbank handed him his personal radio.
Both men clipped them to their lapels and drew their coats
against the cold as they stepped through the massive gate of
the college.

He felt the instinctive resentment of a townsperson as he

walked into the large courtyard, a sudden island of calm privilege just yards from one of Cambridge's busiest streets. A distinguished-looking man in a black suit, white shirt and gray tie approached them from the porters' lodge on their right.

"Gentlemen, are you with the police?" he asked, in a softened East Anglian accent.

"Detective Sergeant Smailes and Detective Constable Swedenbank," said Smailes, figuring that Ted would be gratified he left "Acting" out of the introduction.

"I'm Paul Beecroft, the head porter," he said gravely. "Please follow me."

Beecroft was obviously advanced in years, but he set off around the court at a stiff pace. Smailes jogged two steps to bring himself alongside.

"Can you tell us what happened?"

"Young fellow, research student. Name of Simon Bowles. Strung himself up, seems like. The bedder found him this morning. Called you right away, when I got the okay."

Smailes knew what he meant. Cambridge police were never summoned to a University college without the approval of the senior dons, and they needed a warrant to enter of their own accord. They could probably clean up half the drugs in town if they could ever get approval for a raid, which, of course, they never could. That was another thing about the University that Smailes resented.

Swedenbank had drawn up against Beecroft's other shoulder. He was keeping quiet and the scowl was gone. Smailes realized that if he had to nurse an ADC around, he could do a lot worse than Ted.

Beecroft led them past the ornate fountain in the middle of the court and through a passageway into a second, smaller court. Smailes guessed it was probably eighteenth-century, the first court obviously older. Here were simple, three-story buildings, mullioned windows, plenty of ivy. They made their way around the lawn to a staircase where he recognized

Bert Ainsworth of the uniformed branch through a crowd of students. He was stationed directly in front of the stairs.

"Excuse me, ladies and gentlemen," said Beecroft, with exaggerated courtesy. "Please go on with your business. The police have work to do."

The students backed away slightly, but showed no signs of leaving. There were maybe a dozen, men and women.

"Who is it, Mr. Beecroft? Is it Simon? What's happened?" asked a young man in a bus driver's overcoat.

Beecroft ignored the inquiry and marched up the stairs to the first landing. Smailes was directly behind him.

"Tell Bert to let no one up. No one," he said over his shoulder, and Swedenbank retreated back down the stairs.

On the landing he could see two men in the familiar black uniform of the ambulance service. Over their shoulders he could see another uniformed policeman whose face he knew but whose name escaped him.

The passageway, lit by a single naked bulb, was crowded. Beecroft indicated a door at one end.

"He's in there."

"Smailes, CID," he said, advancing past the ambulance men to the constable. He could feel his pulse quicken, and he was short of breath from matching Beecroft's pace from the lodge and up the stairs. "What we got?"

"He's been dead for a while, sir. Hung himself. I'm Dickley, sir. Just transferred from Huntingdon," said the constable. He seemed embarrassed and at a loss.

"Have you called the coroner's officer?" asked Smailes. The ambulance men were obviously impatient to leave, but someone had to pronounce the subject dead first. No ambulance man would touch an obviously dead body. His unit would have to be decontaminated and he would probably lose overtime while it was out of service.

"No, sir. We just checked him and closed up. Just been here five minutes."

Dickley was apparently hesitant on his first week with Division. It would have been fine for him to get the coroner's wagon over if the man was obviously dead.

"Who found him?" asked Smailes. He knew he was putting off having to go into the room. Beecroft stepped forward. "The bedder, Mrs. Allen, sir. She's in the kitchen." He indicated with a nod a second room down the passageway as a short, bespectacled figure emerged from it.

"Officer? How do you do?" The man edged sideways past the ambulance men and held out his right hand. Smailes saw that his left arm hung uselessly at his side, its fingers buckled into a claw.

"I'm Nigel Hawken, senior tutor of this college. I've been trying to comfort Mrs. Allen. She's quite shaken up, I'm afraid."

Hawken was a man in his middle or late sixties with steel-gray hair, a stubby gray mustache and gold-rimmed spectacles. He was wearing blue pinstripes and a red tie with dogs on it.

Smailes shook his hand. "Detective Sergeant Derek Smailes, CID," he said again.

Hawken looked agitated. He had a florid complexion and an erect, military bearing. Smailes decided he probably smoked a pipe.

"When was he found?"

"About half an hour ago. We called right away," said Hawken. His voice sounded like ripe fruit.

Smailes took the handle of the door and went in, with Hawken on his shoulder.

The room was a small, dark study-bedroom, lined on two sides with books. Immediately inside the door to his left was a desk with a modern typewriter sitting in a pool of light from a desk lamp. Beyond was a single bed, made, although it looked as if someone, or some people, had been sitting on it. It had a plain blue counterpane and was overhung with the first of many shelves of books. Against the opposite wall were two armchairs flanking an electric fire set into an old fireplace. To the right was a black four-drawer filing cabinet and a standing bookcase of the same height. In the center of the room was a stained rug, possibly Oriental.

One reason the room was so dark was that the leaded windows were small and shrouded by a number of hanging plants. Another reason was that they were partly obscured by the body of a young man that hung from a belt from one of the heavy plant hooks screwed into the oak window frame. A small wooden chair was tipped over underneath the body and another potted plant in its hanging basket was sitting on the floor beside it. It looked like an aspidistra.

There was a poster, an enlarged photograph of some white-haired man, pinned to the wall to the left of the windows, near what Smailes assumed was a clothes closet. The scene made him feel terrible.

He advanced to the limp figure of the young man, whose feet swung grotesquely in the air, the head twisted in an unnatural angle against the neck. Despite his bravado, Smailes didn't like stiffs. He didn't like them at all.

Swedenbank came up beside him, breathing heavily. Smailes felt the young man's hand. It was cold. He turned to Hawken, distracted momentarily by the ADC's face, which was turned up toward the dead boy as if in supplication.

"Anything been moved?"

"No. Everything is as Mrs. Allen found it."

"Who has been in the room?"

"Well, Mrs. Allen, myself, the ambulance men and the policemen. No one has touched anything, I think. We were waiting for you," said Hawken.

Smailes could tell from the edge in his voice that Hawken didn't like answering questions. He was the type who liked to ask them. He noted the tone of accusation that they had arrived late, and ignored it. Smailes hated having civilians watch his work.

"Will you excuse us for a few minutes, Mr. . . . ?" Smailes fished for his name.

19

"Dr. Hawken. Dr. Nigel Hawken. Certainly," he said icily, and left the room.

"Poor bugger," said Swedenbank as Hawken closed the door. He had not stopped looking at the grimace on the dead boy's face. Smailes realized it was his first hanging.

"Yeah, well, at least he didn't make a mess of it," said Smailes. "See what you can find. Maybe a note."

Swedenbank retreated toward the door as Smailes knelt under the body. The chair had tipped away after the boy had kicked it. Looked as if he had set the plant down first. Careful type.

He looked up at the body, growing more used to its presence. Longish fair hair over the collar of a rugby shirt. Acne scars. Skinny build, corduroy jeans, tennis shoes. The watch on the boy's wrist was still running. It showed a quarter to eleven.

He reached inside the jeans back pocket and removed a wallet, something that Dickley should have done. In the left front pocket he found some change and a pair of spectacles in a case. The wallet contained seven pounds, a credit card, various library cards and some folded papers.

"Sarge, look at this." Swedenbank was standing over the desk with his back to him.

What he was indicating was a typed sheet in the platen of the typewriter. Smailes took out a handkerchief and rolled it upward. It was fairly brief.

"They came back. I couldn't take it. Simon." It was the first typed note Smailes had seen.

He opened the desk drawer with the handkerchief. Pens, pencils, a roll of tape. A key ring and a checkbook. Further in, a partly used ream of typing paper.

He removed the keys and went over to the fireplace. Six shelves of books in the standing case. The filing cabinet was locked. The small key from the young man's ring fitted and in the first drawer Smailes found neatly arranged hanging files. The first read *Abominable Snowman.*

Swedenbank was examining the bookcase above the bed. Smailes left the filing cabinet unlocked and walked over to inspect the poster of the white-haired gent, who looked familiar to him. It was Bertrand Russell, or one of the Alberts, Schweitzer or Einstein, Smailes wasn't sure which.

"Seen enough, Sarge?" asked Ted. Smailes had to hand it to him. He wasn't doing badly for a first suicide.

"Yeah, I think so."

"How long has he been dead?"

"Maybe eight, ten hours. Joints in the fingers already stiff. Light still on the desk, bed not slept in. Funny thing about rigor mortis. It'll go away in a few hours."

"What do you make of the note?"

"Dunno. Little bit fishy. First typed note I've seen. I'd like to know who 'they' are."

"Prints, pictures?"

"Well, the scenes-of-crimes boys have to come in for the snaps, but forget the prints. It's pretty routine. Get the coroner's officer on the radio and tell them to get their wagon down here. The ambulance boys can scarper. Bert and I can help with the stocking stuffing.

"Tell the SOCO boys we need pictures, then get the full ID, next of kin, from your man Beecroft. Hop a ride back with Dickley and help him with the SD report. He didn't have the sense to empty the pockets or secure the note. Take these things, will you, Ted?"

There was reassurance in the mechanics of police procedure after the untidy violence of Bowles's terrible deed. Smailes handed over the personal effects and pulled the note from the typewriter. He didn't need to tell Ted what to do at the station, and was relieved. Swedenbank was gratified at the deference being shown him. His hands looked as if they were wearing fingerless woolen mittens as he took the belongings from Smailes. There was an odd intimacy in the gesture. The two detectives avoided each other's eyes.

"Thanks, Sarge."

"Sure, Ted."

Smailes could hear Swedenbank issuing orders to the ambulance men: yes, the detective sergeant would verify death; yes, he would send for the coroner; no, they didn't need to stay. Then he heard him in slightly brusquer terms telling Dickley to accompany him to the porters' lodge so they could be sure to get the details right. Ted seemed to have the tone of injured authority just right.

He folded up Bowles's note and put it in his jacket pocket with the dead boy's keys before leaving the room. The typed note was unusual, but from the neatness of the room and the filing cabinet, it didn't seem entirely out of character. He found Hawken in the cramped kitchen off the other side of the landing, standing solicitously over Mrs. Allen, who was drinking tea. Her face was flushed beneath a wreath of gray curls, her considerable weight crumpled onto a small stool. She started to get up as Smailes entered the small room.

"No, please. Rest your legs," he said gently.

She seemed gratified and blinked into the chipped mug, which she held with both hands.

"Would you like to question Mrs. Allen here or in my rooms, Officer?" Hawken asked. He obviously felt he should be in charge. Smailes had not planned to question anyone yet, but Hawken had forced a response.

"I don't want to keep you, Mrs. Allen. I'm with Cambridge CID. Just tell me what happened here this morning." He avoided words like "body" and "dead man."

"Well," she said, gathering herself with a sniff and setting her mug down on the edge of the steel sink.

"I comes up 'ere to the first floor about ten o'clock. I usually does 'is room first, because 'e's usually not there. I knocked, as I always do, because sometimes the young gentlemen are sleepin' or something and they calls out if they don't want you to come in.

"As usual, there was no reply, so I goes in. I don't take the

22

broom and duster in first because I like to get the old coffee cups and plates out to the kitchen before I start on the room.

"I didn't even see him at first. I looked on 'is desk and by the fireplace and there was no mugs and then I looks by the winder and I seen him 'anging there."

Here she faltered and began to wring her hands in her lap. The two men waited in silence.

"So then I runs out down the steps to the lodge and I tells Mr. Beecroft that young Mr. Bowles has 'ung himself. Then I waited while he was on the phone and came back 'ere with him and made some tea while Dr. Hawken arrived. Then all these police and ambulance fellas came. But it's no good. 'E's dead, i'n't he?"

"Yes, I'm afraid he is," said Smailes.

"Such a nice young fella. So quiet and shy and neat, not like some of them. Real slobs they are, Officer. You wouldn't believe some of the things I 'ave to clean up."

Here Hawken interceded. "Well, thank you, Mrs. Allen. Sergeant?"

"No more questions, Mrs. Allen. We may need you to make a statement."

The remark did not seem to register on her.

"Take the rest of the day off, Mrs. Allen. Just tell Beecroft on your way out that you're going home," said Hawken.

Smailes stepped out of the tiny kitchen onto the landing as Bert Ainsworth came up the stairs with the DC from the coroner's office and two mortuary attendants. Ainsworth stepped up and said in a low voice, "We told them to bring the wagon up the drive on the Backs. Less of a crowd."

Derek Smailes had always liked Bert Ainsworth. He was old school; no procedural hand-wringing like Dickley.

Smailes handed him the folded suicide note.

"This is the young fella's note. Give it to the coroner's DC, will you, Bert, and help them get the body in the bag," said Smailes. The other officers had already disappeared into Bowles's room. Mrs. Allen made her way gingerly down the steps as Hawken watched her. He turned to look at Smailes, who noticed for the first time how short he was. The disabled arm made him look almost frail. The light from the overhead bulb made his glasses flash like mirrors.

"Sergeant, I suggest we discuss this matter further in my rooms," he said.

"Certainly," said Smailes, catching part of the formality of his speech. He turned to Ainsworth.

"Stick around for the SOCO boys, Bert, and then secure the room yourself." He handed Ainsworth the dead man's keys. "Put these in the personal bag at the station—and keep an eye on Dickley, will you?" He winked at Ainsworth, who grinned.

He followed Hawken down the stairs and out into the court, where the crowd of students had dissipated.

Two

DEREK SMAILES had never intended to join the police force. In fact, he had resisted the idea vehemently when his father had begun to suggest it after he entered the sixth form and started seeing Yvonne. His father had liked Yvonne from the beginning. She showed Harry Smailes the frank deference he expected from the world, and her father was a fire captain, well within the canon of his acceptance.

His father, with some justification, had always been skeptical of his chances for university, although Derek resented his pessimism. By the time he was seventeen, he had to deal with the insistent suggestion that he should look around for a career, that he should consider alternatives if he decided to settle down. The prospect appalled him. While he was quite determined to find a strategy to conquer Yvonne's sexual resolve, he had no intentions of settling down. He wanted to leave Cambridge and go away to college, like any other teen-ager with half a chance.

He resisted the suggestion of police service as a career with the violent mixture of indignation and remorse that always characterized his dealings with his father. It was absurd for someone with his prospects, however modest, to toss them away on a career that did not require even A levels. And besides, he would never try to follow his father's act at Cambridge police station. It would be an impossible task.

At the same time, he realized that a career in the police appealed to him acutely. He was unsure whether the attraction was the tug of a genetic imperative or that compliance was simply the only way he could ever amount to anything in his father's eyes. He dismissed the idea as ridiculous and told no one of it. He could never fit in over there. For Christ's sake, he liked books. And besides, he would never subject any future offspring of his to the grief and isolation he had suffered as a policeman's child. For some reason he could not explain, Derek Smailes found himself preoccupied with thoughts of his past as he stared at the back of Nigel Hawken's head, the steel-gray hair and the crisp white collar above the blue pinstripes.

Hawken was standing at a modern glass cabinet with his back to the detective. "Sherry?" he asked over his shoulder, the syllables rhyming.

It was only eleven-thirty and Smailes was on duty, but he didn't hesitate. You never really got used to it. You just switched something off in your mind, pretending that the deceased was not someone who had shared your humanity, like air.

"Yes, thank you," he said, resisting the temptation to rock back on his heels and say, "Don't mind if I do."

Hawken looked more like a banker than an academic. He had led the detective to a large suite of rooms overlooking the main court of St. Margaret's. They were in a spacious sitting room with oak-paneled walls and college crests around the

26

picture rail. Former luminaries of St. Margaret's gazed bleakly in oils from the long wall which faced the door. Smailes could see through a partially open door into a cluttered study where Hawken obviously did his paperwork. At the far end was another door, which probably led to a bedroom.

The sitting room was furnished in a combination of somber traditional mahogany and Danish modern. Two large butcher-block sofas faced each other across a low coffee table, on which were stacked copies of *National Geographic* and *Foreign Affairs*. The room reminded him vaguely of the headmaster's study at the Crowe School.

Hawken handed him a small crystal glass and indicated the sofa with a gesture of his hand. Smailes declined, reaching into his raincoat pocket for his first cigarette. He took the coat off and laid it carefully over the back of the couch.

He had been right about Hawken's smoking habits, since he had begun stuffing a pipe skillfully with his single good hand and was regarding him steadily.

"Officer, before we proceed, may I ask you whether we can keep this matter out of the newspaper? I see nothing to be gained from a lot of garish publicity, and these things do tend to bring the college a bad name," he began.

Christ, it was always the same story. Forget the culprit or the victim, what about the reputations of the rest of us? This time he had no inclination to comply.

"I'm afraid not, sir," he said. "We update the press twice daily from the incident book, and there's no way we could keep a suicide from them. Besides, there will have to be an inquest. The coroner's office has already taken over."

Hawken shook his head in resignation. The news seemed to worsen his mood of glacial displeasure. Smailes had seen detachment before, but Hawken's response to this tragic death seemed extreme.

"Very well, then. How can I help you?" he asked wearily.

"Perhaps I should ask first to see the Master of the college.

27

He is the senior official, I think?" He suspected this inquiry was going to annoy Hawken, and he was right.

"Sir Felix Apsley is indeed the head of the college, but the position of Master is somewhat, er, ceremonial, shall we say. Bestowed by the government. Sir Felix is up in town, and I shall of course inform him of this unfortunate event. But for all practical purposes, as senior tutor, I am the administrative head of this college."

"Well, tell me what you can about the dead man. Simon Bowles was his name, I think," said Smailes baldly.

"Brilliant chap, no doubt about it. One of the highest scholarship papers we had ever seen. Mathematics, you know. But unstable, I'm afraid. You see, he had tried it before."

"You mean he had attempted suicide before?" asked Smailes, taking out a small notebook. "When was this?"

"Well, I'm not sure. Before his Finals. Must be nearly two years ago. Jumped out the ruddy window. There was a terrible fuss. He was in the asylum for a month or so. Thought it might be the last we'd see of him. But he made quite a recovery and the faculty committee went and awarded him a research fellowship, even though he only had the *aegrotat.*"

Hawken became distracted by his attempts to tamp down the tobacco in his pipe with a gadget from his pocket. He walked over to the window and began to stare out at the court.

Smailes stopped scribbling in his notebook. "I'm sorry, sir, I don't follow. What was the illness you say he had?"

"An *aegrotat?* Good Lord, no. That's a type of degree. When you're medically unfit to sit your exams, you get an *aegrotat.* Means 'he is ill,' I think," said Hawken impatiently. He began to wave a great flare of flame over his pipe.

"I'm sorry, Dr. Hawken, but could you explain further? How long had Simon Bowles been a student here?" Smailes was irritated by the condescension.

"As I said, Officer, he came up as an undergraduate with one of the highest marks we had ever seen on an entrance paper. As I understood it, he did as well as expected. First in Part One. Looked like he was heading for a double First when he went to pieces.

"I'd rather forgotten about him at the time—I only ever knew him by sight. Heard the story later from his tutor, Professor Davies. Decent chap. Arch. and anth. You should talk to him. Knew a lot more about Bowles than I did."

"Ark and what, I'm sorry?" asked Smailes.

"Archaeology and anthropology. Davies's field. Anyway, seems he was working frantically, Bowles I mean, and then he had some bad news, I think perhaps his father died, and he started to go off the deep end. Always gets to them, Finals term. The unstable types," said Hawken, attempting to sound sympathetic, and failing.

"Had he received help from anyone in the college, or doctors?" asked Smailes.

"Well, Davies knew all about it. Had him under medical supervision. But it didn't do any good. Never does, does it? He was found one night lying in the court. Luckily he had only fallen fifteen feet or so, and broken his ankle. But his mind was completely gone. Babbling about snakes. They took him to the hospital, then out to Myrtlefields."

The name of Cambridge's famous mental hospital sent a chill down Smailes's spine. Since boyhood, it had been synonymous with the direst of fates. He had lived in Cambridge all his life, but had never even driven past it.

Hawken seemed to have hit a stride. He was standing in profile against the window, the four fingers of his good hand tucked into the flap of his jacket pocket, addressing the portrait of some walrus-faced don in a mortarboard and ermine-fringed gown. Smailes realized it was Harold Macmillan.

"I was involved a little at the time, with the family, but I left most of it to Davies. Family is from Rickmansworth, as I recall. His sister is married to a vicar. I suppose we should inform them. Is it my job to call?"

"No, sir. My assistant, DC Swedenbank, is taking care of

that. He will have got the particulars from Mr. Beecroft. We never call. Always send a constable around from the local force. That way there's always someone there, in case of an extreme reaction. You understand."

Like hell he does, thought Smailes.

Hawken turned to face him directly through a cloud of blue smoke.

"So anyway, he missed the Finals, obviously, and the committee gave him an *aegrotat,* no problem about that. But then they decided that he had been so certain to score the highest in his exams that they gave him the research fellowship after all. There were two or three other chaps in the running too.

"I said nothing at the time, but I wondered if the committee wasn't backing a bit of a game horse. Wasn't sure he'd take the pace, you know."

Smailes wanted to get the details straight, so he made Hawken go back over them.

"So, the first suicide attempt was two years ago. He jumped out of a window. The window of the same room he killed himself in?"

"Yes, I'm fairly sure," said Hawken.

"Then he was hospitalized for a time, then returned to the college as a graduate fellow. How had his progress been since then?"

"Well, I hadn't heard any more about him, so I assumed he was doing all right. Davies was out of the country most of last year, but he took him on again as a tutorial student when he came back. I asked him to let me know if he heard he was having problems."

Hawken seemed to find the subject of Bowles unusually irritating. Smailes wondered if it was Hawken's obvious military training that engendered this attitude toward self-inflicted death, or whether it was really the prospective publicity that was annoying him. He passed by the detective on his way back to the cocktail cabinet, and Smailes could see the fine web of burst capillaries in his cheeks that gave his complexion its unnatural glow. Such faces were usually the product of healthy outdoor pursuits or less healthy indoor ones. Hawken looked the Labrador-and-shooting-stick type, but the way he was waving his decanter around at this time of the morning made Smailes wonder.

"Did he continue to see a doctor, the people out at Myrtlefields?" he continued.

"I'm afraid you'll have to ask Davies—I'm really not sure." He held up the sherry decanter and raised his eyebrows. Smailes declined.

"You know nothing that might have precipitated this act—trouble with money, girlfriends, drugs? Was Professor Davies involved in any special surveillance on this man?"

Again, Hawken appeared to take offense.

"Certainly not. The college recognizes the privacy of its members—junior and senior—to a very fine degree. If Mr. Bowles was in some kind of difficulty, it would have been up to him to initiate a discussion of the matter with his tutor.

"I had heard nothing which might suggest Mr. Bowles might be about to make an attempt on his life again. But it does seem to bear out my concerns that he was inappropriate material for a fellowship."

You bastard, thought Smailes. What if young Bowles didn't like this bloke Davies? Where did he go then? What role did the tutor play anyway?

"Perhaps you could explain a little further to me the relationship between the student and the tutor. It might be helpful when I see Dr. Davies."

Hawken assumed an attitude of amused tolerance. "Well, it's a bit old-fashioned, I suppose, but all the men at Cambridge have both a director of studies and a moral tutor. It's a very long tradition. The director of studies concerns himself with the academic affairs of the student, and the tutor—we've sort of dropped the moral bit over the years—is in charge of, well, moral welfare, shall we say. He meets with the student at regular intervals, reviews academic progress, but also goes over more general things, how things are going, whether there are any problems, things like that."

"Is the relationship, er, optional?" asked Smailes.

"Certainly not," retorted Hawken quickly. "Every man must meet with his tutor at least once a term. It's a requirement for graduation. Of course, for a graduate student, it's not mandatory, but in Bowles's case we thought it wise to insist he keep up the meetings."

"So if anyone from the college knew if there was anything troubling Bowles, it would be Dr. Davies?" He found himself acting deliberately slow to aggravate this arrogant, callous man.

"Yes, yes, that's correct," said Hawken. "I have been thinking. Dr. Poole, a botany chap, is away at Harvard on sabbatical this term and you could use his rooms to conduct further inquiries, if you feel that is necessary. I suspect Dr. Davies is in his rooms. I could arrange for you to speak with him now, if you wish."

Smailes assented, and walked over to the window overlooking the court as Hawken made phone calls. The scene was perfectly normal. Two young women locked in earnest conversation were moving hurriedly past a group of Japanese tourists, all wearing identical tan raincoats. A stout man with a walking stick was gesticulating at the large clock above the porter's lodge and haranguing them. Hawken joined him.

"Well, then, that's all fixed. I'm sorry if I seem a little businesslike about all this. But someone has to take the larger view."

Smailes ignored the remark. "Those young women there—I noticed them outside Bowles's staircase too. Are there women students at this college?"

"Yes, I'm afraid so," said Hawken, resuming his tone of wintry displeasure. "Three years ago. Couldn't hold out any longer, although, God knows, I was in favor of doing so. Not that I object to female students, of course. Frightfully bright, some of them. But they have their own colleges, and I never

32

saw any point in mixing things up. Damn distracting for the men, if you ask me."

"Would seem more natural to me," said Smailes casually. "It's mixed out there in the world too."

"Well, indeed, Sergeant Smailes. But St. Margaret's is in the business of serious scholarship, and personally I have never felt that the presence of women enhanced that aim."

"You mean men study better if they're celibate?" asked Smailes in disbelief.

"Damn it, man, if any chap from this college wants a woman, he can ruddy well go up to London and buy one, as we all did," Hawken exploded.

Smailes gaped at him but could find no reply. There was an awkward silence as Hawken strode back across the room to pick up Smailes's coat.

"Just a couple of things, Dr. Hawken," said Smailes, not knowing in quite what tone to proceed. "Did you see the note the young man left?"

"No, I did not."

"It was in his typewriter. It said 'They came back.' Do you know what he meant?"

"No, I'm afraid I do not. As I have told you, I did not know this young man very well," said Hawken.

He took his coat from Hawken's outstretched hand. There was no longer any ceremony in Hawken's manner.

"I will show you Dr. Poole's rooms. Dr. Davies is on his way over."

"One last thing. Will you try to determine if anyone saw Bowles last night? We always try to find out as much as we can for the report to the coroner, and for the family."

"Certainly. I will ask Mr. Beecroft to see to it right away." He led the detective out of the room.

The old spy shifted his weight again on the hard chair and felt nervously for the carbon copy of his memo in his inside pocket. It was unnecessary, since he knew its contents by heart, but he wanted to be prepared if a particular word or phrasing was queried. He had met the chairman many times during the fourteen years of his tenure, but not usually alone, and not usually in the famous third-floor office of the Lubianka. He was aching for a cigarette, but forced his attention elsewhere, to survey the conference room that formed an outer office of the chairman's suite. At intervals along the green baize of the huge table were small crystal goblets, each containing a sheaf of perfectly sharpened pencils. On the wall opposite the windows was the large, mandatory portrait of Lenin. Above the double walnut doors by which he had entered was a modern, rectangular clock, also of walnut. The time was almost ten-twenty. The only other persons in the room were the uniformed guard at attention by the double doors and the rodent-faced assistant seated impassively at the small desk just outside the door to the private office.

He touched the memo with his fingertips and cleared his throat. He was proud of it. He had always had a mature ease with written expression, and had begun and ended his career in the West as a journalist. He had taken considerable pains to learn the nuance of Russian prose, and could now write better in his adopted language than many native officers. He had long dispensed with translators, and now employed only Rufa to review his grammar and syntax. He looked at the handsome paneled door to the chairman's private office and smiled. When the chairman had taken charge in the late sixties, the only means of entry to his inner sanctum was through a *shkaf,* a contraption that resembled an antique wardrobe. The entrant stepped into the *shkaf* and total darkness, then an assistant activated the mechanism that opened the panel into the inner office. His first order as KGB chairman had been to have the *shkaf* demolished and replaced with an ordinary door. It had been a symbolic beginning, for in the ensuing years the KGB had been transformed from a backward troupe of louts and criminals into an elite corps that now attracted the most talented of Moscow's graduates. For

34

all the puzzling contradictions of his character, the chairman was a man of vision, a vision which might yet work a profound transformation on Soviet society.

The assistant responded to a barely audible buzz on his handset and rose to open the paneled door. The ugly little man turned and silently gestured for the old spy to enter.

His nervousness left him as he strode quickly to accept the proffered handshake from the second most powerful man in the Soviet Union. The tall, stooped figure in a dark business suit smiled slightly as he stood behind the huge desk and indicated a chair with a courteous hand. The men sat down in silence, and the chairman resumed his contemplation of the memorandum in front of him. The Englishman crossed his legs and looked around the room.

The office was a reflection of the enigma of the man himself. The only adornments were the large portrait of Feliks Dzerzhinsky above the marble mantel and a beautiful wooden statue of Don Quixote on his desk. Side by side, the images of the fearsome founder of the Cheka, Lenin's secret police, and the hopelessly pure *chevalier*, the emblem of humanity's unquenchable idealism. Is this how the chairman saw himself, a fabulous knight tilting against endless brutish realities of the police state? He was compounded of contradictions: daring and conservative, enlightened and pitiless, a man who wrote poetry to his friends and family and imprisoned dissidents in psychiatric hospitals. The silver hair and black-rimmed glasses made him seem kindly and professorial, but his reputation for cruelty made him universally feared. He stopped reading and looked up.

"You present an eloquent case, Comrade Colonel," he said, making fastidious distinction between the spy's status, which was general, and his rank, which was colonel.

"I serve the Soviet Union," the old spy replied, and both men smiled. It was the standard declamation, usually barked at attention when receiving a decoration or promotion. The old spy pronounced the formula in his quiet, self-deprecating way, and the chairman nodded in appreciation.

"Indeed, most well. But I fear in this case your suggestion seems unorthodox." The chairman's bland expression did not change.

The old spy maintained an even and unassertive tone. "To use Department Five cannot work at this stage. Cambridge is a closed society. Our response must be suitable for such an environment. All we are talking about is a surveillance operation."

"And if enforcement is needed?"

"There has been some training."

The chairman relaxed his gaze and scanned the memorandum again. The old spy felt a trace of concern that he was perceived as merely squeamish, his gentleman's objection to *mokrei dela,* to wet affairs, being well known.

"Some. But our comrades are most proud of their accomplishments at the Sorge Institute. They do not still wear baggy suits and speak English like Cossacks."

The old spy felt discomfited by the accusation, but stroked his cheek and said nothing.

"Do you know what will be said at First? They will say that our British comrade grows sentimental with his years, that he thinks of his university days and his judgment becomes clouded."

"Why would they know?"

"They will know," said the chairman quietly.

Again the old spy chose to say nothing, knowing that the chairman's decision was made, and that this interview was merely a formality, a warning that if the mission was approved and then failed it would be tagged deliberately to him.

"I have given the question much thought, and I believe I am right. Conrad's identity must be protected at all costs."

"Except from our *gebist?*" asked the chairman, using the slang term for agent, and invoking the inevitable question of consequences.

36

"If the danger passes, our *gebist* should be amply rewarded. Would we not do the same for our Sorge Institute comrades?" The rejoinder had no effect on the chairman's expression, and he knew he could take the matter no further. But he felt if the chairman acceded, he would be acknowledging an implicit condition. Again silence spread out between them and the chairman flicked to the second page of the report.

"It is agreed. We will make this our initial response. I will instruct Veleshin to make arrangements. Do you wish to be involved with briefing?"

Suddenly flushed with surprise and embarrassment, the old spy's lifelong stammer, long quiescent, returned. "I th-think not. The t-travel, at my age. Perhaps a word with C-comrade Veleshin."

"Of course." Unexpectedly, a warm smile lit up the impassive Slavic face. "A brilliant analysis, Comrade Colonel, as I have come to expect from you."

"Thank you, Comrade Andropov," he said, still embarrassed, but luxuriating in the unaccustomed praise.

"Come, no need for such formality."

"Thank you, Yuri Vladimirovich."

"Thank *you*, Igor Andreyevich." Both men exploded in laughter at the use of the preposterous alias that the KGB had given him all those years ago when he had first arrived, an alcoholic and nervous wreck, from Beirut.

"Thank you, Kim. Thank you, Comrade Philby."

He rose and returned the chairman's hearty handshake. With the chairman one could never be sure, but Kim Philby felt they understood each other perfectly.

Three

POOLE'S ROOMS were two courts away from the main court, overlooking the River Cam and the Cambridge Backs. The detective sergeant looked down at the sluggish green water flowing between the brick banks. The boatyards would not open until Easter, the following week, and the river was empty of life except for a lone duck. He could just decipher a slogan that had been painted on the bricks in foot-high white letters, long faded. VIETNAM HOT DAMN, it said, in ugly capitals. He looked further across the expanse of lawn which swept across to Queen's Road and down toward King's College.

Derek Smailes watched the tranquil scene and felt the centuries-old antipathy of the town toward the gown. He loathed the University, the arrogance and patronage that Nigel Hawken personified. The acres of lawn and pasture along the river had once been the center of a busy market town, before the University arrived and commandeered everything. Now its ivory towers squatted like a Gothic lizard along the river and on the center of the town, usurping the best land and commercial property, dictating terms to the elected officials of the council. It was Cambridge's largest employer but paid its workers poorly and instilled in them a fawning subservience that infuriated Smailes. The porters' uniforms were a mockery of his own service. Even when they had helped the college authorities in some tight spots, during the student riots of the early seventies, Cambridge police were always made to feel as if they were a distasteful last resort, representatives of the barbarism of the outside world. The tension between the town and the University had erupted into open violence on numerous occasions in history, although not during his time on the force. The most he had ever seen were isolated cases of grad-bashing, when the local skinheads broke a few teeth on Saturday nights. Like many Cambridge policemen, he secretly sympathized with the local toughs. Who was this kid Bowles anyway? Some neurotic, overprivileged brat with too much brains and too little sense. He would be glad to conclude this investigation and get back into the real world.

He took a look around Poole's rooms, or rather Poole's room. It was a more modest version of Hawken's offices; a sofa which looked as if it might convert into a bed, armchairs, coffee table, desk, telephone and bookshelves. He walked over and examined a shelf. It seemed Dr. Poole had the complete works of Desmond Bagley, in a book-club edition. Smailes turned up his nose.

He wondered if his irritation with St. Margaret's College wasn't in part due to his resentment at never having been to university himself. He could have gone, he knew it. He was always near the top in English, and would probably have gotten high enough marks in the languages to get accepted at a redbrick. Not Cambridge. He wouldn't have wanted to attend this place anyway. Moral tutors indeed. And Hawken, tooling up to town for a woman. It was all quite disgusting.

But despite his lack of formal education he had always been a bookish man, which unhappily Yvonne had resented from the start. It had seemed unimportant at first. There had been the excitement of sexual discovery, the strange miracle of Tracy's birth, the sense of a shared predicament as they entered the unknown territory of marriage and adulthood. Sure, there had always been things they didn't talk about, which Smailes accepted as part of the trade-off of marriage. You hang up the hunting cap, you get square meals and regular sex, and you talk about things that don't interest you. But he had never been one to go out with the lads, and when Tracy was small and down for the night, he preferred to sit with a book in the kitchen than watch television night in and night out. Yvonne began to see it as an implicit criticism, which it wasn't. He just preferred Thomas Hardy to stories about the neighbors during the commercials.

When he looked back, he figured it was during the early imprisonment of his marriage that his fascination with America had really taken hold. It had begun much earlier, in his boyhood, when he would choose to accompany his Uncle Roy up to the Alconburys base just north of town rather than go with his dad to the dog track. His mother's brother Roy was employed as a handyman by the U.S. Air Force and would let Derek ride up with him and carry his toolbox when he worked the weekend shift. Roy would become engrossed fixing the massive steam kettles in the kitchen or tinkering with the refrigeration units in the PX, and Derek would be free to roam around. The base was a chunk of an exaggerated alien culture just miles from his home, and he would marvel at the strange accents and mannerisms, and the shocking profusion of goods on sale in the PX store. Roy would give him American coins so he could play Johnny Cash and Bobby Darin on the jukebox as he roamed the aisles along with the Air Force wives and their kids, or as he pressed his face against the

40

windows to watch the huge-finned cars sailing noiselessly by on the wrong side of the road. Best of all he liked to watch the planes, the fighters and bombers and giant transports, and the airmen themselves, which he could when Roy worked in the barracks near the runway. For young Derek Smailes, the American fliers had a mythic status. With their crew cuts and flight overalls and the bowlegged way they walked weighed down by their equipment, they were the real cowboys, infinitely more impressive than their silly counterparts on television. He would daydream about faking an accent and enlisting when he was old enough, and was brokenhearted when Roy lost his job during a budget review and their trips had to come to an end.

To be a fan of America was not to make yourself particularly popular at Cambridge police station, Smailes was aware, where the old resentment from the war years could still be felt. Younger officers too felt that America was a bad influence on British youth, promoting violence and drugs, and in general, people could find angry things to say about the United States, no matter how transfixed they were by its television programs. But for Derek Smailes, the fascination was both enduring and involuntary.

The United States became a safety valve for his imagination, a place of deserts and forests and cities, of cornball decency and shocking excess, a place where things happened. He was particularly attracted to a certain kind of American renegade. He liked Jack Nicholson, who grew defiantly fat and bald while Redford and Hoffman ate grapefruit and pursued romantic lead roles. He liked Mailer, who threw punches on the cusp of journalism and literature. And he liked Willie Nelson, above all, who reminded him of the country singers he had listened to on the PX jukebox as a boy. He would have given anything to be able to sing like that. As he grew older, he realized his Americanisms had become part of an adopted style, a way of defying respectability and the expectations around him.

41

Perhaps there had been an aloofness in his attitude during his marriage. He had been accused of superiority too often in his life to be able to simply shrug the claim off. But he had tried, he felt. He had done all the things you were supposed to do when you were married. But his heart wasn't in it, and Yvonne realized it intuitively early on, which maddened her. By the end of the second year she had begun to brandish the timeworn weapons of marital decay—silence, overspending and the withholding of sex. Smailes might have been able to handle the first two, but in combination with the third, they were a lethal strategy. In bed she wielded enormous power over him. He had always been crazy about her physically, her creamy skin and slightly feral smell, the way she turned her head and stabbed timidly with her pelvis, her girlish pleasure. She began to turn away from him deliberately, rejecting all his ploys. He was stricken by her cruelty. He had tried his best.

His capitulation came about inexorably. Janet in the typing pool started to smile at him a little more than she needed to; he would linger to joke just long enough to let her know he understood, he was interested. He often worked late when he was on special squads, so it was easy to telephone Yvonne with his excuse the night Janet agreed to go for a drink with him after work. She lived out near Cherry Hinton and they would go there, where he thought no one knew him—then the sly preliminaries in the pub before they would saunter in past her frowning flatmates and copulate like the blazes on her frilly bed. But he knew he was doomed, and was almost relieved when a former school friend of Yvonne's spotted them in the pub and called her up. He didn't attempt to deny anything, and his remorse came more from the realization that he was no better than the rest of his sex than from any real feeling of failure.

He had done his best, and it wasn't good enough, but he would have stuck it out if she had wanted to. But then maybe he was unrealistic, because he realized how insulting she

42

found his attitude. She screamed and cursed him and wept pitifully, but he knew that she was also relieved, and was more frightened about what would become of her than heartbroken. He had moved out that week, and within three months Yvonne and Tracy had had to leave the police flat and went back to her mother's. There was the child support, but he didn't mind that. He knew Yvonne would remarry. She was an attractive woman with no greater ambition than to keep a house and raise children and be in the swim. Tracy would be better off too, if Yvonne remarried fast enough. It might be better if he stayed out of the picture altogether.

They had been divorced for six years, Yvonne eventually wanting to push the whole thing through so she could marry an optician who was a friend of her family. She had had two more kids since, and Smailes had decided not to stay completely out of the picture. He saw Tracy twice a month, and she was a fair-haired little beauty. They got along famously, he felt.

There had been others of course. Bernadette from the hospital, who started to get too serious. Paula from the Ops Room, which had been a mistake. He was in no hurry, and had grown used to being on his own. Maybe one day he would leave Cambridge and the police, and try again for a degree. Maybe he would go to Texas and work the oil rigs. Unlikely, but he was determined to visit the States one day, no matter what.

There was a knock at the door and he opened it to a small, sandy-haired man with a high forehead and a paunch who strode past him into the room, visibly distressed. Professor Ivor Davies was about five feet four and wore a brown corduroy jacket and a green rayon shirt with a wide matching tie, which he was wringing with the fingers of his right hand. He wore thick-lensed glasses which made his eyes look like tadpoles. Smailes introduced himself.

"Yes, yes, I know, Officer. Hawken told me you were here.

Do excuse me. This news about Simon is most upsetting. It was not expected. Not expected, you know."

Davies bobbed slightly as he spoke, and stopped worrying his tie to run his hands through his wiry hair, which was long on the sides and very thin on top. Smailes sat down behind Poole's desk and took out his notebook. He gestured for Davies to sit down, but Davies was too agitated.

"I had no idea, you see. I saw him about two months ago, and he seemed cheerful enough. He was working too hard, but then, he always did that, you know. When did this happen? Dr. Hawken only gave me the bare details."

"Last night, we think," said Smailes. "He was found hanged this morning by the cleaning woman, and it looked like his bed had not been slept in. There was a note." He wondered about telling Davies of its peculiar message, but Davies preempted him.

"What did it say, for heaven's sake? Did it say why he did it?"

"No. It just said 'they' came back, and he couldn't take it. Any idea who 'they' might be, Professor?" asked Smailes.

Davies pursed his lips, then grimaced.

"Good heavens. Maybe the snakes. Yes, that would be it, wouldn't it? They came back, and he couldn't take it, you know."

This insight seemed to pacify Davies to the extent that he could sit down. He steered himself absently into the chair opposite Smailes and then blinked at him twice.

"Perhaps you could tell me what you mean, Dr. Davies," he asked softly.

"Well, you see, it's not the first time. I mean, the poor fellow had tried to kill himself before. At least, that's what we all thought, although when Simon was well enough again to tell me about it, he said all he was trying to do was get away from the snakes. Not real snakes, you know. Hallucinations. But real enough to make him jump out of his window. Real enough for that, you know.

44

"It must have been two years ago, nearly. Before Finals. Of course, Simon was heading for a First. Absolutely brilliant chap, didn't need to work nearly so hard as he did. I was always trying to get him to take up some hobby to relax with, stamp collecting or something, but he would never listen. All he ever thought of was his work and his projects."

"Projects?" asked Smailes.

"Yes. Simon was one of those people who loved a mystery, or so he told me. He had been interested in them since he was a boy. You know, flying saucers, the Bermuda Triangle, things like that.

"Anyway, he was also interested in real-life mysteries, if you like. He told me a little about them. Two years ago he was working on President Kennedy. The one who was assassinated, you know."

Smailes indicated with an inclination of his head that, yes, he knew.

"So anyway it was one month to Finals and we all wanted him so much to have the research fellowship and stay on here and I kept telling him to put aside his work on this Kennedy business until the exams were over and he would have the whole summer to write to whomever he liked in America, but of course he wouldn't listen."

Smailes said nothing.

"Anyway, then he had this terrible blow. His father died. Car accident. He was in insurance, I think. The news seemed to throw poor Simon into a loop. A loop, you know.

"I make it sound as if I knew all this as it was happening, which I didn't, of course. The junior members aren't usually very forthcoming about their personal affairs, although Simon was less secretive than most. It was one of his friends that came to me and told me Simon seemed to be very depressed, that his friends were worried about him.

"So I went over to his rooms and found him in bed. Hadn't eaten in days, said he couldn't concentrate on his work, that he was going to fail his exams, that his life was not worth

45

living. Gave me a bit of a fright, you know. So I got my doctor round to him. Selby—wonderful chap. I think he put him on some pills and gave him the name of a psychiatrist to see. I urged him to visit him, but I don't think he did. Said it would do no good.

"I started to visit him two or three times a week. Anything more would have been a little too intrusive, you know. I talked to his sister and told her that I was concerned about him, that he should go home for rest immediately after the exams were over.

"And then he was found one night in the court. I heard about it the next day. Screaming hysterically about snakes. Very upsetting. He was taken off. To Myrtlefields, you know. I went to see him out there. Awful place. Tried to cheer him up about getting an *aegrotat* and how I knew the maths faculty would stand behind him. Of course, he was too depressed to care. Too depressed, you know."

Smailes had noticed his attitude toward Bowles changing subtly during Davies's monologue. He had once blown some pretty important examinations himself after his own father died. He felt an odd link with Simon Bowles.

"But blow me if he wasn't as right as rain within a month, sitting in my rooms laughing and saying it was all like a bad dream to him and he felt absolutely fine whatever the faculty committee decided, and anyway he knew who killed President Kennedy. It must have been the new drugs they have nowadays, because they certainly made the difference for Simon. He was like a new man."

Davies paused and a sudden sadness clouded his features as he remembered that Bowles was no longer a new man, that he was dead. He blinked again at the detective and looked at his hands.

"How often had you seen Simon Bowles since his release from the hospital? Dr. Hawken told me you had been out of the country but that you had resumed your relationship with him. I understand it's not customary for a graduate student to see a tutor."

"Quite right, quite right. Yes, not long after Simon recovered I went abroad for the whole summer. I'm an archaeologist, you see. Hittites, particularly. I'd been working to arrange a dig for years."

"Where was that, sir?"

Davies seemed momentarily disoriented by Smailes's interest in his work. He stammered slightly. "Well, well, Anatolia, of course. Modern Turkey, and a bit of Syria. We were at Halpa. It's called Aleppo today. Part of Turkey until 1914, when Syria annexed it."

"And so you came back at the start of the academic year, when Simon Bowles began his graduate work?"

"Yes, that's right. You can only dig for a season, you see, while the weather holds, although I had hoped to stay until October or November and then perhaps resume the following spring. It had all been approved by the college. But we ran into, well, funding problems, and had to come back early. Very frustrating, actually."

"And you became Bowles's tutor again when you came back? Was that your idea?"

"Yes, yes, it was, although it didn't happen right away. I suggested it to Hawken, to Dr. Hawken, sometime in the Michaelmas term, I think, and he agreed we should, well, recommend it to Simon. Simon agreed, and I saw him usually once or twice a term, I think. I made him promise to come and see me if anything was bothering him. He did promise, and, you know, I believed him."

Davies's manner had grown noticeably agitated again, and there was something about his story that did not make sense. Smailes paused to take notes, and then asked, "So you resumed the relationship, even though you were planning to return to, where was it, Syria, the next year?"

"Oh no, that had fallen through. Still problems with money, you see, then the damned Syrian government began to give me problems about the permit. I had to cancel the whole thing, and go back out there for a month last summer to cajole the bloody people, and see what was left of our work. It's finally all straightened out. I leave again this summer, in July."

"Difficult people to work with, I expect, sir."

"The Syrians? Not too bad, actually. A little sticky, but they want to show they're civilized, I suspect. The Lebanon's a nonstarter, of course, and the Turks, the Antiquities Department people, are hopeless. But I'm digressing . . ."

"Yes, I'm sorry. When was it you last saw Mr. Bowles, sir?"

"I last saw Simon about the beginning of the term, and he seemed fine."

"In your office, sir?"

"In my rooms, of course, yes."

"He didn't seem under any unusual pressures?"

"Well, he told me he was working flat out and that his latest research would make his Kennedy investigation seem insignificant. Insignificant, he said."

"Do you know what he was working on?"

"No. No idea and no interest. Told him again he should take up stamps, but he only laughed."

Smailes paused to catch up with his note-taking and saw that Davies had begun pulling at the green polyester tie again.

"Professor, do you think Simon Bowles would have come and told you if he had been worried or afraid of something?" asked Smailes. To his relief, Davies did not take offense at the remark, as Hawken would have.

"Well, you know, Simon was different than a lot of the men," Davies began. "A lot of them have absolutely no feeling for the place. Just regard Cambridge as a place to mess around before they have to go off and get a job. They certainly don't appreciate having to talk to a tutor once or twice a term, and the meetings are often very difficult, embarrassing. I think those people are most foolish, arrogant, you

48

know, and that they are missing the whole point. I mean, just because we're a bit older and make a living as teachers and scholars doesn't mean that we're not human, that we can't lend a sympathetic ear and perhaps even be helpful now and again. Of course, the fact that we represent the authority of the University can sometimes make things awkward, but basically there's no contradiction."

Like hell, thought Smailes. He wondered if he would want to see this hyperactive Welshman if he really had something on his mind. Compared with Hawken, though, he was all right. He got the impression there was no love lost between the two dons.

"But Simon wasn't like that. Wasn't stuck-up at all. He had a sort of childlike quality to him, tremendous enthusiasms, but very little guile, you know. No guile.

"So I think he was frank with me. He didn't have many close friends and we had gotten along well over the years. Another man might have been offended or embarrassed to meet with a tutor as a graduate fellow, you know, but Simon didn't seem to mind. Yes, I think he would have mentioned it if he was worried about something."

Reluctantly, Smailes unrolled the standard question, as he had with Hawken.

"Do you know of any difficulties with money, girlfriends or drugs which might have got him into trouble?" he asked.

"Simon? No, he really wasn't the type, I don't think. I got the impression he lived quite a quiet life."

"Was he a religious man, to your knowledge?"

"Simon? No, I'm sure he wasn't. Why do you ask?"

"Oh, a poster in his room. It's Albert Schweitzer, I think."

"No, no, that's Russell. Bertrand Russell. One of his heroes, I suppose."

"Yes, that would make sense," said Smailes, writing carefully in his notebook. "So you have no idea why he might have taken his own life?"

"No, Officer, I really don't. It's a mystery. A mystery, you know."

Smailes thought for a moment, then got up from the desk and walked to the leaded window overlooking the soupy water of the Cam. The faded graffiti against the red brick caused a sudden flicker of recognition.

"I know that," he said to himself absently.

"What's that?" said Davies, and Smailes remembered he had an audience.

"That's Norman Mailer," he said.

"Eh, what's that?" asked Davies again, advancing toward the window as if to see the old pugilist punting up the river. Smailes was embarrassed, but he had committed himself.

"Those words—VIETNAM HOT DAMN—they're the last line of Norman Mailer's *Why We Are in Vietnam*."

"Yes," said Davies. "Bloody vandals."

Smailes felt like a fool and the two men stood in silence watching the river. The phone rang and the detective caught it on the third ring. It was Hawken, being businesslike.

"Ah, Mr. Smailes, I thought you'd like to know. Beecroft has ascertained with whom Mr. Bowles spent last evening, or at least the latter part of it. It seems he was in the college bar with two friends—a Mr. Giles Allerton and an unidentified young woman. He is attempting to locate them now. Would you care to interview them?"

Smailes's attention was distracted by Davies, who had resumed his agitated pacing around the room. He asked Hawken to hold, cupping his hand over the receiver. He told Davies he could leave if he had other commitments, that they might need him to make a statement for the coroner.

Davies seemed relieved. "Oh, certainly. Of course, whenever you need me, whenever at all, you know. My rooms are in Second Court, opposite Simon's staircase." He made an awkward bowing movement and turned toward the door.

"Excuse me, just finishing with Dr. Davies," Smailes said into the receiver. "Of course I would like to speak with them, but perhaps later. I should get back to the station and make sure the reports have been filed correctly. Can we arrange a meeting for two o'clock?"

"I'm sure," said Hawken.

"Meanwhile, can you ensure that Bowles's room remains locked and out of bounds to everyone?"

"Indeed," came the dry response.

The truth was Hawken's sherry had whetted his appetite and he realized he was starving for lunch. Death often had this effect on him, it made him ravenous. And it might be prudent to check the paperwork before it went upstairs. It was, after all, his investigation.

Nigel Hawken watched the detective from his window as he strode purposefully around the court, his hands thrust deep into his raincoat pockets, leaning slightly into the wind. He stood to the side so he would not be seen if the policeman chanced to look up. He did not entirely trust his ingenuousness. It would be wise to be cautious around him.

For the twentieth time that morning he rehearsed the possibilities and probabilities that would result from this unfortunate development. The phone call had been a gross error in judgment, but it had at least given him several extra hours to prepare his response. It was all so stupid and unnecessary, but as he looked at the situation dispassionately, he knew it was unlikely anything could be traced to him. He could count on his friend's discretion, he was almost sure, and since nothing was known of the association, the rest would hinge on the acuity, or lack of it, of Mr. Smailes. All things being equal, the matter would probably blow over with the inquest.

Yet he had felt acutely anxious when he saw the second group of policemen arrive with their suitcases and photographic equipment and when he realized that he was powerless now to prevent the police from doing whatever they liked in his college. He hated that feeling. He was also trying to avoid the more painful thought that hovered on the edge of his consciousness, that he was foolish to risk any exposure

51

whatsoever, that his predilection was shameful and weak. Perhaps, but his subterfuge had worked so well for so long, his habits were so ingrained, that he could not believe he could be uncovered now by a provincial policeman, no matter how sharp.

He looked at his watch. It was time to call Sir Felix, to counter his feeble protests that he should return to Cambridge at once to respond to the crisis. It would not be difficult for Hawken to convince him there was no crisis, that there was no reason for Sir Felix to alarm himself, that everything was under control. Sir Felix had deferred to him ever since he had been told that Hawken worked for the government. The knowledge had allowed Sir Felix to relax about whether he was really supposed to do anything at Cambridge and to return to the full-time pursuit of his peerage. The arrangement suited them both admirably, and allowed them to maintain the guise that Hawken was Sir Felix's subordinate.

Hawken considered returning to Bowles's room to take a last look around for himself, but dismissed the idea as too risky. He had examined the premises as thoroughly and as carefully as possible before the first arrival of the police, and had seen nothing remotely compromising. Of course, he had not had time to examine the files themselves, as he would have liked. But it was all now too late. And after all, there was no cause for alarm.

Four

SERGEANT HARRY SMAILES had been no ordinary policeman. His family had been grocers in Newnham village for generations, but he himself had joined the force in his teens after the Depression had put his father out of business. He had served on the beat for twenty years before winning his sergeant's stripes, and by the time Derek was a teenager was a desk officer with all manner of important administrative duties.

The tales of his bravery were legion and he was an almost legendary figure in the town. He seemed to know everyone. On Saturday mornings, when Derek was a boy, if they went to town to Woolworth's or Marks and Spencer, his father would continually stop to swap news with someone from his vast acquaintance. Occasionally, Derek would be examined by some strong-breathed stranger or chucked under the chin by a lady in a hat. He hated these encounters but would endure them in silence.

Harry Smailes was a huge man, with the large hands and feet he had passed on to his son, a bulbous pitted nose and black hair that flowed back from his forehead in brilliantined waves like a washboard. He took great pride in his appearance and his uniform was always immaculate. Derek's first memories of his father were that he was like a fairy-tale giant. He was afraid of him.

His father was never off duty. He translated the sacrifice of police service into an unyielding sternness, and ran his household with a calm tyranny which kept Derek's mother in a continuous state of anxiety. His elder sister Denise adopted sullen defiance, and he himself alternated between conciliation and resentment. He had always been desperate to please his father, who had a heroic and terrifying stature for him, but he had never found how.

Derek Smailes was big for his age and good at sports, and his physical recklessness made him a first-rate goalkeeper. His father rarely missed the home games of the football teams he played on, but no matter how well he played, his father always seemed unimpressed. Derek could never understand why he continued to attend, unless it was to silently remonstrate with him, to remind him that his performance was lacking. He began to prefer the away games, the absence of the accusatory presence on the edge of his vision.

Report time was always an occasion of particular terror. He usually scored well in English, but the other subjects were always in the Inadequate or Must Try Harder category. His father would sit opposite him at the dining table, the report card between them like a felon's statement. Then he would wag the stem of his pipe at it and tell him he was letting himself down. Derek's cheeks would burn with anger and shame. School bored him. He passed most subjects—why couldn't his father acknowledge that? And anyway, his father behaved as if he didn't want him to go to university. His

54

mother, who doted on him, let him know privately that if her Derek didn't do so well at school, it was all right with her. He would ask her to reason with his father, but she would only look at him helplessly. Harry Smailes's household authority was an absolute she dared not challenge.

Derek Smailes shifted uneasily in his chair and stared at the small pile of Simon Bowles's belongings that he had removed from the plastic personal bag on his blotter. The canteen lunch felt like a bowling ball in his stomach.

He poked at Bowles's key ring with a pencil. There were keys to his room and filing cabinet, and two others that looked like house keys. He took out a handkerchief to examine the wallet, but changed his mind. There was no crime here, no need for precautions over fingerprints. The typed note still bothered him slightly, but given what he had learned about Simon Bowles's personality, it could be explained.

During lunch he had found himself ruminating on the note, irked by the knowledge that whereas you could fake a suicide, you couldn't fake a suicide note in someone else's handwriting. But you could use a typewriter. Should he have dusted the machine, just to be sure?

Years of training had made him rehearse these possibilities. What was Bowles's latest research project? Was it connected to his death? Had a third party been involved in the suicide, by contrivance or coercion? Some of these questions would be answered by the postmortem report, which would show any unusual circumstances in the cause of death.

But then, if Bowles's death had been somehow induced, it would be foolish to draw attention by typing a fake note. Just leave no note. After all, Bowles had attempted suicide before. As he stared at Bowles's meager belongings he was puzzled why these questions still nagged at him. Something about the college—Beecroft, Hawken and Davies—made him uneasy. Had Hawken and Davies insisted on bringing Bowles under the tutor's wing out of concern for his welfare, or from other motives? Certainly, the suicide was shocking, but the reactions of both men seemed exaggerated. Davies was able to identify the Russell poster, but by his own account had not visited Bowles's room in almost two years. A good memory, simply? And then his thoughts would turn to the note, the incongruity of it.

The state of the room had swayed him finally. No clothes lying around, no dirty ashtrays, no books or papers out of place. Bowles was a fastidious type. He had set the plant down carefully before climbing onto the chair and looping his belt through the plant hook. He was the type who could have rolled a sheet of paper into his typewriter and written his explanation tidily, without an error. What was it Mrs. Allen had said? *So quiet and shy and neat* . . . The thought of the stricken boy's last moments suddenly filled him with anger and disgust, a sense of waste.

The wallet contained a little paper money, library cards, some book receipts and a dog-eared note card with telephone numbers on it. Alan, Hugh, Lauren, Alice (work). Two of the numbers had long-distance codes he did not recognize. The names were in scrawny capitals and were difficult to read. On the reverse side were a series of doodles around a question that had been overwritten again and again to make it almost illegible. It looked like "Who flagged the fliers from Bletchley?" Derek Smailes was not sure what the reference to Bletchley meant, although he seemed to think there had been some government offices there during the war. It was also the site of a well-known racecourse, which was not far from Cambridge, although a bit further than Newmarket. It seemed peculiar that Bowles might have fancied the horses. Could he have had gambling debts?

No, it seemed probable that, for whatever reason, Bowles's frightening delusions had returned and he had killed himself in panic. The thought made Smailes shudder.

He opened the spectacle case and saw a pair of black-

56

framed glasses. The lenses looked fairly strong. Again, it seemed typical. Bowles typing his final note and putting away his glasses carefully before climbing up on his chair for the last time.

He turned to the Sudden Death report and was relieved to find that between them Dickley and Swedenbank had got it right. Under "Death pronounced by" Ted had filled in the name of Dr. Maurice Jones, the pathologist at Addenbrookes, and not the name of Detective Sergeant Smailes. Under "Relative informed" he read the name of Alice Wentworth. Must be the sister, he thought. He decided to hand-carry the report up to Dearnley, despite its routine nature. He hadn't spoken to George since the Crowe School case and was curious to know its disposition.

"Why'd he do it, Derek? Exam pressure, thwarted in love, any idea?"

"Not really, George. Except he tried it before. Two years ago. Cracked up after his father died and ended up at Myrtlefields."

"Pills?"

"No, jumped out the window. Didn't mess it up this time."

"Any negligence? Doctors, college authorities? We're not going to see any family suits, are we?"

"Unlikely. Apparently he'd been doing fine for the last couple of years. No wind of this at all, according to his tutor. I'm going to interview a couple of his friends who were with him last night. Might give us more to go on."

Smailes could tell from George's manner that he was already losing interest in the case. As long as there was no foul play and the police were not going to get in the middle of any messy litigation, the dead student was just another statistic to George. Smailes told him about the note anyway.

George merely shrugged and glared at the SD report again, shaking his jowls at it slightly.

"Sounds like a relapse. See what the coroner's office wants.

They may want us to talk to the people out at Myrtlefields. Usually do with these 'balance of mind' verdicts. Just cover our arse for the inquest. You know, Derek." He tossed the SD report into a file tray and wiped his nose and mouth methodically with a large blue handkerchief.

George Dearnley was a big man who had obviously been handsome in his youth and had managed to retain a certain swagger into his middle years. It was a matter of pride in the department that the man at the helm was married to his third wife, who was nearly twenty years younger than he. However, George Dearnley was an aloof figure and his staff rarely discussed personal matters with him. Not even Derek Smailes, who had known him all his life.

Dearnley's girth had spread considerably in recent years, particularly since his latest marriage, so that he could no longer sit close to his desk. But he had the nimble step of an athlete and was reputedly still a formidable tennis player. He had introduced Derek Smailes to the game, although the two of them no longer played. Dearnley's office, a mishmash of the institutional and the personal, was full of mementos of his love of the game. His desk stood at the end of his large office, facing into it, and behind his head were calendars from equipment companies and a large framed picture of the Cambridge police team that Dearnley had led to the county championship ten years earlier. Someone had given him a large brass tennis ball, which he used as a paperweight. The coffee table at the far end of the room, next to the orange vinyl settee, held copies of *Tennis* magazine, along with *The Economist* and *Police Review*.

The crown of Dearnley's bald head gave off a pale glow in the fluorescent light. He kept what was left of his hair clipped very short. He stretched back in his chair and rested his eyes on the ceiling. The polyester sheen of his blue Marks and Spencer suit made him look like a huge shark.

Smailes got up and walked to the door, holding a folder, then paused. He drummed lightly on it with his fingertips.

"George, did you see the statements on the fraud job out at the Crowe? Swedenbank's first go?"

"Oh yeah. I'm going to NFA that, if the bus company agrees," said Dearnley absently.

"Yeah, seems reasonable. First offenders," said Smailes, and to his surprise, meaning it. He suddenly realized that his earlier irritation had been misplaced, that he had been annoyed at himself in advance for arranging an embarrassment for the chief super. Who the hell was he to try to make George squirm? Objectively, a minor fraud involving teenage forgers and dud bus passes was not worth hauling through the courts, no matter who was involved. Any kids with clean sheets would have been given an NFA by Dearnley, he realized. But he could tell by the feigned casualness of Dearnley's manner that he knew exactly why Smailes had asked the question and that the connection between himself and the boy's father was awkward for him. Smailes felt as if he had played a mean trick.

Both men looked away as the silence extended. The problem was the expectations they had for each other. Smailes thought to himself that he couldn't have it both ways. If George had an undeclared interest in this Crowe School case, what about his own undeclared interest in George? It was never acknowledged by the two men, but they both knew it keenly, as did most of the CID detectives. He had known George Dearnley since boyhood, and had only stopped calling him Uncle George after he had joined the force. The advantages he had enjoyed at the station were subtle, but real. As she had done moments ago, Gloria usually nodded him through without an appointment when he wanted a word in private. And Dearnley, although he carefully avoided any overt favoritism, always managed to let Smailes know which way the wind was blowing from Hinchingbrooke, so he was prepared when the brass came through with policy changes. Smailes had not won his sergeant's stripes in any record time, but he was fairly sure Dearnley went to bat for him whenever doors were closed. He was an unconventional cop, and was under no illusion that he owed some measure of his success to this unstated patronage.

Smailes had joined the police force because it had seemed inevitable, but had stayed because there was something fundamentally satisfying to him in its simple duties. He found himself confused on many issues, particularly those involving freedom and responsibility, and equity and power in general. But he was not confused about the necessity of the laws of the land or about the desirability of enforcing them. Crooks were crooks, whether they were bullion thieves or neurotic shoplifting housewives. He felt good about catching them, about his small contribution to things being orderly and safe. Let someone else decide the bigger issues. He couldn't even decide which way to vote.

Still, he could not claim to be at ease in the policeman's domain. He had never understood his colleagues' boorish preoccupation with "villains," and their small-minded bigotries and occasional brutalities troubled him. But in his eyes, Dearnley was different, and Smailes knew he felt awkward about anything that appeared to stain the chief super's motives in his eyes. He trusted Dearnley the way he trusted no one else on the force. Dearnley understood him intuitively, had known him all his life, and particularly understood his complex relationship with his father and the mechanism of guilt and resentment that was its hinge. And Dearnley was discreet. Smailes loved to watch George in action in tight situations, the way he could accomplish awkward tasks with few words. Since Smailes's divorce, George would occasionally ask questions about his mother, or Tracy, and even probe a little about his amorous liaisons. But mostly the two men guarded their privacy and maintained the conventions of the junior and senior officer relationship. But Smailes was grateful he finally had a more evenhanded authority to appease, and Dearnley knew it.

He kept his voice even and looked George directly in the

eye. "He did a good job, Swedenbank, for a first try. He's going to be good," he said.

"Good, Sergeant, keep me posted," said Dearnley, returning to the fat computer printout he had been studying when Smailes had entered.

George Dearnley waited until Smailes's footsteps had retreated well down the hall before looking up. "Bloody impertinence," he said under his breath.

It was shortly after one forty-five when Smailes drew up outside St. Margaret's, and the scene had returned to normal, bereft of bystanders and emergency vehicles. He parked his car in the space reserved for the Master, lowering the visor with its *Cambridge Police CID* sign. He checked in his inside pocket for his notes on the next-of-kin arrangements. The wind had dropped and Trinity Street seemed strangely calm. A woman in a headscarf passed by slowly, as if underwater.

St. Margaret's porters' lodge felt like the waiting room of a Victorian railway station. The heat was oppressive, and there were expanses of polished wood and linoleum and a long wooden bench against the wall where people sat with bags next to them. There was a smell of floor wax and shaving soap. Grave men in shirt sleeves and waistcoats stood behind an enormous oak counter that ran down the center of the room. From behind these men emerged Paul Beecroft, wearing his suit jacket, his face flushed and shining.

"Ah, Officer, good afternoon," he said, rounding the counter. "Let me introduce Mr. Giles Allerton and Miss Lauren Greenwald. They were with young Mr. Bowles last night in the college bar. I believe Dr. Hawken informed you."

Beecroft indicated the bench behind Smailes. He turned to notice for the first time the two students who were waiting for him. He was struck immediately by how alike they looked, like twins. The man was twenty-one or two, slightly built with long dark hair. Allerton wore a black blazer with a faded school badge on the breast pocket and yellow piping around the lapels and collar. Inside an open-necked white shirt he wore a white silk scarf which heightened the pallor of his face and accentuated the heavy shadow across his upper lip and chin. He had a strong brow and nose and looked handsome and vaguely famous. He was staring blankly ahead, and glanced mutely up at Smailes when the detective sergeant turned to face him.

The woman was a few years older. She was also dressed in black with a white open-throated shirt, and her hair fell in untidy curls onto her forehead and the collar of a black jacket. She was of similar height and build to Allerton, but her complexion was darker and her features Jewish rather than aristocratic. She wore small, round glasses like the old National Health type, and was slumped almost diagonally across the wooden bench, her hands thrust into the pockets of her jacket, staring sullenly at her black leather boots. She did not look up.

The two of them looked numb with shock, and Smailes was reminded once again that a real person, with friends, lovers and family, was dead.

He considered interviewing them both at once, to save time, but decided to stick with strict procedures. Always interview witnesses separately, he reminded himself. It was important that the stories match independently, no matter what the situation. He turned to Beecroft and asked whether Poole's rooms were unlocked. Beecroft nodded and signaled with his eyes that he wanted a word with him privately. Smailes stepped toward him and Beecroft murmured discreetly, "Please go up and see Dr. Hawken when you have the opportunity, Officer. I think he has heard from young Mr. Bowles's sister and needs your advice." Smailes acknowledged the request, and turned to follow Allerton, who was already leaving the lodge.

By the time they were seated, Allerton had emerged from his daze and needed no prompting.

62

"He didn't do it, Mr. Smailes. Simon. He didn't kill himself. He had no reason," he began immediately.

"Why do you say that?" said Smailes evenly, reaching for his notebook.

"He was fine. He was okay last night. A bit quiet, that's all. Wouldn't he have told us if he was freaking out?" Smailes noticed the uncertainty in his voice, the contrast to the vehemence of his first statement.

"What happened, please? Last night?"

Allerton's story emerged in spurts, as the young man's mood modulated between indignation and disbelief. He would occasionally tug at his long hair and wind it round a forefinger. He avoided looking at Smailes, as if uncomfortable and embarrassed to be talking candidly to a policeman. It was an attitude Smailes had long gotten used to.

Allerton and Lauren Greenwald had met by chance at dinner at the college. He and Lauren were "friends," he explained. They decided to go to an early movie, a Woody Allen film at the Arts. They had returned to the college around nine-thirty and had decided to look up Simon Bowles, a mutual friend, and get him to go for a drink. It had been Lauren's idea. She liked to tease Simon, draw him out of his shell.

"How long had you known Simon Bowles?" asked Smailes.

"Oh, years and years. You see, he was a contemporary of my elder brother Hugh at Oundel. They're both three years older than me. So when I came up to Cambridge, Simon was already here at Meg's. I've known him since I was eight years old."

"How long have you been a student here?"

"I'm in my third year. Modern languages. German and Russian."

"And Miss Greenwald. How long have you known her?"

"Lauren? Just this year. She came over from Columbia in September on a Fulbright. She's American, you know. From New York. That's where Columbia is. I met her in Simon's room actually."

63

"What is the relationship between the three of you? You say you were friends."

"That's right."

"What was your sexual interrelationship?" He felt Allerton was being obtuse.

"Lauren and I are lovers, off and on. We were both just friends with Simon." There was no edge in his voice.

"Please go on with your story."

Giles Allerton seemed to remember the details of the previous night quite vividly. They had stopped in at Simon's room. He was working at his typewriter when they entered and seemed annoyed at their intrusion. This was predictable. Simon always liked to pretend that he didn't like company. But both Allerton and Lauren knew that Simon liked the attention they gave him, the glimpses they brought him of a world outside his books and research.

"Was he an antisocial type? Few friends? How would you describe him?"

"No, no, Simon wasn't antisocial. He was just shy, and tended to live in his own world. He was really brilliant, you know. Everyone knew it, but he was never condescending or patronizing, and I'm sure he often held back from joining in discussions, you know, because he didn't want to utterly demolish people's arguments and make them feel stupid. He could do that quite easily, though. I've seen it happen."

"What do you mean?"

"Well, if he was in the bar, or there were people in his room, and some topic came up that he felt really strongly about, then he wouldn't hold back.

"He had this really pure, almost shocking intellect. He could take some murky issue and turn his high beam on it, and it would appear completely obvious. I remember him once turning on a guy who was spouting some theory of reincarnation and Simon just let him have it. Quite awesome. Something about the physical laws of continuity and discontinuity. But the interesting thing was, you could tell he really didn't like doing it. That's what made him so special. He was basically so modest and kind. He would always rather give you the benefit of the doubt than submit your ideas to his own flawless analysis. I think he valued logic above everything else. But he allowed others to be sloppy about it."

Allerton returned to his description of the previous night. Bowles had put the documents he had been working on into a manila folder and then into his desk drawer. He remained seated at his desk, and Allerton and Lauren sat on the bed. Simon asked them to leave because he was working. He seemed quite serious about it. But Lauren had gotten him to laugh, and he eventually agreed to go for a drink with them.

"Did anything seem unusual about his behavior when you arrived in his room?"

"Not at all. Simon worked all the time. His only recreation was the occasional drink."

"What about his annoyance when you showed up?"

"Oh, that was real enough. He got quite agitated at first. But then, we'd been through the same scene so many times we didn't take him seriously. And then Lauren started him laughing. He really did have a good sense of humor. Then he couldn't put on the pious scholar act again, so he agreed to come out with us."

"Did he lock anything—his desk, his files, his room—when you left?"

"No, I don't think so."

"Go on. What happened in the bar?"

"Well, he did seem a bit quiet. I remember a couple of other people joined us and Simon seemed sort of left out of the conversation."

"You mean he seemed depressed?"

"No, not depressed. Sort of preoccupied. I think he only had a halfpint, maybe two, and then he said he had to go. He left before Lauren and me. Maybe a quarter past ten."

"Did you think that was strange?"

"A bit. But then, I'm used to Simon. I remember Lauren

and I sort of shrugged at each other. Didn't seem like a big deal."

Allerton paused and looked blank for a moment, then rounded on the detective in an animated way.

"You see, Officer, I know what Simon's like when he's depressed. I was here during that dreadful time two years ago, when he ended up in the hospital. His mood last night was nothing like that. Nothing like that."

"No one said anything to him that might have upset him?"

"No, we were arguing about Woody Allen mostly, I think. He just seemed disinterested."

"The former suicide attempt. Did he talk to you about it at the time?"

"A bit, when he was better. I suppose it was his exams mostly, and his father dying like that. But Simon always maintained that he wasn't really trying to kill himself. He had these hallucinations, you see, and they scared the hell out of him. He had to jump out of the window because he saw snakes coming in the door."

"Really?" said Smailes.

Allerton thought for a moment. "Yes. You know, he said to me at the time that if he really meant to kill himself, he wouldn't have made a mess of it. He told my brother later—he was closer friends with Hugh than he was with me—that he wouldn't be able to take it again. That if that kind of delusion ever recurred, he wouldn't be able to take it. I think to someone with such an impeccably logical mind as Simon, such irrationality was completely terrifying, and utterly shameful. At least, that's what Hugh told me."

"Where is your brother now?"

"He's at Merton College, Oxford, studying divinity. We're not really very alike, Hugh and I. I called him this morning, when I found out about Simon. He's terribly upset. You see, Simon had just been over to see him, at the end of last week. Hugh was probably his best friend."

"Did you know what frame of mind Simon Bowles was in

during the period immediately before his death? Had you spent much time with him?"

"No. I hadn't seen him much, although I ran into him in hall on Saturday. He'd just got back from visiting Hugh. He seemed in good spirits, in fact. A bit mischievous. Simon could be like that. Said he had been sharpening his wits on the whetstone of my brother's faith. Something like that. See, Simon was a committed atheist, and my brother is quite High Church. It's a wonder they stayed so friendly, because they would argue all the time."

"How about the research he had been doing? Had he discussed that with you?"

"The latest stuff? No, he didn't talk to me much about that kind of thing. I don't think he saw me quite as an equal, which I'm not, really. I'm not much of an intellectual. Be lucky if I get a degree at all this year, unless I change my ways." Allerton failed to suppress a smirk.

Smailes remembered the Bletchley note he had found in Bowles's wallet. "Do you know if Simon Bowles liked to gamble? Did he follow the horses, for instance?"

Allerton snorted. "Good Lord, no. That's something I would certainly have known about. I'm a bit of a fanatic myself. Like to go over to Newmarket whenever I get the chance. It's sort of a standing joke that I'm a better student of racing form than any modern language. It must be in my blood, I think. No, in fact, I tried to get Simon to go with me a couple of times, but he only laughed. I don't think Simon would be seen dead at a racecourse."

Allerton realized the unwitting poor taste of his remark, and fell silent. Smailes asked casually, "Ever been to Bletchley?"

"Yes, I've seen some races there, but not during term time. It's a bit of a slog over there, when Newmarket's so close."

"Mr. Bowles left a typed note. Does that seem unusual to you?"

"A note? I hadn't thought of that. Does it say why he did it?"

Smailes looked at the young man, but did not respond. A note seemed the first, most obvious thing to expect.

"No, not at all. Simon had terrible, childish handwriting, and was very embarrassed by it. He used his typewriter for everything. That's exactly what he'd do. What did the note say, Officer? Can't you tell me?"

"It said: 'They came back. I couldn't take it. Simon.' "

Allerton looked stunned and passed a hand in front of his eyes. "My God. It must have happened. I can't believe it," he whispered. He gave Smailes a look of mute anguish.

"Mr. Allerton, you began by saying that Simon Bowles did not kill himself. Why do you think that, and what do you think caused his death?"

"That must have been it. He must have got frightened by something that recalled that awful time. I suppose that's why he did it. He used a belt, didn't he? From a plant hook? God, and we had just been there an hour or two before. Maybe if we'd gone back, after the bar, Simon would still be . . ."

"How did you know he had hanged himself with a belt? There has been no official report released."

"Oh, come on, Officer. It's all around the college. The porters, the bedders, everyone's talking about it. You don't think . . . What are you trying to imply?"

"You have not answered my question. You began by saying Simon Bowles did not kill himself. Now you seem to believe he did."

"Well, I didn't know about the note, and I thought that he didn't seem in that frame of mind, that extreme frame of mind. But something must have been going on with him that I didn't know about, obviously. But look, I'm serious. What do you mean by asking me how I know how he died? You don't mean . . . I mean . . . Jesus Christ . . ."

Allerton flushed a deep red and tears welled up in his eyes. He put his hand to the bridge of his nose and looked away.

Smailes had to admit that if he was dissimulating, he was doing a bloody good job. But he did not counter Allerton's protestations.

"Where did you go, you and Miss Greenberg, after the bar? Did you go to bed together?"

Allerton's sudden emotion spilled into anger. "Look, I don't like your tone, and I don't like what you're saying, and if it's just the same with you, I've had enough of this." He began to rise from his seat.

"Well, did you?"

"No, we bloody well did not, you dirty-minded . . ." He hesitated, as if unsure of the repercussions of swearing at a policeman. Smailes remained impassive.

"We haven't been sleeping together recently. We're friends. I have rooms in Axton Court. Lauren lives in digs, a ways out. I left her at my staircase. I assume she had her bike at the front gate. That's where she was headed. Look, are we finished, Officer?"

"For the time being. Please tell your friend Miss Greenberg that I will see her now."

"Greenwald. Not Greenberg. Yes. Look, I'm sorry, Officer. I just don't see this is any of your business. And I'm upset. You understand."

Such breeding. Smailes managed a thin smile as Allerton rose and walked unsteadily out of the room.

Five

DEREK SMAILES could never remember hearing his father laugh. He patrolled the house as if he were policing a public meeting and his children and their friends were unruly demonstrators. Not that Derek had many friends apart from Iain Mack, but they went to his house most of the time.

The only intimacy he could ever remember between them was when his father would read Dickens to him at bedtime. It had been a tradition in his own home, which Harry Smailes chose to continue. He seemed to shed the burden of his severity amid the colorful gallery of characters, adopting accents and mannerisms with abandon. Derek saw that his father could have been a music-hall performer, he came alive with a script in his hands. Derek would lie mesmerized in the grip of Dickens's imagination long after Denise had fallen asleep, pleading with his father not to stop. His father would close the book with a look of guilty pleasure, and return to the glowering part he had chosen in real life. When Derek Smailes became a teenager, he started to read Dickens himself. It was the start of his interest in serious reading, which was probably the only reason he had ever done well in anything at school.

The only other passion Harry Smailes seemed to feel was for his dogs. Those bloody dogs. It was the first thing he and his mother had done after the funeral. They had sold them both.

Harry Smailes kept and raced whippets. Derek had always thought they were absurd animals, prancing around on their toes with their bug eyes like giant insects. His father kept them in a special wire compound at the bottom of the garden, and the two dogs, Lucky and Lady, won from him a devotion which no human seemed able to. The whole family resented the amount of time he spent talking to them and grooming them, and taking them to weekend races in his specially converted Morris van. As they got older, Denise used to complain to their mother about the amount of time and money he spent on them, and how their yelping kept her awake at night. Their mother would tell her to mind her tongue. Derek accompanied his father to a race only once, and he was appalled by the cruel spectacle of the frantic dogs and the harsh-voiced men in mufflers with whiskey on their breath.

Then suddenly at the beginning of May when Derek was eighteen, his father had died, and any real chance of getting into university had been wrecked. The events were blurred in his memory, but he remembered that one morning his father, who had an almost flawless record of attendance in over thirty years of service, had not gone to work. He had been sitting at the kitchen table, drinking tea, when Derek had left for school. His father was still at home in the middle of the afternoon when he came back, standing at the bottom of the garden, talking to the dogs.

He had asked his mother, who seemed crippled with anxi-

71

ety, what was wrong, but she would only say that his father wasn't well, that she didn't know what was happening.

Denise, who was engaged at this time and soon to leave home, was more contemptuous.

"What's he doing, moping around all day? Why isn't he going to work? Have you called the doctor?" she would persist.

Smailes could not remember if the doctor had visited, but he remembered his Uncle George, who was an inspector at the station, visiting the house to talk to his dad and holding a worried conference with his mother at the kitchen table.

The next two days he remembered approaching his house with dread after killing time over at his friend Iain's. His sense of foreboding was overwhelming, and he could not concentrate on studying, although his exams were only weeks away. His father no longer bothered to dress, emerging in his dressing gown to eat in brooding silence, then walking back up the stairs. He looked very old.

Then, on the third day, Derek Smailes had come home from school to see an ambulance with flashing lights parked at the front door. He had rushed in and found his mother at the foot of the stairs, weeping.

"It's your dad. He's had a heart attack. They're taking him to the hospital," she had told him.

He had held on to her in fright. His father had died the same night.

He was shocked by the intensity of his grief and his feelings of guilt. The examinations arrived, and he did miserably. He felt that by continuously letting himself down, he had let his father down, and that the disappointment had killed him.

Smailes looked back at his notes and was reflecting wryly on Allerton's concoction of petulance and manners when Lauren Greenwald came angrily into the room. He doubted he would receive any such deference from her. She slouched across the room and slumped into the chair opposite the desk, not looking at him.

"Good afternoon, miss," Smailes began. "Let me just check the spelling of your name, if I can. Is that G-r-e . . ."

"Let's get this over with. What do you want to know?" she interrupted.

"Now, miss, we could start by being a little more polite. Don't like policemen much, is that it, miss?"

"Cops are cops. I'm pretty sure I don't like you. Giles told me about your wise-ass remarks. I think that stinks. He's pretty upset. Everyone's pretty upset. Maybe you don't appreciate that."

Smailes studied her. The similarity with Allerton was purely superficial. In background, outlook and attitudes this woman was from a different planet. In his most careful tone he rehearsed the spelling of her name, then looked at her mildly.

"I'm just trying to get the facts, miss. Perhaps you'll tell me what happened last night, as you recall it."

Her story tied with Allerton's pretty well, at most points. In her version, it had been Allerton who had suggested the visit to Bowles's room. He had been working at his typewriter, and put his work away in the desk after they entered. It had been her doing to persuade Bowles to go with them to the college bar. Her description of his behavior was the same: aloof, preoccupied, but nothing to suggest he might do anything drastic. She had left the bar with Allerton around eleven, left him at his staircase, and cycled home. She had found out about Simon's death that morning when she picked up her mail after her Wednesday-morning supervision at Magdalene College.

"What kind of person was Simon Bowles?"

Lauren Greenwald's manner had loosened during her narrative and she seemed less sullen.

"Simon? He was, well, a gentleman. You live in the States, you know, and you have this expectation that the whole coun-

73

try's like some giant version of *Upstairs, Downstairs*. Of course, it's not, but it sure is a lot more civilized than what I'm used to. And that was Simon. He had this real civilized, courteous intelligence. You could see he had a mind like a steel trap, but with, er, padded jaws."

"How did you meet him?"

"When I first arrived, there was some hospitality thing for the American students. Simon came to it. I think he liked Americans. He had this whole Kennedy trip."

"What was that about?"

"He was an assassination freak. There's a ton of them in the States. He corresponded with them. I think he was quite an authority on the whole thing. He had his own theory, about the Cubans. I didn't take too much interest."

"Do you know why he was interested in this subject? Did he talk to you about it?"

"Not after he realized I wasn't interested. I think he found unsolved mysteries intriguing, that's all. They offended his sense of propriety."

"Did he tell you what he was working on currently? Did you see the papers he was working on when you came in the room?"

"No, I didn't look. I think he was interested in something about Cambridge and politics, but he didn't discuss it. Said he didn't like to make assertions until he'd worked out his ideas properly. He was a private sort of person."

"What was the nature of your friendship? Were you intimate?"

To his surprise, she didn't take offense, or become defensive like Allerton, but gave a long, low-throated laugh.

"Simon? Of course not. Simon was gay. Pretty firmly in the closet, but definitely gay. He'd even talk to me about it, in the right mood."

Smailes had taken few notes while Lauren Greenwald was speaking, but he wrote down this short, abused word and underlined it. This was a new aspect of Bowles's personality, but he chose not to pursue it.

"And with Giles Allerton?"

"Giles and I were lovers, for a while, until I put my foot down. Giles is what you guys call a cad. A blue-blooded Englishman—horses, liquor and women. Endlessly promiscuous. I sort of got sick of it, his untrustworthiness. But we managed to stay friends."

Smailes found himself intrigued by this woman's assurance, the lack of contrivance with which she presented herself. She seemed quite a bit more adult than the boyish Allerton. She had a delicate face beneath the swath of black tangled curls, dark brown eyes in a foreign complexion, small, even mouth, strong nose. In Smailes's youth, her National Health-style glasses would have been a shameful emblem of poverty, but now they gave her an air of radical chic. Her masculine choice of clothes did not diminish a strong female aura. He realized he quite liked her.

"What are you doing here? I mean, are you studying for a degree?"

"No, I'm a grad student at Columbia. Doctoral candidate—chemical engineering. I won a one-year scholarship, and in recognition of our high academic standards in the U.S., the University lets me take a year of undergraduate course work."

"Chemical engineering? Not very ladylike."

The disdain in her reply was not harsh. "Aw, come on, Detective. Times change."

"Columbia. That's in Harlem, isn't it?"

"Not quite. Upper West Side. You know New York?"

"Not really. I've read about it. Cambridge must be a bit different."

"You bet. I have a studio on a Hundred Eighteenth Street above a Chinese Cuban restaurant with two families of Puerto Ricans on either side. Kinda noisy. Here I live with Mrs. Bilton in a semi-detached with scones every day for tea."

"Lauren, why do you think Simon Bowles killed himself?"

Her face clouded. "I've been trying to think it through, waiting across there in the lodge. It's hard to believe it's really true. You know, not having seen him. Of course, I know about that episode a couple of years ago, what Giles told me. Last night he was kind of quiet, but that's not unusual. I think he had this tortured thing inside himself, about being weird, about being gay. He told me once—we were in his room alone, he'd had a few drinks—that he had this terrible crush on Giles. Then he made me swear never to tell anyone, especially Giles. I never have, until now."

"Did Giles realize this perhaps?"

"Giles is a horny English heterosexual. Believe me, he had no idea. But when Simon told me, it let me know it was a big deal for him, that it was real significant he was confiding in me. I would bet that it had something to do with this, some love affair no one knew about, some big guilt-and-remorse thing."

"Or jealousy?"

"Jealousy? Of Giles and me? Oh, I can't believe that. That would be no reason to . . . I can't really believe that. But then he left the bar so suddenly. Why did he do that?"

"No one had said anything to him?"

"No. He wasn't even paying attention. Some other guys we know showed up, and he just suddenly announced he was leaving. But you know, I think the note is a fake, that he was covering something."

"What note?"

"The suicide note. The typed note. Giles told me about it. He thinks the snake fantasy came back, and that Simon freaked out. It doesn't sound right, does it? You don't sit in a bar, having a quiet drink, and then go back and imagine your room full of snakes, do you? I bet it's a fake."

"Yes, I see." Suddenly Smailes wished he'd kept these two apart after his questioning began. Had they managed to tailor their stories? What was missing here? He agreed that a sudden return of the terrifying hallucination seemed farfetched. The desk drawer had been empty of typed papers that morning. Perhaps Bowles had returned to find his papers stolen. Perhaps their contents had been so intensely personal that their loss was too much for him. Although another, more plausible explanation was that before taking his life, Bowles had simply transferred the manila file and its contents to the cabinet, which after all had been locked this morning. What had been its contents?

He looked again at Lauren Greenwald, whose face had become distracted, and watched as it contorted slowly into a mask of grief. She drew in a long breath as if trying to control herself, and then let out two enormous, heaving sobs.

"Oh God, it's true, it's true. It's such a stupid, fucking waste. Simon's dead. I can't believe he killed himself because he was in love with Giles and saw me and Giles together all the time. I just can't believe that."

Smailes waited until she had composed herself, which took several minutes. He told her quietly that he had finished his questions for the time being. He watched her as she rose and slowly left the room. He could not help noticing that from the rear she was very pleasantly proportioned.

He was disinclined to believe it also. Suicide was rarely a sudden act, but rather the culmination of a terrible process of mounting fear and hopelessness. Most of the suicides he had seen were of people with some type of dreadful history, who had given up thinking that things would ever improve. He had known a couple where prominent, well-situated people had killed themselves rather than face some terrible disgrace for which they were responsible. But neither of these situations seemed to fit Simon Bowles. The young man had been working—seemingly normally—at his typewriter when first interrupted, hardly the behavior of someone overwhelmed by a personal problem. He had put his papers away in a manila folder in the desk, and not locked anything as the three young people left for the bar—or so Allerton claimed. So the ab-

sence of the file in the drawer that morning meant it was
either stolen or filed with the dozens of others in Bowles's
four-drawer cabinet. Assuming the latter, and accepting that
nothing unusual had transpired among the three friends
while they were together, something had happened between
the hours of ten-thirty and one o'clock or so, which, Smailes
was convinced, the postmortem would determine to be the
time of his death. An unexpected visitor? Threats, accusations
or some new, terrible piece of news? Something that had
caused the frightening hallucinations to return when the visitor left? On consideration, Smailes was inclined to believe the
note, that something terrifying had happened to him and he
had indeed taken his life on impulse. But not out of unre-
quited love for Giles Allerton.

On this occasion, Smailes was compelled to wait in
Hawken's outer office before the senior tutor would see him.
The electric clock on the wall told him it was just before
three. To his surprise, he found that Hawken's secretary was
not the desiccated matron he would have expected, but a
young Australian woman who had the figure of a beauty
queen and the tan of a surfer. She also had an openness of
manner that seemed out of place in the Cambridge college,
and asked him frank questions about Simon Bowles and why
he had done such a dreadful thing. Hawken leaned through
the doorway, waving his pipe with his good arm.

"Ah, Detective Sergeant, do step in. Sorry to keep you."

Hawken expressed his concern that Simon Bowles's sister,
who had called him almost immediately after being informed
by the Rickmansworth police of her brother's death, was
planning to visit the college on Thursday, the following day,
to take care of her brother's personal effects and to make arrangements for a funeral service. He had told her he would
call back, when he had checked with the police that it was all
right for her to dispose of the things in his room. Hawken
assured Smailes that he had put no pressure on the woman to

take care of such details right away. She could have the rest of the academic year, as far as he was concerned.

Smailes hesitated. In a different environment, he could simply seal off the room and take as long as he liked before deciding on a more detailed forensic examination or a physical inventory of the room's contents, for example. To make such a move now would probably mean upgrading the classification to Suspicious Death, amending the paperwork and going back in to George to explain his actions. But while Bowles's sudden death was peculiar, he had found nothing to indicate that it was suspicious, and didn't fancy going toe to toe with George with anything as loose and uncorroborated as his uneasy feelings. He decided he ought to check the room once more, to see if there was anything he had missed. But there was no reason to hold up the family. He told Hawken it was fine if Bowles's family wanted to straighten out his affairs.

"How did she sound, the sister, when you spoke to her?"

"Well, I think she was in shock, naturally. She said it was going to be a terrible blow to her mother. But she seemed in control, I must say. Quite businesslike." This term of Hawken's was obviously one of the strongest approbation.

"Did she say anything more?"

"She said she was sorry that her last conversation with him had been so unpleasant. He was apparently due to go home for a family gathering last weekend and had called to cancel at the last minute. She had been angry with him. She did ask how the police were treating the affair. I told her your name, that you were making inquiries. I trust you have spoken with the friends who were with him last night?"

Hawken had taken a seat on one of the butcher-block sofas and seemed considerably more relaxed than during their earlier conversation. There was almost a manner of apology about him, that he regretted his earlier tone. He shifted his weight on the sofa and winced slightly as he positioned his crippled arm into his lap with his good hand. Smailes had taken a seat opposite and watched the painful maneuver as he

79

leaned forward, his hands clasped between his knees. He too felt the weight of his prejudices, a sense of embarrassment.

"War wound, sir?" he asked quietly.

"No, I'm afraid not," said Hawken with a sigh. His story was obviously one he had told many, many times.

"Skiing accident while I was an undergraduate. Bavaria. Too much schnapps at lunch, then missed a turn and hit a tree doing about fifty. Lucky to still have the arm at all. My own fault of course. Kept me in desk jobs all through the war, unfortunately. But one learns to live with one's limitations," he said without conviction.

"Well, Mrs. Wentworth—that's her name—said she would contact the coroner's people as the woman police officer had told her to do. Plans to come to the college tomorrow, around one or so. Have you discovered anything about what might have precipitated this? I have told Sir Felix I will give him a full report, and I should do the same for the college council."

"I'm afraid not. According to his friends, his behavior was quite normal. Reserved, as usual, but nothing that worried them. He had been studying, his friends went to his room, and then took him to the bar for an hour or so. He left before them, and he returned to his room alone, I assume. Has his room been locked since this morning?"

"Oh yes, I asked Mr. Beecroft to check the room was locked securely after the last of your people left. What were they doing in there, may I ask?"

"Scenes-of-crimes officers. Photographs and fingerprints. Forensics, those kinds of things," said Smailes evenly, suddenly concerned why Hawken would want to know. He decided at that moment that lifts should have been taken from Bowles's room, and that the omission was a mistake that he would remedy as soon as he was able, and that he would make sure Hawken would not learn of it.

"Surely you don't suspect crime here, Mr. Smailes?" Hawken asked.

"No, I don't," said Smailes. "Scenes-of-crimes procedures

80

are routine in any sudden death case, particularly a suspected suicide. The coroner's office, well, their requirements are quite strict. But what we don't know is why this guy Bowles actually did it. His friends think the note could refer to the hallucinations about the snakes, that something made them come back. He had apparently told someone, not a friend here at the college, that he couldn't take it if they ever did. But I'm not sure. The reference in the note could be covering the real reason he hanged himself."

"Real reason? How can we possibly know the real reason? And does it really matter?" asked Hawken evenly.

"Actually, for the coroner, not particularly. The fact that Bowles had attempted suicide before, and that he had left a note, no matter how enigmatic, will be pretty persuasive. And there appear to be no suspicious circumstances."

Smailes paused as if to concentrate on extracting his notebook from the inside pocket of his jacket. In fact, he leaned forward and from under his brows kept his eyes fixed on Hawken's expression. He saw no trace of relief or concern pass across it.

The detective made a production of licking a thumb and finding Hawken's earlier remarks. "April two years ago you said, I think?"

"What?"

"The first suicide attempt. When he was found in the quad, shouting about snakes. When he jumped out of the window the first time."

"Court. Found in the court. Quads are at Oxford. Yes, two years ago, before Finals. Around this time, late March or April. I'm sure the hospital or his family can give you the exact date."

Hawken's annoyance was returning. Smailes was gratified that he could disturb this man's balance so easily, merely by acting the stupid policeman, which he knew Hawken thought he was. As the senior tutor gave way to his agitation and walked over to the window, Smailes resumed.

"But normally we like to find out as much as we can, for the family. It's my own feeling that something happened between ten-thirty and one or so that made him do it. I don't think the two friends can help us much more."

"Davies. He didn't have any clue?" Hawken addressed the remark to the ancient casement window, and Smailes wondered again about the two men's motives in imposing the tutorial relationship on Bowles. Perhaps it had been Hawken's idea in the first place.

"No. He apparently had not seen young Bowles in a couple of months. Seemingly Bowles had promised to let him know if anything was seriously bothering him. But it's my guess that this was something sudden, unexpected. Or something so sensitive that he was unable to discuss it with anyone. You knew, for instance, that he was homosexual?"

Hawken wheeled on him angrily. "No, I certainly did not. Detective Sergeant Smailes, I assure you the sexual proclivities of our junior members are no business of mine, and of no interest. I think you have quite the wrong idea of the degree to which we college authorities interfere with our men. And I suggest you go very carefully with such allegations before you divulge them. To his family, for instance."

Smailes returned the notebook to his jacket pocket and rose from his seat contritely. "I'm sorry, Professor, if I have given the wrong impression." He wasn't sure if Hawken was a professor, but was fairly confident the title would conciliate him. "This may have some relevance to his death. It may not. Can you think of anyone else in the college I could speak to? Mr. Beecroft, for instance?"

"I can't think what Beecroft would have to add." Hawken had regained himself after his outburst, and turned again to look out over the manicured lawn of the court. A weak sun had broken through the clouds. Smailes stood off to his right and looked out also. An elegant elderly man in an academic gown was walking slowly on a diagonal course toward the porters' lodge. The sight puzzled Smailes, as he had distinctly

82

seen the *Keep Off the Grass* signs posted around the lawn's perimeter.

"Well, *he* might, of course," said Hawken, nodding toward the figure ambling across the grass.

"I'm sorry?"

"G-L. Sir Martin Gorham-Leach. Everyone calls him G-L. I believe he was supervising Bowles's thesis. Most unusual. You've heard of him of course?"

Smailes indicated that he had not, from which Hawken appeared to derive pleasure.

"Nobel Prize for physics, back in the sixties. One of the most brilliant men here. Certainly the most eminent fellow of St. Margaret's. We've been lucky to keep him all these years, really, but it's probably because we don't tie him down with teaching duties. In fact, he has little contact with the junior members, which is why it was so unusual he agreed to look over Bowles's doctoral work. At least, that's what I've been told. Didn't Davies tell you?"

Smailes replied that Davies had not mentioned the relationship, and he wondered what an old scientist, no matter how distinguished, might be able to add to what he already knew about Bowles. But he had an intuition that by alternately pacifying and provoking Hawken, he might get this self-important little man to betray something about Bowles's death that he might be holding back. It could be that his agitation that morning was simply displeasure at the adverse publicity that would result from the suicide, but it was clearly something that affected Hawken directly, personally. Perhaps there were deeper political issues of which he, Smailes, was unaware. He agreed that he would be pleased to meet the eminent physicist the following afternoon, if Beecroft could make arrangements.

"Why is he ignoring the signs, walking on the grass like that?" asked the detective. The question seemed to delight Hawken.

"Oh, that notice is for the tourists and the junior members.

One of the quirks of a St. Margaret's fellowship is that it confers the right to walk across all the lawns. A tradition dating back to the eighteenth century, I gather. It allows our aging fellows to simultaneously exercise their limbs, and their prerogatives." Hawken beamed at Smailes.

"I think I'll visit Mr. Bowles's room again. I'd like to take another look around before the family comes in," Smailes said impassively. "Can I get a key at the lodge?"

"Yes, of course," said Hawken, a little too politely.

Andrei Petrovich Orlovsky stood at the sixth-floor window of the huge steel-and-glass building and gazed across the ribbons of traffic on the Moscow ring road. Winter was lingering, and still in mid-April the limbs of the birch trees surrounding the distant lake were bare, allowing glimpses of gray water. In summer, the dense foliage would prevent his seeing the foreign diplomats who came from the city to row and swim. It would also prevent prying eyes with binoculars from examining the building.

Unlike many at First, he had not bridled at the move to Yasyenevo, to the giant seven-story building in the shape of a three-pointed star. Many felt an almost mystic attachment to the building at Dzerzhinsky Square, but he had been irritated by its cramped offices, the unreliable heating and communications systems, the increasing crowds of tourists with their guidebooks and telephoto lenses. The move to Yasyenevo had brought the expansion and privacy those at the top of First had long sought, and had confirmed the First Chief Directorate, the KGB's foreign intelligence section, as the elite domain within the world's largest security agency. It had also allowed him to settle some scores, to encourage retirements and advance promotions, to try to mold the higher echelons of the directorate to his liking. It was now no secret where Chairman Andropov was aiming, and Orlovsky's boss, Gryslov, as head of the First Chief Directorate, was a logical successor when the move came. That left himself and Veleshin as the two leading candidates for Gryslov's seventh-floor office when reorganization came to Yasyenevo. He was a major general and head of the Scientific and Technical Directorate, and senior to Veleshin by three or four years. Veleshin was only a brigadier general, but was in charge of the Third Directorate, which included the prestigious Western Europe beat. It could be a close call, and Veleshin's overt jockeying for the chairman's favor was beginning to annoy him. But it was a ploy that could well backfire.

There was one retirement he had been particularly pleased to accomplish. He had never shared in the fawning admiration of the so-called Five Stars. They were supposedly shining examples of the triumph of communist ideology over capitalism, but he had known the three who had escaped to Moscow well enough to know they were dissolute, sentimental fools. The fourth, now exposed to the world, seemed no better. The identity of the fifth was a mystery to him, as to everyone else at First, except he knew that he worked in Whitehall. He seemed made of sterner stuff.

He had always distrusted Philby. The self-conscious, stammering manner, the affectation of gentleman's distaste for the modern world and its unpleasant necessities, the peculiarly British arrogance that assumed infallibility for his bland analyses. And for all the glamour of his reputation, no one had raised a protest when he had lobbied in the relocation committee against the assignment of an office. Many of his contemporaries were veterans of the Patriotic War and their xenophobia ran deep, no matter how loyal a particular foreigner may have been to the revolution. Orlovsky had thought he had gotten rid of him for good.

Then his source at headquarters had begun to tell him of the private correspondence between Philby and Comrade Andropov. Not only did Philby continue to submit his irrelevant position papers, but occasionally the chairman would actually solicit his opinion, as if to counter the prevailing views at First. Then the free-lance material. Profiles of politi-

85

cians and businessmen, even jazz musicians, pandering blatantly to the chairman's private tastes. He had heard rumors of weekends at the chairman's dacha, which thankfully turned out to be false. Now he heard that between them the chairman and Veleshin had turned to Philby over the routine question of a protection operation in Britain. He had not seen the recommendation, and did not know the principals involved, but his friend Maschenko at Department Five had seemed excited at the prospect of a challenging foreign mission. Although he had not been consulted, he would have concurred that Maschenko's men were the most able and the best trained, and their deployment was the most logical response in such a situation. Orlovsky did not know of the disposition of the case, except that the recommendation had been overridden and that Veleshin had seemed particularly smug of late. For his part, Maschenko was smoldering over the insult. Orlovsky watched as his breath clouded the reinforced window. He reflected that Veleshin and Philby were both ambitious men, and seemed to have secured an inside track with the chairman. He thought with sudden disgust that the grandiose Englishman might even consider himself a candidate for rehabilitation at First, then dismissed the idea immediately. But he would dearly like to know the response they had cooked up between them. Perhaps it would give him an opportunity to fire a shot across both their bows.

Six

THE SUMMER Denise had married and moved out, Derek grew closer to Yvonne, whose chastity had yielded to the entreaties of his unhappiness. He could not face the idea of another year in school just to retake the examinations. He enrolled in a Liberal Studies program at the Cambridge College of Technology and stayed home with his mother. He hated the Tech. He felt older and more intelligent than the other students, and cut off from their hedonism. His few school friends, and particularly Iain, had left for college, and he had his mother to think of. Financially she was all right, with his father's half pension, and was making a brave attempt to adapt. But she was lost without Harry Smailes's monumental self-regard as her reference point, and in her loneliness appreciated Derek's staying at home more than she would say.

At the beginning of his second year, Yvonne became pregnant. They had never been that careful. Oddly, he never considered any option other than marriage. It was as if the glad promise of his youth had given way to the obligations of manhood with a momentum he was unable to resist. And within two months he had asked to see George Dearnley about the possibility of joining the force.

In time he got used to being called Harry's boy. He knew it would be a long shadow to walk in, but he got the firm impression his father had not been much liked on the force, which gratified him. But it had all seemed inevitable. His father's admonition from the grave had been too strong.

Immediately on leaving Hawken's staircase Smailes strode over to the porters' lodge, signed for a pass key, then asked for a private telephone. He was shown into Beecroft's office, which was vacant, and arranged for the prints officer to meet him at the college within the hour. He took the precaution of phoning directly through to the lab and giving precise directions to Bowles's court and corridor. He did not want anyone at the college to know he was having second thoughts. He figured that Alex Klammer, the duty officer, could carry his nondescript briefcase past the porters' lodge without being questioned.

Bowles's room was as gloomy as before. The SOCO boys and coroner's people had left the lamp on over the desk, and had replaced the belt in the plant hook above the window, where it hung limply. The chair had been righted and stood expectantly next to the potted plant on the floor. Smailes stood on the chair and carefully replaced the belt with the aspidistra, holding the plastic plant pot with his handkerchief and working the belt hole off the hook with his free hand. He placed the belt on the desk beside the typewriter and studied them both slowly. He doubted the leather of the belt would take a decent print, and anyway, it had probably been handled by several others already besides himself. Same for the chair. The typewriter was a different story, of course. He knew the metal body and plastic keys would take the tiny sweat prints beautifully, and it was unlikely the machine had been touched since Bowles had supposedly used it to type his last message to the world. When he squatted next to it, the detective could see distinct whorls lit by the compressed light from the desk lamp on the space bar and return key. The lamp would take good prints too, and maybe the plant pot. He would have Klammer dust the whole desk, the hanging plant and the chair.

The filing cabinet was a possibility too. He swung open the first drawer and again he saw the first file, labeled *Abominable Snowman*. There were several hanging files which seemed to contain papers and clippings. Further back was a file labeled *Extraterrestrials*. For a mathematician, Bowles certainly had had a speculative curiosity.

The second file drawer was introduced by a typed tab that read *Cambridge* and by a smaller tab on the first hanging file labeled *Apostles*. The drawers and files were obviously arranged alphabetically, which made sense for such an organized mind as Bowles's. Smailes pulled the *Apostles* file. The notes were typed, and obviously quite recent. They seemed to describe some secret society at Cambridge University in the thirties, which meant nothing to him. He replaced the file and looked through the other subdivisions. The file headings seemed to reflect a dry sense of humor—*Fellows and Travelers, Golf Club and Chess Society, The Trinity Homintern*—and a personal code that was impenetrable to him. The file drawer was full, with twelve or thirteen fat files. Toward the front he found a more recognizable file, labeled *Communist Party of Great Britain*, which he pulled. It contained pages and pages of typed notes. He wondered whether any of this stuff would be of interest to the Special Branch, and made a mental note to check out the second drawer more thoroughly.

The third drawer was arranged similarly. The file label at the front said *Kennedy*, followed by a series of supporting files marked neatly with colored tabs. Smailes scanned the headings: *The Geometry of a Murder, The Hall of Mirrors, Hands Off Cuba!, Jack Ruby—The Jew Who Had Guts.* Again, he was struck by the quirky style. The last title seemed particularly odd, so he pulled out the fat folder and moved to the desk to examine it. He spread the pages carefully and saw a series of photo-copied articles, handwritten and typed notes and a collection of black-and-white photographs. At the front of the file was a typed document stapled together which bore the same title as the file itself. Smailes flipped it open to the second page and read:

"The Warren Commission concluded that Ruby's murder of Oswald was a freak accident that changed history, that premeditation could only be inferred if there was evidence that Ruby had been stalking Oswald from the time Oswald was in custody. Yet that is precisely what Ruby had done. He was observed at the Dallas police station the Friday evening Oswald was arrested, attempting to enter the room where Oswald was being interrogated. He was there the following day, at the precise time Oswald was first scheduled to be moved to the county jail. Then he appeared in the station basement with split-second timing on Sunday morning to murder Oswald in front of scores of armed police and a tele-vision audience of millions.

"Jack Ruby had led a life of seamless venality, uncluttered by any demonstrated concern for other human beings. The notion that he killed Oswald out of compassion for Jacqueline Kennedy is nonsense. So is his later assertion that he in-tended to show the world that a Jew could have guts. He killed Oswald because he knew he would be tortured and killed himself if he did not, believing desperately that he could escape a murder charge and receive a light sentence because he would be seen as a hero by the American people. In fact, he only escaped the electric chair on a technicality, and died of lung cancer while awaiting a retrial."

Smailes had been ten years old when John Kennedy was shot. He remembered he had been playing at Iain Mack's house, with their model trains, when Iain's sister had dashed into the room and told them in a superior way that they had shot the American President. The two boys had thought it was a joke, barely knowing who the American President was, but Janet had started to cry.

Days later he remembered seeing the shooting of the President's killer on television. Oswald, a greasy little man surrounded by gangsters, was walking through a concrete basement when one of the gangsters stepped forward and shot him. Then the other gangsters jumped on the killer. The news announcer had told them excitedly that the gangsters were Dallas policemen.

Over the years Smailes had paid little attention to the intermittent sensational accounts in the press and on television of plots and conspiracies in the Kennedy murder. The assassination seemed part of the incomprehensible way that American society worked, an example of its deep, repulsive violence. What he *had* learned, years later as a policeman, was that there was no way Ruby could have gotten into that police basement without the active collusion of someone on the force. With a prisoner like Oswald, those kinds of mistakes didn't happen. And sure enough, it had come out that Ruby was a minor hoodlum and a cop glad-hander. He provided the police booze and women, and they in turn knocked down the assault and traffic charges on which he was continually being hauled in. Which meant there were probably other, more serious charges on which he was never hauled in, Smailes knew. He knew that score. There were a few like Ruby in Cambridge these days. Wide boys, the Cambridge cops called them. A crate of beer and scotch at Christmas, big donations to the benevolent fund. It was a measure of your integrity as a cop, how much slack you cut them.

Thinking about the Kennedy assassination after all this time made Smailes pause as he replaced the file. He wondered if it was true, after all, that Oswald had been the killer. He opened the bottom file drawer, which began with a file labeled *Marie Céleste.* Then a large *Miscellaneous* file. Then a big alphabetic jump to *UFOs.* He closed the drawer, leaving the cabinet unlocked. If the family were due the following day, it would be simpler if they didn't have to hunt around for keys. He scanned the outside of the case carefully, but could see no distinct prints with the naked eye.

The standing bookcase to the right of the file cabinet was filled almost exclusively with mathematics and physics textbooks, with a row of binders on the top shelf. Smailes removed one and found work papers which contained an incomprehensible series of formulae and equations. He replaced the book and shuddered slightly. Mathematical formulae had always looked like barbed wire to him.

Across the room the bookshelves above the bed contained more varied titles. He noticed also that Bowles had them arranged into a kind of private library, with identifying labels taped to the base of each spine. They seemed to reflect the subjects displayed in the files, meticulously arranged by subject and author. Bowles had obviously been a lover of books. Most were hardbacks and had been kept in excellent condition. He removed an old volume on Himalayan travel and noticed that the dust jacket had been carefully repaired. On the inside cover was written *Simon Bowles, 1967,* a conspicuous sign of pride of ownership.

There was one whole shelf of books relating to American society and to the Kennedy assassination in particular. There were almost two shelves of books about World War II, international espionage and communism. In this section were also biographies and memoirs about Cambridge University in the twentieth century. There was nothing to suggest to the detective what might have been preoccupying the young man on the night of his death. He checked the desk drawer again, and confirmed that there were no files or papers on which Bowles might have been working. He decided to check the clothes closet on the far side of the room. It contained a modest selection of clothes, and an old briefcase lying on the floor. Smailes removed it expectantly and sat down in one of the armchairs in front of the electric fire.

He was disappointed. There were a lot of handwritten notes in a childish hand which the detective found practically indecipherable, some mathematical work, bank statements and a collection of personal letters all received within the last six months. He glanced through one from Bowles's sister, one from his mother and one from a friend called Hugh. They contained nothing of any significance as far as the detective could ascertain, and he felt no relish for examining Bowles's papers further. He replaced the briefcase and sat down in the armchair again to wait for Klammer, the fingerprint officer.

He drummed his fingers on the arm of the chair, irritated by the pique he felt at this case. It was just a suicide, after all. Bowles was undoubtedly a bright young man, but he was also unstable, and not particularly communicative about his feelings. Maybe something particular had happened in the hour or so after he got back from the bar to compel him to take his own life. Maybe nothing had happened, except that whatever well of misery and grief he had in his life had suddenly and unexpectedly spilled over. Davies and Hawken had both been testy and agitated, but it was perhaps understandable given the fact they had tried deliberately to monitor Bowles's emotional state, and failed. Smailes lit a cigarette and reached down for an empty ashtray in the hearth of the old fireplace. He glanced at his watch, saw that it was almost three-twenty, and realized he might have a long wait for Klammer.

Smailes reflected that this was probably his last visit to the room before the family came to dispose of the belongings, and took out his notebook to sketch the relative positions of the furniture in the room, and the position in which he had discovered the body, which he would need for the inquest. He considered going further, making a list of the contents of the drawer, the briefcase and the filing cabinet, but felt no enthusiasm for such a fruitless task. Besides, the notes on the Kennedy murder had aroused his curiosity. How was it that

Bowles had described Ruby? "Seamless venality, uncluttered by any demonstrated concern . . ." Pretty florid prose for a math student. Needing to kill time, Smailes reached back into the file drawer and removed the first Kennedy file, the one called *The Geometry of a Murder.*

By the time Klammer arrived forty-five minutes later, Smailes hardly heard the knock on the door. He was completely engrossed in Simon Bowles's exposition of the events in Dealey Plaza, Dallas, on November 22, 1963. Through Bowles's depiction, the detective felt that he was there at the scene, hearing the gunfire roar, flinging himself to the sidewalk in panic, rushing up the grassy knoll with the other cops, finding nothing. Despite the awkwardness of Bowles's writing, he painted a vivid and gripping picture of the physical circumstances of Kennedy's murder. He had made many drawings of the configuration of buildings, cars and people on that Friday lunchtime, and the relationship between these components was stated in terms of geometric and algebraic equations that Smailes could not understand. Bowles's notes, however, were typed and were relatively easy to follow. Occasionally they presumed some knowledge about the Kennedy assassination that Smailes did not have, but more often they presented a patient, step-by-step description of his conclusions. Smailes found the reconstruction quite fascinating, his professional curiosity engaged by Bowles's painstaking reasoning. It seemed that Simon Bowles, by claiming to apply strict mathematical and physical rules to the known evidence, concluded that three gunmen fired on Kennedy that day. Didn't the official account state conclusively that Oswald was the lone gunman? Smailes wondered if anyone else had ever subjected the assassination scene to such laborious mathematical analysis. If Bowles was right, his theory disproved the accepted version. As the detective sergeant considered the implication of this discovery, he realized that the soft tapping behind him was in fact the lab officer knocking at the door.

94

He hurriedly replaced the file in its drawer and let Alex Klammer into the room.

The two policemen completed their work with little discussion between them. Klammer was an industrious man a little older than Smailes, whose professionalism seemed to have a barb to it, as if confronting Detective Sergeant Smailes with his unorthodox reputation by soundly repudiating it. His technique was thoroughly proper and unhurried, and his manner respectful and distant. Smailes also knew that Klammer and his wife were neighbors of Yvonne and her new husband, that they played whist or something together, and the connection made him uncomfortable. Klammer had completed his work on the typewriter and other objects on the desk and was standing on the chair dusting the plant hanger.

"Nothing but smears, Sergeant," he said, squinting at the plastic pot, with his back to Smailes. "It's either been wiped or handled recently with a cloth."

Typically, Klammer had not attempted to move the evidence at all, but was holding it lightly with his surgical gloves. Smailes concealed his annoyance that his own brusquer handling of the pot might have obscured good prints, saying instead that he had figured as much, that the filing cabinet might be better. Klammer climbed down carefully and proceeded to work on the cabinet in his absorbed, self-conscious way. As Smailes imagined, there were some good lifts from the case and drawer fronts, but nothing from the knurled metal pulls of the drawers themselves. The lifts from the typewriter would be the best, he knew, and he reassured himself that he had done the right thing, even if it was second thought, by bringing in the fingerprint officer. As Klammer was methodically returning his instruments to their case, he felt a momentary concern that the lab man might have parked a marked car in the college's restricted car park, and thereby given his presence away. If Klammer was offended by the question, he carefully concealed it, answering casually that he had parked at the foot of Trinity Street and walked to the main entrance, heedful of Smailes's wish to keep his visit secret. He had not been challenged entering the college, he explained. Was that all? he wanted to know.

Klammer's deadpan manner must be an asset at the card table, Smailes decided. He asked the officer to call through to the coroner's DC and make sure that prints were lifted from Bowles's hands before the undertaker's people got hold of the body, if possible. Such a procedure was not always routine in a suicide, and Klammer was to refer any objections to him personally. He asked how long it would be before Klammer could run comparisons and confirm any unknown prints.

"Oh, a couple of days, Sergeant, depending on the quality, you know. Are there any others we need to take, for elimination?"

Smailes had already thought of this. Hawken had said no one had touched anything, which meant there had only been himself and the scenes-of-crimes and coroner's officers in the room. The others had touched only the belt, he guessed.

"Let's wait and see. Maybe mine." Smailes grinned. If Klammer thought the remark was funny, he did not show it. He told Smailes he would get him a report as soon as possible, and left unobtrusively, leaving Smailes alone once more in the bleak little room.

There was something about the willing efficiency of Detective Constable Klammer that Smailes found depressing. It was the same with Ted Swedenbank—a sort of uncontrived eagerness, a buoyancy that Smailes himself was unable to muster. He knew at times his colleagues on the force thought his manner stuck-up or conceited, that his cynicism and humor were in some subtle way designed to put them down. He honestly did not think this was fair, and it hurt him when these rumors got back to him. The fact was, he thought *they* were dishonest, the Klammers and Swedenbanks, who denied ambiguity and uncertainty with their bright professionalism. How could you not be somewhat cynical if you took two seconds to look around you? After all, they worked for the police, not the church. If cops couldn't laugh at the contradictions of their work they were a pretty pathetic institution, in Smailes's view. He simply was not a true believer, he realized, and it pained him. It meant he could never fully belong, or fully relax with the rules. And while he felt a certain defiance in the superiority of his judgment, he also sometimes felt dejected and isolated. He looked at his watch, noticed it was well after five, and decided it was time he went home.

Much later he decided it was his mood after Klammer left that afternoon that was decisive in the unraveling of the whole extraordinary business. He was not sure whether it was characteristic or uncharacteristic, but he went back to the third drawer of Bowles's filing cabinet and removed all the typed summary files from the Kennedy file, which together made up a manuscript five or six inches thick. He put them under his jacket and raincoat, and held them against his body with his hand in his coat pocket, and then left the room, locking it carefully behind him. He met no one in the corridor or as he strode around the two courts on his way back to the lodge. However, as he spoke with the duty porter behind the counter and handed back the pass key, he did think it strange that in his inner office Paul Beecroft was listening intently to Bunty Allen, Bowles's bedder, whom Smailes had questioned that morning. The detective could not hear what was being said, but Mrs. Allen looked considerably more animated than earlier that day, as she emphasized a point with a thrusting motion of her hands. Blue smoke curled from a cigarette parked in an ashtray in front of her as Beecroft, impassive, leaned on the back of a chair which held his suit jacket, listening. Smailes was surprised because he distinctly remembered Hawken telling her to go home for the day, many hours ago.

The dogs strained at their leash and the young man could barely restrain them as they pulled him along the street. A sharp wind made his eyes and throat ache, and his shoulder socket felt wrenched and damaged. The houses seemed to stretch forever, and at every opening in a wall or hedge, the whippets would pull more fiercely to explore the terrain inside. The sky was a sickly purple color.

Suddenly the animals found a narrow aperture beside a gatepost and surged through into the garden beyond. The young man braced his shoulder against the concrete post to stop them, and began pulling them slowly back into the street. Their squirming strength diminished and became a leaden mass. He pulled and pulled, and saw at the end of the leash a leather belt. And then, inexorably, the head and shoulders came into sight. He saw the thin, fair curls, and then he saw the awful grimace on the face of Simon Bowles.

In the courtyard at the base of Bowles's staircase, Hawken and Beecroft were speaking to two ambulance men who held a stretcher between them, pointing to the far side of the court and the exit to Great Court and the street beyond. Their gestures unfurled in slow motion, and though their mouths moved, there was no sound beyond the soft swirling of the wind. The wind stirred the hair at Hawken's temples. Beside them stood Ted Swedenbank and Bunty Allen. She held a yellow cloth duster and wore a scarf on her head, a familiar green scarf with a check pattern. Smailes looked more closely and saw it was his mother's scarf, and the woman was not Bunty Allen but in fact his mother, who seemed to be crying noiselessly as she leaned against Swedenbank's arm. He glanced down at the stretcher and the covered body it held. The wind began to stir the cream-colored sheet that draped the corpse. A sudden gust lifted the top of the sheet into the air, and inert on the stretcher he saw the face of his father, blue with toxemia. The myocardial infarction had already shut down his heart. He saw his mother cup her face in her hands in despair. He woke up and snapped on the light.

He sat up and listened to the pounding of his heart and the faint sound of rain on the roof of his neighbor's shed. After a minute his eyes adjusted to the light and the faded roses of the bedroom wallpaper solidified into their familiar pattern. He reached for the packet of Marlboros and the lighter on the nightstand, lit a cigarette, and inhaled deeply. He got up to fetch the ashtray from the top of the dresser, and felt a damp patch of sweat at the base of his spine. He sat up again in bed and saw that his hands shook slightly as he raised the cigarette to his mouth.

The dream was a variation of one which he had had for nearly ten years now, but less frequently of late. It always involved the dogs and the feeling of being pulled out of control by them, and then the discovery of something unspeakable at the end of their leash. The part with his father on the stretcher had been a new embellishment.

His heartbeat began to still but he guessed it would be hours before he felt like sleep again. He took his ancient tartan dressing gown down from the back of the door, stepped into a pair of rubber sandals, and padded out into the hallway and into the tiny kitchen. He turned on the electric kettle and wandered into the living room, snapping on lights as he went. He went back to the bedroom for his cigarettes, put a Willie Nelson album on the turntable, and sat down in the lounger. A feeling of dread still gripped at the muscles of his chest, and he felt an oceanic loneliness.

Derek Smailes looked around at the living room. He liked the featureless bachelor conformity of his small, one-bedroom flat. He had moved there five years ago, the second place he had had since the divorce, choosing it because it was closer to the station and far away from the neighborhood in which he had grown up and lived after his marriage. The houses of the gray terraced streets off Mill Road were so different from the development where his parents had lived in their police house, or where he and Yvonne had begun their marriage in their small police flat. The houses made no pretense at middle-class expansiveness, had no gardens front or back, and were relieved in their uniformity only by the occasional brightly painted door or defiant window box. The place had come furnished, and Smailes had accepted wholeheartedly the jumble of cheap furniture, the tasteless faded wallpapers and fitted nylon carpets that went along with the lease. The landlord was Les Howarth, a fish-shop owner in Histon Smailes knew vaguely, who left him completely alone. Les himself had the lease on the upstairs flat, which Smailes knew he kept to cavort in the afternoons and the occasional evening with a shapely blonde whom Smailes had met a couple of times in the hallway. Smailes would know they were up there when he heard strains of Engelbert Humperdinck or Frankie Vaughn drifting through the ceiling.

He remembered with distaste the arduous succession of meaningless choices which his marriage had seemed to require. Should they choose the folding Habitat dining chairs or the conventional oak set from Eaden Lilly? What about the bedspread and the sheets, or should they choose a duvet, more expensive but more efficient? Yvonne had wanted blue in their bedroom and yellow in Tracy's room, what did he think? In truth he did not care a damn about any of these issues, but could not say so or Yvonne would get upset, so he stroked his chin in feigned reflection and gave considered, thoughtful replies. What a relief to escape such pretense! Now his furniture was Naugahyde, his color schemes unmatched, his environment untended. He adjusted himself in the vinyl recliner that he had inherited with the place, and looked over at the wooden clock on the tiled mantel shelf above the fireplace that held the gas fire. It was twelve forty-five. Willie's low wail felt apt, companionable. He bent down and turned the dial on the side of the gas fire, the single pillar of flame appearing with a low hiss. He thought again of Simon Bowles, the luminous intellect extinguished, the sadness and the waste. Almost without thinking he reached for the manuscript which he had left on the green plastic footstool when he retired for the night, and began reading again.

Smailes had finished the *Geometry of a Murder* chapter and had started on *The Hall of Mirrors* before he had gone to bed.

100

This second chapter detailed Oswald's potential intelligence links and was as meticulously researched as the earlier work. The detective had been impressed by Bowles's analysis, the combination of biting scientific insight and common-sense fairness that made his interpretations particularly persuasive. It was plain that Bowles discounted the theory that Oswald acted alone, but he also dismissed the claim that Oswald might have been an active intelligence agent of any government. He was intrigued by Oswald's links to volatile Cuban exile groups on both sides of the impassioned Cuba debate, and speculated that the theatrical Oswald might have been manipulated by agents from one of the opposed camps. Separate accounts placed Oswald in the company of a stocky Latino man at different sites before the assassination, and Bowles was obviously frustrated by his inability to identify the presumed Cuban. The young mathematician clearly had an encyclopedic grasp of the issues surrounding the murder and of the research and theories that had been advanced to date. Smailes found himself steadily more engrossed as Bowles's reconstruction of the extraordinary events surrounding the assassination unfolded. He drank several mugs of tea that night to keep himself awake as he made his way to the final, frustrating chapter, titled *Conundrum*. At times he wondered whether Bowles had prepared the manuscript for publication, the material was so scrupulously organized and presented. But as the first wash of light began to seep into the room he realized that this was impossible, since Bowles's work had failed in the same way for which he criticized all previous analyses. While proving to Smailes's complete satisfaction that Oswald could not have performed the feat required of him that day, the manuscript was frayed with countless loose ends and could not answer the simple question: if Oswald had not shot Kennedy, who had, why and how? In fact, the final *Conundrum* chapter was simply a succession of tantalizing questions that remained unanswered after twenty years, which Bowles had simply succeeded in restating with telling force. If Bowles had claimed to Davies that he had solved the Kennedy murder, then it was not apparent in the work Smailes had just spent most of the night reading.

He heard the ghostly whir of the milk wagon in the street and the chink of bottles as he tossed the manuscript down on the footstool in disgust before heading back up the hallway for a few, insufficient hours of sleep. He was angry at himself for staying up so late, and despite a grudging admiration, angry at Simon Bowles for disappointing him. Bowles had set himself a question that he had been unable to answer, despite the brilliant analytic and investigative technique. Smailes reflected that if a mind like Bowles's could not crack the Kennedy mystery, maybe no one's could, but it was a thought from which he drew no comfort.

Seven

ACTING DETECTIVE CONSTABLE Edward Swedenbank was pleased. He now had official instructions from
Chief Superintendent Dearnley to leave the Bowles inquest
preparation to Derek Smailes, and to work with Detective
Sergeant Godfrey Howell on the cigarette lorry theft. Howell
had his hands full with at least two other cases, and was likely
to leave a lot of the investigation to him. And he wasn't such a
peculiar bastard as Smailes. Not that the sergeant bothered
him as much as he bothered others in CID, but you never
quite knew where you stood with him. Howell was a type he
understood better, a cop who had served with the Army
abroad before joining the force. Stickler for the rules, not
much sense of humor, but that didn't matter much.

Now they had a report that the lorry had been found abandoned in Walthamstow, in East London, empty of course.
The owner of the truck stop had called in with a claim that

103

his attendant had noticed three men waiting in a parked car around the side of the café in the hour or so before the theft was reported. The men were all wearing turbans, which made them Sikhs, he guessed. The implications were significant. These new circumstances meant that he would have to deal not only with the Metropolitan Police about the discovery of the lorry but maybe even with the Yard or Special Branch. If Sikhs had pulled off a big lorry theft, it might well be connected to all that political trouble happening over in India. The Sikhs were usually a law-abiding lot, let's face it. They were probably after money for weapons for the lads back home. At least, it was a possibility. However the case turned out, it looked like he was going to rub shoulders with the brass from town, and if he pulled off his end of things all right, well, he could chalk off this probationary period and get the bloody "acting" out of his rank.

Swedenbank was studying the report from the Walthamstow station when Derek Smailes came noisily into the small room the CID detectives shared, carrying a mug of coffee. He looked bleary and bad-tempered, and Swedenbank wondered how he would take the news that he was on the St. Margaret's suicide alone, whereas Swedenbank, a lowly ADC, had been assigned to Howell and the lorry theft. To his surprise, Smailes already knew about it, and made some decent remarks about the opportunity it offered. It was one thing you had to say about Derek Smailes—he had bloody good contacts when it came to knowing what George Dearnley was up to.

In truth, Smailes didn't mind, and actually preferred to wrap up the rest of the Bowles suicide inquiry himself. He had shown no surprise when Gloria, George's secretary, had stood behind him in the breakfast line in the canteen, silently raising her eyebrows and a file flap showing the memo she had just typed on the reassignment. Swedenbank was a little earnest for his taste, and he didn't fancy tugging him around today on two hours' sleep. Besides, he had to somehow get Bowles's Kennedy notes back into his files, preferably unnoticed. The thought irritated him. Hawken had said the sister would be by around one, and he had the other don to try to interview. And then there were the Myrtlefields people, the doctors who had treated Bowles when he was out there. He picked up his telephone and began calling.

It was a raw Thursday morning when he arrived again at the stone portal of St. Margaret's, but the heat of the porters' lodge was stifling. He recognized the duty porter from the day before, but the man failed to acknowledge him as he strode up to the counter. He seemed engrossed in his newspaper, whose headline told of ominous events in the South Atlantic, where Argentina was making threatening noises about the Falkland Islands. No bloody wonder, thought Smailes. How would we like it if Korea occupied the Scilly Isles? The porter slowly looked up, then returned to his reading.

"Sorry, Officer. Someone's already come for the pass key for Mr. Bowles's room. I can't give you my key—it's not allowed unless I come with it and I'm here by myself until one. I suggest you just go over there, if that's what you want. Otherwise I can call Dr. Hawken . . ."

The porter, a small bald man with thick glasses, was obviously uninterested in calling Dr. Hawken or having his routines, or his reading, disrupted.

"Who came for the key, if I might ask?" he inquired, trying to keep sarcasm out of his voice.

"Allerton. Friend of Bowles, I think." At this point, the porter deigned to look up again. "He said he had Dr. Hawken's permission."

"No doubt," said Smailes. He was carrying Bowles's notes in a small, zippered portfolio under his arm, which suddenly felt conspicuous. "How long ago?"

"Oh, ten minutes," the porter said, and gave an incongruous, expansive smile. Smailes looked at his watch. It was barely twelve-thirty; either Allerton was on some mission of his own or the family had shown up early.

There was a small crowd in Simon Bowles's room. Allerton

sat with his back to the desk, smoking a cigarette. A woman sat on the rug in the middle of the floor, with the contents of Bowles's briefcase spread before her. A shabby-looking man with his back to the room was inspecting the books in the bookshelves above the bed. No one was talking.

Smailes studied the woman. She seemed in her late thirties, but the long, light brown hair that fell across the side of her face made her look younger. It was a strong, intelligent face. She was intent on reading the letters that Smailes had found in the briefcase, and did not at first look up. Smailes could make out nothing of the man inspecting the bookshelves. Allerton was the first to notice him.

"Uh, hullo," he said awkwardly. "Alice, it's the CID man I was telling you about."

The woman looked at him impassively for a moment, then got to her feet and held out her hand.

"Mr. Smailes? I'm Alice Wentworth, Simon's sister. Pleased to meet you."

Smailes was uneasy about shaking hands with women, unsure how to grasp their limp parcel of fingers, but Alice Wentworth's grip was firm and confident. She looked at him directly but without hostility. He wondered what Allerton had told her of their confrontation the previous day. He could see the family resemblance in the strong nose and small mouth, and the hair coloring was the same. She was wearing a fawn polo-neck sweater with a belt at the waist and brown slacks. She wore a little discreet makeup. Her manner was formal, and her voice was firm, with the featureless Home Counties accent of the upper middle class.

"Perhaps we should sit down." She gestured to the armchairs flanking the fireplace. "I'm early. The business at the hospital took no time at all. Giles and I were just trying to straighten things out. The senior tutor said that was all right. It is all right, isn't it?"

"Yes, of course," Smailes said, and paused. "I'm very sorry about your brother."

The remark seemed to provoke her. "Yes, thank you, but I'm more cross with Simon than anything at the moment. He had promised to speak to people if he was feeling depressed, you know. Someone here at the college, or me, you know. He could have called me. Of course, he refused to see anyone on a regular basis. Said it was unnecessary."

She made a scoffing movement of her head and swept her hair out of her face with her hand. "It seems so cruel and selfish, that's all. My mother is beside herself. My father died just two years ago, I don't know if you know. And I'm afraid I'm rather old-fashioned about suicide. I think it's a sin."

Smailes had seen the reaction before. Anger and recrimination as a means of stemming grief. That would come later, inevitably.

Allerton, who had been looking sullen and embarrassed, seemed shocked by her last remark. "God, Alice. Come on," he protested.

"No, I mean it, Giles. I can't think that anything justifies taking one's own life. Anything."

Smailes realized that Alice Wentworth could probably provide him with more information than anyone so far about Simon Bowles. But this was hardly the place. He wondered if he could remember how to get to Poole's office, his interview room. The man examining the bookcases turned to Alice Wentworth and began to speak. Smailes had assumed that this was her clergyman husband, but he seemed much too young and disheveled to be married to this carefully groomed woman.

"I can give you a hundred quid, the lot," said the young man, in the voice of a Shakespearean actor. He wore a battered velvet jacket, from the pocket of which protruded the neck of a pint of vodka. The detective realized he represented a secondhand bookstore. He probably was an actor, fallen on hard times, consoling himself with vodka at noon.

"They would be worth more, but most are, er, adulterated,

107

I'm afraid. I mean, they have labels on their spines that will be hard to remove."

"Well, quite," said Mrs. Wentworth, disinterested. "Look, I'll have to think about it. I may want to keep some myself. Can we call you? I mean, does Giles have your number?"

The man fished around in his top pocket with a forefinger and pulled out a grubby business card, which he handed to Allerton.

"Yes, Michael, we'll be in touch, okay? Might be a day or two," said Allerton. The men obviously knew each other.

Smailes had walked across the room to examine again the poster of the old philosopher next to the closet. He was a little surprised that they were moving to liquidate Bowles's belongings so quickly. Hadn't Hawken said they could have the rest of the year?

"How long has this been here?" asked Smailes.

"The poster? I've no idea. Giles?"

Allerton shrugged. "Dunno. As long as I knew him, I think. At least three years. Sort of forgot it was there. Shall I take it down, Alice?"

"Yes, yes, I suppose so. We should clear everything, I think. Is there anything else, Officer?"

Smailes asked her if she could spare the time to answer some questions in private, and she agreed. The portfolio with her brother's files felt heavy underneath his arm as they made their way to the adjacent court and Poole's corridor. Smailes found the room without difficulty. Alice Wentworth began talking as soon as she sat down.

"Look, I know that it's part of your business to try to find a motive for what Simon did, but I think it's somewhat pointless to speculate, don't you? I was probably as close to my brother as anyone, and he didn't say anything to me about what was troubling him." Smailes guessed that Allerton had given her words of warning about his interview technique.

"When was the last time you spoke to him?"

"On Saturday. And I was annoyed with him. He was sup-

posed to come and stay with us that night, in Rickmansworth, because Sunday was my mother's birthday and we
were planning lunch together. Simon is my only brother, you
see, and these things are important for my mother, now that
she is getting older. Well, he said he wasn't going to come,
that he had to go down to London on Monday and he needed
to do a lot of preparatory work in the library. I thought it was
a really stupid excuse."

"Did he say where he was going?"

"Yes. Somerset House. I didn't ask why. No doubt it was to
do with his latest theorem."

"His academic work?"

"Oh no, not his mathematics. It seemed Simon was getting
less and less interested in that. No, solving his latest mystery,
I mean. Do you know what a theorem is, Mr., er . . . ?"

"Smailes."

"Mr. Smailes."

He thought back to the vague geometric concepts he had
retained from his school days. "Er, some theory that can be
proved to be self-evidently true, something like that."

"Not quite, that's an axiom. A theorem is a proposition that
you can logically deduce from known postulates, that is not
self-evidently true. But it can be proved logically, you see.
Well, my brother, as long as I can remember, was fascinated
by the notion that every mystery could be solved by logical
analysis, that every truth could be known, or at least inferred.
Something to do with the mathematical law of decidability,
he said. Simon felt you could apply the mathematical method
to all kinds of unsolved puzzles and arrive at probabilities, if
not definite truths. He started when he was quite small, with
mysteries like the Loch Ness monster, you know, and then
developed an interest in more political things as he got
older."

"Like the Kennedy assassination."

"Oh, so you know."

109

"Well, his friends told me a little about it. And Dr. Davies, his tutor."

"You mean Giles?"

"Yes, and Miss Greenwald."

"That must be his American friend. I haven't met her, although Simon had spoken of her. What's she like?"

The question surprised him. "She seems very pleasant," he said lamely.

"So, anyway, I assumed he was going down to London because he was working on his latest theorem. That was the general term he used for his research projects. It didn't seem a very good reason to miss Mother's birthday."

"And what was his latest theorem?"

"He was researching the penetration of the security forces by the Russians. Particularly by people who had been communists at Cambridge in the thirties. You know, all this Blunt business. Simon was convinced that all the truth had not come out, that perhaps there were still moles, you know, in the Establishment, who were still being protected. He had quite a bee in his bonnet about it."

This information made sense, in view of the books and files Smailes had seen, but the detective kept his face impassive.

"How did he sound? Worried, upset?"

"Preoccupied, certainly. Simon is, I'm sorry, was . . ." Alice Wentworth stopped and took out a Kleenex from a brown leather handbag and dabbed lightly at her eyes. She regained herself quickly. "Simon was forgetful, but fairly conscientious. It was unlike him not to come home for a family occasion for such a pathetic reason. I thought he sounded strange and asked him if he was all right. He said he was, it was just important for him to do this. I'm afraid I wasn't very sympathetic."

"Did he say why he wanted to go to Somerset House? You don't know if he went, do you? That would have been the day before his death."

"No, I don't think he told me why he was going. To look

110

up birth records, I would imagine. I have no idea if he went or not, I'm afraid."

"Would he have told you if something in particular was bothering him?"

"He might. He obviously didn't, though, did he? Although he was quite candid with me around that dreadful time two years ago, when he ended up in the hospital. I'm sure you know about that."

"Yes. So you have no idea why your brother took his own life?"

"Well, he was depressed again, I'm sure. But specifically why, no, I don't have any idea."

"You said your brother was not seeing anyone, a psychiatrist or anything, on a regular basis. Did he take any kind of drugs or medicine?"

"For his nerves, you mean? No, no, I'm sure he didn't. He had to take pills for a few months after he came out of the hospital, but I remember him telling me he had stopped. He didn't like taking them."

Smailes thought for a moment before his next question. "Did you know that your brother was homosexual?"

"Yes, yes, I did, Mr. Smailes. You see, I might be a Christian, but I am not completely unprogressive in my thinking, and it didn't shock me too much when Simon told me. It must have been a year or two ago. Nothing specific, you understand. But he wanted to know whether my mother was expecting him to get engaged and married soon, and he told me that was unlikely to happen. When I asked him why not, he just said: 'I'm gay.' Well, if he had accepted it, there was no reason for me not to, was there? I don't think we spoke at length about it, or have mentioned it since, but I was gratified that he wanted me to know. As I say, I wasn't surprised. He never had girlfriends during his teens, but then he went to that dreadful public school, which hardly gave him much opportunity, did it? I told Peter, my husband, about it at the

111

time, and he agreed that it was brave of Simon to tell me. But you see, we were quite close, in our own way."

Smailes found himself admiring this straightforward, intelligent woman, despite his prejudices. She was not unattractive, in a horsey sort of way.

"What exactly happened two years ago?" he asked.

"Well, it was a combination of things, really, as far as I could tell. Simon always tended to get neurotic around exam time, despite the fact that he always did so well. And then there was all the Kennedy business. He kept reading and reading and getting completely obsessed with trying to work out what had happened. He would call me wildly excited about this or that lead that I really couldn't understand. Then he found that he couldn't give it up, you know, and he became more and more driven and depressed. And then, of course, my father died suddenly, with no warning, and it seemed the last straw for Simon's sanity. It was quite awful for us when we heard he had jumped out of the window, although he did recover quite quickly in the hospital, thank goodness, and then the college gave him the fellowship, so everything was all right in the end, it seemed. And he did solve it, you know, his Kennedy Theorem."

"I'm sorry?" said Smailes, stunned.

"Oh yes, while he was in the hospital, these documents arrived from America. Released by Freedom of Information, or something. And some things from a Cuban study center too. It was all to do with the Cubans, according to Simon. I'm afraid I never paid too much attention. But after he got better he spent a week or two completing his research and actually wrote up his Kennedy Theorem. I think I even read it, although a lot of it I didn't understand. Mr. Smailes, why are you looking at me like that?"

"You say your brother actually completed this research?"

"Oh yes. He was very proud of it."

"Well, I have a slight confession to make." Smailes lifted the portfolio from where it was resting against his chair leg

112

and extracted the manuscript he had read the night before. "I took the liberty of reading some of the material I found in your brother's filing cabinet yesterday. The Kennedy murder has always interested me professionally, and I thought I might get some insight into your brother by looking at it. I meant to return it all this morning, before you arrived."

Alice Wentworth did not seem unduly perturbed by the policeman's peculiar behavior, although she did hold out her hand in a proprietorial way to take the fat document back from him.

"Did you understand it all?" she asked.

"Oh, I knew most of it already," he lied. "But it was interesting to see a fresh perspective. He obviously had a keen mind, your brother."

"Yes, quite," she said, riffling through the typed sheaf. "You must have missed it, I think."

"What?"

"Well, *The Kennedy Theorem*, of course. The summary of all this stuff. I would have thought you would have seen it, since you obviously removed these documents quite carefully. It would be odd if it wasn't there. I must check." There was now an edge in her voice.

"Yes, of course." The detective tugged at his ear and glanced over at Poole's bookshelves with their sad collection of thrillers. "I'd be interested to see it, if it's there," he added.

"Well, of course," she said, and silence filled the room.

"What about this latest project—what did you say it was about?" asked Smailes eventually.

"The Cambridge spy ring—you know, those dreadful men who went to Moscow and our famous Mr. Blunt. They were all at Cambridge here in the thirties, although not at St. Margaret's, I think. Mostly at Trinity. Anyway, I think Simon became interested via his Kennedy project, because he got quite fascinated with the intelligence services and how they operate. He got quite impassioned about it, and said things like secrecy was the only true villainy in a free society. Then

113

of course there was all that scandal surrounding Blunt when he was exposed, and all the speculation in the press that not everything had come out. Simon thought it was worth looking into. He had probably been involved with this for a year or so, off and on. I think he had become more interested in these investigations than in mathematics, frankly, but then he was always so effortlessly brilliant at maths, it didn't matter. I don't suppose any of it matters now, does it?"

Smailes had followed the stories in the press three years earlier when Sir Anthony Blunt was finally revealed as the Fourth Man in the Burgess, Maclean and Philby spy ring. He was appalled when it emerged that the authorities had known of Blunt's espionage activities for fifteen years, but had allowed him to continue to hold his position in the royal household as Surveyor of Pictures in the interests of avoiding scandal. Of course, the old bugger was stripped of his knighthood, and hounded to death by the press, but because of whatever immunity deal he had been given for his confession in the sixties, the courts could not touch him. It had made Smailes and many others in the police force furious. They spent their time locking up ordinary criminals while well-connected and well-heeled bastards like Anthony Blunt, who had jeopardized the country's security and probably sent good men to their graves, were given a finger-wagging and cocktails before briefing the press. Derek Smailes was pretty sure such disgraceful injustice would not happen in America—there just wasn't the same fawning in front of privilege, the same self-perpetuating network of snobs running the country, the same loathing of scandal. Pass the gin and bugger the enlisted men, but keep the tent flap closed, the motto of the British Empire. If anything, America went too far the other way, scouring everywhere for Reds. But at least you couldn't claim unimpeachable credentials by waving the right school tie at someone, the way you still could in Britain. It made him sick.

"And had he got anywhere with this research, to your knowledge?"

"Well, he was certainly well informed about the whole subject. That was his first approach—to read everything that had been written on a topic. But as for any theories of his own—no, I don't think so. Although I know he had done some investigating in Oxford, which not many people had. Look, Mr. Smailes, is all this really relevant for my brother's inquest? How much information do you need?"

Smailes explained that his investigation was not simply a preparation for the inquest, which would be handled for the most part by the coroner's office. He was preparing an internal report which CID required in any unusual death. But he conceded to Alice Wentworth a personal interest in her brother's research. He hoped she did not object.

"No, of course not. Excuse me. It has been a little trying for me, you understand, and Giles, well"—here she offered Smailes a thin smile—"he advised me not to tell you anything I didn't think was necessary."

"Oh, really?"

"Yes, I think you upset him yesterday, with your questions. But don't worry, you haven't upset me."

"I see he is helping you with your brother's affairs."

"Yes, thank goodness. I know it might look unseemly, but I wanted everything taken care of by the time my mother gets here tomorrow. She's traveling up with my husband for the funeral service. Peter is going to conduct it, at the crematorium, and then we'll have a gathering at the Cambridge Arms. The college offered a room here, but I think that would be too upsetting, don't you?"

"What are you doing with everything?"

"Well, sell the books, I suppose, although I didn't care much for that unsavory character Giles got hold of. I think he runs a secondhand bookstore over by Magdalene College. Do you know it?"

"No, I don't think so."

"Tell me, do you think a hundred pounds is too little for all those books?"

"I'm really not sure," said Smailes weakly.

"And then give away the clothes, I suppose. Peter and I will take the typewriter—it's really the only thing of value that we can use. And of course, his files. I couldn't bear to throw out all those notes—he's been keeping them since he was eleven years old. The family gave him the filing cabinet as a gift, when he was sixteen, I think. He could already almost fill it up then. But that's about all we can manage, in the Volvo."

"How long have you known Mr. Allerton?"

"Giles? Good Lord, since he was a boy. You see, Simon was at school with Hugh, his elder brother, and they lived nearby when we were growing up. So they were often around in the holidays, and Giles would tag along. I think he rather looked up to Simon and Hugh. He's not like them at all."

"How so?"

"Well, he's awfully irresponsible. Gambles on horse races, gets into scrapes with the police, drinks a lot. Always has lots of girlfriends, it seems. Hugh, his brother, is completely different. Studying divinity at Oxford, and has the makings of a first-class theologian, I think. Peter and I find him fascinating. My husband has a parish, you know. Church of England. We always found it interesting that Simon and Hugh retained their friendship, because Simon was really quite a convinced atheist, unfortunately, and Hugh is a committed Christian, obviously. Do you have a faith, Officer?"

"Sort of," said Smailes awkwardly.

"I do find it helps in such a terrible time as this. I don't know how I could face such a tragedy without it. You see, I know that although Simon was not a believer, and although I feel suicide is a mortal sin, I know that God loved my brother and will forgive him. And I know that Simon now is no longer suffering."

Smailes felt self-conscious. "I have no further questions," he said.

When they returned to the room, both Allerton and the

116

bookseller had left. Bowles's papers and letters were still strewn on the rug in the middle of the floor. The room felt abandoned. Alice Wentworth went straight to the filing cabinet and began replacing the notes that Smailes had borrowed. When she had finished, she looked in the front of the drawer and pulled out a hanging file.

"Yes, here it is. You must have missed it." She handed Smailes the file. It had no index tab. Inside was a stapled document, about fifty pages long. The title page said *The Kennedy Theorem.*

"Would you like to borrow it?"

"Well, if I might," he said offhandedly. "Give me your address so I can send it back to you."

"Yes, certainly," she said, reaching inside her handbag for a pen. "Or you could come tomorrow. The funeral service. If that's not inappropriate. You could return it then."

"Yes, perhaps," said the detective, knowing he could call for the address if he needed it. "By the way, that's an IBM typewriter, isn't it? Pretty expensive, I think. Did your brother have money for this kind of purchase?"

Alice Wentworth was not troubled by the question. "We both inherited some money when my father died. An insurance policy. That was his profession, you know."

"A car accident, wasn't it?"

"Yes, that's what was decided at the inquest. But there was no other vehicle involved, and I think some people thought it might have been suicide. The insurance company certainly did, because they didn't want to pay out. It was quite a lot." Her face betrayed no emotion.

"How much?" asked the detective.

"My mother, Simon and I each received fifty thousand pounds."

"What did you and your brother think about your father's death?"

"We thought it was an accident," she said impassively.

"There's one more favor I'd like to ask, if I may," said

Smailes, but it seemed that Alice Wentworth had anticipated him, because she walked to the filing cabinet and opened the second drawer.

"Help yourself," she said.

Derek Smailes began quickly and somewhat self-consciously to remove the typed summaries from the hanging files on Bowles's Cambridge research. In his haste he could hardly be aware that there was one file fewer than on his inspection the previous day.

Eight

"SO TELL THE TRUTH. What's he like to work for?"

"Now, Detective. That's really none of your business."

Her name was Tiffany Pollock and she said she came from Adelaide. Smailes found her straightforward manner engaging and had begun flirting with her immediately. She told him she had come to England on a visit the year before and had decided to stay. Then she found the job as Hawken's secretary, which she said she liked. Smailes wanted to know if she had decided to stay for romantic reasons, and again she warned him, with mock severity, to mind his own business. With her dark skin, white teeth and makeup of primary colors, she seemed exotically female in the stiff male redoubt of the college administration. He liked the way she called him "diticktive," it was so un-British. He toyed with the idea of asking her out for a drink, but he could not imagine that such a lovely creature would be available or, if she was, would be interested in him, a tall, doughy policeman. He realized that he did not really need to see Hawken at all, that he had contrived this visit largely as an excuse to see her again.

"Does he teach? Dr. Hawken? I mean, could I go hear him lecture on my day off?"

Tiffany made the error of assuming he was serious. "Naw, I don't think so, at least not since I've been here. He's officially with the History Department, though, I know that much. Why don't ya ask him?"

"Modern American history. That's my field. We could hold a discussion."

Tiffany looked at him archly from behind her typewriter. "That's right, and I'm a cultural attachée for Tasmania, didn't I tell ya?" She gave him a gleaming smile and a wink that made his heart quicken. Her telephone handset buzzed and she leaned on a button, still smiling at him.

"Ask Mr. Smailes to step in, Miss Pollock," said Hawken's voice metallically.

Smailes and Hawken faced each other cagily, like contestants who had already gone several rounds. Smailes told him that after his interview with Gorham-Leach, his inquiries would be concluded and that he would file his report within a few days. He had found nothing to change his opinion that young Bowles had taken his own life while his sanity was disturbed. It seemed unlikely that they would discover the cause of the specific disturbance, but this would probably not trouble the coroner, who would no doubt arrive at the same conclusion. And Smailes had to admit to himself, despite a few nagging doubts, that the conclusion was logical. He wondered what would happen to the remainder of Bowles's wealth, the inheritance from his father. It would doubtless go to his sister or mother. It did not seem significant.

Nigel Hawken felt placated by this information and allowed himself to rest against the back of the sofa with his good hand. The affair would not damage the college further, it seemed. The report of the death in the local paper had been a modest piece hidden in the inside pages and there was little reason to expect follow-up coverage. The inquest would be weeks away, and by then the death of Simon Bowles would be of little interest to anyone. He could probably begin his report to the college council later that day. And he would finally be rid of this annoying, obtuse man from Cambridge CID.

There were a number of things Smailes could pursue at what he assumed would be his last interview with Nigel Hawken. The nature of Bowles's latest research project, for instance, or the fact that the dead man had in all likelihood traveled down to London the day before his death to visit Somerset House. Or that Bowles's father was also perhaps a suicide. Or that yesterday he had seen Paul Beecroft talking with Bunty Allen, the bedder, hours after she had been sent home for the day. But he was disinclined to discuss any of them. He wondered if he felt intimidated by Hawken's scornful manner, or whether he knew that privately he was not quite ready to conclude this case and did not want to play any of these cards at present. He hoped it was the latter.

Instead he asked about Gorham-Leach. "So is there anything in particular I should know about this chap before we meet?"

"G-L?" asked Hawken. The very mention of his name seemed to give him pleasure. "A marvelous man, is about all I can say. I've known him myself for years. He was a young don here when I came up before the war. Brilliant, of course. Been with the Cavendish and the CRI, off and on, all his life. I saw him a little, during the war—we both had desk jobs for a while with the War Office. Then he was in America for a time, after the war. Top nuclear man, I think. He's been back at St. Margaret's since the early sixties. Won the Nobel five years or so after he joined us. Semi-retired now, although he likes to stay in touch with college affairs. Teaches hardly at all, but always has to have a special auditorium when he does. Thousands show up, you know. It really was unusual that he

agreed to supervise young Bowles's thesis in whatever it was
—maths or physics, I assume. Shows you what a bright fellow
he was, I suppose. But for all G-L's eminence, I think you'll
find him a charming, modest man. My wife and I are particularly fond of his company. He's a widower now. His wife
died of cancer, must be four years ago. I think he has a son,
who's a lecturer somewhere. Is that enough?"

Smailes had recognized the name of the world-famous Cavendish laboratory, where British scientists had first split the
atom. The other institution was new to him.

"What's CRI, if I may?" he asked.

"Cambridge Research Institute. In the science park up the
Bedford Road. Basically a spin-off from the Cavendish. Works
pretty well exclusively on government defense contracts.
Top-end theoretical stuff, you know. G-L has been one of the
leading figures there for twenty years or so."

Smailes made some further notes in his book and looked up
at Hawken.

"You've been very helpful," he said, "and thank you for all
your cooperation in this, ah, unfortunate business."

"Not at all," said Hawken, smiling his thin-lipped smile.
"Not at all."

Smailes was a little surprised to find the door to his interview room open when he returned and to see a tall, soberly
dressed figure standing at the far end of the room, staring
silently out onto the River Cam. The man faced away from
Smailes, who assumed it was Gorham-Leach, a few minutes
early for their appointment. He tried to suppress any facial
expression when the man turned around and he saw it was
the head porter, Paul Beecroft. Probably something about
keys, or paperwork, or dealings with the press. Smailes closed
the door quietly behind him.

"Mr. Beecroft, please sit down. How can I help you?"

He took the chair behind the desk, but Beecroft made no
movement. Smailes took out his cigarettes and offered them

to the older man, who waved his hand slightly. He seemed to be considering how to begin.

"I wanted a word with you, in private, Officer, before you leave. You are finishing your inquiries today, I understand?"

"Probably."

"Yes, well. Excuse me, but this is rather difficult for me."

"Does it involve what you learned from Mrs. Allen yesterday afternoon?"

Beecroft looked shocked and actually stepped back a pace.

"I saw you talking to her when I stopped by the lodge on my way out yesterday. I assumed you had called her back to question her about Bowles. Am I right?"

Beecroft seemed relieved at the explanation. "Yes, yes, you are. She put up quite a fuss at first, until I offered to pay her fares. I'm glad I did, though."

"Really?" Let him find his own words, Smailes told himself.

"I don't quite know how to say this, and, believe me, I'm not accusing anybody. But it's to do with one of our junior porters. Alan Fenwick. He's called in sick the last two days. But yesterday I learn that he has, well, a friendship with Mr. Bowles. One of the other junior men in the lodge, Mr. Givens, told me that he thought, you know, Fenwick and Bowles had been seeing each other a bit. I called Bunty—I'm sorry, Mrs. Allen—back in to see if she'd ever seen Fenwick around Bowles's room. Bedders see a lot of things, you know, Mr. Smailes, that they don't talk about."

"And?"

"Well, she doesn't know Fenwick by sight, as he works the late shift and she's always done by two, but when I describe him to her, she says yes, she thinks she's seen him on the corridor a couple of times early in the morning and just assumed he was someone new in the lodge she hadn't met yet, delivering a message or something."

"Describe him to me."

"Fenwick? Blond, slim build, nineteen or twenty. Bit effeminate."

"Homosexual?"

"Well, could be. But I aren't pointing any fingers, you see. It's just, he's been out the last two days, starting the day after Bowles kills himself, and then I'm told he's been friendly with the chap. I thought I'd give him the benefit of the doubt, you know, see if he shows up today, and talk to him myself. It's serious, you see. Strictly forbidden."

"What?"

"Any kind of, well, friendships with the junior members. Male or female. Strictly forbidden. May I?"

Smailes had left the Marlboro packet and his lighter on the desk top. Beecroft took the seat across the desk from the detective and lit one slowly. He looked a little shaken.

"Why are you telling me this? Why not Hawken?"

"Well, I don't want to accuse anyone unfairly, you see. It could be that my chap is mistaken, that Mrs. Allen is mistaken, and that he's just out sick, see. To tell you the truth, I'd rather not have Hawken on the warpath on this one unless I know it's true. He would sack young Fenwick automatically. Then there'd be a big palaver, I know it."

"And you would be in the hot seat?"

"Well, there'd be an inquisition. He'd want to know how Fenwick was taken on, and how come I didn't know his background, even though he always has the last word on new hires. And then, I thought, maybe he does know something."

"Fenwick?"

"Yes. Maybe he's not telling the truth calling in sick. Maybe he's left town, you know. It's possible. I talked to the switchboard man and apparently he's called in both days from a call box. Could be from anywhere, couldn't it? So I thought you'd be a better person to tell, all round."

"I think you're right. Do you have his address?"

Beecroft reached into the jacket of his dark suit and pulled out an index card.

124

"He's not on the phone, apparently. Lived with his mother until recent, but I think this is a flat."

Smailes looked at the address and saw it was near his own. "Does anyone else know about this?"

"Well, people in the lodge know he's out sick, but I think only this other chap knows about him knowing Mr. Bowles, you know. I've not said anything."

"Please don't, okay, until I've spoken with him. But if it's true, that he had a relationship with Bowles, or knows something about why he killed himself, Hawken will have to be informed, you understand."

"Well, of course." There was an obvious distaste in his voice. "And he'll be sacked, like I say, no doubt about it. But, like I say, the rules is quite clear. Nobody's fault but his own."

Smailes gathered his cigarettes, and chose his words carefully.

"Must be a demanding bloke to work for. Hawken."

"Yes, well, we go back a long way," Beecroft replied cautiously. "He can be difficult, yes."

"I met Davies yesterday. Got the impression he doesn't care for Hawken too much."

"Not half."

"Really? They've obviously worked closely together. Got Bowles to keep his tutor while he was a fellow anyway. Did Davies resent having to do that?"

"No, that's got nothing to do with it. That's not that unusual, given the young fella's history. No, it goes way back." Beecroft looked at Smailes steadily, seeming to weigh how far he should let his own animus push him. "Not long after he first got here, must be eight, nine years ago, Davies changes his name, and asks for the signboard on his staircase to be redone. You've seem 'em, I expect, at the foot of each staircase?"

"Yes, I have. What was the change?"

125

"Shortened a double-barreled name, that's all. From Forse-Davies, or Furse-Davies, something like that, to just Davies."

"I see. Go on."

"Well, Hawken says okay but Davies has to foot the bill since the college only pays for them to be repainted once a year, at the start of Michaelmas term, see. Davies was livid, but went ahead anyway."

"Why the rush?"

"Well, as I recall, his mother had made the original change, which he never liked, and then when she died, he couldn't wait to 'ave it changed back again. Then there was all that business two years ago."

"About the dig out in Turkey?"

"Wherever it was. He tell you about it? See, he'd been planning it for years and the college was fronting most of the necessary cash from the general fund, see, but Hawken writes in this condition that the second-year money depends what happens the first year. Well, Davies comes back to report in, I dunno, August or something, and Hawken persuades the council that it's not worth it, that Davies hasn't found nothing, and they voted down the second year. Least that's how it was explained to me.

"Well, Davies was furious. Had to wind it up and come back and has spent the best part of the last two years trying to raise his money elsewhere. Then the bloomin' government out there starts to give him grief. He lays it all at Hawken's door, of course."

"He tells me he's going back again, he's raised the money."

"So I hear, but no one knows where he got it. Gotten pretty tight-lipped about the whole business." Beecroft looked at him anxiously. "This is all confidential, you understand."

"Of course, Mr. Beecroft. Davies told me most of it himself. You've just filled in a few blanks. Where would you guess the money's coming from?"

"Can't say for sure, of course, but there's been a lot of correspondence of late with the British Academy. That's my bet."

"Who're they?"

"Sort of government place in London. Gave him a bit for the first trip. I expect he's gotten them to cough up some more."

"What's behind Hawken's attitude?"

"In my opinion? Politics, pure and simple. He wants to be known he's a tightwad, tough manager, reining in the free-spending dons, you know. Hawken's got his eye on the Council of the Senate, see, the mucketymucks."

"So that's why he's so upset about the suicide, eh? Scandal won't improve his chances, I shouldn't think."

"Absolutely. But you wait. He'll get there, my guess."

"Which won't make you sorry, Mr. Beecroft."

"I'll not answer that, if you don't mind," said Beecroft stiffly.

"Of course, excuse me. Thanks for the information. And, Mr. Beecroft? You've done the right thing. I think I'll pay a visit to our Mr. Fenwick right away."

"Leave by yourself, will you, Officer? I'll stay and tidy up Dr. Poole's room a bit. I don't want people to know I've been talking to you, in case nothing comes of all this. You know how tongues wag."

Smailes opened the door to leave and startled an elderly man who was about to knock on it. He had completely forgotten his appointment with Sir Martin Gorham-Leach. He stood in the doorway, confident his big frame would hide Beecroft, who was still sitting by the desk. He began brightly: "Ah, you must be Sir Martin. I do apologize, but I've been called back to the station unexpectedly. Can we reschedule this meeting for tomorrow?"

Gorham-Leach looked bemused. He was a frail-looking man, probably in his early seventies, with a high forehead and rimless, octagonal glasses. His face looked slightly flushed, perhaps from the exertion of the stairs, and there was

127

a shine on his angular cheeks. He had pursed, fleshy lips and an almost birdlike way of holding his head slightly cocked to one side. He wore an old houndstooth jacket and a neat blue tie. He made a fastidious gesture with his hands.

"Oh, well, let me see. I suppose it's possible. Except I don't usually come to college on Fridays." His consonants rang with academic precision. He was obviously a creature of habit.

"Well, I was about to give up Dr. Poole's room today anyway," said Smailes. "Can I visit you at your home?"

"Certainly, certainly. You know where it is?" he asked trustingly.

"Can I ask Mr. Beecroft?"

"Oh yes, Beecroft knows, I'm sure. I think everyone in Cambridge knows where I live. Park Parade, overlooking the Green. Shall we say ten o'clock?"

"That sounds okay."

"It's best for me. You see, my housekeeper leaves at half past ten and she makes a much better cup of tea than I do. Do you prefer tea or coffee?"

"Tea's fine." The detective smiled. He shook his head slightly as the old don ambled away back down the staircase. He assumed he represented a vanishing breed. He closed the door carefully, not looking around at Beecroft.

Like all of CID, Derek Smailes drove his own car on police business, a three-year-old Austin Allegro. Police detectives liked the anonymity of driving private cars, and they liked the expenses they were able to claim. He lit another cigarette and thought about what Beecroft had told him. If Fenwick worked the night shift, perhaps he had a tryst with Bowles after getting off work. Perhaps they had quarreled, like any lovers, and Bowles had ended his life in forsaken anguish. Perhaps here was the missing motive, something to tell the coolly-controlled Alice Wentworth. Then the note was indeed a fake, something to make family and friends think his delusions had returned, to shield his lover from suspicion or

128

exposure, to protect his job. But hadn't his sister said that he sounded strange on Saturday, three days before his death? Was this just coincidence? And what about Beecroft's story of the resentment between Davies and Hawken? College politics, or something else, something Bowles got wind of? Loose ends were inevitable in any investigation, he reminded himself. Simon Bowles had learned that.

Smailes had a slightly sour taste in his mouth as he contemplated the prospect of interviewing Fenwick. He was not completely immune from the savage prejudice with which most of the British police regarded homosexuals, but he felt they were entitled to live their lives in peace without harassment from the authorities. He thought it absurd that their way of life, until recently, had been illegal, and felt more pity than outrage that in their loneliness they were obliged to seek out furtive contacts in shabby public places. One of his most distasteful duties when he first became an ADC was the stakeout operation at the Chesterton Lane cottage, the public lavatory over on the river that everyone knew was a meeting place for queers. The police had sniggered and jeered as they had snapped their Polaroids of the sad couplings in the cubicles, knowing that the teachers and civil servants they caught would have their careers wrecked, their marriages destroyed. He despised the self-righteousness with which the evidence had been presented in court, the sergeant mispronouncing words like "fellatio" and "anal," the prim woman magistrate doling out her petty fines, probation and ruin. What was the crime here? he wondered. He had hated his colleagues, their hypocrisy and glee.

Alan Fenwick's flat was the ground floor of a newly converted row house about a mile from Smailes's own place. There was a small apron of concrete in front of the bow window, on which sat a late-model Austin Mini. Fenwick answered the door himself. He looked ghostly pale and was wearing a light blue shirt open at the neck and dark slacks, and had a haggard look as if he had not slept. The dark pouches beneath his eyes contrasted with the pallor of his skin and the thin, light hair. His hands and features were delicate. He leaned against the green painted doorframe with unconvincing defiance and asked why the police wanted to see him. Smailes explained that he was conducting investigations at St. Margaret's and would like to question him. Fenwick led him through a dim hallway into a small bed-sitting-room.

The room was tastefully furnished in an understated way. There was a sink, refrigerator and hot plate on a counter against the far wall, with yellow Formica cabinets above and below. The furniture was all modern, and newer than his own. Nothing was out of place. The single bed was carefully made, and there were a couple of dishes and glasses draining beside the sink. There were no pictures or photographs on the walls, which were newly painted. Fenwick had evidently been sitting in an armchair beside a small standing lamp, since there was an open magazine on the seat. Smailes could not make out the title. He walked over to the black plastic chair standing beside the small dresser. Here the only decorative touch was a small vase of freshly cut flowers. He did not see a telephone in the room.

"Mind if I sit down?" he asked, grabbing the chair and turning it to face the armchair.

"Please, go ahead," said Fenwick, remaining standing. He looked terrified. Smailes reckoned he was no older than nineteen.

Smailes slowly extracted the small, dog-eared notebook and began: "So tell me what you know about the death of Simon Bowles."

"I don't know anything about it, except what I read in the paper yesterday. I was terribly shocked."

"Why have you been away from work the last two days?"

"I called in. I think I have a virus. You know, light-headed, feverish."

"Have you been to the doctor?"

130

"Not yet," said Fenwick wretchedly. He was gripping the back of his armchair and trying to control himself. Now his face had turned red and Smailes thought he might be about to break down. Smailes looked at him pointedly and raised his voice.

"None of this is true. You went there on Tuesday night, didn't you, after your shift? Simon Bowles was your lover, wasn't he? You quarreled about something, didn't you? Did he threaten to kill himself right then? How did you learn he had killed himself? Did you go back to see him? Did you . . ."

"Stop, stop," said Fenwick. "It's not true. He was already dead when I . . ." Here he succumbed to the wrenching sobs that had been building within him, and had to steady himself against the chair. Smailes got up and helped him sit down, and then filled a glass with water and handed it to the pathetic young man when his sobbing subsided in intensity. After a few moments he gathered himself and gulped a mouthful of water. He wiped his eyes with his sleeve.

"I'm sorry. I haven't slept in two nights. I don't know what to do with myself. I just don't know what to do with myself."

"Just tell me the truth," said Smailes gently. "You are under no obligation to say anything, but I must tell you that anything you do say will be taken down and may be used in evidence. Do you understand that?"

"Yes."

"Go on."

"I went over there Tuesday night, as usual."

"What time?"

"About ten past one. I go off duty at one Tuesdays and Thursdays. I usually go right over after I lock up the lodge."

"How long have you been doing this?"

"About three months or so. Since Simon and I met."

"How long have you worked at the college?"

"About six months."

"Go on."

131

"Well, I knocked on the door. I always do. And there was no reply. So I knocked again, and then I went in. And then I saw him."

"What did you see?"

"He was hanged. Over by the window, from the plant hook." Here Fenwick covered his face with his hands and began sobbing again. He regained himself slowly and drank again from the glass. Smailes waited.

"What else did you see?"

"Nothing. What do you mean?"

"What did you see in the room? Any sign of struggle? Were all the lights on? Was the gas fire on?"

"I don't think there was any sign of struggle. I think I saw a plant on the floor, the one from the hook. The light on the desk was on, I think, not the overhead light. I don't know about the fire. I'm sorry, but I panicked. I ran."

"Ran where?"

"Just down the hall and the stairs. When I got to the court I started walking, in case anyone saw me and got suspicious. I don't think anyone did."

"Where did you go then?"

"I walked out the main gate and over to the market square and got a taxi home. I get the taxi fare, you see, when I work late."

"Alan, why didn't you tell the police, or the college authorities, about this?"

"I was scared. I knew I'd get the sack, you see, that people would get the wrong idea about me and Simon. There was nothing I could do. I could see he was dead."

"What is the wrong idea? That you and Simon Bowles were romantically involved? It's not illegal, you know." Smailes was unsure that Fenwick was not telling an edited version of Tuesday night's events.

"Simon and I were friends, that's all. I had only known him for a few months. But we had to be secretive about meeting because it wasn't allowed by the college. I could get into trouble, you know."

"Alan, are you gay?"

"I don't feel that's any of your business," he said petulantly.

"So you say you were not romantically or sexually involved with Simon Bowles?"

"That's right. We were friends. I would go over to his room a couple of nights a week and we would just talk, maybe have a drink." Smailes could not quite understand the preposterous denial, since the lesser offense would not pardon him at the college.

"Then what?"

"Then I would leave, walk over to the market, and get a taxi home, like I said."

"So how come the bedder, Mrs. Allen, says she saw you in the morning, on Bowles's corridor?"

"I suppose I stayed a couple of times, on the floor, when it got too late for a taxi. They're gone, you know, by three."

Smailes shook his head in exasperation. There was no point trying to get the wretched man to confess. It wouldn't matter to Hawken anyway.

"Alan, what you did is extremely serious. Willfully leaving the scene of a crime is a criminal offense. Failure to report is also a crime. Do you realize what you have done?"

"Well, I don't say I should have done it, but can't you see it my way? I panicked and ran. Then I stopped. I realized there was nothing I could do. Simon was obviously dead—you could tell by the way his body was, the angle of his head. It wasn't a crime, was it? Suicide isn't a crime, is it? And I knew that the bedder would find him in the morning. No one had seen me, had they? And what could I do, except get myself into trouble? I thought I would go into work next day and pretend I knew nothing about it. But I was too upset. I was very fond of Simon. I was too upset to go in, you see. And then I couldn't sleep again last night, so I didn't go in again

133

today. I'm sorry. I know I should have told someone. Only, I like my job. I don't want to lose it. You don't have to tell Mr. Beecroft, do you, Officer?"

"He's the one who told me."

"Mr. Beecroft? How did he know anything?"

"Apparently one of the other junior porters told him about your friendship with Bowles, after you didn't show up yesterday."

"Ooh, that Michael Givens. I knew he suspected us." Fenwick gave a theatrical pout. Smailes thought it ridiculous that this man should attempt to deny his sexuality, or the nature of his relationship with Bowles.

"Let me go over this again. You came off duty at one o'clock and walked over to Bowles's room. You had been in the habit of doing this on Tuesday and Thursday nights for two or three months. You knocked, and when there was no reply, you went in. You saw Bowles hanged and left in a panic. You think no one saw you arrive or leave. Is this correct?"

"Yes."

"You didn't touch anything in the room?"

"No."

"Or talk to anyone about what you saw?"

"No."

"And you intended to keep quiet about what you saw and go to work as normal. Only you were unable to because of your emotional condition."

"Yes."

"Alan, what instructions were you given, as the night porter, for dealing with emergency situations? To call the police?"

"Definitely not. First you tell the duty tutor, and they decide whether to call the police."

"Who's that?"

"There is a tutor who sleeps in his rooms every night at the college during term. He's the duty tutor after the administra-

134

tion offices close. He makes all those kinds of decisions. The tutors rotate the duty every week."

"Who was it two nights ago?"

"I don't know. I hadn't checked. I had already locked up the lodge and just kept going after I left Simon's room."

"So, obviously, regardless of whether technically you have committed a crime, you did not perform your duties as they were expected of you."

"No." Fenwick was staring at the floor.

Smailes said nothing for a minute, and reread his notes.

"It's not my decision whether to charge you with anything, Alan. That's up to the chief superintendent. But you will have to come to the station and make a full statement. And you may be required to testify at the inquest. Do you understand?"

"Yes," said Fenwick, without raising his eyes.

"And I will have to let Mr. Beecroft know that we have had this discussion. It'll be up to him to decide what to do with the information, you understand."

"Yes."

"So. Do you know why Simon Bowles killed himself?"

"Honest, Officer, I've no idea. No idea." He looked up at Smailes with angry, red-rimmed eyes. "If he was upset about something, I don't know why he didn't wait to talk to me about it."

"Did he feel guilty about your friendship?"

"I don't think so. He felt frustrated that we couldn't be more open about it, that's all."

"Did he tell you about any other relationships he had, about other men he would like to be, er, friendly with?" Smailes thought of the Giles Allerton theory.

"Definitely not. There was nobody else, for either of us."

"How about problems with money, or drugs, anything?"

"Not at all. Simon was from a very good family."

"Did Simon Bowles confide in you?"

"I thought so."

135

"Had he told you of anything that was bothering him lately?"

"No."

"Did he tell you why he went down to London the day of his death?" asked Smailes mildly.

"It wasn't Tuesday. It was Monday, the day before. No, he just told me he was going down for the day."

"How did he tell you?"

"The usual way. We left notes for each other in Simon's pigeonhole. He left me a note when I came in Monday lunch-time. Said he would be back by Tuesday, 'as usual.' That was our signal."

"That you would meet as usual."

"Yes."

"How about his reason for missing the gathering at his sister's house on Sunday?"

"In Rickmansworth?" Fenwick seemed genuinely sur-prised. "I had no idea he was supposed to go there."

"How about his latest research project, on communism at Cambridge?"

"I don't know what you're talking about, Officer," he said primly. Smailes had heard enough to know that Bowles did not confide in him in any significant way.

"Mr. Fenwick, I'd like you to come with me. To the sta-tion."

"Am I under arrest?"

"No. I'd like you to make a voluntary statement."

Fenwick stood up and heaved a sigh. "All right. Let's get it over with. Shall I drive?"

"That your Mini outside?"

"Yes, it is."

"Make the payments on your salary, Alan?"

"I used to, just," said Fenwick gloomily.

"No, I'll bring you back," he said gently.

Fenwick walked to a wardrobe and extracted a yellow zip-pered leather jacket. Smailes doubted that he wore it to work.

Nine

GEORGE DEARNLEY removed his glasses and rubbed his face vigorously with his hand, then gave his jowls a strong tug. Then he put the glasses back on and pursed his lips. He looked at Smailes quizzically.

"You believe him, Derek?"

"Yes, I do, unfortunately."

Dearnley looked down again at the printout of Fenwick's record and the handwritten statement. Three soliciting arrests, two while still a juvenile. One shoplifting arrest nine months ago, from a clothing store. Hardly an exemplary citizen.

"So the Bowles kid hanged himself between ten-thirty and one, and we don't really know why. Except he was an unstable type, right? Fairy too?" asked Dearnley. Smailes nodded.

"So it's a question of whether we charge"—Dearnley

looked down again at the statement—"Fenwick with failure to report, or maybe obstruction, something like that."

"Yes."

"Teach him a bloody lesson, wouldn't it?" Dearnley mused. Smailes said nothing.

"So what's the downside?" asked Dearnley, anticipating opposition.

"Well, you spoon-feed the bloody *Evening News* a tailor-made scandal, don't you?" said Smailes forcefully. " 'Dead student in midnight tryst with porter,' all over page one. When Fenwick's previous convictions come out, and that he was a regular visitor of the deceased, it'll be hard to maintain he was delivering a phone message, won't it? I'm not saying Fenwick doesn't deserve it, but it seems hard on the family."

Smailes knew George would have to chew on this one. It had caused a minor scandal around Cambridge when George had left his second wife and set up house with Jill Wilde, who was the crime reporter for the *Evening News* and a well-known figure around the town. When they had both divorced and married each other, she had been forced to resign from the paper out of potential conflict of interest, and had eventually found a job on the crime desk of a Fleet Street daily. Smailes doubted she was entirely happy about it, though, commuting nearly three hours a day, and altering her career so George wouldn't have to alter his. So George probably had mixed feelings about the *Evening News*. Like all policemen, Dearnley had an intense distrust of the press in general, and had no wish to dish up a juicy and damaging story if it was avoidable. He probably also resented the management of the *News* for the way they had forced Jill out, inevitable though it had been. Smailes felt he was probably on firm ground.

"So you suggest?" asked Dearnley disinterestedly.

"Tell the family how Fenwick found the body and panicked. Suppress the statement from the report to the coroner, and tell the family that we are doing so to avoid a scandal. Let the record show that the bedder was the first person to find the body. Let Fenwick take it in the neck from the people at St. Margaret's. He'll be fired, which is probably enough punishment."

"Yeah, except we can tell Baddeley what we want him to do. He'll toe the line." Oscar Baddeley was the Cambridge coroner who would conduct the inquest. Like magistrates, coroners were simply private citizens of good character with no special medical or legal training. They usually deferred to the police in the strategy for conducting inquests, particularly a chief superintendent. Smailes realized that while it would be hard to sell Baddeley on suppression of evidence simply to deny the press, he would probably accept the desirability of protecting the family, and no doubt the college, from unnecessary scandal. He would also appreciate the appeal to his discretion and compassion.

"Fenwick will have to know he's not going to be called, and agree to keep quiet. Will he do it?" As Smailes had hoped, Dearnley had picked up the ball and run with it.

"Sure," said Smailes. "He'll be getting off light."

"You mean yes, do you?" George, in particular, loathed his Americanisms.

"I mean yes, George," said Smailes, smiling.

"So what else? Can we give Baddeley any idea why he did it?"

"I don't think so. I've got to talk to this scientist guy tomorrow, who supervised him. Then the Myrtlefields people, I suppose, but I don't think we'll turn up anything specific. One thing worries me, though."

Dearnley leaned forward on his elbows and adopted his most paternal tone. "Say 'concerned,' Derek. 'One thing concerns me.'"

"One thing concerns me," he repeated obediently.

"Yes?"

"Bowles was a bit of an amateur detective. He'd worked out a theory about the Kennedy murder. Quite clever. Recently he'd begun work on Russian spies from Cambridge.

139

You know, the Blunt business. Were there any left, that sort of thing."

Dearnley said nothing, listening skeptically.

"Well, the day before he hanged himself, he'd been down to London, to Somerset House. We don't know why. Canceled out of a family celebration to do it. Maybe he learned something there which made him do it."

"You mean found out that one of his ancestors was a spy and the shame was too much for him?"

"I don't know, but . . ."

"Derek, really." Dearnley made a scoffing gesture with his hand.

"Could be just coincidence, but . . ."

Dearnley's voice was firmer. "Damn right it could be coincidence. It's nothing, Derek. Nothing. Don't let me see any expenses for trips to London, understand?"

"Okay, George." Smailes felt slightly embarrassed.

"Let's wrap this up." He swung around in his chair and glared at his Slazenger wall calendar. "Report by Tuesday. I'm gonna need you on the Royston lorry job."

"The cigarette lorry?"

"Yeah. It's Sikhs, seems. You know what that means."

"No, what?"

"Think about it. Probably gunrunning. You read the papers, don't you? Howell and Swedenbank are beginning to mess their britches about it. Finish this up so we can get you on it, okay?"

"Okay, George," said Smailes, turning on his heel. As often with his meetings with George Dearnley, he came away feeling both chastened and flattered. He did not see that, as he left, Dearnley pulled the Fenwick paperwork again and stared at it pensively before reaching for his telephone.

There was no one in the detectives' room. The ranks of gray metal desks and green filing cabinets stood silent and empty, like abandoned weaponry. The table just inside the glass-paneled door had become a graveyard for dead typewriters and had collected another newly expired model, which was tipped over on its end, its key bars lolling like a parched tongue. Smailes ran his hand over it. There must be only a couple of working models left in the whole department.

Two reports were waiting for him in his in tray. He examined the first, the postmortem report from the pathologist at Addenbrookes. He saw the familiar signature of Dr. Maurice Jones, who had performed all the postmortems in Cambridge for as long as Smailes could remember. He skipped the preamble, where Dr. Jones always spoke about the physical condition of the cadaver and the presence or absence of major diseases, and jumped to the probable cause and time of death. Jones had time of death between midnight and 4 A.M. No doubt, thought Smailes. For cause, he had rupture of the spinal column between the first and second vertebrae, resulting in massive neurological trauma. A broken neck, in other words. He referred to the contusions on the neck and found them consistent with constriction caused by a thick strap or rope. Or belt, thought Smailes. There were no other marks of injury to the body. He read carefully the blood and stomach contents analysis. A blood alcohol count of 0.06—or about a pint and a half of beer, Smailes calculated. No other unusual chemicals or substances. Dr. Jones's summary was eminently reasonable—that whereas the neck bruising and abrasions suggested the possibility of strangulation, there was no evidence of asphyxiation. Thus the cause of death was the sharp, traumatic injury to the spinal column, which was consonant with hanging. Dr. Jones found it likely that the young man's injury was self-inflicted.

The second report was from Klammer. He was a little surprised the lab had worked so quickly. It probably meant the coroner's people had taken the lifts from Bowles's hands without being asked, and Klammer had been able to run comparisons right away. Smailes was disappointed. As Klammer had predicted, there were nothing but smudges and fragments from the plant pot—Klammer had written "Wiped?"

141

in the "Comments" column. The leather belt had a number of poorly defined prints from different sources—some definitely belonged to Bowles—and Klammer had written "Need eliminators" under "Comments." From the desk lamp there were again only smudges and fragments—Klammer had no comments. From the filing cabinet Klammer had pulled many distinct prints, all identified as belonging to Simon Bowles. And finally, the typewriter keys had yielded good prints of all of Bowles's eight fingers, with fat, full thumbprints from the space bar. So much for someone else typing Bowles's suicide note. It made sense that Bowles would type properly, using all his fingers. George was right, it was time to wrap up this case and move on. He looked over the report again and decided no further action was needed. He knew for sure that the belt had been handled by the coroner's officers, and he himself had taken it down and placed it on the desk, without using precautions. It also made sense that the plant pot would seem wiped, as he had manipulated it with his handkerchief. There was no point bothering with eliminators, because there would be no unidentifiable prints, he was convinced. He jotted down these comments and removed his Bowles file from his portfolio and inserted the reports. Time to think Sikhs, he said to himself.

His portfolio felt fat and heavy on his knee, containing all the notes that Alice Wentworth had let him remove that morning. He examined the slim document he had missed yesterday, Bowles's Kennedy Theorem. He yawned mightily, and remembered again how little sleep he had had the night before due to Simon Bowles.

An hour and a half later he finished the document with a racing heart. He was almost sure Bowles was right, that Héctor Martínez had killed Kennedy, or at least masterminded the murder. Bowles pronounced it the crime of the century, and Smailes was inclined to agree. He also had to agree that it was likely this improbable young man in his Cambridge study had solved a crime that had defeated all other public

142

and private investigations. He felt an involuntary surge of admiration.

As Alice Wentworth had said, her brother's breakthrough appeared to come after the arrival of a number of documents from the States during the time he was in the hospital. Bowles had corresponded with an independent researcher in California, who had sent him a stack of FBI and CIA documents released through the Freedom of Information Act. Many of these apparently dealt with the activities of the Cuban exile community in the months preceding and following the Kennedy assassination. There were even photographs of Oswald taken with some Cubans at one of the paramilitary camps in Louisiana. Then there was a long report by a UN-affiliated Latin America Research Group examining upheavals in Cuba in the mid-sixties, in particular a damaging rift between the Castro brothers which some analysts had thought might lead to an open power struggle and even civil war. He had no idea how Bowles had located this document, which was nearly twenty years old. Together the documents seemed to represent to Bowles the missing pieces of a jigsaw puzzle that he had known must be lying around somewhere, and he had latched on to their significance with awesome intellectual speed.

The loops and turns of Bowles's exposition were hard to follow, but his breakthrough had obviously come with the identification of the mysterious Cuban with whom Oswald was seen in the months preceding the shooting. From the photographs he'd received, Bowles tagged him as Héctor Martínez, an agent run personally by the Cuban intelligence chief, Raúl Castro, Fidel's brother. It appeared Oswald had known Martínez years before in Minsk during his stay there, when Martínez was enrolled in a KGB language school.

The plot to murder Kennedy was apparently an elaborate triple bluff hatched by Martínez as a free-lancer, without approval of either of the Castros. Mafia money bankrolled the job, which entailed the murder of Kennedy by three profes-

143

sional assassins, including Martínez, and the setup of Oswald for the fall, while pinning the conception on the anti-Castro exiles. Martínez's game was to neutralize both Kennedy and the exiles, the two biggest threats to the survival of the revolution, and to become a hero himself on his return to Cuba. Oswald had been sold a story that he and Martínez would escape together, the blame falling on the lunatic Cuban right wing that they had infiltrated. Meanwhile, Martínez had conspired with the exiles to arrange for Oswald, a known Marxist, to be taken out trying to escape. Apart from Oswald's unexpected survival of his arrest, the plan worked perfectly. Martínez had counted on the Mafia's code of silence as a fail-safe, which kicked in when Ruby, the mob's bagman in Dallas, gunned down Oswald in the police basement. This was the story, Bowles speculated, that Martínez told Raúl Castro after his documented flight from Dallas to Havana on the afternoon of the murder.

Simon Bowles claimed that Héctor Martínez was still in a Havana jail, his execution stayed only by the personal intercession of Raúl Castro. The other assassins were not so fortunate; Fidel Castro insisted they each be located and eliminated. Indeed, the Cuban leader had been enraged when he learned of the crazy plot, and hourly expected invasion after Oswald's Marxist background became known. That Raúl had not authorized the murder did not excuse him in Fidel's eyes, and a dangerous rift opened up between the two brothers. Only when it became clear that the U.S. Establishment would close ranks behind the "lone nut" theory, and that the fascist Texan who had inherited the White House would not invade, did the division heal. The official investigation suppressed any evidence that might have tied Oswald to the exiles, and likewise the Warren panel dismissed notions that Oswald was an agent of Havana, despite LBJ's private doubts. Luckily for Cuba, the U.S. military leadership soon persuaded Johnson that his main communist threat lay elsewhere, in Southeast Asia, and the danger of reprisals passed.

After Raúl Castro, retreating to his power base within the Cuban military, was rehabilitated, the threat to Cuba's stability receded. Fidel Castro even met later with congressional investigators to explain Cuba's innocence in the affair. It would have been folly, he argued, for Cuba to provoke its superpower enemy through such a lunatic act. The congressmen accepted the sorrowful analysis, and conceded that a traitor's murderous actions had indeed prevented better relations with this troublesome neighbor. It was one minor note in the greater tragedy of that brutal crime.

Derek Smailes thought back over the entire reach of Bowles's Kennedy work and was thrilled by what it showed. Starting with the application of mathematical rules to known evidence, he had patiently refuted the official version of a deadly accurate lone assassin. He then illuminated each contradiction created by the false premise. Then, with his new knowledge of a key player in the crime, went back and resolved each loose end one by one, so the final analysis shone with an irrefutable logic. The detective could not imagine that Bowles had been content to allow his extraordinary work to sit unappreciated among his files—unless, perhaps, he had become absorbed in new research that overshadowed his accomplishment. After all, Oswald, Ruby and the Cuban assassins were all dead and Martínez languished in a Cuban jail. Smailes speculated that perhaps only one goal could make such an achievement seem insignificant—the solution of a similar crime whose perpetrators were still at large. He resolved to look into Bowles's Cambridge research as soon as he was able, despite the blandishments of George Dearnley.

The small, weasel-faced young man climbed into the passenger seat of the Volga sedan without a word. As the car sped away he stared gloomily out at the passersby on Kutuzovsky Prospekt. It was October, and some Muscovites had already begun wearing topcoats and their distinctive fur hats. Orlovsky maneuvered the car into the center lane, reserved for the vehicles of the *vlasti,* the bosses, and gathered speed. His broad Kazakh face contrasted sharply with the angular features of his passenger.

"I could be shot for this," the man muttered.

"Come, come, Mischa. You always exaggerate. You must not forget where your friends are. You will come to no harm."

Mikhail Pavelovich Popov needed no reminder of his uncle's status and influence. His wife's uncle, he should say. He had secured Mischa the position in the chairman's secretariat and the apartment out by the airport. They had leaped over at least a five-year wait.

"Petra tells me you have news finally."

"Something, I think," he said, in the same sepulchral tone. He had not minded passing on the odd pieces of gossip, confirming and denying rumors. As long as concrete information was not involved, he felt as if he was merely indulging in Moscow's favorite pastime. If his uncle, the big man out at Yasyenevo, was the beneficiary, so what? But now he had glimpsed a memo, overheard a remark, which confirmed for him a code name. He felt like a spy.

"Well?"

"Veleshin and the chairman were together yesterday, and they had been discussing a briefing at the Englishman's apartment."

"Yes?"

"I heard the name Painter, that's all. I saw a memo last week with Veleshin's name on it and thought I saw the same name. That's all, Andrei Petrovich."

"Very good. Which exit do I take now? The third left? You and Petra are comfortable out here? And the baby?"

"We like the apartment, yes. That's all. This has taken me a long time," Popov said suddenly, seeking acknowledgment. "It might be significant."

"Might be, yes," said Orlovsky, ignoring his nephew's en-

146

treaty. "And the three of you, are you coming to the dacha this weekend? That will be nice."

In truth, it was he, not this unpleasant young man, who was risking the firing squad if he persisted with the plan he had nurtured all summer. The cryptonym was little to go on, but if he was able to cross-reference Veleshin's recent travel vouchers with files from that particular *referentura*, he might find recruitment details, and if not an identity, enough clues to fill in an outline. The next step would then be the most delicate, how to plant a kernel of fact without its appearing to be disinformation, and how to cover his tracks to ensure that such a treasonous act was not traced back to him. But he could not consider it treason when the reputation of his directorate was at stake. And if it eliminated rivals as a side effect, so be it. Enough of insults.

Ten

THERE WAS A QUIET ELEGANCE to the Victorian terrace of Park Parade, whose bay windows looked out across small, tidy gardens, a narrow causeway and wrought-iron railings to Jesus Green, Victoria Avenue and Midsummer Common beyond. Such central Cambridge properties had doubled in value in recent years, and were owned mostly by University professors who had occupied them for decades. Few students could afford the rents in these gentrified neighborhoods.

Smailes grabbed the old-fashioned bell pull at Gorham-Leach's door and heard a weak trickle of sound from the hallway as he eased the knob against its spring. The door was opened by an elderly woman in a housecoat, who invited him in by name. From the back of the house he could hear the whistle of a kettle.

148

Gorham-Leach's housekeeper did not introduce herself and gestured simply to the first door on the right.

"Sir Martin's in his study," she said, and turned quickly back toward the kitchen. Smailes knocked lightly with a knuckle on the door, which stood ajar.

"Do come in," he heard Gorham-Leach respond.

Martin Gorham-Leach was seated in a modern leather revolving chair behind a desk set back in the bay and facing into the room, and was almost completely hidden by a wall of books piled in front of him. As Smailes looked around the large study, it seemed less a place of work than an exhibit in a museum, a vast and eccentric reliquary of knowledge. The reason was the number of books, which were strewn throughout the room in almost comical excess. The walls were lined from floor to ceiling with shelves, which were all haphazardly full. Books stood in piles on the windowsills, on the mantel shelf and on the floor next to an ugly electric fire. Gorham-Leach himself seemed trapped at his desk by the stacks of books that surrounded his chair, and the only other chairs in the room, a pair of ancient green wingbacks that faced the hearth, were at least a foot deep in a jumble of books and magazines. The air in the room was acrid with the aroma of decaying paper. Between Gorham-Leach and the wall on his right stood a battered-looking manual typewriter on a metal table, which seemed to have the only horizontal surface with any virgin space. Gorham-Leach got to his feet and made a vague circular gesture in the air.

"Ah, Detective Sergeant Smailes, so kind of you to be punctual. Do move some of those books aside and have a seat."

Smailes, unsure whether this was physically possible, hesitated.

"I'm sorry to be so cramped," G-L added sheepishly. "You see, the study is the one place Mrs. Gilbert is not allowed, and I do tend to neglect things. To the left of the fire I think there's room. Let me help."

149

Gorham-Leach maneuvered around the books at his feet and began to clear off both armchairs. Smailes helped him make two awkward piles next to the hearth, smiling as he did so. He saw titles on philosophy, political science and mathematics. All the books Gorham-Leach owned seemed to be hardbacks. The elderly physicist grinned back at him guiltily.

"It's my only vice, you see. I buy far too many, more than I can ever read. But I've never been able to resist buying books, I'm afraid, and I'm incapable of throwing any away. Please be seated," he said after the two chairs were finally cleared. At that moment Mrs. Gilbert, the housekeeper, entered with a tea tray equipped with folding legs, which she erected precariously on the hearth rug in front of Gorham-Leach. She retreated with a loud sniff, as if to emphasize her disavowal of this particular environment. Gorham-Leach smiled at the policeman as she left, and began pouring tea.

"I'd be lost without her, I swear. But she will never forgive me for not allowing her to clean and straighten up this room. She is always offended when I receive visitors here. It's quite touching really."

He handed Smailes a teacup, his face clouding. "So where shall we begin?" he asked.

"Well, Sir Martin, I'd like to know anything you could tell me about Simon Bowles that could help us explain his suicide. For the coroner, you understand. I've been told you were supervising . . ."

"Do call me G-L," interrupted the professor. "Everyone does."

"I understand you were supervising his academic work."

"Yes, that's true, that's true. Not entirely my field, but one which still interests me considerably."

"And what was that?" asked Smailes guardedly.

"The properties of the transfinite ordinals," responded G-L. "It's pure maths really, whereas I have been much more involved in applied maths and physics in my own career. But

150

this young man had such a reputation, I thought it might be stimulating to work with him."

"So the relationship was your own suggestion?"

"Yes, indeed. It may have had some influence on the fellowship committee, I think, but that's not why I offered. There has really been very little original work in the field since Bertrand, so I thought it was high time."

"I'm sorry?"

"Bertrand Russell's work in the thirties. The second edition of the *Principia*."

"Oh yes, of course," said Smailes. "I think perhaps Simon Bowles had a poster of Mr. Russell in his room."

"Well, that would make sense. I think Bertrand was his personal model, and you know, Simon reminded me of him more than a little." It seemed natural that Gorham-Leach should have been an intimate of the most famous British mathematician and philosopher of the century.

"What do you mean?" asked the detective, sipping tea. He rested the cup on the arm of his chair and studied the scientist's features. Gorham-Leach was about seventy, he figured, but was aging with dignity, and held himself erect in his chair as he spoke. He seemed to Smailes the antithesis of Hawken: courteous, modest and amiable. The strong nose and brow gave him the appearance of a large bird.

"Well, Simon had this unusual combination of a powerful logical mind, a very strong technique and an intuitive faculty that all the greatest mathematicians have shared. You know, the ability to set aside the conventional approaches to a problem, a kind of daring. He really did show remarkable promise."

Smailes thought of the deductive powers Bowles had shown in his Kennedy research, the admiration he had felt toward the young man as an investigator.

"Did you meet with him often?"

"No, not often. Every two or three months, we would review his progress. I couldn't really offer him more, I have been so busy myself of late."

"You're with the Cambridge Research Institute, I understand, sir," said Smailes.

Gorham-Leach seemed surprised, a little annoyed. "Who told you that, if I may ask?"

"Dr. Hawken, when I asked for information about you."

There was irritation in G-L's voice. "My word, that man really can be impossible at times. Excuse me, Officer, I'm not criticizing you, but the very existence of CRI is supposed to be confidential. Hawken, of all people, should know that."

"Why so?"

"Well, let me see." Gorham-Leach set his teacup down carefully on the arm of his chair and stared at it for a moment. "I'm afraid I can't talk about it. I'm not allowed to. If I say that this is because of the Official Secrets Act, I think you may understand." He looked at Smailes steadily for a moment, as if for confirmation.

"Did the news of Simon Bowles's suicide surprise you?"

"It most certainly did. I had no idea, no inkling. I knew there had been some, well, difficulties in his past, but I had no suspicion that there was anything the matter with him recently."

"When was the last time you saw him?"

"Just ten days ago, a week past Wednesday. I checked my diary this morning before you arrived."

"And how was that meeting?"

"A little unsatisfactory, I must confess. Simon seemed to have done very little work so far this year, and I'm afraid I remonstrated with him a little. We expect our fellows to earn their doctorates, you know."

"Did he tell you why he had been neglecting his work?"

"What do you mean?"

"Did Simon Bowles confide in you at all? Did he tell you about the research projects he undertook outside his academic work?"

152

Here again Gorham-Leach paused to examine his teacup before continuing. "Yes, he did to a certain extent. In fact, he even tried to get me to cooperate, to give him my opinions."

"About the recruitment of Soviet agents at Cambridge University in the thirties?"

"I thought you might know. Yes, it seemed to me that Simon had grown quite preoccupied with the question. Really quite an inappropriate way for a research fellow to spend his time and the college's funds, as I told him."

"What else did you tell him, sir?"

"There was very little I could tell him, even if I wanted to. I think you may appreciate, Officer, that I have been involved in sensitive government work practically my whole career. When I arrived in Cambridge in 1937, this place was a hotbed of socialism. Our most celebrated traitors had already gone down, for the most part, but there was still plenty of activity. I have always found the intrusion of politics into the academic world repellent, and have never understood the attraction of the utopian rantings of that boil-ridden Jew. I'm afraid I was a rather vocal opponent of my communist colleagues during that time. Believe me, if I thought there was still anyone with allegiance to the Soviets in any prominent position in our society, I would have told the authorities long ago. I myself submit to regular positive vetting every few years or so, and quite rightly. But I was not in a position to tell Simon any of these opinions."

"Why not?"

"Because to do so might draw me into discussions that I am simply prohibited from conducting. Simon knew from my record that I was at Cambridge toward the end of that period, and wanted to know my general opinion about whether all those who were recruited had been exposed. He even tried to ask me about specific names. I'm afraid I may have been indiscreet anyway, despite my caution."

"Really? With respect to what?"

153

Gorham-Leach looked distinctly uncomfortable. Eventually he said quietly, "Nigel Hawken."

"Hawken?"

"Let me try to explain to you, Detective Sergeant. I saw Simon Bowles as a protégé. Oh, I tried to disguise from him any personal feelings, but otherwise I would never have agreed to take him on as a supervisee. I think I can say without immodesty that my time is quite important. This young man showed spectacular gifts which could have been invaluable to his country in any number of ways. So I was irritated and annoyed that he spent so much time chasing ghosts. I know they are ghosts, believe me. And so does Nigel Hawken."

Smailes said nothing. He became aware of the hum of the electric fire, the distant sound of a vacuum cleaner. Gorham-Leach perched quietly in his chair, his head slightly cocked, choosing his words carefully.

"Simon asked me a couple of months ago if it was true that Hawken was still an intelligence officer. It really wasn't such a startling deduction, believe me, since Hawken's entry in Who's Who simply lists "attached to War Office" from '41 to '64. To anyone who studies the British Establishment, such an entry is like a flag indicating the individual has been with the security services. Simon had been analyzing the careers of dozens of people who had been here in the thirties, but that was the only name he asked me about directly. And I'm afraid I told him to ask Hawken himself. Well, I think Simon took it as a confirmation, because I know he subsequently tried to interview him. I should have simply refused to discuss the question, but I wanted Simon to stop this fruitless quest. And I thought Hawken might actually be able to stop him, or give him information that would stop him. I wanted to see Simon get through his doctoral work and get into the applied fields where his skills could really be put to use. Mr. Smailes, I cannot tell you how tragic it is that a talent such as Simon Bowles showed is lost to us. His death is a terrible waste."

154

Smailes tried not to appear taken aback by this extraordinary news. "Dr. Hawken is an intelligence officer?" he asked mildly.

"I think I have said enough, Officer. But I regret having inferred any such thing to Simon. I can imagine Hawken's wrath if he were confronted by such an inquiry. It was foolish of me to think that I would be doing anything except whetting Simon's appetite. At our last meeting he wanted to tell me of his meeting with Hawken, but I refused to entertain the subject. I felt I had already done enough damage."

Smailes's brain was racing through the implications of this disclosure. Hadn't Hawken claimed hardly to know Bowles, to have had no personal dealings with him in years? He kept his tone even in his next question.

"Do you think Simon might have been on to some new information at the time of his death? Do you think he may have uncovered something?"

G-L's reply was weary and dismissive. "If Simon Bowles discovered anything about Soviet penetration of Cambridge intellectual circles that wasn't already known, then he did better than scores of government investigators and the most talented of Fleet Street's diggers. There wasn't anything left to come out, Officer, believe me. In fact, there has been tremendous overkill in this whole area. The closets are empty, I'm afraid." He gave Smailes a tired smile.

"So you can't help me as to why Simon Bowles might have killed himself?" said the detective. He recalled that the same assertions had been made by government authorities about the Kennedy investigation.

"No, I really can't, except there is one aspect to his death that I find particularly tragic."

"Yes?"

"I was duty tutor on Tuesday, the night of his death. My rooms are in Axton Court, just a minute's walk from Simon's corridor. If he had known that, that I was nearby, perhaps he would have come to speak with me about whatever was troubling him, instead of taking this reckless action."

Smailes was puzzled. Why would a don of Sir Martin's prominence be on such a duty roster? Hadn't Hawken said he was semi-retired?

"Is this a duty you have to perform often, sir?" he asked.

"No, not often. One's turn only comes round once a year or so, and it really is little imposition. It's quite rare that anything happens. The duty is for one week, and I always use the opportunity to catch up on my internal paperwork. I'm sure the college would waive the requirement for me at this stage, but I've never felt right about those that accept the privileges of a college fellowship without the responsibilities. Do you know what I mean?"

"And you heard nothing that evening, sir? No incidents were reported to you?" Smailes had already decided to make no mention of Fenwick and his discovery of the body. They would leave that to the discretion of the college authorities, which was the same as saying his involvement would be covered up.

"Nothing, as I said. It was a completely routine evening. I retired around midnight, I think. I didn't learn of Simon's death until later the following day, when I came back from the lab."

"And you didn't call the lodge during the evening to check in, did you, sir?"

"Call in? No, there's no need. The porter always contacts one if there's anything to report. The only requirement is that one stay in one's rooms for the whole evening and the whole night. To be able to take calls."

"Yes, quite," said Smailes. He wanted to conclude this interview, and he wanted to see Nigel Hawken again. His uneasiness about Bowles's death only grew the more he learned.

"Have you lived in Cambridge long, sir?" asked Smailes.

"Practically my entire adult life, with a few interruptions," said G-L. "My family is from Surrey, and I did undergrad work at Oxford. At that time Cambridge was stronger in maths and the natural sciences, and I came over here in the late thirties for doctoral work, and stayed as a fellow. There were interruptions for the war, and then there was a spell in America, at Princeton in the fifties, but mostly I'm a Cambridge man," he said equably.

"Where did you see service in the war, sir?"

"I'm afraid I can't tell you that, Mr. Smailes," Gorham-Leach replied with a sad smile. Smailes did not feel thwarted by G-L's reticence. He had learned far more than he had expected. Graciously, Sir Martin Gorham-Leach accompanied him to the door and shook hands. He gave a small shrug when Smailes thanked him for his cooperation.

Paul Beecroft sounded disappointed but resigned as Derek Smailes recounted Alan Fenwick's story on the telephone. Beecroft said there was no need for a written report, he would report to Hawken verbally at his first opportunity. Smailes told him that Bowles's family had been informed, and had acquiesced in the chief super's decision not to call Fenwick at the inquest or charge him with any crime. Beecroft said he did not doubt the porter would be suspended pending a formal decision of the college council. He thanked Smailes for handling the matter with discretion. Smailes asked to be put through to Hawken's secretary.

Tiffany Pollock came on the line with her breezy good humor, but Smailes kept his tone neutral. He asked if he could get in to see the senior tutor that afternoon.

"I'm sorry, Detective. He will be out all afternoon at the service for young Mr. Bowles, and then the gathering afterward at the Cambridge Arms. I can fit you in sometime next week . . ."

Smailes suddenly remembered the service to which Alice Wentworth had invited him. He didn't usually attend funeral ceremonies for persons involved in his investigations, it often was not welcomed by the family, but he decided then and

157

there to make an exception. He told Tiffany not to bother, he would call back later. He hung up and dialed the crematorium. He had met the director there on two or three occasions, and was sure a private room would be available if he asked.

The crematorium on the northern edge of Cambridge looked like an uneasy combination of a light-industrial facility and a modern church. It did after all serve a twin function, Smailes reflected. The gray wisp of smoke from the disguised chimney told him a cremation was in progress as he pulled into the small car park. Three ancient hearses were parked in the curved driveway in front of the building.

There were two huge vases of flowers standing on fake Greek pedestals on either side of the tiled foyer, whose walls were painted a discreet institutional green. At its far end were the stained-glass panels of a small chapel, which, in presumed deference to the variety of religious belief, were of abstract design. He took his position respectfully next to one of the pedestals as the service in the chapel concluded, and stood quietly as the mourners slowly filed out to the strains of "Abide with Me." His watch told him it was almost one-thirty, which allowed a decent interval before the next service, the one for Simon Bowles, was due to begin. Among the mourners he caught the eye of Andrew Mull, the lugubrious Scot who managed the place. The man came over and guided him gently by the elbow to the corner of the foyer. He opened a door and ushered the detective inside.

"I think this will be to your purpose, Officer," he said in his professionally grave voice. "You may use it as long as you wish."

Smailes looked around. It probably was Mull's own office, containing a desk, a credenza and several large filing cabinets. There were pictures of hunting scenes on the wall. "Yes, thank you, Mr. Mull. I'll only use it for a few minutes," he said. Mull bowed awkwardly and retreated back into the chapel. Smailes resumed his wait in the foyer. He was hoping Hawken would be early, that they could conclude this interview before the service actually began. Otherwise Smailes would have to wait through the entire event to speak with him afterward, which he would rather avoid. He had no doubt Hawken would be angry to be confronted on unfamiliar turf, but there were contradictions Smailes needed resolved immediately. He wanted Hawken to be off guard, to know that he regarded his deceptions seriously. His anticipation of Hawken's anger only strengthened his determination. He did not like being lied to.

The first party through the double doors was Bowles's family. Alice Wentworth was wearing a dark gray suit and pearls, and was holding by the elbow an older woman who was dressed in black with a hat and veil. This was Simon Bowles's mother, he realized. She looked frail and disoriented, but her daughter still wore an expression of determination and displeasure, not grief. With them was a tall, sandy-haired man in a clerical collar carrying a briefcase. Peter Wentworth, Smailes told himself, the vicar. Alice Wentworth noticed him almost immediately.

"Mr. Smailes, how thoughtful of you to come. Have you brought Simon's file? Mother, this is the man from the Cambridge police who has been in charge of inquiries. You know, the one I told you about."

Mrs. Bowles held out her hand and Smailes gripped it briefly. "Yes. Thank you," she said weakly.

"No, I thought I would send the files back to you by post, if that's all right," said Smailes. He felt awkward, unsure whether to offer the conventional sympathies. Mull rescued him, stepping up quickly from the entrance to the chapel.

"Is this the family of the deceased?" he asked. "Mr. and Mrs. Wentworth, and Mrs. Bowles? Please step this way." Mull guided them toward the chapel, but Alice Wentworth paused long enough to invite Smailes to the reception follow-

159

ing the service at the Cambridge Arms. Smailes said he would try to make it, knowing he wouldn't.

Hawken and Davies were next. Both walked briskly into the foyer, as if they were about to address a meeting. Smailes stood quietly, waiting for the men to notice him. Hawken nodded to him with a frown, but did not slacken his pace. Smailes stepped forward and placed his hand on the arm of Hawken's overcoat. The senior tutor halted, glanced down at the detective's hand, and then looked up at him in disbelief.

"Yes?" he asked, with difficulty.

"May I have a word or two with you in private, sir, before the service begins? It really won't take a moment."

Davies suddenly looked terrified. He had turned white as a sheet and looked around as if he were about to bolt for the exit. Then he regained himself, cleared his throat, and said stiffly, "Well, I'll save you a pew, Nigel." He turned quickly and entered the small chapel.

As soon as the office door was closed, Hawken snarled, "What the hell is the meaning of this? This is a funeral service you are interrupting. I am here to represent the college officially. Why on earth couldn't you wait?"

"What's the matter with Davies?" asked Smailes, ignoring him.

"Nothing on earth's the matter with him. Answer my question, man."

Hawken's expression slackened as Smailes explained his meeting with Gorham-Leach, his discovery that Bowles had been investigating Soviet espionage at Cambridge at the time of his death, his understanding that Bowles had met with Hawken to discuss the issue not long before his death. He was careful not to attribute the source of his information. His chief super wanted a report by Tuesday morning. He was just trying to ascertain whether any of this new information was relevant to Bowles's suicide. He tried to gauge from Hawken's body language whether Beecroft had told him yet of the Fenwick connection. His guess was that he hadn't.

160

"I don't see what possible relevance this can have. And this is neither the time nor the place . . ." Hawken began.

"So you did meet with him, if I'm correct, sir," said Smailes evenly.

"I would not really call it a meeting," said Hawken.

"But you told me you only knew the young man by sight, sir, and had not spoken to him in years, I think. Why the deception?"

Hawken's color rose. "This impertinent young man had deduced from somewhere that I had worked in intelligence in my past and had the cold nerve to ask me about it directly. He wanted to know my opinions about his research, of all things. I could not believe it."

"And what did you tell him, if I may ask?"

"I sent him away with a flea in his ear, and told him such matters were none of his business."

"And apparently none of mine either, sir."

"Listen, Mr. Smailes, I'll tell you a couple of things that I did not tell Mr. Bowles, which must not go further than this room, do you understand?"

Smailes nodded.

"I was posted at St. Margaret's in '64 when we first broke Blunt. You do know who I mean, I assume?"

Smailes nodded again.

"It became clear that the penetration at Cambridge had been much worse than we thought."

"Who's 'we,' sir?"

"The security service. MI5 is the official title."

"For whom you still work, sir?"

"Yes, if you must know. But I certainly was not about to tell our pimply little amateur detective that. Neither was I going to tell him that he could save his efforts. We have spent the better part of the last twenty years identifying every last communist sympathizer who was at Cambridge at that time, interrogating them, and removing them from sensitive posi-

161

tions if we had the least suspicion, the least suspicion, of their loyalties. Do you understand?"

"Understand what, sir?"

"You really are an infuriating man, Officer. The files are closed, Mr. Smailes, the files are closed. And I have stayed in place at this university ever since to ensure that there are no repetitions, no repetitions, you understand, of the thirties. The harm that was done to this country and its allies is irreparable . . ."

"Not to mention the scandal."

"Yes, as a matter of fact, I think the scandal has been despicable, and terribly injurious to the security of this country. The KGB might as well have the whole of Fleet Street working for it. You can perhaps imagine how I reacted to a self-important neurotic fool like Simon Bowles asking me questions."

Hawken's chest was heaving, and he put out his good hand against a filing cabinet to steady himself.

"Perhaps you can imagine how I react when I am misled in my inquiries into an unusual death," Smailes replied.

"I knew Bowles might have told someone, one of his friends, of our meeting, and if you brought it up, I was resolved not to dissemble, if you must know. But I was not about to volunteer this information. The interests of the state supersede the interests of a provincial CID, in my opinion. What I have told you is known to very few individuals in this town. I trust I can rely on your confidentiality."

"Certainly, sir."

"Since Blunt, we have kept a very close eye on the academic community, both the professors and the students, believe me, Mr. Smailes. I have my counterpart at Oxford. And our work has been successful. We have finally purged our society of a whole generation of traitors, and no one, no one with extreme left-wing sympathies will be able to penetrate the British government ever again. Simon Bowles and his preposterous inquiries. I could not believe my ears."

162

"But you don't believe his investigations had anything to do with his death?"

"I certainly do not. The fellow was obviously unstable, damnit. What do you think?"

"I happen to agree with you. I just like to get all the facts. And since you were holding some back, it just raised questions for me, that's all. Did you know, for instance, that he went down to London the day before his death?"

"No, I did not. Why would I know or care about his movements?"

"Good point, sir, why would you? I don't think there's anything else. You can rely on my discretion, believe me, sir." He glanced at his watch. "The service is probably about to begin. Sorry to catch you off guard like this, but I don't think you've missed anything." Smailes gave a smile as Hawken stared at him icily and turned to the door. He remained in the room with his thoughts for several minutes before leaving Mull's office.

There were about thirty mourners in the small chapel. The simple wooden casket stood at the front of the room on a raised platform next to the pulpit. The platform extended backward to a curtain behind which was the business end of the crematorium, Smailes surmised. At some juncture in the service, an unseen hand would press a button and the specially muffled motors would activate the conveyor that took its cargo to the furnace. Much less primitive than burial, let's face it, he told himself.

About half the mourners were students. He recognized Giles Allerton and Lauren Greenwald. The conservatively dressed young man next to Allerton was probably his brother Hugh from Oxford. He did not see Alan Fenwick. Representing the college were Hawken and Davies, who sat stonily behind the more colorful ranks of the junior members. It seemed to Smailes that the tension between them was almost palpable. He wondered if Davies had also known more about Bowles's activities than he had conceded. He certainly had

163

seemed stunned to see the policeman again, and had only regained himself with difficulty. Should he speak with him again? Across the aisle were Alice Wentworth and her mother and a few other relatives and friends from the older generation. He wondered whether the family harbored any suspicions that they had not confided in him. Peter Wentworth was holding forth from the pulpit, his ample voice filling the small room.

"And accept unto thee thy son, Simon, we beseech thee. Pardon his sins, as we beseech thee also to pardon ours . . ."

Smailes was not sure he could continue listening to Wentworth's discourse. He had been telling the truth when he told Alice Wentworth that he had a faith of sorts, but it certainly wasn't anything he could recognize in the pieties of the Church of England. He had always thought the notion of a divine being listening to the simultaneous entreaties of five billion souls was nonsense, as were notions of God as some sort of eternal housemaster, meting out punishment and reward. The Victorian manners of the Church had always exasperated him, the dreadful hymns and the stiff admonitory language of the Bible. He had not taken a seat and was able to leave unobtrusively, he thought.

"Nearly finished, are they, guv?" asked the driver of one of the funeral cars as Smailes stepped out into the sharp cold of the afternoon. There were three of them, dressed in dark overcoats, leaning on the side of the limousine, smoking.

"I dunno, the casket's still sitting there, so I guess not," said Smailes, pausing to light up also.

"You riding with us?" asked the same man. "Cambridge Arms, isn't it?"

"No, no, I've got to get back to work. I just had a professional interest in this, that's all. They a decent family to work for?"

"Don't ask me, mate. I just drive, that's all. Don't speak unless spoken to, you know. He was a youngster, I hear. Usually more upsetting when they're young," he said.

164

"Yes, quite young," Smailes said, and had begun to move off toward his car when he heard a voice behind him. He turned. It was Lauren Greenwald, and her face looked angry.

"Mr. Smailes, are you driving back to Cambridge?" she asked.

"Sure."

"Can I get a ride back with you? I can't take any more of this."

"If you like," said Smailes, surprised. "Where are you going?"

"The college will do," she said. Nothing more was said until they had been driving for five minutes. "It's not just the Christian bullshit, it's the whole fucking dishonest attitude toward death," she said suddenly. She looked straight ahead as she spoke, recounting an angry story of her meeting with Bowles's family, of their emotional repression, of their treating Simon Bowles's death as an embarrassment. "They're so bloody British, emotion is something distasteful to them. I just couldn't face going back to that hotel and drinking sherry with them, making small talk." She turned to Smailes, and he could see the pain in her eyes. "Thanks for the ride. I could have waited for Giles and his brother, but I didn't want to get into explanations. They're almost as bad."

Smailes was unsure what to say. "Well, weeping and wailing isn't everybody's way, you know," he volunteered. But he thought of his father's funeral, the way he had cried and cried. The words sounded hollow.

"Oh, sure, stiff upper lip and all that. Can't we just admit that Simon's death is a tragedy and share grief? What's the matter with these people? Do they think grief is something shameful? His sister seems more angry than sorry that Simon is dead."

"Are funerals different where you come from, miss?" he asked.

"Oh, I guess not. But as a culture we're not so hung up

165

about emotion. And Jews are good at suffering. I just didn't want to be the only one crying in that chapel."

They had stopped outside St. Margaret's, but Lauren Greenwald made no move to get out of the car. She seemed to have gathered herself.

"So what are your conclusions, Detective?"

"About what, miss?"

"Simon's death."

"It's not my job to make conclusions, miss. That's for the coroner."

"You know what I mean."

"There seems to be no foul play, I'm sure of that. As for the real reason he took his life, I've no idea. Do you, miss?"

"I don't think he took his life," she said softly. "And I don't think he typed that note."

"Ah, well, there we'll have to differ, miss," said Smailes carefully. "Unless you know something that you haven't told me."

"No, it's just a hunch. Because I can't figure it."

"You give me a call, miss, if you get anything more than hunches, okay?" He smiled at her and she gave him an awkward smile in return.

"Okay," she said, opening the door of the car.

166

Eleven

THERE WERE TWO DISTINCT HALVES to Myrtlefields Hospital. The Old Hospital was a fortresslike Victorian asylum built behind a high stone wall on a knoll outside the town. In the summer ancient elm trees shrouded the grim turrets and barred windows almost completely from view. Now in the early spring the bare limbs of the trees, capped with the bell-shaped nests of a rookery, formed a gray curtain in front of the brown stone of the buildings. At the rear of the hospital a huge chimney rose from the heating plant, as from a textile mill. This was the original hospital, where the worst cases, the chronically mentally ill, were housed. The modern half of the hospital had been built in the late sixties on flat farmland between the Old Hospital and the main road, and its trim, low buildings, unwalled and unfenced, with expanses of lawn like playing fields on three sides, spoke of the bleak civic optimism of that era. Smailes pulled into the car park outside the new wing. Bowles had been a short-stay resident, a month-long rehab job; he had not needed to ask in which wing Dr. Julius Kramer, Bowles's psychiatrist, had worked.

Kramer had agreed to see him late Monday afternoon, and Smailes expected to learn nothing to justify keeping the case alive. He was intrigued by the disclosures of Gorham-Leach and Hawken, and felt he now understood better the bile that Hawken had displayed throughout the investigation. But he did not find himself surprised. He had always assumed that the British security services kept a much closer watch on domestic activities than anyone really knew, and it made sense that they would have their men in the breeding grounds of the ruling class. He wondered if Hawken had any academic credentials at all, how his cover worked. He wondered what else the astute Mr. Bowles might have found out, and knew that although the report he would hand up the next day would officially close the file, he personally would not close this case until he had read all Bowles's Cambridge files, the files Alice Wentworth had allowed him to remove, the files that he had begun plowing into that weekend.

Smailes was quite familiar with institutionalized misery, and the smell of disinfectant, urine and overcooked food which greeted him as he entered the double doors of the hospital was the same as in any orphanage or juvenile prison he had visited. He turned to the right down a low corridor, following a sign to Reception, clearing his throat out of uneasiness. A young man appeared at the far end of the corridor and shuffled toward him. He was wearing pajamas and a carelessly tied dressing gown, and scuffed the floor with his slippers as he walked. "Hey, you," he almost shouted, and Smailes felt his stomach tighten, wondering how he should deal with this encounter. As the man drew closer it was clear he was no more than nineteen or so, with an unnaturally pale, waxy complexion and a dark stubble on his chin and top lip. Smailes checked his step, but the young man stumbled past, not seeing him, absorbed in a delusion in which the detective played no part.

"That's what I said, goddamnit!" he yelled toward the end of the corridor, and then began laughing softly.

Smailes rounded the corner toward a counter which seemed to be the staff station. Behind was a glass-walled office in which a group of people were talking. In front of the counter was a low table which held a number of newspapers and magazines. Below the table sat an old woman, also in nightclothes and a dressing gown, seemingly asleep. Smailes leaned on the counter and peered into the office. The old woman asleep under the counter smelled awful.

A young man with light brown hair, beard and spectacles was seated at a desk, resting his chin on his hand and watching the antics of another man with an air of bemused tolerance. A young woman sat on the desk watching with similar concentration. They were both dressed casually in jeans and sweaters. The woman had straight blond hair pulled back into a ponytail and wore no makeup. The other man was seated across the room and was gesticulating wildly. He was older than the other two, perhaps in his forties, with unkempt black hair and beard. He wore glasses fastened at the hinge with tape, an old sweater and corduroys. He seemed quite overweight. Whatever his ailment, it did not seem to trouble the two orderlies, who listened to him with a sort of rapt weariness, as if they had heard whatever was his tale many times. Although the door was closed, Smailes could catch the occasional syllable as the speaker's cadence swelled. He considered knocking when he heard a door open behind him.

A small, middle-aged Oriental man emerged from a ward and asked if he could help. He was not dressed like a typical hospital worker either. Smailes mentioned he had a four o'clock appointment with Dr. Kramer.

"Please wait in here. I'll tell him you're here," he told him in an accent Smailes could not place. He opened another door

169

off the reception area to what was clearly some kind of waiting room. The heavy steel door with its vertical panel of reinforced glass swung shut on its spring.

Smailes chose one of the battered vinyl armchairs and sat down. Cigarette smoke still hung in the air. None of the chairs or sofas matched, and some were in terrible shape, with their plastic torn and folds of dirty batting hanging loose. He supposed the National Health could not quite stretch to regular furniture replacement, but the state of the room enforced a sense of depression and neglect. The walls had not been painted in years and were adorned with graffiti. Across from his chair someone had scrawled "Nutters Rule OK." The heavy door opened.

Smailes tried to contain his surprise that Dr. Kramer was in fact the energetic bearded gentleman he had just witnessed regaling his younger colleagues. He had thrown a white coat over the old sweater and trousers. He pushed his long black hair off his forehead and shook Smailes by the hand. In his other hand he held a large file folder.

"No, don't get up, Officer," he said as he pulled out a pack of cigarettes and sat down opposite him. "Mind if I smoke?" He tossed the folder down lightly on a small Formica table.

Smailes's preference was apparently academic, since Kramer lit a cigarette without looking further at him. He inhaled deeply, protruding his tongue as he did so. He was the most unsavory-looking doctor Smailes had ever seen.

"You want to talk to me about Simon Bowles, I gather." The psychiatrist had settled back into his chair and was regarding Smailes pleasantly. "We were all very sorry to hear the news. A number of us remember Simon quite well."

"How did you hear the news?"

"Well, one of the orderlies spotted the notice in the paper and brought it to work next day. Then I had a call from the coroner's office. I understand I may be called at the inquest. Which is quite understandable. Unfortunately it's a duty I have had to perform before. Is that why, ah, you need to interview me?"

"Not entirely. I'm with Cambridge CID. We normally conduct our own investigation in cases of unusual death. The coroner's officer will probably contact you directly about your testimony at the inquest." Smailes shifted his weight and the plastic chair gave a sharp squawk.

"Were you surprised at the news that Simon Bowles had taken his own life?"

"Yes, yes, I was," the psychiatrist began, prefacing his remark with his unsettling tongue movement. "Simon seemed absolutely fine when he left here, and since we had heard nothing in the interim, one always assumes the best. Of course, he had technically attempted suicide before, and there is an unfortunately high relapse rate among patients who have suffered a major depression."

"Why do you say 'technically'?"

"As I recall, and I did take the opportunity to review the file after the coroner's people called, Simon was not trying to harm himself when he jumped out of his window. He was in the grip of a powerful delusion in which snakes were entering by the door of his bedroom. He chose the logical way to escape them, by leaping from the window. He landed on his feet, quite deliberately so, and broke an ankle, I believe. There were also a couple of crushed vertebrae, because we were unable to administer ECT, which would have been the treatment of choice. We had to rely on drugs, which worked quite well, actually."

"ECT? What's that?"

"Electroconvulsive therapy. More commonly known as electric-shock treatment."

Smailes shuddered inwardly at the image of some unfortunate wretch strapped to a table while an orderly wired up his skull to an electrical socket. He could not believe such practices survived in modern hospitals. Lucky Bowles and his crushed vertebrae. It seemed Kramer was able to sense his

171

distaste, for he crushed out his cigarette and continued amiably: "And the most commonly misunderstood and maligned practice in modern psychiatry, I might add."

"How so?"

"Well, I think I detect in your expression the usual impression that ECT is some barbarous and primitive practice, a violation of individual rights, a mistreatment of the mentally ill, that sort of thing."

"Perhaps. But I don't really know anything about it."

"Precisely, Officer. Precisely. I concede that we don't quite know how it works ourselves, except that it rapidly alters brain chemistry in a way that alleviates depression almost immediately. It is quite safe, harmless, and has few lasting side effects now that we are able to administer the charge to the nondominant side of the brain. You probably have the image of a struggling patient held down as his body convulses uncontrollably. That is all wrong, all wrong."

Kramer's tone had become more urgent. He lit another cigarette.

"The patient is given anesthesia and a skeletal-muscle relaxant. The voltage that is administered is quite low and usually causes only a slight contraction of the digits. The patient wakes up with little discomfort and whatever fears he may have had allayed. Most patients will show significant improvement after one or two treatments. The majority will recover completely."

Kramer reclined in the chair and made an expansive gesture with the hand that held the cigarette.

"Fortunately in Simon Bowles's case, the modern antidepressants worked quite quickly and well, so there was significant improvement within a few weeks. But I stress, with ECT we would have expected improvement within days."

Smailes said nothing for a few moments. "Perhaps we could go back to that time two years ago when Bowles was

172

admitted. You may be able to help reconstruct the young man's state of mind the night he killed himself."

"Well, it was some time ago, but the case was somewhat unusual, and it was also one of the first I handled after I became a resident here. I've also been looking at the file, as I mentioned. One of the most vivid dietary defaults I've ever seen." Kramer reached down for the manila file, removing his glasses by the taped hinge as he did so.

"I'm sorry?"

"Oh, I thought you would have known that. Simon Bowles's psychotic episode—you know, the delusional thinking—was caused by violation of the dietary restrictions of the medication he was taking. He had been put on one of the older generation of drugs—they are generally slower-acting and have more potential side effects. He obviously did not understand the seriousness of not strictly following the dietary constraints that applied.

"The snake hallucination was really quite powerful at first. He was brought here from the Royal Cambridge after the emergency room set his ankle and then realized that he should be in a, well, more appropriate environment. By the time he was admitted here he could not move his limbs—you see, he thought he had become a snake himself."

"Really?"

"Yes, poor chap."

"Excuse me, Doctor, I'm not trying to be clever, but he must have seemed really crazy when you first saw him."

"Quite. With such a severely disturbed individual, our policy is to administer a major tranquilizer to encourage any delusions to subside. Then we proceed with discussions with the patient and his clinicians to try to arrive at a diagnosis and a course of treatment. Of course, we would not have considered administering ECT as a treatment until we discovered that Simon was depressed, which became clear quite quickly."

"It sounds a lot worse than that."

"Not really. Through his family we quickly found out which doctor had been treating him and with which medications. One does not like to criticize a professional colleague, but it really was surprising to find that Simon had been prescribed an MAO inhibitor as an antidepressant. A little old-fashioned, one might say. Although not entirely surprising that a practitioner of family medicine might be a little behind the psychotropic times, so to speak.

"Simon's hallucinations subsided quite quickly, and he was able to describe them quite candidly, although with considerable embarrassment, the file notes."

Kramer had become quite animated and was about to quote further from the file when the detective held up his hand. He kept his eyes on his notepad.

"I'm sorry, Doctor, you've lost me with some of these technical terms. You'd better try to explain them to me, if you can. Just tell me in layman's terms what happened to Simon Bowles two years ago."

Kramer studied the file for a few moments, flicking through its pages impatiently. Smailes suspected he actually enjoyed this appeal to his professional abilities.

"Yes. Okay. Well, Bowles had sought treatment from a family doctor for anxiety and depression. This was in March, two years ago, about six weeks before his Finals, I think. This alone is significant. We regularly see an increase in undergraduate admissions here around exam time. The stress, you know.

"According to the file, he was put on an antidepressant, one of the monoamine oxidase inhibitors, as I mentioned."

"What's that?"

"Well, how technical do you want me to get?"

"Not very," said Smailes evenly. "I just want to get a sense of what happened to him two years ago, and whether what happened was some kind of repeat performance."

"Okay. When Simon saw his doctor, and described his symptoms, which I gather were sleeplessness, loss of appetite,

174

anxiety and, ah, gloomy ruminations, he was diagnosed, I believe correctly, as suffering from depression. What was incorrect perhaps was the prescription of Parnate."

"Why so?"

"This family of drugs—the MAO inhibitors—works to counteract a chemical deficiency in the brain which we are now sure plays a significant role in depression. Unfortunately, it can have serious side effects on the cardiovascular system and the liver. It can also have most unpleasant consequences when ingested in combination with certain common foods—notably fish and cheese. So its use needs to be carefully monitored. Since a much safer and more effective drug family—the tricyclics—has been discovered, most physicians would only turn to the earlier drugs if other methods had failed. One of these drugs helped Simon recover quite nicely, we found.

"What we found out was that the night of his admission Simon had eaten a cheese sandwich, the only thing he had eaten that day. So he either was unaware of the restrictions that applied or did not take them sufficiently seriously. The psychotic episode, I am quite sure, was obviously a direct response to this, although Simon, poor fellow, was convinced that he had gone quite mad. Naturally, we took him off this medication and substituted one of the more sophisticated drugs, as I mentioned."

Smailes was silent for a moment as he caught up with his note-taking, and then studied the psychiatrist's face. He was obviously an oddball, but then he supposed you would have to be to choose this kind of work. Despite his appearance, he obviously knew his stuff. The detective was aware that he was laboring under a strong prejudice, a severe distrust of this man's profession and its efficacy in the treatment of simple human unhappiness. Look at young Bowles and the muck they had pumped into him. His next question emerged somewhat involuntarily.

"How are you defining depression, in Mr. Bowles's case?"

175

"Well, depression is an organic condition whose symptoms include profound feelings of sadness and worthlessness, inability to sleep or eat properly, loss of interest in sex and intense feelings of guilt and self-blame."

Smailes shifted uncomfortably in his chair. There had been times in his life when that description pretty well summed up his own state of mind, particularly after his divorce. Uncannily, the doctor seemed to sense his discomfort.

"This should not be confused with normal feelings of sadness or despondency, which everyone experiences. Depression in the psychiatric sense is a disease, which can be treated as a disease quite successfully, thank goodness. But clinical depression should not be confused with simple loss of spirits. Depression is a loss of all perspective, where the sufferer cannot conceive that life will ever improve. He cannot recall ever having felt contentment or joy, and will revive all manner of ancient memories to confirm his sense of worthlessness and inadequacy. For the depressed person, suicide becomes a real threat, which is such a tragedy since depression is one of the simplest psychiatric disorders to treat.

"We classify depression as an affective disorder—that is, a disorder of mood—but since as humans we are biopsychological organisms, as it were, there are changes in brain chemistry that accompany such severe mood alterations. They may not have caused the depression initially, but they reinforce its tenacity. Studies tell us that untreated, ah, depression will lift organically in, say, six to eight months. What our modern drugs do is to accelerate the recovery process by restoring the chemical balance in the brain so that our natural resilience, the tendency of our organism to heal itself, can take over. The first indication is often the restoration of the sense of humor. Incidents that previously confirmed a patient's sense of shame or worthlessness can be seen as funny or absurd. I remember in Simon's case this was the first indication of recovery. One morning in group he said that if he was not allowed to speak first, he would jump out of the window

176

again. He had a big smile on his face, and most people appreciated the joke, if only because we only have the ground floor here."

The Oriental orderly Smailes had already met stuck his head around the door and told Kramer he had a phone call. The detective flicked back through his notes, and then tapped his top lip as he tried to absorb all this information. You ate a cheese sandwich, then turned into a snake. It didn't seem to add up. Could this delusion return spontaneously? When Kramer came back, Smailes steered him in this direction.

"This business of the snakes. What's all that about?"

"Well, a panic delusion often takes the form of the thing that an individual finds the most distasteful or upsetting. So Simon saw snakes. Then, because he was ashamed of this, he thought he had become one himself. It makes sense that you imagine yourself as something rather nasty if you are upset with yourself."

Smailes marveled at Kramer's understatement.

"Could this hallucination, whatever, recur spontaneously?"

"Most unlikely. You see, a major depressive episode is really a traumatic response to a sustained period of stress. Simon's psychotic incident happened within the context of a longer-lasting trauma, that of his depression, which is in itself a terrible stress, quite a terrible stress. But depression does not come on suddenly, like the flu. It is something that seems to gather strength gradually, often following some unfortunate life event. Of course, I have no information on what Simon's psychiatric history may have been immediately preceding his suicide. It is possible that he had become depressed again. Quite possible. But I think it is most unlikely that the particularly frightening delusion about the snakes would recur without some specific event which precipitated it. Simon Bowles's illness was basically a neurotic disorder, not a psychotic one."

Smailes decided to tell Kramer what he knew of the days and hours preceding Bowles's death, and then about the suicide note and the interpretation that people who had known Bowles had put upon it. Kramer listened intently, hunching his shoulders in concentration. He regarded the detective with a genuine expression of puzzlement.

"My word. It does sound as if something may have happened like you suggest. But his behavior sounds quite normal, from what you say. I know that one of the symptoms that Simon found most distressing before was his inability to concentrate. This doesn't seem to have been happening in this case, does it?

"Well, I'm not sure. He was not under any form of care before this, was he? No medications? All I can think is that he was really quite severely depressed at this time, but had been able to mask his feelings most successfully from everyone. But frankly, I doubt very much that his delusional thinking had returned. I doubt that very much."

"What kind of a person was he, Simon Bowles? Do you recall your impressions?" the detective asked, still looking down as he wrote rapidly in his book.

"Not too much. It's really a long time ago. We don't concern ourselves too much with personality analysis, you know. Don't have the time. We concentrate more on making an accurate diagnosis and prescribing the right therapeutic intervention. I may have some notes here. I remember he was quite an engaging personality."

Kramer flicked through to the back of his file. "Well, 'unipolar syndrome, possible narcissistic tendency' is basically all I wrote. I don't know if that helps."

"Not much."

"Well, as I recall, Simon displayed some of the classical personality attributes that our profession has identified as depressogenic. Roughly, these could be described as inability to constructively channel feelings of hostility, a highly developed superego and an unusual sensitivity to loss. I also detected some tendencies toward a grandiose sense of self-importance, which was counterbalanced by feelings of special

178

unworthiness. This is what I'm referring to as a unipolar syndrome with a narcissistic tendency."

Smailes stopped writing to consider whether this sounded like a description of himself. He convinced himself that it didn't.

Smailes asked a couple more routine questions, then concluded the interview by reviewing the discharge procedures for Bowles. They confirmed that the young man had been recommended to stay on his medication for six months to a year, and was released to the care of Selby, the doctor who had prescribed the drug that had gotten Bowles into trouble in the first place. Smailes wondered whether the young man had complied with these terms, and Kramer confirmed that there was little follow-up from the Myrtlefields end—they had no outpatient facility. All that was required was that Selby confirm that Bowles had visited him within ten days of his release, which he had done. From that date nothing further was known, and Smailes had a strong hunch that Bowles had dropped the good Dr. Selby like a brick at his first opportunity. He had probably had no contact with a medical professional since.

As he was leaving, Smailes asked the question that had been formulating in his mind since he had been told the genesis of Bowles's earlier psychotic lapse.

"Doctor, as far as we can tell, Simon Bowles had been receiving no medical attention in the period before his death. But if he had been, if he had been prescribed the same drug as before, he might have had the same psychotic reaction again, mightn't he?"

"Well, yes, of course," said Kramer dubiously. "But Simon was a smart fellow. I doubt very much whether he would have consented to take Parnate again, and if he had, he would certainly not have made the same dietary mistakes. Certainly not."

"Okay. That's what I would have thought. But if he had been taking the drug *without his knowledge,* then the same delusion might have returned when he inevitably ate the wrong thing."

"My word, Officer, what on earth are you suggesting?" asked Kramer, a little flustered. Smailes waited for the psychiatrist's answer, saying nothing.

"Very unlikely indeed. You see, all antidepressants take at least two weeks to have any effect, which includes any major side effect. So this young man would have had to take the drug in considerable dosage for an extended period of time before any such thing could have happened. It hardly seems likely he could have done this without his knowledge, does it?"

Smailes agreed. It hardly seemed likely. Neither did it seem likely that the delusion of the snakes had returned, according to Kramer. So why had Simon Bowles taken his own life? He felt frustrated that no one seemed to be able to answer that question.

Twelve

DEREK SMAILES first began reading Bowles's Cambridge files during the weekend after his encounter with Hawken and Davies at the crematorium. In the days following the trip to Myrtlefields he renewed his efforts. It was his way of keeping the case alive, of trying to understand the young man better, of trying to determine whether there were clues in his research that would help explain his death.

As with the Kennedy material, Smailes had removed only the typed summaries from the hanging files, leaving the handwritten notes, newspaper clippings and magazine articles in Bowles's filing cabinet for Alice Wentworth to take back to Rickmansworth in her Volvo station wagon. He felt an obligation to her—she could have easily refused his request to see her brother's work—and wanted to get the material back to her as soon as possible.

From the start, he was hampered by his lack of knowledge

of the period Bowles was writing about and a basic lack of interest in the subject matter itself. The periodic contortions of the British Establishment over traitors in its midst had never really captured his imagination and had ceased to even surprise him—the phenomenon seemed emblematic of Britain's decline in the world, a fact Smailes had long taken for granted. He could remember his father's wrath over the successive scandals during his boyhood, the defections of Burgess and Maclean, the Profumo affair and then the furor when Philby finally turned up in Moscow. His father would recite the litany of their names along with those of Gormley, Scargill and Benn, contemporary figures he was convinced also wanted to create a communist Britain. The disclosures about Anthony Blunt, coming more recently, had won his attention briefly, and he had been sickened to learn about the immunity Blunt had been granted. There followed disclosures about all kinds of smaller fry, and there always seemed to be the common denominator of the Oxford or Cambridge education and the impassioned conversion to communism in the thirties. It was extraordinary how many of these men had then entered the mainstream of political and diplomatic life without their allegiances being known, or judged to be of significance.

Smailes had begun systematically with Bowles's *Apostles* file, which described the activities of the elite secret society at the University in the thirties. The Apostles Society was founded by the poet Tennyson and his brother in the nineteenth century, and restricted its initiates to those of special intellectual or artistic distinction. Membership was small and by invitation only, and new members had to swear all kinds of terrible oaths of loyalty and secrecy. In the thirties, the club's guiding light was John Maynard Keynes, the world-famous economist at King's, and although homosexuality was not a requirement of membership, it seemed that many members, like Keynes, had distinct and open preference for their own sex. Whereas Blunt and Burgess were both homosexual

182

and prominent members of the Apostles, Maclean and Philby, although students at the same time, were not. Bowles had been able to identify all the members of the club between 1930 and 1939, and then had written extensive profiles of their careers since leaving the University. Smailes had to admit that a surprising number of them had been Soviet sympathizers, and quite a few had been active agents. Bowles seemed satisfied that he had accounted for the activities of all of them.

The *Communist Party of Great Britain* file represented Bowles's research into the way the Communist International, or Comintern (merely a front for the KGB, Smailes was to learn), used leading communist academics to identify promising student recruits for Soviet espionage work. The strategy had been stunningly successful, for it seemed that volunteers had been recruited in scores, who then proceeded to take up their rightful positions in the corridors of power in government, industry and academia. What puzzled Smailes was why so many young men, heirs to the traditionally conservative ruling class, should have embraced revolutionary socialism with the intensity of commitment that allowed them to spy for a foreign power. Wasn't the nature of Stalin's regime already clear in the thirties? But again, Bowles seemed confident that the activities of the Soviet recruiters had been sufficiently traced and documented.

A slim file elliptically entitled *The Gang of Four* . . . represented Bowles's examination of the Cambridge careers of the four traitors who had attained such notoriety in their later years. Burgess and Maclean had come up in 1930, a year later than Philby and four years later than Blunt, whom Bowles portrayed as the *éminence grise* of the student communist movement. Surprisingly, Bowles had chosen not to dwell at length on their recruitment and subsequent development, although it was clear they had all known each other well, itself a departure from recognized Soviet recruitment practice. He was more interested to track down previously undocumented activities, and particularly to identify friends and associates who might have escaped official scrutiny. "If you want to discover a person's true nature, find his friends," Bowles had asserted somewhat haughtily at one juncture in the notes. But apart from a few contemporary accounts and anecdotes, Bowles seemed disappointed in this quest, and seemed to get sidetracked by the somewhat distasteful question of whether Burgess had in fact slept with each of the other three. It seemed Blunt and Burgess had become lovers early in their acquaintance, and remained firm friends for the rest of their lives, and it also appeared likely that the bisexual Maclean had been compromised by Burgess and was later blackmailed by him. But Bowles apparently believed that the shy, pipe-smoking Philby had also succumbed after a reputed meeting in Philby's economics supervisor's rooms, although Bowles's physical description of the garlic-chewing Burgess gave him pause in his account. Whether this little-known fact was significant in Philby's later rise to general's rank in the KGB was left unclear.

Bowles's next step had been to turn to the University archives themselves. It seemed that the University Library, the ugly fortress off Grange Road that looked like a power station, contained copies of all literature produced by University societies stretching back into the nineteenth century. Bowles had obviously spent weeks poring over publications of left-wing groups in the thirties, checking on authorship of articles, the members of editorial boards and internal references to individuals. In a file called *Bolsheviks and Gentlemen* he had traced the activities of the members of the executive committees of the Socialist Society, the Labour Club and the Union Society for all the relevant years. He had checked the participants in debates, who took the pro- and anti-socialist sides. He had even checked college magazines for political gossip about college members and pored through reports of the University administration, the Council of the Senate, for accounts of political demonstrations and upheavals during those years. The sheer volume of detail was overwhelming for Smailes, and made for much less compelling reading than Bowles's Kennedy research, which had read like a detective novel. Most of the names Bowles had researched meant nothing to him, but he did recognize the names of a surprising number of people who had become prominent in later life in politics, business and the arts. It seemed that almost anyone with talent or brains during those years before the war had been on the left. Bowles had selected out a few names for further research, but there was no indication that the research had been completed.

In the *Trinity Homintern* file Bowles had been able to document the particular activities of the communist cell at Trinity during the thirties, and had examined in detail a number of events that he thought might be of special significance. It appeared there had been a series of labor disputes at the University in 1933 and 1934 that had been orchestrated by the cell, in which students and college workers joined together to protest wages and conditions at the University. It was clear that organizers from the Communist Party in London were also involved, and several of the strikes and demonstrations had ended in violence with numerous arrests. Bowles had attempted to identify both the student and the worker organizers from contemporary accounts and to trace their later careers.

It was clear that he was also interested in the various pilgrimages made by parties of communist students from Cambridge to the Soviet Union in the mid-thirties. Compatriots from Oxford often participated in these trips. For some, the ghastly conditions they found in the Russian countryside and cities were enough to wean them from their socialist faith permanently; others merely saw what they wanted to see, interpreting the obvious suffering of the Russian people as the heroic and necessary struggle of the proletariat. One of these trips was led by Max Gottlieb, the fiery student organizer from Oxford, who was a member of a famous communist dynasty. Born in Russia to a communist German engineer, Gottlieb retained his Soviet citizenship even though he was educated privately at an English boarding school in Switzerland and at Oxford. His father, Karl Gottlieb, became a government official in the Department of Industry and was one of the few nonnatives to survive Stalin's purges. Karl Gottlieb's eldest son, Peter, became a daring and highly successful spy for Russia in Japan during the war, before his capture and execution in 1944. The younger Gottlieb never returned from Moscow after the Oxford trip he led there in 1935, and since had pursued an illustrious career in the Soviet Academy of Sciences as a leading metallurgist and crystallographer. He was awarded the Order of Merit, the highest Soviet scientific award, in 1975. Bowles was particularly interested in following the careers of those who returned from Russia with newly declared antipathy to the Soviet system. Clearly he was skeptical whether these renunciations were in fact real.

As he read Bowles's Cambridge files, Smailes found himself thinking again and again of Iain Mack, and wondering what his opinion might be of the whole business. His boyhood friend prided himself on an intimate knowledge of the foibles of Britain's ruling class and was particularly well informed about any kind of scandal. Iain might have opinions on the pertinence of Bowles's research, the directions it might have taken. Iain Mack now worked in advertising in London, and Smailes actually called his flat in Highgate a couple of times that first week, but got no reply. It was time they got together again anyway, Smailes felt.

Smailes's research into the Bowles files did intensify one mystery for him. There were many internal references throughout the files to Bletchley Park and the Government Code and Cipher School which Smailes gathered had been stationed there, which confirmed his suspicion that an intelligence facility had existed at Bletchley during the war. This in turn suggested that the cryptic note he had found in Bowles's wallet must have referred to the code-breaking center rather than the racecourse. Given the poor quality of the handwriting, the detective could easily have misinterpreted the text, which might just as easily have read "files" as "fliers," which would make more sense. Smailes felt embarrassed that he might have jumped to the wrong conclusion. He made a mental note to himself to check the contents of the wallet again, if the family had not yet picked up the personals from the coroner's DC out at the hospital.

However, despite the wealth of references to "See Bletchley" or "See GCCS," there was no individual file with this title. Given Bowles's penchant for mordant file headings, he checked them all carefully more than once, but of the twelve files he had removed, there was none that had such a title or that dealt directly with the wartime institution. He wondered whether he might have missed a crucial document, as he had with the Kennedy Theorem file, but he was sure he had been careful and methodical in removing the summaries from every hanging file in the second drawer. As he racked his memory, he thought he had seen in his first examination of the Cambridge drawer something about golf and chess, which might have been one of Bowles's oblique references to Bletchley. He had not physically removed the files until the following day, when Alice Wentworth had given him permission. A cold fist struck Smailes below the rib cage. Had the files been sabotaged? Had a crucial piece of Bowles's research been removed between late Wednesday afternoon, when he first inspected the file drawers, and Thursday, when Alice Wentworth gave him permission to borrow them? If so, by whom? The cabinet had been left open, but the room had remained locked during that whole period, according to the college, until Allerton and the sister had taken a key from the lodge ten minutes before his arrival. Had Alice Wentworth some motivation to doctor her brother's papers? He remembered the cool, proprietorial manner she had assumed when he presented her with her brother's Kennedy files, her unhes-

187

itating gesture to allow him to remove the Cambridge documents. Or Allerton and his sleazy bookseller friend, while he and the sister were conducting their interview in Poole's rooms? Hawken, of course, would have a pass key, as would Beecroft, and what about Davies's alarmed reaction at the crematorium the following day? Was he the culprit? Smailes kicked himself for disavowing the instinct to inventory the contents of the room. He could have done so easily in the forty-five minutes he waited for Klammer to dust the room, or after Klammer had left. He felt angry, negligent, incompetent. He could not swear to George Dearnley that a file was stolen, but perhaps he could persuade him there was sufficient suspicion to reopen the case. Except Dearnley would probably get angry that he had free-lanced again, had removed evidence without observing proper procedures or completing the proper forms, and had felt the files significant enough to remove, yet had omitted to inventory them. Smailes cursed inwardly, and realized that he had jammed himself up. To barge into Dearnley with his doubts would only get him further into hot water. His alternative was to pursue his inquiries independently, and find out what he could about Bletchley Park. He could go to the library, or perhaps track down the texts that Bowles himself had used. He did not doubt that the young man's books had been sold to the shabby bookseller who was Allerton's friend. He resolved to visit the bookshop as soon as he could.

Derek Smailes cursed under his breath as he hunted along Chesterton Lane and its side streets looking for parking. He eventually found a space in Magrath Avenue and walked slowly back to the lights at Magdalene Street, then turned left toward the city center. He found the façade of the dilapidated little bookshop without difficulty, opposite the front gates of Magdalene College. In the window was a dusty display of first editions about Scott of the Antarctic, behind an eerie

188

poster of a man in an overcoat with no head, with a legend in Polish. He pushed the door and stepped in.

Behind a high counter immediately inside the door to the right sat the character Smailes had met in Simon Bowles's room. There was no heat in the shop and the man wore a red tartan scarf over the faded velvet jacket, his hands cupping a cracked mug of tea. He stared at Smailes painfully. The detective looked around and saw that apart from a rotund, bearded student scanning the science-fiction racks, the place was empty.

He stepped up to the man, who gave him no sign of recognition, and asked for the titles on espionage. The face was light gray and unshaven, with dark pockets beneath the eyes.

"Fiction or nonfiction?" he replied, barely audibly.

"Nonfiction," said Smailes, and the man mumbled something about the back of the store.

"I'm sorry?"

The man gestured with his head to the racks at the rear left of the store, his eyes actually rolling backward into his skull. Smailes realized suddenly that he was laboring under a poisonous hangover and retreated quickly.

It was not difficult to find the titles Bowles had owned. They were each distinguished by thick marks from a black felt-tip at the base of the spine, and they occupied almost three whole shelves. Smailes scanned back and forth for several minutes, aware that the small shop was slowly filling up. He finally picked out a generic history of the British security services and two titles specifically on Bletchley Park. He turned toward the front of the store and hesitated. Leaning against the counter with her back to him, talking earnestly with the proprietor, was Lauren Greenwald.

Smailes stuck the books back in the rack and stepped immediately to his right to begin examining a shelf of mystery novels. He glanced at her surreptitiously and was struck by her careless grace as she leaned on an elbow, one foot supporting her weight, straining to hear what her unfortunate friend was saying. She was wearing a New York Mets baseball jacket, jeans and a thick woolen scarf. She began to turn around and Smailes went back to examining the racks of Desmond Bagley and Ngaio Marsh.

"You're into mysteries. Makes sense," said a voice to his left.

He turned and smiled at her. She was tall, maybe five-eight, and the thick strands of dark hair, streaked with lighter tints, fell forward onto the rims of the round glasses. The effect was both artful and unkempt, and Smailes wondered how she accomplished it. The complexion was sallow, the mouth small and even. Her chin was tilted toward him.

"Now and again. For recreation. How about you? What do chemical engineers read before they put out the light?"

She looked at him quizzically. "Magazines mostly, I guess. I haven't read a novel in years."

"No science fiction?"

"You really do have a lot of stereotypes," she said, but not harshly. "What are you doing here? This is mostly a student hangout."

"I could ask you the same, since you don't read books."

"I have supervision at Magdalene on Wednesday mornings, and I usually stop by afterward. I'm friends with Michael," she said quietly, indicating with a glance the front of the store. "I know him through Giles. He's having a tough time. Estella, that's his old lady, has threatened to kick him out if he doesn't quit drinking, and Michael won't even admit he has a problem. We're trying to get him some help. You know how it is."

"Yeah," said Smailes absently. Lauren did not move. "Well, you can find the occasional bargain here," he said weakly. "I sometimes drop in, on a day off. Thought I recognized the guy the other day, at St. Margaret's." He hoped he sounded more convincing than he felt. He would not want anyone,

190

particularly not a friend of Bowles, to know of his suspicions or the real reason for his trip to the little shop.

He felt her eyes on him and became suddenly self-conscious. He turned to look at her. Despite himself he asked, "How do you get your hair to look like that?"

She smiled at him broadly, unembarrassed. "Easy, Detective. I wash it every morning, and I don't comb or brush it."

"Ah, I see," he said a little foolishly.

There was a pause, and she said, "Well, see you around."

"Sure," said Smailes, unable to prevent himself from watching as she swung away, the jacket billowing above the tight jeans, waving to the proprietor as she left. He stood lost in thought a moment, and then retrieved the nonfiction titles, paid for them without ceremony, and headed back toward Chesterton Lane.

"Sure," he said to himself again as he sat behind the wheel of the Allegro, squinting at himself in the rearview.

Smailes interrupted his review of Bowles's notes to educate himself about Bletchley Park. It was a strangely intimate feeling to be reading the same books that Simon Bowles had used in his own research. Occasionally there were underlinings or notes in the margin that reminded Smailes that he was following in someone's deliberate footsteps. All his hostility and skepticism toward Simon Bowles had left him, and he now felt him almost as a peer, a colleague. And the first chapter of the first book he opened convinced him that his suspicions of tampering with Bowles's files were correct.

The Government Code and Cipher School, housed in its wartime premises of Bletchley Park, a rambling mansion fifty miles north of London, had been known informally to the intelligence community as the Golf Club and Chess Society. That was the name Smailes had seen as a file heading the first day he had inspected the second drawer of the filing cabinet, he was convinced. It meant a file had been stolen, and meant that someone was obviously interested in the suppression of

191

evidence surrounding Bowles's death. Had he been murdered? Or had his suicide meant that damaging revelations
from his research might now come to light? What had Bowles
written in his Bletchley file that was not in the public domain, that someone would risk exposure to remove? Derek
Smailes stayed up late two nights in a row to read through
the literature. In the end he was no nearer finding an answer
to his question.

Smailes read with interest the accounts of the stunning success of the British cryptanalysts at Bletchley, who were able
to crack most of the encipherments of the fearsomely complex Enigma coding machine, which was used by all the German armed forces, including the High Command. This had
been one of the best-kept secrets of the war, and gave the
Allies priceless intelligence, code-named Ultra, on enemy
strategy as the war progressed. Ultra intelligence was
credited with turning the tide of the U-boat war in the North
Atlantic, reversing the damaging successes of Rommel in
North Africa, and allowing the Allies to know that their deceptions over the site of the D-Day landings in Normandy
had worked. Knowledge of the intelligence breakthrough at
Bletchley was restricted to very few of Britain's wartime
leaders, and none of those involved in the massive undertak-
ing—the staff at Bletchley grew to ten thousand at its peak—
leaked a word about the project until the government authorized the first account of the center in 1974, almost thirty
years after the war's conclusion.

Smailes noticed an irony while reading the accounts of the
wartime triumph at Bletchley, and suspected it had struck
Simon Bowles in much the same way. It appeared that the
top cryptographers at Bletchley were nearly all recruited
from Cambridge University, and that at least one, Alan Turing, who had designed the first prototype computer to perform the bewildering number of calculations needed to break
through the German codes, had been homosexual. Yet for all
the venom Smailes remembered spilled in the press around

the time of the Blunt affair about the links between Cambridge University, homosexuality and treason, the Bletchley scientists had achieved one of the most significant intelligence coups of all time in a total secrecy that had lasted a generation. Bowles had drawn a fat line down the margin of the page where this was pointed out, and had written three large exclamation marks beside a particularly poignant footnote. It appeared that Turing, having returned to academic life sworn to secrecy and with his wartime heroism unsung, had taken his own life in 1954 following prosecution under Britain's barbarous public decency laws for homosexual conduct with a consenting lover. Had Simon Bowles, in some bizarre way, repeated the self-destructive act of his wartime predecessor? The triple exclamation marks stood as mute witness to the bond Bowles had clearly felt with the dead mathematical genius. It was a provocative question, and one more that Smailes could not hope to answer.

Thirteen

IT WAS WITH A MOUNTING SENSE of irritation that Derek Smailes resumed his study of the dead student's files. Part of Bowles's technique seemed to have been to examine the careers not only of known communist sympathizers but of whole groups of individuals from which known agents had been recruited. In a long file called *Fellows and Travelers* he had extended his investigation to cover scores of Cambridge dons who may have had contacts with active communists in the thirties. For each individual he would reach a conclusion about his attitude toward communism—the range seemed to span from "member" and "sympathizer" to "neutral" and "hostile." Since most of the Bletchley code-breakers had been recruited from Cambridge science departments, and since many prominent Cambridge scientists had been overt communists, Bowles had written evaluations of the careers of many of the senior figures at GCCS. These profiles appeared

194

under the subheading "Cantab Junction and the Golf Club and Chess Society," and Smailes suddenly wondered whether this reference was not the one he had noticed on his first examination of the files, in which case his alarm at potential sabotage was misplaced. The possibility only succeeded in making him more annoyed that he had neglected the simple task of a physical inventory. However, his frustration was quickly replaced by excitement when he began reading the entries. Two of these first profiles were of peculiar interest to him, those of Nigel Hawken and Sir Martin Gorham-Leach.

It seemed that both Hawken and Gorham-Leach had seen wartime service at Bletchley Park after being recruited as research fellows at Cambridge. According to Bowles, both men had studied at Oxford as undergraduates, although their careers there had not overlapped, Gorham-Leach graduating in mathematics and physics in 1934 and Hawken going up in 1935 to study history. The two men might have met later at Cambridge, because Gorham-Leach was recruited to join the Bletchley code-breakers in early 1940, and Hawken was recruited by the War Office in 1941 after completing a doctorate in history. According to Bowles's research, Hawken wound up at Bletchley in mid-1942 as a military intelligence liaison officer, whereas Gorham-Leach seemed to have spent his entire wartime career as part of the front-line code-breaking team. No doubt this was why G-L had been unable to tell him of his assignment during the war years, although much of the record of the Bletchley triumph was now in the public domain. The Official Secrets Act simply prevented a signatory from discussing the nature of his work in perpetuity, and Gorham-Leach was obviously the kind of man who would regard such a commitment solemnly. Smailes wondered whether there was any personal animosity on G-L's part toward Hawken that had caused him to push Bowles in Hawken's direction. The action seemed slightly out of character. Hawken had also claimed the two men were friendly, social acquaintances, which struck Smailes as incongruous.

195

The profiles also answered another question for Smailes: Hawken did appear to hold a bona fide doctorate, so was at least nominally qualified to be a Cambridge professor.

According to Bowles's research, Hawken had seen considerable service abroad with the Secret Intelligence Service—MI6—after the war, in Washington, Ankara and Bonn, before officially leaving the intelligence service in 1964 to take the position at St. Margaret's. It was clear that Bowles had been skeptical that Hawken's intelligence role had ever formally ended. As Gorham-Leach had indicated, he had been at Cambridge, officially with the Cavendish Laboratory as a fellow of St. Margaret's, since the war, apart from three years at Princeton University in the fifties. Nothing was mentioned about the Cambridge Research Institute.

At this juncture in his notes, Bowles had written "See *Oxford Blues and Reds*," which referred to the research the young man had completed in the Oxford University archives. The volume of material was not so great as the Cambridge research, comprising one relatively slim document. It seemed that not as much was known about Soviet recruitment efforts there, although it was clear that pro-communist sentiment among undergraduates was just as strong as at Cambridge. With his characteristic thoroughness, Bowles had identified clubs and societies to which both Hawken and Gorham-Leach had belonged, none of which seemed particularly provocative. Hawken had belonged to the History Society, the Oxford Union and the Pistol Club. Gorham-Leach apparently had not been a member of any political groups, but belonged to the Oxford University Alpine Club and something called the Blenheim Hunt. The conclusion reached about each man's communist sympathies at the time was the same: "hostile," which seemed eminently reasonable to Smailes. Once again, he recognized the names of a number of well-known political figures among Bowles's profiles of those who had been active socialists while at Oxford University. Smailes wondered what the young man planned to do with

196

all this information, and whether any of it was of interest to the authorities. But to believe Hawken, such information was all already known and Bowles was fruitlessly treading waters that had been thoroughly plumbed at both institutions. While Smailes found himself reluctant to believe Hawken on principle, he had to concede that it seemed unlikely that persons who had showed overt communist sympathies at Oxford or Cambridge would not by now have been identified and questioned.

One question continued to gnaw at Smailes as he completed his first review of Bowles's Cambridge files. Nowhere in the material he had read was the newly explained question he had seen on Bowles's note card, about the flagging of Bletchley files, discussed, or even mentioned. It might have no more significance than a doodle, but the fact that he could not confirm or deny its significance exasperated him.

It was around six on a Friday afternoon after his visit to Myrtlefields Hospital, and Derek Smailes had straightened the papers on his desk and was about to leave for the day. He had just filed his duplicate of the request to the coroner's office for a reinspection of Bowles's personal belongings when his phone rang. He picked it up on the first ring.

"Smailes, CID," he said gruffly.

"Del baby. Nabbed any bank robbers lately?" Only Iain Mack was allowed to use the hated diminutive or to tease him about his work. Smailes grinned into the receiver.

"Iain, you old bastard. I called you twice this week. Where are you? I've got a raft of questions for you."

"You'll never make it stick. I deny everything. I'm at the bleeding railway station. Where do you think I'm calling from? Filial-duty time, you know. You free tonight?"

"I'm free right now. What are your plans? You here for the Easter weekend?"

"No, just until tomorrow night. I've got to put in the obligatory with the Aged P's for a bit tonight. Dinner at least, I

197

suppose, but I can see you later on. Where are you drinking these days? The Lamb and Flag?"

The Lamb was a pub where off-duty Cambridge cops went for refreshment, which Smailes had begun to frequent less and less.

"No, let's say the Masons. Around eight."

"You got it, Kojak," he said, and hung up.

Smailes sometimes wondered how his friendship with Iain Mack had survived into adulthood. It was now more than ten years since they had left school and their paths since had been so divergent. Iain had done well enough in A levels to make it to one of the progressive universities on the South Coast, where he had somehow managed to secure a degree while living a life of energetic debauchery. Smailes had been married with a baby daughter when Iain had first started coming home during the long summer vacations, so they had not seen much of each other during that time. They had felt embarrassed by their differences and defensive around each other, Smailes with the shorn hair and stiff manner of a police recruit, and Iain Mack with the scruffy beard, weird clothes and indulgent habits of a university student. But somehow the friendship had stuck, perhaps because each represented qualities the other yearned for. Certainly, Derek Smailes had always envied Iain Mack's flamboyance, the adventures and embroilments that he seemed able to negotiate without the trammels of self-doubt that complicated Smailes's life. After university, Iain had taken a position on an East London daily, eventually becoming an investigative reporter of some minor celebrity who broke a series of stories that went national. Then, in the last year, he had surprised everyone by taking an advertising job instead of moving on to Fleet Street, pronouncing journalism to be a venal, cynical and undignified profession. Smailes was amused that Iain found advertising a satisfactory alternative. He was currently laboring under a one-year driving suspension that he insisted was the result of a faulty Breathalyzer bag.

198

For Iain's part, Smailes did not doubt that he, the hard-working detective, somehow represented to him a solidity and dutifulness that Iain, in his more wistful moments, wished he could emulate. He had been genuinely distraught at Smailes's divorce, and had even offered in a semi-serious way to try to mediate between Derek and Yvonne. Smailes had thanked him but remarked that Iain's seducing Yvonne would only complicate the issue, at which Iain had pretended to take offense. There was in fact little rivalry between them, and although their lives had taken such different courses, Smailes becoming steadily more conservative and Iain less so, they were able to relax with each other. In particular, Smailes loved to listen to Iain gossip. He had specialized in modern history at university, and his career in newspapers had intensified his interest in, and knowledge of, the inside story of how the country was run. Smailes was convinced that Iain, if anyone, could fill in some of the blanks of Simon Bowles's research for him.

The Masons was a lowbrow pub that catered to a mixed clientele of students, working people and professionals who liked to slum it after work. The lounge was not crowded when Smailes took his seat. The aroma of spilled beer and tobacco helped him to relax, and he glanced over at the next table, where a young man wearing a scruffy beard and eye makeup was waving his hands in the air and haranguing two young women wearing black lipstick and bored expressions. He couldn't catch the words. He looked over toward the door and saw Iain Mack squeeze past a large bus driver in the doorway and squint around the bar until he spied him. He was suddenly reminded of the one quality that really irked him about his friend—his overweening personal vanity. Iain waved and strode toward him, and Smailes saw that he was wearing a blue leather safari jacket and matching blue ankle boots which he wore outside his pants, and had had a white streak dyed into the front of his black hair. Smailes thought he looked ridiculous but said nothing, standing and returning

199

his friend's awkward slaps on the shoulder. Iain pulled away and pushed his hair back with his hand.

"What do you think of my groovy hairstyle?"

"Groovy," said Smailes.

"Yeah," said Iain, and they bought beers. Iain made sure to make admiring comments about Smailes's lizard-skin cowboy boots, which the detective always wore off duty. That Smailes could relax about his own eccentricities around Iain was a quality of the friendship he really treasured.

They spent time catching up on news. Iain's latest advertising account was a new dog-food line called Regal, for which he had devised the campaign slogan "Treat your pet like a king." He complained bitterly over his beer of that afternoon's filming session, the difficulty of getting a tiara to stay on the head of a hungry poodle while the technical people hung around at terrifying hourly rates and his boss nearly had a stroke yelling at people. Iain maintained seriously that he found the work much more creative than newspapers. He wanted to know about Smailes's love life, which the detective described gloomily as the Gobi Desert. Then they talked about his work, and the Bowles suicide came up.

"Was he a philosophy student?" asked Mack.

"No, maths. Why do you ask?"

"Well, Cambridge has the highest suicide rate of any university in the country, and the highest incidence of suicides there is among philosophy students, so it's the best odds, you know." This was a typical Iain Mack assertion, one that required improbable knowledge but whose veracity seemed unimpeachable.

"He was a bit of a detective, it seems. Worked out a whole theory about the Kennedy assassination that was quite persuasive."

"The Cubans?" said Iain predictably.

"Yes," Smailes replied, "but he seemed to actually name the culprit. Or so he claimed." There was a pause.

"Then there was the project he was working on when he

200

died. Soviet intelligence links to Cambridge University. You know, the Blunt business."

"This what you were calling me about earlier? Why are you interested in this kid's theories? You think it's connected with why he killed himself? Or maybe he didn't?"

"No, it seems pretty clear that he did, although there were some unusual circumstances, including the lack of any warning that he might try it. No, it's more that I have a sense that he was on to something. But whether it was related to the suicide, I dunno."

"So that's what you wanted to talk about. Skeletons in the closet? Spies recruited in the thirties still roaming around? Right?"

"Yes, I suppose so," said Smailes, feeling a little sheepish.

Iain took a slow swallow of beer and wiped foam from his top lip with the back of his hand.

"Unlikely. You see, after Blunt finally confessed in '64, and they shook a lot of names out of him, the services finally realized that they had better clean under that rug once and for all. Up till then there was continuing disbelief that there could still be rotten apples in the barrel. You know, Burgess, Maclean and Philby were just aberrations, traitors to their class. But Blunt, a servant of the royal family no less? Some of the newer officers, the Young Turks, insisted that they had to go back and examine every file since before the war, that no one should be above suspicion. Five and Six tore themselves apart for the best part of fifteen years, and anyone with a Cambridge background was particularly suspect. I can't think any stones were left unturned. But there has always been the suspicion about a Fifth Man . . ."

"What?" asked Smailes.

"A number of defectors in the sixties confirmed that the Kremlin had operated a spy ring in Britain known as the Ring of Five, that all five were recruited at Cambridge and had penetrated the British Establishment. Philby was finally identified as the third man when he defected, and Blunt made

201

four, but no one as important as the first four has ever been revealed since."

"No kidding?"

"Yeah. For a long time, the Turks thought it was one of the old guard at the head of Five, and there were all kinds of morale-damaging mole hunts, but nothing was ever proved. Of course, all this has only come out lately, because the Turks took out their frustrations with leaks to the press right, left and center. You see, both services are almost pathological about secrecy. In fact, it's not even officially recognized that Britain *has* domestic or overseas intelligence services. And after the Burgess and Maclean fiasco, then Philby slipping through their fingers like that, you can see why the old guard wanted to keep the Blunt business secret, can't you? Every scandal made them look more incompetent, and put more pressure on their relations with the Cousins."

"Who?"

"The Americans. They were furious about the whole business because through Philby and Maclean a lot of U.S. operations had been compromised. Then, when the British are trying to make out that they've cleaned house, another high-ranking agent is exposed, and the Yanks get apoplectic. Believe me, British intelligence is now completely dependent on American signals surveillance, American funding and American cooperation. They just can't afford to look compromised or second-rate anymore. But the Blunt affair would never have seen the light had not there been some serious leaks in high places."

"But why did the Fifth Man have to be someone still active, someone at MI5?" asked Smailes.

"Partly because of a string of embarrassing counterintelligence flops and partly because the defectors dried up, which indicated that no one would risk defecting to Britain because there was still a high-ranking Soviet mole in counterespionage. Get it?"

202

"I suppose," said Smailes, pausing over his next question. "Why the hell did they do it, Iain?"

Mack grinned and stretched before beginning his answer. This was the kind of question he liked.

"You can't understand because you didn't go to public school, old man."

"Neither did you."

"No, but I've studied the phenomenon. First, you have to understand the political climate of the thirties. Parliamentary socialism had been discredited by the capitulation of Ramsay MacDonald's government, the failure to prevent the Great Depression. Fascism was on the rise everywhere in Europe, while millions were unemployed at home. For a lot of people, the Soviet Union looked like a beacon of hope for the future. So the center fell apart, and increasingly you were one or the other, communist or fascist. But that doesn't really explain it, does it?

"You see, spying for Russia appealed to two powerful elements in the psyche of the ruling class—puritanism and snobbery. If the patient was sick, damnit, he needed stiff medicine. Only a generation raised on castor oil and cold showers could see things quite as simply as that. Then the Soviet recruiters played up the KGB as an elite force, like a sort of international Apostles Society. Have you heard of them?"

Smailes explained that he had, and told him something of Bowles's research papers that he had been reading.

"Well, so you can understand how the whole secrecy thing appealed to them all. Then, of course, there's the quasi-religious aspect of communism, the mythopoetic aspect. A lot of people turned in their party cards after the Hitler-Stalin Nonaggression Pact in '39, but those that didn't literally kept the faith. For them, nothing Stalin did could be wrong, because Stalin was infallible, like the Pope."

"I still don't understand how they were able to nail down their jobs in Whitehall and then proceed up the ladder.

203

Didn't anyone realize they were security risks?" asked Smailes.

"You're complaining with hindsight, old man. See, one of the Kremlin's cleverest moves was to tell them all to renounce their beliefs and then move along into government with exaggerated contrition. So they staged various nervous breakdowns, theatrical crises of faith and the like, and enrolled in right-wing groups. Burgess and Philby joined the Anglo-German Fellowship, of all things. So it was relatively easy to convince recruiters that their student beliefs had been merely the folly of youth. They all came from such good backgrounds, you see. A lot of the old guard found it impossible to believe that any of them were traitors, even when the evidence was undeniable. Gentlemen just didn't behave that way after all." There was a wicked gleam in Iain Mack's eye as he warmed to his theme.

"Iain, what would 'Who flagged the files from Bletchley?' mean?"

"No idea. Why d'you ask?"

Smailes explained about the note he had found in Bowles's wallet and his subsequent research into the code-breaking operation. He found himself unable to mention his suspicions of theft from Bowles's files, because to do so would involve an admission of his own negligence. He did confess guiltily that he had thought at first that the Bletchley reference was to the racecourse. Mack guffawed at this.

"Ah, Bletchley. The British at their best."

"What do you mean?"

"I just love the whole story of how that came about, the code-breaking thing. When war broke out, the Code and Cipher School occupied one room somewhere in the Admiralty. Then they got hold of a captured Enigma machine and decided they needed to draft some brainpower to crack the bloody thing. So they just put out the call.

"To whom?"

"To just about anybody they could think of. Just about the

204

whole maths faculty and many of the brightest undergraduates from here, for a start, as you seem to know. Then the entire British chess team. Then the top crossword puzzle fanatics. Any loony British eccentric who might have some notion how to crack a code got a job at Bletchley. I can't think of any other culture that could have thrown up such a bizarre institution that worked so brilliantly. You know, the deference to the impassioned amateur, the tolerance of oddity, it's so British. Bletchley was like a Sherlock Holmes story come to life. And they kept it secret for so long, that's the amazing thing. Not that that really mattered to the Kremlin, they got the information anyway."

"Really? I read that everyone was so proud that Bletchley wasn't penetrated."

"It wasn't. Churchill called them 'the geese that laid the golden eggs and never cackled.' But Churchill himself deliberately fed the Russians the information until the tide of the war turned in the East. Then he dried it up—he didn't want the Russians barreling toward Berlin and taking over Eastern Europe until the Second Front had broken through and the Allies were almost there themselves. But that's not what happened, as we know." Iain Mack paused here for effect. He finished his beer slowly and suggested Smailes fetch more. Smailes said he would, after Iain finished his story.

"Well, you see, the funny thing was, Stalin wouldn't believe Churchill was telling him the truth about the German plans to invade. After all, Ribbentrop and Molotov had signed the Nonaggression Pact and Stalin was so paranoid about Churchill that he dismissed the warnings as disinformation. So the British decided to feed Stalin the information through a double agent in Switzerland, so that it would look like the information was being uncovered by Stalin's own spies listening to German radio traffic. Then he believed it. But it was almost too late. When the Germans invaded, Stalin panicked, and at first his conduct of the Russian defense was appalling. The Swiss spy ring kept feeding information from Bletchley and gradually the Russian generals began to recover the initiative. Then Churchill had the Swiss spies rounded up, because he wanted the Russian and German forces to remain stalemated on the Eastern Front so the Allies could break the Germans in the West and then end up as the occupying force in Eastern Europe as the German army in the East was surrounded. But it didn't happen. Either Stalin suddenly became a brilliant commander or he was still getting access to Ultra, because the Russian tank regiments were able to outmaneuver the retreating Germans at every crucial battle. So when the Big Three met at Yalta, the Russian occupation of Eastern Europe was a fait accompli. Hell, Monty was barely able to break through to the Baltic in time to prevent the Russians getting Denmark.

"The jury is officially still out on whether Uncle Joe had become a great, battle-hardened tactician or whether he was still reading the opposition's hand. But the likelihood is that by the time the tide turned in the East, the Ring of Five were sufficiently advanced in their wartime agencies to have access to Ultra material. Blunt at MI5 probably was, and Philby at MI6 definitely was, and by 1944 he was promoted to the head of section nine, the bloody Soviet counterespionage division. In fact, the British government didn't authorize an official version of the Bletchley operation until the KGB announced Philby was going to publish his memoirs in Moscow—so they obviously thought he knew the whole story, didn't they? No, it's a tragedy really, but the fact that the British weren't able to plug Ultra when they wanted to was probably the single most decisive factor in the political division of Europe today. Makes you think, doesn't it? Don't believe the stories you read about espionage just being a game, that it doesn't affect the big political issues. It certainly does."

"Maybe Bowles thought the Fifth Man was someone at Bletchley," said Smailes tentatively.

"Maybe, maybe," said Mack. "But that's one place that has been pretty thoroughly checked out, and the official word is

206

still that there was no leak at Bletchley itself. The boffins might have been weird, but disloyal they weren't. Patriots to a man. Now what about those beers?"

Smailes got reluctantly to his feet, shaking his head in disbelief at Iain's story, at the whole sordid affair. He resolved to delve again into Bowles's research, to see if there was anything he had missed, any obvious leads untraced. He felt a curious sense of obligation to the dead student, and the more he learned, the stronger it became.

Fourteen

MARTIN GORHAM-LEACH drew the blinds on the bay windows of the study carefully before turning on his desk lamp. He moved slowly to the electric fire set into the hearth, released the catch underneath the bottom front right of the grille, and swung the fire open on its hinge. Moving mechanically and without haste, he reached up into the ledge of the flue and removed the parcel of equipment in its worn cloth wrapping. Kneeling on the hearth rug, he unwrapped the outer layer and uncovered the thick rubber pouch inside. This he carried over to his typing table and set it beside the battered typewriter. Then he moved the typewriter onto the floor beside the desk. Only then did he permit himself to sit down in the revolving chair.

His fingers performed the methodical task of unzipping the document camera and erecting it on its stand with the familiarity that came from countless repetitions. He focused the

208

machine approximately and bent to reach his briefcase. He unbuckled the flap and removed the sheaf of documents, smiling as he did so. This should keep us busy for a while, he thought to himself. His work on the miniaturization of the laser resonator was now almost complete. It really was a much more satisfactory way of intensifying a beam than the bomb-pumped X ray. He did not care that the broad outline of the physics involved might also be conveyed to the scientists at Lawrence Livermore Laboratory in California. He felt he had mounted a vigorous argument with Sir Keith, the government's science adviser, and thought his arguments might even fly in the xenophobic climate of Whitehall. Still, he reflected, the Germans in California were probably only a matter of months behind in the refinement of the same process. All that mattered was that we keep pace, he reminded himself.

He loaded the tiny Minox camera and carefully fed the documents across the brightly illuminated plate, snapping once with the cable release for each page. Then he rewound the film, unloaded it, and set the tiny spool on the desk. He had one more task to complete before he and Winston took their nightly walk. He reached inside the pouch and produced the pad, tearing off the top page with its bunched rows of Cyrillic characters. He withdrew from his desk drawer a foolscap pad and began the slow process of encipherment.

When he had finished, he folded the page again and again, and then wrapped it around the film spool. The whole parcel fit neatly inside a standard plastic film canister, which he produced from the bottom drawer of the desk. He still felt little cause for alarm, but given the delicate status of his research and the persistence of this obtuse policeman, it was probably wise to be cautious. His identity need not be compromised, he felt sure, and it was prudent to leave the decision to the chairman himself.

The initial response had shocked him a little at first, but then he was able to see Kim's old devilry in its unorthodoxy.

It must mean his old friend was still a force to be reckoned with at the Lubianka. He wondered if Kim shared his knowledge of the fate of those few who had learned his identity over the years, and doubted that he did not. It made the move even more curious.

Bowles had had to die. When he had started nosing around at Oxford, G-L had known it was only a matter of time before the tiresome young man unearthed something telling in the bowels of the Bodleian. The odds were still heavily against the worthy Detective Smailes being able to duplicate this feat, but caution should prevail. "Unimaginative but thorough" was the description he had used in his message, but the chairman would know that the very mention meant that consideration should be given. He, G-L, might never know what that consideration was.

Carefully Gorham-Leach moved back to the fireplace with the torn code sheet between his fingers. He knelt to place the paper in the open hearth, then removed the wooden matches from his pocket and set it on fire. He let the match burn almost down, then grabbed the cooling tip with moistened fingers and allowed the flame to consume the stem entirely. With delicate movements he gathered up the wafer of ash from the hearth until he held all the burnt fragments in his cupped palm. He walked methodically out into the hall and into the downstairs bathroom, where he flushed the ashes away in the toilet. Bowles's file had required several trips, he remembered.

He returned to his desk and slowly repeated the familiar process in reverse, stowing the equipment and the pad in their rubber pouch, folding the pouch back into the cloth wrapping and reaching the package back into the flue. The fire swung shut on its catch with a soft click, and Gorham-Leach got to his feet with a slight grunt. He was getting old for this business, he thought ruefully. He walked to the door of the study and called Winston's name and the old black

210

Labrador came shuffling down the hall from the kitchen, eager for their evening ritual. He took the leash and his overcoat from the coat stand that stood outside the downstairs bathroom and extracted his walking stick. He heard Winston's tail beating its steady *whump whump* on the hall carpet as he stepped briefly back into the study to make his call. The number, which he always consigned to memory, was changed every three months or so. From the prefix G-L guessed this one was in the Coventry area. He called, let the number ring three times, and hung up. He called again, and let it ring twice. He wondered how many operatives had served this tour over the years. He had never met a single one of them.

Martin Gorham-Leach and his dog stepped briskly into the evening air and across Park Parade to Jesus Green. Winston knew that he did not get unleashed until Midsummer Common, and padded obediently along the path after marking his territory at the entrance post. It was a mild, dark night and there was already a scent of spring in the April air.

Across Victoria Avenue, Winston strained until G-L uncoupled him and he lumbered off heavily into the darkness. Habit made the old don follow his pattern of taking a wide skirting walk past the noisy pub at the edge of the common and onto the towpath near the footbridge over the Cam. Then he walked slowly back toward the avenue, sure that he was not followed, calling to Winston occasionally as the old dog checked up to examine a particular scent or tree. A group of students walked past him toward the pub, and then the towpath was clear in both directions. About fifty yards from the avenue, near the base of the third elm from the road bridge, a small concrete post marked the existence of a hydrant eight feet away. Behind the post a large flat stone covered a small crevice. G-L eased the stone to the side with his foot and then stooped to drop the film canister silently into the blackness. He positioned the stone again with his foot and then stretched casually and looked about him. The one-time pad

211

and the dead letter drop, still the staples of fieldcraft after all this time, he thought to himself.

"Come on, Winston. Time to go home," he called.

Derek Smailes was examining carefully the contents of Bowles's wallet. His request to the coroner's office to reinspect the personal bag had reminded the DC at Addenbrookes that he had neglected to tell the family to pick up the belongings at the inquest. Derek Smailes had volunteered to make the call—he owed it to Alice Wentworth anyway.

In addition to the small amount of bank notes, there were several different types of library card in the wallet. There were cards for the City of Cambridge Public Library and the University Library and a card that showed Bowles had reader's privileges at the Bodleian Library at Oxford. There was also a small green card, marked "Public Record Office—Reader's Ticket," that Smailes did not recognize. The card was signed with Bowles's scrawny signature and dated March 1982, the previous month.

The dog-eared note card was now understandable to him, since he now knew who Alan, Lauren, Alice and Hugh were. As he examined the scribble on the reverse it was clear that the doodled question could as easily read "files" as "fliers." He felt embarrassed that he had jumped to the wrong conclusion, that since his primary association with Bletchley was horse racing, he had assumed it meant the same to Bowles.

Smailes walked to the photocopy machine again and copied all the contents of the wallet, then replaced the wallet, the keys and the spectacles in their case in the plastic evidence bag. Then he called Information, got Alice Wentworth's home number and waited until he heard the crisp and efficient voice answer at the other end.

"Mr. Smailes. What a coincidence. I was just about to lift the receiver and call you."

"Well, yes, if it's about your brother's files, I've just finished and wanted to send . . ."

212

"No, no. Something, well, more disturbing, I'm afraid. About Simon."

"What?" asked Smailes, his heart quickening.

"Well, it may be nothing, but we just heard from Mr. Bird, our solicitor, and actually, I thought I should call . . ."

"What has happened?"

"Mr. Bird called with a preliminary figure for Simon's estate. He was intestate, of course, and the whole thing has to go through probate, but the family decided—that is, Peter and I decided—that whatever was left should go to my mother."

"Yes."

"Well, there wasn't quite as much as we would have thought. A little less than forty-four thousand. I think I told you about our inheritance from my father's policy."

"Yes. Fifty thousand, I thought."

"Quite. Well, it seemed odd that Simon would have spent so much, so I went to his recent bank statements and checkbook, and there are a couple of payments I really don't understand."

"I see."

"Yes, there's one transfer from his savings account in January for a thousand pounds, and a check written for that amount to Alan Fenwick. That's the man you told us about, isn't it? Simon's friend?"

"Yes. And the other?"

"Well, it's even bigger. Just three weeks ago, a transfer of three thousand pounds and a check written to the bank itself for twenty-nine hundred fifty-two pounds and fifty pence. What could that mean? Could he have been buying traveler's checks or something?"

Smailes did some quick calculations. "Possibly. Or he could have been buying a cashier's check for twenty-nine fifty, with a two-pound-fifty fee."

"Cashier's check? Whatever for?"

"For the purchase of a high-ticket item, like a car."

213

"Car? Simon didn't drive."

"No, but his boyfriend . . . I'm sorry, Alan Fenwick did."

"Good grief, do you think this could be, well, blackmail or something?"

"I think that's a very good question. Let me talk with Fenwick again, all right, and I'll get back to you. Of course, it could be the payments were completely voluntary, no law against that, but we should check, definitely. Look, thanks for the call."

"Oh, that's all right. But, Officer Smailes, why were you calling me?"

Smailes had forgotten. "Oh, right. I just wanted to thank you again for letting me see your brother's research and to take your address so I can post the files back to you."

She dictated the address and inquired whether Smailes had found the contents of any use, and he answered truthfully that they had not shed any light on her brother's death, and he had chosen not to refer to them in his report. He did not indicate to her that he had any unresolved feelings about the case, or that he had photocopied the entire manuscript earlier that day.

"There's something else. Did you receive notification of the inquest date yet?" he asked.

"Yes, it's in two weeks, I hear," she said. "I'll see you there, I suppose."

"Yes, you will," said Smailes. "Did the coroner's office also tell you to stop by the hospital to pick up your brother's personal effects, the contents of his pockets on the day he was found?"

"No, they did not," she said irritably. "What on earth is there?"

"His wallet, a little money, his spectacles and keys. Nothing of any great value. I was just looking at the contents again myself, as it happens."

"This really is a nuisance. Can't you just send the things by post, along with the files?"

"I'm afraid not, Mrs. Wentworth. They have to be signed for, you see."

"I'd rather not have to make a trip out there. Can I get someone in Cambridge, one of his friends, to pick them up from you?"

Smailes thought for a second. "Yes, that would be all right, if you tell me in advance who it is."

"Does it have to wait until after the inquest?"

"No, not at all. It's just a formality."

"Fine. I'll have Giles do it. You remember Giles Allerton?"

"I do indeed," said Smailes. "I'll make a note with the paperwork on the bag. Just have Allerton tell the desk officer what he's there for and sign off the personal property form. I'll let the DC know."

"Fine," said Alice Wentworth in her businesslike way. "I'm sorry if I sound suspicious about this money business. It's not the money, of course. Simon can do whatever he pleased. It's just, in the circumstances . . ."

"You did the right thing," said Smailes. He wondered what she would say to the doubts he entertained, and what Mr. Fenwick would have to say about this latest development.

When his phone rang later that evening, after his second unsuccessful attempt to find Fenwick at his flat, he thought at first it was probably Yvonne, calling to remind him that Tracy was with him on the coming Saturday. Not that he had ever or would ever forget, but Yvonne liked to maintain that it was a possibility. Still, Smailes could not criticize her too much, because at least she and her new husband didn't run him down to the little girl, and Tracy seemed to enjoy their time together. The divorce and custody arrangements could have been a lot worse, he realized.

But instead of Yvonne's usual distrustful tones, the female voice was unfamiliar, and her first words were: "So you're not unlisted."

"Who's this?" asked Smailes.

"This is Detective Smailes, okay?" she asked.

"Yes."

"This is Lauren Greenwald. You know, I saw you in the bookstore last week? Well, you told me to call you if ever I got any information about Simon's death that was more than a hunch, right?"

"Right."

"Well, I have." There was a moment of silence.

"Yes?" asked Smailes.

"I don't want to talk about it on the phone, okay? It's too creepy. Will you come over?"

"That's a little irregular, miss. Can you stop by the station in the morning?"

"No, I can't. If you're serious about looking into Simon's death, you'll come over. It won't wait till tomorrow."

"I see, miss. And where is it you live?"

Smailes pulled up outside the semi-detached house on Harvey Goodwin Avenue and rang the bell three times, as she had instructed. Lauren Greenwald answered the door to him with lowered eyes and turned and led him up the stairs. She turned sharply on the landing and led him into the room at the front of the house. She said nothing until she had closed the door behind him.

"Thanks for coming. I'm sorry if I was a bit weird. Do you want to take off your coat? Hang it on the back of the door. Here, sit down."

She showed him to the single armchair that faced the fireplace. He looked around the room and saw a fairly featureless student bed-sitter. A desk and chair stood under the window, where heavy green curtains had been pulled closed. A single bed was against the same wall, above which hung a poster of a rock musician Smailes vaguely recognized. The only other furniture was a small standing bookcase which was only partially filled with books, but held a stereo unit and some bottles and glasses, and a standing lamp by the chair. There was also a sink and mirror in the corner of the room, and a small

216

hot plate. Smailes sat down and Lauren Greenwald sat on the half-moon-shaped rug in front of the fire. He looked at her closely.

She seemed to like black. She was wearing black pants, black tennis shoes and a black waistcoat over a white blouse. The dark eyes looked at him intently behind the round spectacle rims.

"Well?" asked Smailes eventually.

"I just got back from the college, right? I saw Giles there. You know, Giles Allerton, the guy who . . ."

"I know who you mean."

"Well, it seems that Simon's sister called him today, or left a message for him and he called back, I guess, and asked him to drive over to the police station and get the things that were found on Simon's body that day, when Simon was found."

"I know, I made the arrangements with her."

"So you know what the contents were."

"Sure," he said. He hoped he didn't sound ingratiating.

"Well, Simon's glasses were in their case. That meant they were in the case in his pocket when he was found, right?"

Smailes thought for a second. "Right. I found them there myself."

"Did you see how strong those lenses were? Simon was blind as a bat without his glasses. He would never have taken them off before doing something as intricate as threading his belt through a hook to hang himself. Don't you see? It means that someone else had to be involved."

Smailes had not thought of this. He said nothing for a minute.

"Not necessarily. It's the kind of maneuver you could do just by feel. Or maybe he hooked the belt on the hook, then put his glasses away in his pocket before he kicked the chair away. He was a careful type, you know."

"No way, no way. Someone helped him do it." Lauren's voice was starting to waver.

217

"Come on, Lauren. You don't help someone commit suicide."

"Right. Maybe the whole thing was faked. Maybe he was unconscious or doped up or something and someone strung him up. Don't you see? Christ, you're the professional."

"Lauren, the postmortem would have shown if Simon was unconscious before he died. There were no injuries to his body. And there were no unusual substances in his blood. The evidence is that he was fully conscious when he hanged himself. And even if he wasn't, do you know how much strength it would take to lift a man even of Simon Bowles's build up to that height and suspend him there? More than one person has, that's for damn sure. Lauren, I appreciate what you're trying to say, but what you're telling me is completely inconclusive. You must see that."

"Shit, Giles was right," she said angrily. "He saw it first, but refused to talk to you. Said you were too hostile to students to believe anything we came up with. I thought . . . I dunno. I thought you were different." She looked up at him defiantly and tears welled up in her eyes.

"I'm sorry, that's not fair," she said. She got up and walked to the bookcase. "Look, I'm going to have some scotch. Do you want some?"

"Sure," said Smailes. "Don't apologize. It's okay. Look, I've given this case a lot of thought, and confidentially, I'm not ready to give it up yet. There are a number of, well, inconsistencies that bother me. What you have said throws a little more doubt on exactly how he met his death, I agree. But it's not conclusive. Anyway, what motive could anyone have for wanting to kill Simon Bowles?"

She came and sat down again and handed him a small tumbler of whiskey. "That's the question I can't answer, except I keep thinking that maybe he was involved with something or someone we knew nothing about, something really heavy. He was real secretive, you know. He'd make these trips to Oxford and London, and we really didn't know why. He wouldn't say anything about the research he was doing."

"Did you know about the trip he made to London the day before his death?"

"Sure, I saw him on Sunday. He told me about it, he was going down the next day."

"Did he tell you why?"

"No."

"Did he mention it Tuesday night, when you saw him?"

"No. I knew better than to ask." Lauren paused, and then asked urgently, "Are you leveling with me? Won't the inquest find it a suicide?"

"Oh, sure, but that doesn't mean unofficially I can't keep the file open. I found those glasses in his pocket myself, and didn't get the incongruity." He looked at her and smiled a little. "I guess it's because I don't wear them myself. I can't think what it's like to function without them if you're dependent."

Lauren looked through her spectacles at him and smiled weakly. "Right, right," she said. "So seriously, you're still asking questions?"

"Not actively. But I'm still asking questions in my mind." He thought momentarily of telling her of Bowles's research notes he had copied, of his suspicion that a file had been removed, of the relationship with Fenwick, which she had almost guessed, and the unexplained payments to him, but dismissed these ideas quickly. It was already unprofessional enough for him to be sitting drinking scotch in this woman's bedroom, technically a material witness in an unusual-death investigation, telling her information in confidence. He felt a little uneasy.

"Great boots," she said unexpectedly.

Smailes held out one of the Tony Lamas and cocked his ankle. "Yeah, I like them," he said.

"You're a pretty bizarre policeman," she replied quietly.

He did not recognize the impulse that made him ready to

219

confide in this person, but suddenly he found himself telling her the whole story of his involvement with the police force, about his father's career and death, his marriage and divorce. She would prompt him from time to time, or murmur comments, but mostly it was monologue. He had not recounted these thoughts and feelings to anyone in years, and he felt strange as his story gathered momentum. He took his account right up to the present, and tried to explain the equivocation he felt about police work, but how it was difficult for him to imagine doing anything else. When he had concluded he felt embarrassed, and asked politely, "What about yourself? Tell me the real reason you're in Cambridge."

When he looked back on the evening, Smailes could not remember at what point his desire for her became unmanageable. It must have been at some point in her own monologue, as he watched her staring at the pillars of flame in the gas fire, tugging at her hair. He remembered looking awkwardly at the point where the sallowness of her throat met the white fabric of her blouse, and his mouth becoming dry. He was painfully aware that she did not wear a brassiere, how her breasts rocked when she shook her head and its dark curls in emphasis of some memory that exasperated her.

His concentration on her story faltered, but he heard her describe her conventional middle-class Jewish upbringing in a suburb of New York, how she had felt compelled to study and achieve for her parents, Howard and Mimi, to reward their expectations as the only child of their old age. She said she understood his painful feelings about his father, that she had had a classical Freudian fixation herself, before her father had died in her early teens. He had enjoyed brief success as a screenwriter, but then had settled down to teach English in a high school on Long Island, until his sudden death from a stroke. Her mother was a Sephardic Jew, a first-generation immigrant from Turkey, from whom Lauren drew her exotic looks. Her parents had spoiled her and she had not been a particularly rebellious teenager.

220

Some survival instinct told him his lack of professionalism had already gone far enough. He should not have come to her digs in the first place. He felt regret that he had confided in her. He shifted in his chair and tilted the whiskey tumbler, as if to confirm it was empty, a prelude to leaving.

She turned and rested her dark eyes on him, and then caught herself, embarrassed. "I'm sorry. I've been going on and on. It must be late."

"Yes, I must be going."

There was a hiatus in which he felt a mounting constriction in his throat and a pain in his stomach. Wordlessly, he got up and walked to the door, and reached for his raincoat hanging on the hook.

Afterward, they agreed that he might have actually left if his larynx hadn't given way. Standing with his back to the door and the handle in a backhand grip, he tried to say, as Lauren walked toward him, "Call me if anything comes up."

What he actually said sounded more like "Cock-a-doodle-doo."

She threw back her head and laughed, a free and melodious laugh. He didn't have time to feel mortified because as he released his grip on the door handle Lauren took a step toward him and then the blade of her nose was against his cheek and her lips against his, softly at first, then more urgently. Her arms rose around his neck and he felt the soft, untethered weight beneath her waistcoat with his hands, his excitement surging. She broke away and held him close.

"Oh, I've been wanting to do that," she said to his shoulder. She stood back and helped him with the reverse process of removing his raincoat, then his jacket. She ran her hands over his shoulders and kissed him again.

"You don't wear a gun," she said. "All the cops in the States wear guns."

"Of course I don't wear a gun," he said softly.

She left him standing there and went to turn off the standing lamp, then the lamp on the desk, then sat on the bed and

221

turned off the lamp on the nightstand. He heard the light popping of buttons.

As he sat beside her and began to tug at his boots he did ask himself briefly what the hell he thought he was doing, but it was a token protest. Her long nakedness waited for him as he climbed in beside her, and he felt exultant.

The preliminary moves were familiar and delightful, until suddenly a surprisingly strong arm pushed him over onto his back and he became a baffled spectator. She knew what to do and Smailes found himself in entirely new territory, with all kinds of room for his hands. He had not made love in this way before and wondered with alarm as he approached his climax if gravity was going to be a problem. It wasn't.

Lauren kept moving against him and in the glow from the streetlight he saw her face, distracted and intent. Then she gave a low moan, and her body shuddered, then relaxed against him. There was a long silence.

She had moved away and lay curled against him in a fetal position when her voice interrupted his thoughts.

"Sorry. To be so pushy. It's more of a sure bet for me that way."

He found her modesty lovely, after such assurance. He found her hand. "No problem. No problem at all. Are you okay? I mean, I didn't ask . . ."

"Sure. I'm a modern girl. I have an IUD. You know, I don't know what to call you."

"What?"

"Your name. You're just Detective Smailes. I can't call you that. What's your name?"

"Derek."

He felt her shoulders rock with suppressed laughter. "What's wrong with that?" he asked.

"Nothing. Nothing. I've never known anybody with that name, that's all. It's sort of an old man's name." She cupped her hand over her nose. Derek Smailes had never liked the name either, but he didn't tell her that.

222

"Call me anything you like, Lauren."

"Okay, Plod. You can be Mr. Plod." Now it was his turn to laugh at the preposterous caricature of the British bobby. She laughed too, and then it was still again.

Smailes lay in the dark, his thoughts streaming. He had never had such a strange, illicit encounter, or felt such an overwhelming excitement. He had broken no laws, only an unwritten code. There was no crime here, only suspicions. A brilliant and lonely young man was dead, by his own hand, and his friends felt cheated. They contrived motives, criminals and plots, to blame someone for their own failure to prevent the waste. A file may have been removed, it may not have, he could not be sure. Officials at the college had behaved strangely, pursued personal agendas he could only guess at. He felt irked by the loose ends, but then, he always did. It went with the turf.

His thoughts turned to the girl who lay beside him, her breath soft against his shoulder. My God, a sexually assertive female. Smailes had thought they were inventions of the letters pages of girlie magazines, or inhabited a different realm than his own. Yvonne had never done more than gently return his thrusts, her face averted and absent. Bernadette had been more adventurous, but inexperienced, and his other encounters had been too brief to be anything more than fleeting contests. But he had known that sex was not just a male obsession. What would she say if she knew it was the first time he had made love this way? He knew, instinctively, she would laugh.

But what on earth did she see in him, an ungainly provincial cop with white flesh and strange vowels? He turned to her and she murmured something. He felt a surge of tenderness toward her, her Jewish strangeness, her strength. They made love again, and this time Smailes led the way.

He awoke in a strange room with no idea where he was. Bruce Springsteen looked down on him from the poster on the wall, and he remembered. He felt a moment of triumph. You just bonked your first Yank, he told himself. What time was it? It was no matter, he was on late mornings this week.

Lauren was not around. He saw their discarded clothes on the chair. He heard the distant sound of water running in a bathroom. He needed to relieve himself.

He got up and walked to her sink and used her toothbrush and towel. Then he wrapped the towel around himself and went back and sat on the bed. The door opened and Lauren came in wearing a cotton kimono. Her hair was wet. He suddenly felt embarrassed, an intruder, but her smile reassured him. She looked vulnerable without her glasses.

She came and rested her hands on his shoulders and asked if he had slept well. He asked her if she would get into trouble with her landlady, and she told him no, but they should wait until after nine for him to leave, the time she went to the shops. He asked her what they should do and she laughed and he pulled her down on the bed and they made love again.

When Smailes stepped out of his car outside his flat he had a giddy, unreal feeling and had to steady himself with his hand on the roof of the Austin. He could not suppress a huge grin.

"Shall I see you again?" he had asked.

"I hadn't thought that we wouldn't, Derek," she had said. "I'll call you. We have to find out why Simon died."

That was when Smailes realized that he had forgotten all about him.

Lauren Greenwald listened to the voice of the lecturer droning on and on about elementary organic chemistry that she already knew, and cupped her hand over her nose to hide a smile. She sat with her feet up on the bench in front, and in her folder she doodled the distinct shape of a British policeman's helmet. It really did look like the head of an erect penis, she had to agree.

224

She felt sore in a way she hadn't for years, but it was not an unpleasant sensation. She was very pleased with herself, and wondered what her mother would think if she could see her now. A British policeman! Talk about cutting your teeth.

Fifteen

DONALD WEST had been on the job with the Immigration Service at Prestwick Airport for barely three months when on the Tuesday after Easter the unlikely happened—two of his passengers turned up on the White List. He had undergone his training in London, naturally, and what he was told was that for every hundred names he found on the Black List, he might find one on the White List. But here he was, barely out of his probationary period, and the two Danes were definitely there, names and passport numbers on the White List.

The instructor for that particular training seminar had put it like this: the Black List was for people who were just that—blacklisted. They were to be denied entry into Britain and held in Immigration and told the reasons why, and how they could appeal if they wanted to. Nine times out of ten they were undocumented aliens making a phony immediate-relative claim. Mostly Pakistani and Indian passports, trying for a second or third time. Then there were others, expelled for various crimes, barred from returning to Britain for life. Whatever the reason, that was not your concern. You found their name, nationality and passport number (if known) on the printout, and you asked them to take a seat and you called the duty supervisor to explain it to them. You didn't trouble yourself with the arrangements after that.

The White List was something different. It was a much shorter printout than the Black List, of course. It was for people who were to be allowed into Britain without query, but who were to be followed after leaving the airport. These were not simply wanted criminals, it was explained. They were suspects in various crimes (often terrorist-related) or couriers for different conspiracies (usually narcotics) who might lead the authorities to bigger fish they were involved with. Again, it wasn't your decision. You were to let them through to the baggage area, then close your window and go immediately to the Special Branch station and report that you had let through a whitelisted person and point that person out as discreetly as possible. More often than not, if you moved quickly enough, the person was still waiting for his bags at the carousel, or if he just had carry-on, was in the line for the customs. That was all that had been explained to them, although after the session one of the other recruits told him that he'd been told the White List was put together mostly by MI5 and a lot of the names were suspected legends, cover identities for agents of foreign powers. Donald West didn't pay too much attention to that. He just wanted to be sure that he had the procedure right.

The problem was that at the smaller airports like Prestwick there was no Special Branch station, there was just an office for the regular police, which they shared with the airport security people. In that case your instructions were to explain the details to the officer in charge. There would usually be someone in plain clothes attached to the unit who could take it from there.

He thought he did a pretty good job of disguising any reaction when he handed the two Danes back their passports. Their names were there all right, among the dozen or so listed under Denmark. One was tall and dark, in his thirties and balding at the temples. The other man was older, a squat, overweight figure with short, fair hair and a red complexion. They were both listed as "businessman" in their passports, and spoke the good, unaccented English that all the Scandinavians seemed to speak. When he asked them how long they were planning to spend in Britain, the tall one said one week and gave as their address the name of one of the big hotels in Glasgow. He thought he had handled himself well as he smiled and wished them a profitable stay. He turned immediately to the next passenger and saw them leave the Immigration Hall out of the corner of his eye. Then he quickly pushed his "Closed" sign in front of his window and let himself out the back of the booth. The other passengers in his line shrugged in annoyance and went to join other lines. He thought of running over to the supervisor's office first, but decided to stick to the procedure he had been taught.

He didn't know the police sergeant who was sitting at the desk, and he tried to contain his excitement as he told him about the two businessmen on the noon flight from Copenhagen who were on his White List.

"And what's that, then?" asked the sergeant suspiciously.

West was appalled that the sergeant did not know, but tried to explain patiently about the two lists and what he had been instructed to do about listed people. The sergeant rubbed his chin and thought for a moment.

"We've only got McCann in plain clothes and he's in the freight hangar this week. They should be followed, you say . . ."

"That's what I understood. I'm just supposed to report it to you, and you're supposed to know what to do," West said testily.

"It's a new one on me," said the sergeant flatly. West began

228

to feel agitated. The pair would be through customs and off if they did not do something quickly. West did not doubt that their "business" was drug smuggling.

"I can hardly go out there, can I, in uniform, and have them pointed out. Here, you'd better let me have their names and a description and where they said they're staying, and I'll tell McCann about it when he comes in. He usually does, around two. Or I could call through to Special Branch in Glasgow . . ."

Donald West said, "Forget it," and ran to the door. He should have trusted his judgment and gone to the duty supervisor first, someone who would at least have known what the White List was. They needed to act right away if the pair were not going to disappear entirely. Maybe he should follow them himself, he thought in panic.

He ran down the stairs, down the corridor and into the customs area. He could not see them. He ran out onto the concourse of the airport, which was crowded with people checking in for flights to New York and Toronto. He pushed through the first ranks of passengers to where he could see out onto the pavement, where the two Danes were already getting into a taxi. By the time he reached the doors they were gone, he couldn't even make out the name of the taxi firm, let alone the number plate.

"Damnit," he said to himself angrily. "This is no way to run a bloody country."

Smailes found Fenwick at his flat on the third attempt, the lunchtime after his encounter with Lauren Greenwald. The young man did not seem surprised to see him, and told him gloomily that he had been suspended pending review of his case by the college. He became defensive when Smailes said he did not seem to be spending much time at home. He had been round at his mother's the previous evening, all evening, he maintained.

"Drive over, did you, Alan?"

"Yes, of course," said Fenwick suspiciously. "What's it to you?"

Smailes had decided not to beat about the bush. "Bowles bought it for you, didn't he? Clean cash. Just like he gave you the grand to set you up in this place back in February. What was it for—deposit, furniture, that kind of thing? What did you have on him, Alan, that you could shake four grand out of him in two months?"

Fenwick made no attempt to deny the payments. "Nothing. Nothing. Weren't like that, see."

"Oh, it weren't. How was it? Why don't you tell me, Alan? And it'd better be good, or you'll be telling it to the chief super."

Again Fenwick's story had a plausible ring, if an unpleasant smell to it. After their friendship began, the two men became frustrated at the secrecy with which they had to conduct themselves. Fenwick was living with his mother, so there was no chance to meet outside the college. It had been Bowles's idea to set up Fenwick in the flat. Fenwick could afford the rent, he just hadn't been able to come up with the start-up costs. He hadn't wanted to take the money, but Simon had insisted. Like hell, thought Smailes.

The car had also been Bowles's idea, so they could take trips together on the weekends. Simon didn't drive, so they had put the car in Fenwick's name. He went into a dresser drawer and showed Smailes the deed.

"Not logical, Alan. He could've retained ownership even if you were the driver. Why didn't he do that?"

"Wanted to make it a gift. He insisted."

"You lied, Alan, first time I came here. Said you could afford the payments. There are no payments, right? It's yours, outright. Why d'you lie?"

"Didn't want no questions like these, did I? It's my business."

"It is bloody hell your business, mate. This is a suspicious

230

death we got here, and your behavior's one of the most suspicious things about it. You know what it looks like?"

"What?"

"Blackmail, that's what. That you had the screws on him and he was coughing up to keep you quiet. What'd you do, threaten to expose him as a fairy?"

Here Fenwick produced the waterworks and Smailes had to do his glass-of-water routine again.

"No, no, it weren't, I swear. Simon wasn't ashamed of what he was. We loved each other," he said defiantly when he'd recovered himself. "He was very kind, and very generous, that's all. That's all."

Smailes broke off the questioning and eventually told Fenwick that he was going to put his side of the affair to the chief super and to Bowles's family. The whole issue of his involvement, and his appearing at the inquest, would be brought up again. In the meantime, he might think of selling the car and giving the money back to Bowles's family, where it belonged. It might make things look better.

"I've thought of that," said Fenwick moodily.

"Sure you have, Alan," said Smailes.

Derek Smailes began seeing a lot of Lauren Greenwald. For the most part, they would go to pubs that he liked to frequent and spend their nights at Lauren's digs. She explained that Mrs. Bilton, the landlady, lived downstairs and was hard of hearing, or pretended to be. She had never said anything to Lauren about overnight guests and one of the other students who lived upstairs, a horny undergraduate from Fitzwilliam, often had his girlfriends stay over. The other resident was a married graduate student whose family lived in London and whom she hardly ever saw. Somehow, Smailes felt reluctant to invite her to his flat, it was such a bachelor's redoubt, and she didn't seem to mind. Her bed was a bit small for both of them, but it was the kind of discomfort Smailes liked.

He found her intriguing. She had a strong sense of fun and

began playing tricks on him from the start. On the Saturday after their first night together, he had been at the swimming baths with Tracy, their regular venue, and Lauren had caught him completely by surprise by sneaking up behind him and grabbing the girdle of fat that hung at his waist. At first he felt annoyed that she had intruded on his time with Tracy, but she was so good with his daughter that he could not hang on to his mood. Her bathing suit, predictably, was black and Smailes could only admire how terrific she looked in it. She had an athletic figure and was obviously a strong swimmer, but she took lots of time to play with Tracy in the shallow end, which Smailes soon tired of. As they were all sitting together on the bench before going to the changing rooms, Tracy had asked coyly whether Lauren was Daddy's girl-friend, and Lauren had said yes, without a second thought. At times like that, he was struck by the implausibility of their relationship.

They never had trouble finding subjects to talk about. She was not at all what he would expect of a female engineer, and had interests in a lot of the same areas that he did. He quickly noticed a sort of angry intensity about her when she brought up certain subjects. She was vehement about what she called the withering of idealism in the United States and in Britain, and spoke heatedly of the materialism and shallowness of young people her age. Once when Smailes arrived at her digs she was listening to *Abbey Road* by the Beatles and held up her arm to silence him when he tried to speak. She turned the stereo up louder and together they listened to the whole second side in silence before she would speak. She looked at him almost angrily and said, "They're so fucking *elegiac*. See, there was a chance back then that something lasting might happen." Smailes did some mental arithmetic and said he thought she was a little young to like the Beatles and she told him impatiently that no one was too young to like the Beatles. When they spoke about respective plans for the future, she told him that after graduating she wanted to become an engineer somewhere in Africa, which made Smailes wince. Whenever he thought of Africa, he saw flies, heat and death. He couldn't imagine volunteering to live there. She explained that it was something she and her father had discussed before his death, and she felt it was a commitment she had to see through. He realized that her year at Cambridge would be over soon, in June, and she would be going back to New York. It crossed his mind that she might be a reason for his finally visiting America, but warned himself to presume nothing. Lauren was delighted by his eccentric love of Americana and called him cowboy and teased him about country music, which she said she loathed.

They didn't talk often about Simon Bowles. Lauren had backed off from her insistence that the discovery of the spectacle case cast the whole suicide theory in doubt. Smailes was now involved full-time with investigating the cigarette lorry theft and a couple of smaller robberies and maintained his interest in the case only by rereading parts of Bowles's files from time to time. He had vacillated about going to Dearnley with his suspicions about a missing file, but had finally discarded the idea—the whole thing was too prejudicial. He withheld from Lauren any knowledge of Bowles's research or the unlikely double career of Nigel Hawken. After a week or so he did tell her of Alan Fenwick's involvement, which he immediately regretted, because Lauren latched on to this disclosure forcefully and insisted the relationship must be directly involved with why Simon Bowles had died. Smailes omitted the information about Simon's payments to Fenwick and the negotiations that had ensued between George Dearnley and the family. George, of course, had been appalled and was inclined at first to renege on Fenwick's immunity. But the crafty young man had sold the car immediately and forwarded the check to Smailes. Dearnley realized it would be a considerable loss of face with Baddeley, the coroner, to change channels at this stage, and Alice Wentworth lobbied heavily for proceeding in the agreed way, particularly when

233

she heard there was another two thousand on its way. Smailes felt uneasy that Fenwick was buying his way out of a jam, but Dearnley had allowed Alice Wentworth to prevail. He did not doubt that George felt distaste at being outflanked by a venal punk like Fenwick, but he seemed to write it off as a wrong call to which he had committed too soon. If he blamed Derek Smailes for his predicament, he did not say so, which struck Smailes as slightly odd.

For Lauren's part, she did not believe the version of Fenwick's story Smailes told her, and was disgusted that the police had suppressed his involvement from the record. Smailes realized that he would have to keep his work and his love life separate, given Lauren's volatility. She had become angry at him and he had shouted back, insisting that they knew what they were doing. He told her she knew nothing about police work and the hard decisions it involved, that he was a fool to confide in her. She was mollified and apologized, but Smailes had learned a lesson from his indiscretion.

She was a playful and energetic lover, the best Smailes had ever known. She liked to dress up and act out all kinds of bizarre fantasies, which he resisted at first but quickly began to appreciate. One evening she disappeared to the bathroom and came back wearing a judo suit. She practiced karate with the University club, and after closing the door, approached him across the room with her eyes narrowed, one forearm horizontal and the other raised vertically, one foot in its flat black sandal lifted toward him. Then with a howl she executed a leap and brought her back foot driving through the air to within an inch of his chin. After intimidating him with a number of other moves, any one of which could have knocked him cold, she threw him deftly to the floor and began to undress him. Then she made love to him in the same violent and intimidating way and Smailes loved it.

Occasionally Smailes would feel rueful about the disparity in their ages and lifestyles. One Friday evening at Mrs. Bilton's gate he bumped into one of the fellow lodgers, the

234

married graduate student, a huge, red-haired bear of a man with a Rob Roy beard and thick black glasses, who was carrying an armful of books and a brand-new teddy bear out to his car. He was a man of Smailes's age, doing what men of Smailes's age ought to do, going back to a wife and kid. On another occasion it was particularly humiliating to him when he went to pick up Lauren as planned and found Giles Allerton sitting in her room, as if he belonged there. He realized that Allerton must have spent considerable time there when he and Lauren had been lovers, but he believed Lauren when she told him that was all in the past. Still he couldn't suppress a surge of jealousy and resentment at this unexpected meeting, and was barely able to be polite when Allerton grunted a greeting. The feelings were no doubt mutual, since Allerton got immediately to his feet and left, hardly pausing to speak to Lauren on his way out. Smailes realized that Allerton represented for him the indolence and privilege of a whole generation from which he had been excluded, and he was annoyed that he felt any rivalry with this shallow, insignificant young man. Lauren had understood the chemical reaction between the two men immediately and had merely said, "Forget it, Plod. He's a child," at which Smailes felt a sudden flush of embarrassment. She was able to read his thoughts and moods with an uncanny precision, which he found unsettling.

One particularly filthy night when Smailes was on late evenings, he was sitting in his armchair reading after getting off duty around ten. Since the late tour could often extend past midnight, he and Lauren were not scheduled to meet until the weekend. Squalls of rain rattled against the windows, and Smailes was glad he was home instead of driving around somewhere out in the storm. His armchair was a particularly ugly mauve plastic recliner that had come along with the place, but it was the most comfortable reading chair he had, the one he always chose to sit in. As often happened when he was alone at night, he had begun thinking again of the Bowles case and of his own clumsy investigation. Almost out

235

of a sense of guilt he had begun reading the dry history of the British security services that had belonged to Simon Bowles, but he was finding it repetitive and only moderately interesting. He found he couldn't keep track of all the names and dates and wasn't sufficiently interested in the subject to put out the effort needed. He was distracted by a rap at the window that he thought was the wind, but the noise was repeated, so he walked over and pulled back the curtain. Lauren's contorted face was pressed up against the streaming windowpane and she was wearing a ridiculous yellow sou'wester. He was delighted and annoyed at the same time, and went to let her in. He saw that her overcoat was soaking as she strode past him into the flat.

"Lauren, what the hell?" he asked as she marched around his living room inspecting the furniture, looking at the books on his shelves, the pictures on the wall.

"I came to beard you in your den, you fat old bear," she said. "If I'd called, you might've put me off, admit it. I wanted to see how you lived. So I just came."

She looked absurd. Her overcoat was an old-fashioned, tight-bodied type that was gathered at the waist and then flared almost to the floor. She wore black laced boots and a long dark skirt and a sou'wester that was far too large and came down over her eyes and ears. She pushed it back off her head and the cord caught it as it draped down her back. She shook her hair and laughed.

"Are you mad?" she asked.

"No," he said unconvincingly. "But I'd have invited you if you'd asked."

"Sure," she said, and resumed her inspection of his home. She turned her head to read the titles of the books on his shelves. The two volumes on Bletchley Park with the defaced spines were on the top shelf, but Lauren apparently did not recognize them. Hunting further, she found the fat folder containing the xerox of Bowles's notes sitting on top of the bookcase. She opened the file and said, "What's this?"

"I've got a friend in London who's writing a book on espionage and he asked me to look at his rough draft. It's a bit dry," he said.

"Isn't all this what Simon was into?" she asked, riffling through the papers.

"I dunno. Was he?" said Smailes. He didn't want to get into it again with her. He knew if he told her it was Simon's work she would immediately formulate all kinds of wild theories that he didn't want to listen to. Bowles's inquest was now only days away and he was committed to letting that machinery work. Lauren had said she was going to boycott the proceedings because she was annoyed at the suppression of the Fenwick evidence, and Smailes hoped she kept her word.

"How'd you get here?" he asked, changing the subject.

"Bike, of course," she replied. "Perfect night for a spin." She continued her inspection of his home, lifting the Indian cotton print that he had draped over the Naugahyde couch.

"Boy, do you have awful taste," she said. Smailes realized he was embarrassed by the shabbiness of the flat, and he found this inspection vaguely demeaning. Lauren walked over to the chair and squinted to see the title of the book he had been reading, then took a sudden step backward.

"Yuck, Plod, it's a recliner." She hooted with delight as she found the catch on the armrest that released the mechanism of the chair. It groaned on ancient springs and elongated itself into its humanoid shape. "You old fart, you've got a recliner."

He felt angry and defensive. "Yeah, well, I didn't know that when I got it. It came along with the place. And for your information, I don't use it as a recliner. Did you find me in it when you showed up?"

Lauren was not going to be cowed. She took him by the arm and positioned him in front of the chair and shoved. He toppled backward into the chair's vinyl embrace and she climbed up on the armrests, straddling him. He started to

237

laugh. He loved it when she pushed him around. She began to kiss him hungrily.

"Sweetheart, take off your coat," he said.

"Take off my pants," she replied. He reached up under her coat and skirt and slid the panties down and over one boot, then the next. He stroked her and her breath became more shallow and she kissed him so hard their teeth met. She climbed down and they made love right there, fully clothed, on Smailes's hearth rug, Smailes kneeling behind her and Lauren arching her back toward him. He felt like a highwayman, ravishing some rain-spattered traveler. Her alternation between aggression and submission won him completely, and he felt drunk with his desire.

Later, as they lay together in his small dark bedroom, he asked her if she always got what she wanted. She seemed completely at rest, but he felt tense and uncertain.

"What do you mean?" she said sleepily.

"I just don't see what you see in me. I'm a thirty-year-old divorced policeman with child-support payments and a secondhand Austin. I'm overweight, have lousy taste and a five-hundred-quid overdraft. Do you regularly have affairs with men you have nothing in common with?"

Lauren raised herself on an elbow in the darkness. "Derek, what are you saying? Don't run yourself down. You're a special guy. You're strong, but you're also gentle. You've seen a lot and you're real smart, but you're not bitter or conceited. You really think we have nothing in common?"

"Sure, in terms of background."

"What does that matter? I feel more like myself when I'm with you than with all these overprivileged kids at the University. You're only the second man I've known that made me feel this way."

Smailes was gratified by her frankness, but piqued at the thought of a rival. He felt for her jaw in the darkness and squeezed it. "Oh yeah, and who was the other guy? Somebody with the FBI?"

238

"No, Ari. He was a lover I met in Jerusalem last year. He was married. He was a very brave, idealistic man, and there was absolutely no pettiness about him. But it was real brief, only a couple of weeks."

"Jewish guy?"

"No, Jordanian. A diplomat. We met at the hotel. He had to go back to Amman. He was nearly forty."

Smailes felt this rival's threat recede. "What's a nice Jewish girl like you doing with an A-rab?" he said, choosing the Texan pronunciation deliberately.

"Derek, I don't give a shit about that stuff," she said pointedly.

"Tell me some more. How did you meet him? What did he look like? What were you doing in Jerusalem anyway? A pilgrimage?"

Smailes had felt himself relax and was on the edge of sleep, but he wanted to extend this intimacy, because it reassured him. He wanted her to reveal herself emotionally, the way she did so readily physically.

"Not really. My family's not religious at all. It's more a tribal thing, a roots thing. We have some relatives in Tel Aviv. It was my second visit. I spent a year on a kibbutz, after school, after I graduated. It was great."

"You a commie?" Smailes asked. It was a silly remark, but she took it graciously.

"Hardly, but I really respect the kibbutzim. Those people work really hard. I didn't like the rest of Israel. It's basically a U.S. puppet state, sort of like Florida with bunkers and antiaircraft batteries. I hate those hysterical Zionists that run the place. Fleshy, heartless old men, they're disgusting."

"Did you visit the Arab states?"

"Are you kidding? With my name and looks?"

"I guess you have a point," said Smailes, as he began to fall asleep.

The Bowles inquest was the pantomime that Smailes expected, in which everyone played their part as rehearsed. He was glad Lauren kept her pledge to stay away, because even he found the proceedings a little distasteful. The life and death of Simon Bowles was duly sanitized and recorded, a tiresome legal ritual that no one relished, except Oscar Baddeley, the coroner. Baddeley had the affected gravity and precision of the minor official, and Smailes could almost mouth the words that the coroner pronounced as he went through his inflexible routine.

The first witness called was always Maurice Jones, the postmortem surgeon from Addenbrookes, and Baddeley's technique was to confer as much information as possible for the record in rhetorical questions, to which the witness simply assented. This contributed to the coroner's air of unflawed efficiency, which was what was desired.

"You are Dr. Maurice Jones, consultant morbid anatomist at Addenbrookes Hospital, Cambridge?" asked Baddeley.

"I am," said Jones obediently.

"And on the morning of Wednesday, March 24, 1982, did you examine the body of a young man identified to you as Mr. Simon Bowles of St. Margaret's College, Cambridge?"

"I did," responded Jones.

"Please tell us what you found."

Smailes knew the next line because Jones always described his cadavers as well nourished, unless they had actually died of starvation. The fact that Bowles weighed little over nine stone would be immaterial to him.

"I found the body of a well-nourished young gentleman," Jones said, and proceeded to read from his postmortem report that Smailes had seen weeks before. He noted the absence of major diseases and abnormalities on the body, and the absence of any contusions or injury in any region except the neck. He described the modest blood alcohol reading, and the absence of any other foreign substance he had tested for. He gave the approximate time of death and described the nature

240

of the neck injury as a rupture of the spinal column between the first and second vertebrae, commensurate with an injury caused by hanging. Contusions in the area of the neck supported this judgment.

Baddeley went through a few other questions designed to eliminate other possible causes of death, and then excused Jones, who left to return to his morgue. Obviously a doctor's time was more valuable than a policeman's.

Derek Smailes was the third witness called, after the hesitant testimony of Police Constable Roger Dickley established how the body had first been found. Baddeley had decided to spare Bunty Allen the discomfort of testifying, which was probably wise. Since hearsay evidence was allowed in a coroner's court, unlike a judicial court, Dickley had been permitted to describe his conversations with both Mrs. Allen and Paul Beecroft. He described how they had closed up the room and waited for CID to arrive. He did not tell Baddeley about omitting to call the coroner's office, which Baddeley had no doubt realized and decided to overlook. Just as he had been persuaded to overlook the whole question of Mr. Alan Fenwick, Smailes thought to himself as he sat down in the witness chair next to Baddeley's table. Opposite him sat the court recorder, crouched over her stenotype machine. Looking out, he could see Alice Wentworth, the sole representative of Bowles's family, seated impassively in the first row. Next to her was Giles Allerton, who kept a scowl on his face throughout the whole proceeding. An uncomfortable-looking Ivor Davies appeared to be the sole official of the college present, although to his surprise Smailes made out the striking figure of Tiffany Pollock, Hawken's secretary, seated in the back. Dr. Julius Kramer was there, wearing a shabby blue suit, looking as unkempt as before. There were two or three students in the room that Smailes did not recognize, and a couple of young journalists representing the *Evening News* and one of the weeklies at the press table. Smailes doubted this story would make the front page, or even a page lead. He

241

turned to face Baddeley, who went through Smailes's rank and the circumstances of his arrival at St. Margaret's on that same morning. Smailes assented to Baddeley's descriptions firmly and professionally.

"Please tell the court what you found when you inspected Mr. Bowles's room," said Baddeley, and Smailes took out his small notebook. He was quite glad that Lauren wasn't there.

Derek Smailes went over the details of Simon Bowles's room, including his removal of personal belongings from Bowles's pockets and the discovery of the note in the type-writer. He described the arrival of the mortuary attendants and the arrangements for scenes-of-crimes officers to examine the room. Baddeley then produced the large glossies taken of Bowles's room and Klammer's fingerprint report, and asked Smailes to identify them, which he did. He then described his discussions with Mrs. Allen, Hawken, and the friends with whom Bowles had spent the previous evening. He omitted his discussions with Davies, Gorham-Leach and Kramer and any reference to his inspection of Bowles's files. Baddeley asked Smailes about the reported state of mind of Simon Bowles on the evening of his death, and Smailes read from his notes that both Mr. Giles Allerton and Miss Lauren Green-wald had described Simon Bowles as aloof and preoccupied. Baddeley excused Smailes and to his surprise called Alice Wentworth to the stand.

Baddeley must have picked up on the last phone call be-tween Alice Wentworth and her brother, because it was all he chose to ask her about. She described the strangeness of her brother's mood, the cancellation of his plans to attend a fam-ily gathering on the Sunday before his death, his announce-ment of his plans to study instead and spend Monday in Lon-don. Smailes wondered if Baddeley was going to ask about the reasons for the London trip and was alarmed that the whole question of Simon Bowles's research might come up. That would certainly rouse the two bored-looking reporters,

242

who were dutifully taking notes. It would make for a whole other angle on the story, Smailes knew. But Baddeley merely jotted some notes and excused Alice Wentworth, and Smailes could see what he was doing, steadily increasing the evidence that Bowles's mood before his death was somehow disordered and abnormal. The last witness called was the psychiatrist Julius Kramer, who looked every bit as unsavory on the witness stand as he had weeks ago out at the hospital. His testimony, however, was clear and succinct, and he basically reiterated his belief that his former patient had become severely depressed again but had succeeded in masking the fact from his family and friends. When asked about the significance of the suicide note, Kramer referred to the delusion from which Bowles had been suffering when first admitted to Myrtlefields Hospital two years before. He expressed the opinion that under extreme stress, it was possible that the frightening hallucination might have returned, although he, Kramer, personally doubted that that had occurred. Baddeley concluded by asking Kramer for statistics about how many depressed patients experience a second episode of major depression in their lives, and Kramer answered sixty percent. With unnecessary baldness Baddeley then asked whether suicide was a serious danger among depressed patients, and Kramer replied that it was a concern, although not always a major one. Baddeley thanked Kramer and the psychiatrist stepped down.

Baddeley barely waited a minute before beginning his summing-up. Its fluidity convinced Smailes that, as usual, it had been rehearsed and that nothing unanticipated had emerged during the inquest, which was what Baddeley had intended. He heard Bowles described as a brilliant but unstable young man whose mood had seemed strange to family and friends immediately before his death. The circumstances in which the body was found, together with the postmortem examination, convinced him that Simon Bowles had taken his own life by hanging while the balance of his mind was disturbed.

243

He expressed conventional sympathies for the family and pronounced the inquest closed. It was such a reasonable conclusion, Smailes wondered why he felt there were any questions unanswered.

Sixteen

THE REGIONAL NEWS gave way to a game show and the stocky Russian stuffed a handful of pizza into his mouth and got off the end of the bed to turn down the volume on the television. He cocked his head to listen to a noise outside, chewing slowly, moving first to glance out through the drawn curtains, then to the door. There were two soft raps, a pause, followed by two more. He unlocked the door and went back to his perch at the end of the single bed, next to the flat pizza box.

"You're very late," he said to the television screen. He wiped away tomato sauce with a paper napkin, picked up another piece, and then leaned forward to turn the volume back up.

"Problems?"

The man who had entered the small hotel room dropped a heavy canvas duffel to the floor, then took off an English-style flat cap and began unbuttoning a gray raincoat. Rain glistened on his shoulders. He was younger and taller than his colleague, with dark hair brushed straight back and high, thinning temples. He tossed the coat and hat onto the second bed.

"GRU bastards," he said forcefully. "They are a worse enemy than any Western intelligence agency. The instructions were intentionally misleading. I will write a full report, tonight."

"Don't waste your energy," said the older man. "I warned you it would be difficult. They do it deliberately, to let us know they are doing us a favor. I presume that in time of war there would be no such games. You got everything?"

"Yes," said the other grudgingly. "Once I found the chest—on the third attempt, I might add—I was quite impressed. Every piece individually wrapped and well greased. It should last for years." He began opening the duffel.

"Each site is supposed to last for thirty, I think, although the contents are replaced more often. What did you get?" he asked, beginning to show interest.

"Just two machine pistols and an automatic. It's a Beretta, I couldn't resist. Ammunition, of course. And two transmitters, in case of failure. I left the heavier stuff, the Kalashnikovs, the Israeli semi-automatics . . ."

"Of course, of course. Let me see." The older man took one of the wrapped pistols from the bag and began to carefully unfold its protective cloth.

"How did you disguise the site again?"

"I stuck red flags all around it," said the taller man, offended.

"Just tell me."

"The site is a wooded hill outside Norwich. Very isolated. You have to walk across two fields, but there are tall hedgerows and no one sees you from the road. I filled in the pit again and stamped the earth down. I used turf from a little way off, branches. The rest of the dirt I scattered around. You

246

could go there tomorrow, not find it. Then I returned to the car."

"The tools?"

"There's a pick, a shovel and a one-meter probe still in the boot. I'll dispose of them tomorrow."

The older man thought for a moment. "No. Leave them. They might be useful later." Then he changed the subject. "Well, our comrades in military intelligence understand their work, I think you have to say, even if they like to make things difficult for us. How does it drive?"

"The car? It runs well, very fast. A little stiff through the gears. The other vehicle?"

"I called today. We get it tomorrow, a place called Leyton-stone, east of London. Then we meet Painter, tomorrow night."

"That should be interesting. What do you have to eat? I am half starved."

"Help yourself," said the older man, replacing the pistol and turning again to the television, which gave out a sudden roar as a contestant advanced to the next round. "I couldn't wait, so I went and bought something."

"Pizza? Pizza? We get to go abroad for the first time in two years, we have unlimited expenses, and you buy pizza?"

"What can I do? You are late with the car, this shit hole is miles from anywhere, I am on foot. Go out and get something else, if you like."

The taller man stepped over the bag of weapons and wireless equipment at his feet and took a position opposite his friend on the end of his bed. He tugged a slice of pizza free and raised it vertically until the strands of cheese snapped.

"You have beer or vodka?"

"In the bathroom. Ah, look, this is sickening. This man, he gets everyone excited about these toast makers and televisions he gives away to this idiot. It is not even a Japanese brand."

His friend was walking to the bathroom. "The fish and chips is better than pizza, you should know, Alexei," he said, his mouth full. "Or the pork pie. The pork pie is especially good."

Smailes had been right about the news value of the Bowles inquest. The *Evening News* that day was preoccupied with page after page of news of the British task force which had set sail for the Falklands and the furious diplomatic efforts to avert war. The report on the inquest had merited a few paragraphs on page six under the weak headline "Dead Student Was Brilliant but Unstable—Coroner." Smailes was relieved that nothing had emerged about Bowles's research, because the absence of any splash meant he could continue to test those waters discreetly, if he chose. Although it was nowhere stated explicitly in his files, Smailes had become convinced that Simon Bowles had been seeking to identify a British spy of the same importance as the four Cambridge compatriots who had been unmasked to date. That would square with Iain Mack's theory of a ring of five spies who had burrowed into the Establishment and had been the crowning accomplishment of the Kremlin's courtship of British intellectuals in the thirties. It might also explain the ellipsis of Bowles's *Gang of Four . . .* file heading, if the "gang" was generally accepted to comprise five. Smailes felt somewhat frustrated that Bowles's file did not discuss the careers of these men after they left Cambridge, and in his curiosity turned to other sources.

In one of the Bowles research texts, Smailes found a compelling section that recounted in detail the activities of the four men who had done so much damage to Western interests throughout their careers. It was an improbable tale. The most unlikely was Guy Burgess, flamboyant homosexual and drunkard, who would often boast of his work for the Comintern at the wild parties he threw at his West End flat. Meanwhile he had pursued an erratic career in the BBC and Whitehall before his defection with Maclean in 1951. The feckless and neurotic Maclean had risen steadily through the diplomatic service until he held a senior post in the British Embassy in Washington after the war. He returned to take a position in London in 1950, by which time an error by a Soviet cipher clerk had alerted the CIA to a high-ranking spy inside the British diplomatic mission. By the time British intelligence had conclusively identified Maclean as the mole, serious damage had been done. As a member of the Committee for Joint Atomic Development in Washington, Maclean had access to high-grade scientific intelligence that helped accelerate Soviet development of the atom bomb in the late forties. When Philby learned of the impending interrogation of Maclean, he dispatched Burgess, who was staying at his house in Washington, to orchestrate his escape. Burgess effectively blew Philby's cover and career when, against orders, he accompanied Maclean all the way to Moscow. Blunt, it appeared, had refused to defect when encouraged to do so by his Soviet masters after suspicion had settled on both him and Philby after the disappearance of Burgess and Maclean. He had left active intelligence work at the end of the war, and now relished his eminent position as head of the Courtauld Institute of Art and Surveyor of the Queen's Pictures. He was also in a happy, stable relationship with a former guardsman who shared his flat above the Institute. In all he survived eleven interrogations before he was definitively unmasked in 1964 and forced to confess. When the story was finally told in 1979 he was stripped of his knighthood, his official duties and his Trinity fellowship in the furor that ensued. He was not punished in any other way and asserted to the end that he had not betrayed his conscience.

The most successful and damaging of the Cambridge spies, however, was Philby. He had succeeded brilliantly in disguising an overtly communist past (he had even traveled to Vienna in 1934 to join the communist guerrillas fighting the fascist Chancellor Dollfuss) and adopted the mantle of a neoconservative in London before the war. He traveled to Spain as a free-lance journalist during its civil war, from where he wrote pro-Franco dispatches. Then, under Burgess's aegis, he was able to join the burgeoning intelligence community at the beginning of the war, eventually finding himself head of the Iberian section of the Secret Intelligence Service, or MI6, by 1941. His crowning accomplishment, of course, was to inveigle himself into the position of head of the newly established section nine, the Soviet counterintelligence unit, in 1944. Thus Philby was able to effectively neutralize any measures contemplated against Russia or its satellites in the closing stages of the war, and was strongly suspected of betraying the Bletchley intelligence to his employers. In the cold war that began immediately after Germany's surrender, Philby's treachery defeated a number of counterrevolutionary moves attempted by Western intelligence, including a joint MI6/CIA-backed invasion of Albania. He had duped his colleagues so successfully that he began to be groomed as a future director-general of MI6, first as station chief in Turkey and then as the prestigious liaison officer with the FBI and CIA in Washington. And despite the suspicion that fell on him following Burgess's disappearance, he was able to defy his interrogators and even achieve partial rehabilitation as a field agent in Beirut, where he worked under journalistic cover for four years. He finally defected in 1963 when incontrovertible evidence of his treachery was provided by the high-ranking Soviet defector Anatoli Golitsin and confirmed by a former party member in London.

Smailes read that another distinguishing feature of Philby's career was that he was neither homosexual like Burgess and Blunt nor bisexual like Maclean, despite Burgess's occasional drunken claims to the contrary. Indeed, he seemed to have considerable heterosexual charisma, was married five times and fathered seven children legitimately—five in England by his second wife, Aileen Furse, and two in Moscow by his Russian wife, Rufa. It was also suspected that Philby, a tireless womanizer, may have fathered other, illegitimate offspring. And whereas Burgess and Maclean were given sinecures in Moscow and led dreary, aimless lives, Philby was made a general in the KGB and remained close to its inner circle, and was rumored to be a confidant of its current chairman, Yuri Andropov. It had been asserted that Philby had been the most successful and damaging Soviet agent in history, and even with his limited knowledge, Derek Smailes could understand why.

Smailes had two basic concerns when he contemplated the circumstances of Bowles's death. The first was that there was little evidence, despite Baddeley's assertions, that Bowles had been in any extreme frame of mind in the days and hours that led up to his presumed suicide. He had made trips to Oxford and London during those days, the second of which was important enough for him to cancel out of a family reunion, but the results of both trips were unknown. His second and more serious concern was that whatever Bowles had learned had seemed to inspire him to some sort of work from which he was loath to be interrupted on the evening of his death and to which he returned from the college bar as soon as he was politely able. That work either was buried somewhere in the files Smailes had removed—Bowles never dated his work—or was missing altogether. Derek Smailes could not resolve in his mind the question of the stolen file, but it seemed a strong possibility that if someone had not tampered with Bowles's files while he was drinking in the college bar with his friends, they had done so the following day after Smailes had completed his inspection of the room. What had been stolen? The incriminating file that Bowles had completed before he committed suicide? Or was this after all a murder? What was most tantalizing to Smailes was the possibility that Bowles, as with his Kennedy investigation, had found missing pieces of evidence that had allowed him to compose a Cambridge Theorem as telling in its conclusion as the Kennedy Theorem had been, and that the discovery had somehow cost him his life. Had a Cambridge Theorem file, a triumphant summation that in fact identified a Fifth Man, been stolen from the room

251

together with a Bletchley file? Had a Bletchley file been stolen to disguise the theft of a Cambridge Theorem file? Try as he might, Smailes could not remember seeing a file with this distinctive heading. He was convinced he would have remembered it.

He wondered whether the Bletchley note was not some pregnant truth like the geometric analysis of Dealey Plaza, a postulate that insisted on a formulation other than that accepted by the Establishment, and whether the precision tool of Bowles's intellect had turned over a rock from beneath which something had leapt out to kill him. But if Simon Bowles had been murdered, then the circumstances were peculiar indeed, because it seemed certain that Bowles had typed the suicide note himself, and if he had been overpowered and forcibly hanged, then the act had been accomplished without damage to the room or to the victim's body. Smailes contemplated making inquiries with Allerton's brother in Oxford and at Somerset House in London, but he knew Dearnley would never approve the trips. He could make visits on the sly, but he ran the risk of alarming Bowles's family and angering George if word got back to either of them. And objectively speaking, Smailes had to concede that the truth was probably more ordinary, that the likelihood was still that something horrifying had happened to Bowles between the hours of ten-thirty and one on the night of his death to cause him to take his own life. The conclusion rankled.

Doubts about the real circumstances of Simon Bowles's death continued to grate on Smailes like a toothache. One evening at home he was scanning Bowles's archival work from the Oxford library, hoping to strike something unusual, when he realized suddenly that for all his thoroughness Simon Bowles had overlooked one excellent source of information about activities in the thirties that was available to him. This was the files of the Cambridge police force. All criminal records had been computerized for many years now, but the old manual files containing hard copies of all the criminal

252

investigations conducted by the police force since its inception were stored in one of the government buildings out on Brooklands Avenue, Smailes was fairly sure. There might even be Special Branch files, he realized. Special Branch activities had come and gone at Cambridge over the years, but it seemed likely that there were some Specials stationed in town during the thirties, given the political turmoil of those years. They had certainly had a detachment at the station during the student unrest of the early seventies, and Smailes was aware that a couple of officers had begun operating out of the Cambridge station recently, to monitor the political activity of the peace movement people around the American bases at Molesworth and the Alconburys. The new cruise missiles were not due to be deployed until the following year, but the women down at the Greenham Common base were already beginning to attract a lot of publicity with their continuing demonstration. Nothing major had happened yet in the Cambridge area, but he knew the Specials liked to be on the scene early so they could infiltrate a group while it was still in its formative stages. No one said anything about the plain-clothesmen who operated out of an office on the third floor, but no one needed to. All the CID detectives knew who they were and what they were doing.

However, one big obstacle Smailes faced if he wanted to dig around in the old records was George Dearnley. Dearnley would have to sign off on any request to visit the archive, and he was unlikely to react favorably if Smailes told him he was following up leads from the Bowles case. The case was thankfully closed as far as George was concerned, and he was certain to get irritated if he thought Smailes was still spending time on it. Neither could Smailes legitimately claim that twenty- or thirty-year-old records had any relevance to an investigation of a Sikh lorry hijacking. Any scenario he could think of had the same outcome—George would refuse to sign the authorization. Smailes chewed on the question for a couple of days and then made his decision. The afternoon before his next day off he strolled into Gloria's office when he knew George was away at one of his regular meetings at headquarters. He asked her casually for a Criminal Records Division Authorization Form, which she produced from the bottom drawer of one of the filing cabinets in the bank behind her.

"The chief super's out for the rest of the day, Derek," she told him suspiciously.

"Oh, that's right," said Smailes absently. "Well, I haven't decided yet whether it's worth the trip or not. It's not an urgent thing. Don't tell him I took the form, okay, Gloria? I may just decide to return it and drop the idea."

Gloria looked at him impassively and he knew she was unconvinced. But he knew he could count on her silence for a couple of days at least, by which time he would have decided which way to act. Gloria had always enjoyed her conspiratorial relationship with Derek Smailes and he occasionally felt guilty about exploiting her. But as far as he knew, he had never got her into trouble with George, and she probably trusted that he never would. Smailes had resolved upon an unauthorized visit to the Records Division. If he found nothing, he would contrive a way of removing a blank form from Gloria's files and returning it to her later, telling her with a shrug that he had decided to cancel the trip. If he did find something, then he would go toe to toe with George on the importance of pursuing a lead from the Bowles case. He would have to claim an anonymous tip, or even play the stolen-file card. He might have to threaten to go to HQ with the request if Dearnley stonewalled him, but it might be worth it. He was also aware of potentially perilous consequences.

The next day Smailes pulled into the ugly complex of squat government buildings that sat anonymously on the eastern edge of town. He had not visited the archive before but thought he knew where it was housed, in one of the buildings toward the rear of the compound. He eventually found a

254

small sign announcing the Division of Governmental Records, parked, and looked at his watch. It was a little after eleven.

The archivist was a bored little man with wiry blond hair and long sideburns who sat in an office immediately inside the heavy metal door. The building seemed relatively small and Smailes was puzzled about where the miles of records were physically stored. The man was seated at a standard metal government desk on which sat a large pile of manila files and a fat, contented-looking marmalade cat. The archivist turned in his chair as Smailes leaned inside the door, his face as expressive as the cat's. He was wearing a purple sleeveless sweater and a yellow paisley tie. He wore his glasses pushed onto the crown of his head and was reading a newspaper.

"Hello, guv," said Smailes. "I need to poke around in some of the old criminal records. Can you point me in the right direction?"

The man made an expansive gesture at his newspaper and lowered his glasses onto his nose. "We're going to blow the bastards back into the sea, aren't we, Clive?" he said, apparently to the cat.

"I'm sorry?"

"The Argies. Leave it to the Marines. They'll mow 'em down by the ton. Teach 'em to fool with us."

"Oh yeah," said Smailes. "Looks like there's going to be a dust-up. Unless Haig pulls off something."

"Bleedin' wanker," said the archivist. "He should stay out of it. Name's Prideaux. Albert Prideaux. You got authorization, then, identification?"

Smailes produced his CID card and introduced himself to Albert Prideaux. Then he took out a manila file folder from his portfolio and showed the authorization form, with George's neatly forged signature. Underneath were selections from the Bowles file, with a series of names marked with a highlighter.

255

"What years you want? What type offenses?"

"Let's say '31 through '35, political-type offenses. Disturbing the peace, riotous assembly, maybe criminal damage."

"Constabulary or Special Branch?"

"Both."

"You got a lot of work, mister. You know how this system works?"

"No."

"You got files by name and year, with cross-references on the case number and known associates. What you got, a lot of names?"

"A few."

"Well, I suggest you start year by year, you might have different files in different years. Understand?"

"Sure."

Albert Prideaux frowned at this reply. "Take a look," he said, and with a forceful backhand swept the cat off the desk. He produced from his desk drawer a three-page map, which he spread on the desk in front of him, reversed so Smailes could read it. "We got approximately thirteen miles of files, see, on three levels."

"Underground?"

"Yeah, the vaults stretch all the way under the whole site. Not just police records, see, you got city and county government too. Course, it's all on microfilm nowadays, but not as far back as you wanna go. Look, you want Vault Three, East Four. That's criminal records between '29 and '40, Constabulary. Special Branch is a bit smaller, see, all of 'em through '60 are in East Six."

He was pointing to the map of the lowest basement level, which showed a network of corridors and storage rooms. The directions seemed clear enough.

"How long are you goin' to be?" asked Prideaux.

"A few hours, I suppose. Can I keep this?" he asked, holding up the map.

256

"Of course, but hold on. You not goin' anywhere without a key." Prideaux struggled with the bottom drawer of his desk and produced a huge key ring with an immense number of keys on it. Each was marked with a worn plastic tag. Prideaux furrowed his brow and began pawing through them. After some minutes he gave up and tossed the bunch down on his desk with a crash. The cat, which had begun rubbing against Smailes's legs, flinched at the noise.

"Really must sort these out someday," he said to himself. He fished in his trouser pocket and produced a much smaller ring, with five or six keys on it. He slowly extracted one.

"This is unofficial, see, because it's the master, understand? I'm not supposed to give this out, but if you can't trust a policeman, what's the country coming to? Just make sure you don't drop it and you give it back here to me personal. Understand? I'm here till five."

"No problem, Mr. Prideaux, just show me the way."

There was an eerie silence in the sub-sub-basement of the Cambridge government archive. Corridors stretched in four directions. Smailes aligned himself with the map and headed east. He found a door marked "East Four" and let himself in. He flicked on a light switch and looked in awe at the rows and rows of metal shelves, floor to ceiling, and the endless expanse of files. The smell of acidified paper was almost choking. Maybe this wasn't such a good idea after all, he said to himself.

His first hour and a half was completely fruitless. None of the names Bowles had marked down for further inquiry had any history of arrest or criminal records of any kind. He decided to try a different tack, heading out of the Constabulary file room for the Special Branch files. He referred to the date in Bowles's notes of a college servant strike in 1933 that he knew the Trinity communist cell had orchestrated. After a little searching he found the file of Guy Burgess, as good a place as any to start. He read with some amusement a description of the subversive behavior of the improbable Burgess, and his association with known communists in Cambridge and London. And he actually ended up in the bloody Foreign Office, Smailes said to himself. There was then a description of a violent confrontation between a picket line of students and servants and University faculty, and an account of the arrests that ensued. Smailes read Burgess's subsequent statement to the police, which was a shocking and insolent document. But the real surprise for Smailes came in the listing of Burgess's known associates, where he found the name of a young college waiter, Paul Beecroft. There was a criminal record number and a bald designation: "Known member of the Communist Party." Smailes stared at the page in silence, his thoughts racing.

Higher up in the same bank of files Smailes quickly found the case file for Paul Beecroft. He had been arrested during the picket-line incident for assaulting a police officer and eventually fined five pounds. There were statements and court documents, and a closing note indicating that, by agreement with the Trinity authorities, no college servants had lost their jobs as a result of the incident. It seemed Beecroft had no further record of arrests. He had a list of known associates that included many of the more famous student communists of their day. The last entry in his file indicated that he left his employment with Trinity College in 1936.

Paul Beecroft a communist? Smailes's mind surged at the implications. Was he still a party member? Had he known of Simon Bowles's research? Did he know something about Simon Bowles's death that he had not divulged? And what about Hawken? Did he know about his head porter's past? And what was his role in the present? It was clear Smailes would have to pay another visit to St. Margaret's, whether George Dearnley had closed the file or not.

Smailes snapped off the light as he left the room and oriented himself using the map. He made his way to the staircase and began putting the map away, when something caught his eye. In the first basement level were file rooms marked "Personnel—City," "Personnel—County" and "Personnel—Police and Fire." That would mean that his father's personnel file was probably stuck away somewhere in there. He felt a sudden urge to find it—he wondered if Harry Smailes's evaluations were always as brilliant as he implied, or whether his superiors ever had the kind of reservations about him that Smailes knew they had about his son. He found the corridor quickly and guiltily let himself in. It took some half an hour of searching before he found the right year and alphabetical listing, but then there it was, nestling before Smethwick and after Slater. He pulled out the file and opened it greedily.

The first puzzling discovery was a cover sheet signed off by the chief constable of Cambridgeshire—a recommendation by the chief superintendent of his father's day that survivor benefits be approved. Why should there be any question about his mother's entitlement to his father's police pension? The next document gave the explanation and hit Smailes like an iron bar in the chest. It was a report by then Detective Inspector George Dearnley detailing all the evidence he had compiled against Sergeant Harold Smailes of corruption, extortion and bribe-taking. It was pages long. It listed police station vendors, pub owners, businessmen and minor criminals as associates. It alleged that Harry Smailes had been on the take for a good ten years. And it stated that had his sudden death not intervened, Harry Smailes would have been thrown out of the force, prosecuted as a bent cop, and likely served a prison term. Smailes felt his face go crimson, the blood in his ears singing.

Suddenly the events of so long ago made sense to him. The unexplained absence from work, the moping around the house, the strange visits from his Uncle George. What had his mother known? Why had he never been told anything? And what had his father's contemporaries on the force, those men who still called him "Harry's boy," known of this investigation? Another shocking thought struck him. Had his father

259

really died of a heart attack, or had he taken some drastic action to avoid the scandal and humiliation? And George Dearnley, cultivating Derek Smailes's police career all these years when he knew his father was a fraud, a crook, a phony? He read Dearnley's report through twice. It was a pathetic catalogue—kickbacks from the companies that supplied the station vending machines while the elder Smailes was station officer, payments from pub owners on his beat to let them serve after hours while Harry Smailes was still a PC, suspicion of bribes to suppress evidence in a couple of criminal cases, unauthorized gifts of goods and services. But Dearnley had been unable to get Harry Smailes to make a statement, to sign a confession. He had been suspended without pay while the investigation had proceeded, and then had suddenly died. It was Dearnley himself who had first brought up the issue of survivor benefits, knowing that if Harry Smailes had been convicted, all his pension rights would have been void and Smailes's mother would have been practically destitute. His initial reaction of shock had turned to cold anger. He needed to see George Dearnley. He needed to see him right away.

He was barely able to be polite to Prideaux as he returned the key and thanked him for his help. He ignored the question of whether he had found anything of use, just as he ignored the ten-miles-per-hour speed limit in the government complex as he roared around to the exit. Within fifteen minutes he was standing in Gloria's office, his face still burning. He asked if George was available.

"He's on the phone, I think. You look a little strange, Derek. Are you going to ask him to sign the authorization?" she asked anxiously.

"Yeah, something like that," said Smailes. "I'll just go in and wait," he said, waving her aside. He stepped into George Dearnley's office and walked toward the desk at the end of the room, where George was seated with his feet up, growling something into the phone. He saw Derek Smailes and frowned, and then looked away. Smailes stood patiently.

To express his annoyance Dearnley spent a long time wrapping up his phone call, looking away from Smailes at the wall that held his tennis calendar. He hung up the receiver slowly and lowered his feet. Then he leaned forward heavily onto his elbows and said, "Derek, didn't expect to see you today. Tuesday's your day off, isn't it? Did Gloria tell you to come in?"

"No, she didn't, George. I'm sorry to barge in. But I just found out something that I wish I had known about a long time ago. Maybe you can guess what I mean."

Dearnley gave a weary shrug and shook his head. "Sit down, Derek. You look agitated."

"About my father. About why he was off work that week before he died. Was it really a heart attack, George, or did he do himself in? He bloody well should have, if he didn't." Smailes stayed on his feet.

Dearnley's face remained expressionless. "Who told you about this?"

"How many people could have, George? How many people knew? How many people still know, people I've worked with for ten years, who know I'm the son of a bent cop? Am I the only one who didn't bleeding well know?"

"Watch your tone with me, Smailes," Dearnley warned. "How did you find out?"

"I found his personnel file in the Records Division. I suppose I owe you thanks, helping get my mother the pension and all that. Thanks a lot, George." Smailes had never spoken to George Dearnley like this and felt a strange exhilaration. Maybe he was going to get fired, he reflected. He didn't care.

"I didn't sign any authorization for a Records visit, did I? How did you get in? What were you doing there anyway?"

"I took a form from Gloria and forged your signature, George. She didn't know what I was up to. I wanted to follow up on some leads from the Bowles case. Criminal records from the thirties. I'm not sure we got the story straight there, and I knew you'd probably turn me down if I asked. I shouldn't have done it, I know. Then I went to check personnel records, and found my father's file, your report, everything. I came straight over."

George Dearnley got slowly to his feet. "Sit down," he said quietly. Smailes did not move. "Sit down when I fucking well tell you," Dearnley roared, and Smailes obeyed. Dearnley came over to him and put one foot on the chair, lowering his face until it was about six inches from Smailes's nose.

"How dare you, you arrogant piece of shit," he said under his breath. "After all I've done for you, year in, year out. You know what people say about you, don't you? That you're too fucking arrogant to follow procedures, that you think you're better than everyone else, that you talk with a stupid fucking American accent and that you're a lousy cop. Well, I'm sick of defending you, Sergeant Smailes, because maybe people are right. That case is closed, like I told you. You're suspended, as of right now. I want a full report on your visit to Records, and I want it within one hour. Then it's time to think about whether there's a place for you on this force, sonny."

Smailes said nothing. He licked his lips and swallowed slowly.

"For your information, hardly anyone knew about the investigation into your father. Not even your mother, although she might have guessed. Maybe a few senior people here guessed too, although I for one have never breathed a word. As far as I knew, it was just between the chief super and me. Frankly, Detective Sergeant Smailes, I never cared too much for your father, and neither did many others here in this station. Too officious by half. Behaved like he had a board up his arse. Then we find this out about him, and his whole act fell apart. But when he died like that, I saw no reason to put his family through all the shame and disgrace that would have gone with going public with it. The only thing he would own up to was the vending-machine caper. Said he'd got into trouble at the dogs, needed cash. But the more we looked, the more we found. It had been going on for years. Technically, we had no conviction, not even a statement, so your mother was entitled to the pension, I thought. And your family was entitled to protection too. So you found out. Too bad."

"How did you rumble him, after all that time?" asked Smailes.

"Got greedy, like they all do. Let some new guy bid up the payoff, and the first one blew the whistle. Stupid mistake, considering." Dearnley stood up and walked away, then turned and looked at him coldly. "Yes, I'd thought of telling you, somehow. It *was* a heart attack that killed him, and in a way, I thought it was a blessing, at the time. And I wondered that something, someday, wouldn't come out. But if it didn't, if I hadn't told you, it was not because of lack of respect for you, Derek Smailes. I always had that up until now. I've looked the other way at you bending rules before. Not any-more. I suggest you get yourself some legal advice. Get me that report, understand?" Dearnley stood silently for a long moment, and Smailes sat still, respectfully. "Get out," he said quietly.

It only took him twenty minutes to write his report of his activities that day. His strange sense of exhilaration did not go away. Gloria looked frightened and bewildered when he handed her the typescript, and avoided his eyes, but Smailes gave her a big smile.

"I'm taking a bit of a break, I guess you heard, Gloria. See you around," he said. She looked at him nervously. "I told him I tricked you. It's okay, Gloria, don't worry about it."

"Derek, I'm really sorry," she said.

"Don't be. I don't seem to be," he said.

As he drove home, Smailes felt strangely buoyant. At one point, he let out a loud guffaw. That old fucking fraud, Harry Smailes. All these years, he had been trying to emulate a petty crook. He felt as if an enormous burden had been lifted from him. So he had been suspended. Like father, like son, he thought, and snorted again. For the first time in his life, he realized he didn't have to be a cop. Maybe he was going to have no choice in the matter. What was the procedure with a suspension? A disciplinary review board, wasn't it? Maybe he should just quit now, save them the trouble.

As he tried to pull into his usual parking spot in front of his flat, he was annoyed to find a Post Office Telecommunications van parked there. They had one of those little canvas huts erected over an open manhole, and he had to drive a little way down the street to park. He sat in the car for about five minutes, thinking. Then he drove off again, heading for St. Margaret's.

264

Seventeen

IT WAS ALMOST SIX when Smailes pulled up outside St. Margaret's College and he wondered whether he would still find Paul Beecroft on duty. He knew that continuing to conduct investigations while under suspension would only worsen his predicament if he was found out, and he hoped Dearnley would make no moves like warning people at the college against talking to him. He had to concede that was unlikely. George, despite his anger, could probably not conceive that Smailes would compound the insubordination charge against him, and obviously believed strongly in the futility of further inquiries in the Bowles case. Smailes was probably on safe ground, he thought to himself, although the metaphor sounded wrong.

He was prepared for a difficult interview with Paul Beecroft, but he was not prepared for what greeted him when he entered St. Margaret's porters' lodge. Standing at the

265

counter, working intently on a clipboard checklist, was Alan Fenwick, dressed in his porter's uniform. Fenwick looked up as the door swung shut on its heavy closer, and flushed scarlet when he saw the figure of Smailes enter. He put down his pen and cleared his throat.

"Can I help you, Officer?" he asked a little hoarsely. Smailes looked at him silently for a moment, and then said casually, "Is Mr. Beecroft available? I'd like a word, if possible."

Fenwick didn't need to reply. From his office behind Fenwick, Beecroft emerged at that moment, wearing his overcoat. He too seemed taken aback to see Smailes standing there, and stood motionless, watching him. Another junior porter, who was seated talking on the telephone, finished his conversation and said something to Beecroft, who did not reply. The young man became aware of the tension in the room and looked over at Smailes also. Fenwick broke the silence. "The officer here asked to speak with you, Mr. B.," he said. "I was just going to tell him I thought you was leaving for the day."

Beecroft stood to the side and indicated his office to Smailes. "Step right in, Mr. Smailes," he said, and followed Smailes back into the room, closing the door behind him. He did not take off his coat.

"What the hell is *he* doing here?" Smailes began in an angry undertone. He did not want Fenwick to hear any of this exchange. Beecroft chose his words carefully.

"His suspension was lifted and the college council recommended him reinstated with a reprimand only. Last week," he said.

"Isn't that a little unusual? Didn't you think fit to tell me, Mr. Beecroft? The main reason we didn't press charges against him over the Bowles business was because we were assured he would be fired. You told me so yourself."

"Well, I was a little surprised. But I didn't see how it was any of your business anymore. The inquest finished that

266

whole affair, didn't it? How is it your business how St. Margaret's chooses to discipline its porters, tell me? That's purely an internal matter," Beecroft said testily.

Smailes decided to change the angle of his questions. "You still a member of the Communist Party, Mr. Beecroft? Had any further brushes with the law since that assault conviction in '33? Or is that none of my business either?"

Beecroft looked as if he were about to speak, but changed his mind and turned to look out of the glass panel in his door at the two porters working in the lodge. It seemed a long time before he turned around to face the detective.

"No, I'm not, Mr. Smailes," he said wearily. "I turned in my card in '37, when I got back from Spain. I'd seen enough there."

"Did Simon Bowles know you had been a party member?"

"I doubt it. I doubt it very much. Of course, I knew what he was looking into. Could've told him a few things too, if he'd asked me."

"Like what, for instance?"

Beecroft looked at him steadily. "Can I trust you, Mr. Smailes? Trust you not to do anything without my say-so?"

Beecroft had obviously decided to talk, but then he had to. Smailes had him cornered on two counts. But it was clear that Beecroft had revealed little voluntarily and Smailes would weigh his explanations with caution. Trust was a two-way street.

"I don't know. You trusted me over the Fenwick business before. Why don't you just tell me what you know?"

"It's hard to explain, even to myself. And to someone of your age . . . You can't know what it was like here in the thirties, what the mood was. Then what so many of us had to go through when it became clear where Russia was heading." Smailes said nothing.

"A lot of us joined the party back then. I mean, college servants who gave more than a second thought to what was happening in the world, to what was happening right here at the University. And there was a lot of recruitment going on, by some of the students and dons, and by people up from London. But joining the party in them days was not like today, something you would have to be secretive about. Joining the party was something you did openly, out of principle. It looked like Russia was the only hope for the future in them days, I can tell you. As for the Labour Party, democracy, Parliament, well, it was a bloody shambles." There was an edge of bitterness in Beecroft's voice.

"Of course, some of them I couldn't stomach. Toffee-nosed socialists, we called them. The kind of communist who'd cringe if you ate with the wrong fork. But there was a lot of decent lads here too who had a genuine wish to improve things, not just for us. A lot of us went to Spain. And a lot didn't come back neither. I was lucky.

"Some of us was already having second thoughts about Stalin, through the show trials and that, but it was Spain what opened my eyes. The communists were just not interested in the working people creating something for themselves. You see, I got laid up with dysentery when I first got there and couldn't get to the Madrid front. I had to stay in Barcelona and signed up with one of the workers' militias when I felt right. So I was right there when the street fighting began, when the word came down from Uncle Joe to smash the independent militias, accuse 'em of collaboration, being Trotskyite, whatever. I was wounded in the leg and lucky to get out into France in one piece. That was the only fightin' I did in Spain, and it was against my own side, the bloody Republicans. And of course, everyone at home, the left, just whistled whatever tune Joe said. It seemed to me that if the communists were as interested in stopping a revolution as they were in stopping Franco, they were just fascists of a different stripe. I'd been proud to be a party member up till then, but when I got back from Spain I was just sickened. I'd given back my card by the time of the Nonaggression Pact, but that really was the last straw. So I joined the Labour Party—not

268

that I didn't think there was plenty wrong with it. But by the time I enlisted in '39 I knew that if we was to save Britain from Hitler, then I'd just as soon keep the institutions we had. I thought it was worth fighting for. I was with the infantry in North Africa and Italy. I'd made sergeant by the time I was discharged.

"And then I came back here, got married, and started working at the University again, and never really had much to do with politics anymore. No, I never got arrested again, if you'd like to know. How the hell did you know about that anyway?"

"Criminal records. We keep archives, you know."

"Only one person round here knows I was a communist, and I'd like to keep it at that, if that's all right."

"And who's that?"

"I'm coming to it. I'm coming to it. Well, I was in the lodge here at St. Margaret's when Hawken was appointed senior tutor. I thought there was something fishy about that from the start. It's usually someone from inside you know, and when they said he's from the Foreign Office, well, it got me thinking. It was only a bit after all the stuff about Philby going over, and it seemed too much a coincidence."

"Did you know him?"

"Philby? No, but I knew Burgess all right. Everyone knew that bleedin' creature. He was one of the ones I couldn't stand.

"Well, then there's the rumor that Hawken is talking to people—dons, you know—who'd been in the party before the war, and I put two and two together. That's when I went to him and started workin' for him."

"You work for Hawken?"

"Don't get me wrong. I've never liked the bloke. Never liked him at all. But I thought what he was doing was necessary. I told him about those I'd known back when I was a young man, those who came to party meetings, who was still around. I don't feel bad about it, even now. I just wish I'd

269

known more, could remember more. Of course, some was too high and mighty to come to meetings, and I just didn't know them. That old queen Blunt, for one. I was as surprised as anybody about him.

"Then we—that is, me and Hawken—sort of had an informal agreement that I would keep an eye on the students, as much as I could. I'm in a good position to intercept the post, you know, and I get to hear a lot of gossip, about this college anyway. I'm not proud of it, but I'm not sorry either. Plenty of young people make the same mistakes I made, and that's their privilege. I just felt we should know about 'em, make sure they did no harm."

"What's all this got to do with Fenwick?"

"Well, that's the difficult part. You see, almost since he was hired on, I've had complaints about Fenwick, mostly from the other blokes on the late shift. Seems that he was always disappearing and gave as his excuse that he was doin' errands for Dr. Hawken, you know, odd jobs, buying things in the town. Well, it was irregular, but if he was busy for Hawken, well, there was not much I could do about it, was there? But I thought there might be something, well, unusual in that arrangement. See, he wasn't my first choice for that position, call it prejudice if you like, but like I told you, Hawken has the last word on new hires, and he said we should take him on. Seemed peculiar at the time—not that I said nothing. But I wondered about his persuasion, if you like. That's why I knew it might be sticky if it turned out Fenwick was associating with young Bowles. I didn't want to believe it when Givens told me about it. That's 'im out there in the lodge now. He was one always complaining to me about Fenwick, and I thought it might be, well, just malicious gossip. But when you told me that Fenwick had admitted to it, well, I had no choice but to report the whole thing to him, to Hawken, and he tells me to suspend him right away. Like you would expect. But then after the last meeting of the council, just this last Thursday, he tells me that Fenwick's been reinstated with just a reprimand, and I couldn't believe it. You see, the reports of the meetings aren't published, but I don't believe it ever came up. I don't think they ever discussed it, and then Hawken is able just to give him his job back, like that. And he was counting on me to say nothing. Not just because he has things on me, like, but because he knows I'm up for retirement this summer and I'm not likely to rock the boat by calling you or anything like that. And he was right, I didn't, although, believe me, I thought about it. Something's not right here. Not right at all."

Smailes had sat on the corner of Beecroft's desk during this revelation. He was having trouble adding it all up.

"Mr. Beecroft, do you know something about Simon Bowles's death that you haven't told me?" he asked carefully.

"No, I swear. The first I knew about it was when Bunty Allen ran in here that day. Of course, I knew what young Mr. Bowles was lookin' into. Hawken had told me himself, after he'd tried to interview him. Asked me to keep my eyes and ears open about him. I did, as much as I could, but I didn't know anything about him, well, knowing Fenwick until one of the other porters told me about it, like I told you."

"But you think Fenwick's kept his job because he can blackmail Hawken, right?"

"Well, you said that, Officer, not me. But it's a very peculiar decision, that's all I can say. There's been some raised eyebrows in the lodge about it, and the men are all talking about it, I know. No one's come out and asked me about it plain, but if they do, I don't know what I'll say. I'm in a very sticky position, you see. I don't want people in this college to know I've been informing on students for nearly twenty years, and I don't want to do anything to upset my pension. I've earned that, you know. That's why I want you to go cautious with what I've told you. You understand?"

"Yes, I understand. But let me ask you straight. Do you think Hawken or Fenwick had some involvement with how Simon Bowles met his death?"

271

"That I can't say, Mr. Smailes. I don't know what he had found out, you see, about the two of them, so I'm just guessing. But I don't know if the inquest got the full story, you know. That I don't know."

"Mr. Beecroft, who had a pass key to Simon Bowles's room?"

"Why?"

Derek Smailes recounted to him his suspicion that someone had removed a file from Bowles's cabinet in the twenty-four hours after his first examination of it, during the time the room was locked and Bowles's keys were at the police station. Beecroft's expression clouded.

"All members of the college council. One stays in the lodge, authorized sign-out only. The duty porter, which is unofficial like. One on my ring. That's it."

"How about the duty tutor?"

"No, he has to use the one in the lodge."

"No one else?"

"No one else. Key can't be duplicated without college say-so either. Stamped right on there."

Smailes turned again to look out into the lodge, pondering this new information. Fenwick was no longer around, and the other porter was talking to two students who were writing their names in a fat ledger. "So what are you going to do?" Beecroft asked nervously.

"I don't know," said Smailes. "I'm going to think about what you've told me. But if I go anywhere with this, I'll do so in a way that protects you as the source of information, okay? Because I believe what you've told me. But whatever I do, I can't guarantee I'll tell you in advance, do you understand that? I can't operate that way." The truth was, he was not sure Beecroft was telling him the whole truth. He was not sure at all.

"Please, Officer. I've got more than thirty-five years' service with this place."

"I know that, Mr. Beecroft. You've been able to trust me so

272

far, haven't you?" Beecroft looked uneasy, but could see he was not going to get further guarantees from Smailes.

"I'm not asking you to understand what I've done. I don't know if anyone can understand unless they had put their faith and their life on the line for the party like I did. It's got to do with betrayal. It makes you angry somewhere, very deep down, and you need some kind of revenge, even if it goes against your grain. I never enjoyed being an informer, but I've never taken a penny or gotten any considerations for it. I just feel that putting my trust in the party was the biggest mistake of my life, and even if it's the likes of Hawken that is working to stop it doing any more damage, then that's no matter. The Communist Party is about consolidating its own power, pure and simple, and it has no respect for anything or anyone that gets in its way. I would do the same thing all over again, believe me.

"So in a way I wasn't put out of joint by what Bowles was up to, like Hawken was. More power to him, I thought, because he was a very bright bloke and maybe he would turn something over that'd been missed all these years. And if he'd found out about my past, well, I think I would have told him everything I knew, frankly, because he was a careful and trustworthy individual, I felt."

"But he never did?" asked Smailes.

"Not to my knowledge, and I wasn't about to volunteer."

"What do you mean when you say the inquest didn't get the full story? You mean about Fenwick finding the body?"

"No, I mean about why he did it, why he killed himself."

"You have a theory?"

"Yes, I think maybe he found out that Fenwick was Hawken's lackey, and that had something to do with it. I'm only guessing, mind, but that's what I've been thinking. As for someone from here going into his files after your fellas had been round, well, I'd be very surprised about that. Very surprised indeed." He paused, then frowned at Smailes and

273

said, "Well, I'm going to be off, then, unless there's anything else."

"No, what you've told me is plenty," said Smailes. He reflected that Beecroft was an astute man, and considered talking to Fenwick yet again, probing his version of that night's events and the circumstances of his reinstatement. Then he thought again of the precariousness of his own position, what would happen if Beecroft or Hawken were to call Dearnley. He decided to do nothing at present and not tempt his fate.

Smailes called Lauren as soon as he got home and they agreed to meet for a drink. She sounded pleased to hear from him, but he felt uneasy about how much he should let her know of the day's developments. Either she did not know who Fenwick was or she did not know that he had been reinstated, otherwise she would have let him know already and would have been down on him like a ton of bricks. He guessed that since Fenwick worked the late shift and since Lauren lived out of college and checked her post in the morning, she had not yet run across him. When she did he knew it would be difficult to contain her. She would jump to the same conclusion he had, that Fenwick's reinstatement was somehow linked to Bowles's death, and she would want to make a stink. That could get him in further trouble at the station. Smailes started to feel that his situation there was looking hopeless.

He checked suspension procedures in his CID handbook. In a paid disciplinary suspension, which was what he assumed he was on, he was entitled to a hearing within thirty days before a disciplinary panel. He was also entitled to free legal representation through the union, if he wanted it. He didn't know if he did. He could not invent much of a mitigating case for his deception in getting into the archive, and if George Dearnley was not going to stand up for him, he doubted anyone else would. If it came out that he was sexually involved with someone connected with the Bowles case, and had divulged confidential information about it to her, then forget it. He was history. He was surprised he did not feel more anxious at the prospect of getting fired from the force. He made himself think of what he would do. His brother-in-law Neil had been at him for years to join his real estate agency, where he said there was good money to be made. Smailes couldn't quite see himself as a salesman, trying to sound enthusiastic about the new semi-detached estates in Histon. Then, of course, there was always the living death of the corporate security world, playing rent-a-cop. He didn't like the thought of that either. Maybe he should call the union, see about a solicitor.

What troubled him more was where to take the information that Beecroft had given him that afternoon. Assuming it was true, then there was definitely some kind of complicity between Hawken and Fenwick that was unethical, if not illegal. But what if Beecroft was simply aiming a knife at Hawken and wanting Smailes to throw it? He could understand the level of resentment Beecroft might feel if it was true that he had been one of Hawken's informants for twenty years. What if the issue had been presented at the college council and the dons had genuinely decided to let Fenwick off with a reprimand? Smailes would look a complete fool if he tried to cry foul over a decision that was completely legitimate, if peculiar. And who would he tell? George? Tell George that right after he had slapped him on suspension he had gone back to St. Margaret's to pursue the very same case for which he had been suspended? Or should he pick up the phone and dial MI5 and try to tell the director-general that one of his senior men was being blackmailed by a homosexual college porter? What exactly was the relationship between Hawken and Alan Fenwick, and had Simon Bowles known anything about it? This was what troubled Smailes the most, his ever-growing suspicion that there was some kind of foul play involved in the death of Simon Bowles, and that somehow Hawken and Fenwick were tied into it.

275

He was still chewing over these issues when Lauren arrived at the pub and came over to join him. He got up and brought her a whiskey, and she leaned over and kissed him behind the ear.

"You seem in a good mood tonight," he told her.

"Why, aren't you?" she asked him.

"Surprisingly good, considering I just got suspended."

Lauren expressed her horror in her predictably dramatic way and pressed him so hard for his story that Smailes had trouble getting out even his edited version. He told her he had followed up on a long-standing curiosity to inspect his father's personnel records in the government archive, but had had to forge the authorization to get in. He told her all about what the file had revealed, and how in his anger he had been unable to sit on the information, but had gone back to the station to confront the examining officer, who was now his direct boss. And that had earned him his suspension.

"So what's gonna happen, Derek? Are you gonna get thrown out?" she demanded to know. Smailes conceded it was a strong possibility if he could not think of a better defense than he had so far, and if George Dearnley stayed as angry with him as he was. This news seemed to make Lauren pensive, and they got into a discussion about Smailes's feelings in the light of the new information about his father. He said he could not decide whether to tell his mother or sister what he had learned, but that he would probably talk to his mother someday. He wanted to know if she had guessed but had stayed silent to protect him, or to protect the reputation of his father. But if she had not guessed, then the information would be painful for her. He described his curious feelings of anger and elation, about how he now felt released from his lifelong need to meet his father's expectations, which were now revealed as a complete sham. He told her he felt the whole basis of his commitment to police service had been undermined.

276

"Aw, come on, Plod. You're a cop through to your bones, what the hell else are you gonna do? Eat shit, tell them you really regret what you did, all that crap. Don't lose your job over something as stupid as this. I sort of felt the same when my dad died, that my motivation had dried up because he wasn't around to pat me on the head anymore. That's bullshit. You do what you have to, inside."

Smailes wanted to tell her the real reason he had put his job in jeopardy, but he couldn't. Instead he asked her if she had any photographs of Simon Bowles.

"Simon? No, I don't think so. Why on earth do you want a picture of Simon?"

"Well, it seems that I'm going to have some time on my hands, and I've often thought it would be interesting to try to find out what he did in London the day before he died. You know, take his picture around Somerset House, see if anyone remembers him."

"So you are still looking into the whole thing, huh? You never told me. What else haven't you told me? What else have you found out?"

"Nothing, Lauren, I swear," he said, and he knew then that when she found out about Alan Fenwick she was going to be very, very angry. He would deal with that when it came, because he had a strong intuition that if he was going to save his job, he needed to present some kind of new evidence in the Bowles case to justify his actions. And if he was to find new evidence he needed secrecy, which meant he had to keep Lauren out of the picture. But he felt awkward at the baldness of his deception, and thought she sensed it.

"Giles might," she said. "You know, have a picture of Simon. I don't even have a camera. And I still don't understand why you're doing what you're doing. You're not leveling with me," she accused.

Smailes met her gaze and then said quietly, "Let's just say it's something I have to do, inside."

277

There was a palpable coldness between them, and he could sense Lauren's anger with him.

"Look, Lauren, I've had quite a day, and I've got a lot on my mind. Maybe tonight we shouldn't . . ."

"Yes, let's forget it," she interrupted. "I was going to suggest the same myself." She drained her glass and began to gather her coat. Smailes looked down at his glass and felt uncomfortable. But as she was leaving she stopped and held him by the arm.

"Derek, it's okay. I'm real sorry about what you found out, and I'm real sorry that you're in trouble at work." She leaned toward him and kissed him firmly on the mouth. "Call me soon, okay? I want to know what develops."

"You bet," said Smailes.

"Okay, cowboy," she said, and was gone.

It was before ten when Smailes got home and he had one more call to make that night. He realized that unless he discovered what the college council had decided in the Fenwick matter, he could not take his suspicions any further. He looked up a number in the Cambridge directory and called Sir Martin Gorham-Leach.

G-L was his normal, affable self and did not even seem surprised that Smailes wanted to speak with him again, or curious about why. He said he would be at his lab all the next day but was planning to take dinner in college and would be in his rooms around six-thirty.

"You know where they are, Axton Court, B staircase?" he asked mildly.

"I can find it."

"Fine, I'll expect you," said Gorham-Leach. "We can have a glass of sherry."

Smailes hung up and reflected that he was stepping further into uncharted, unauthorized territory. But if his commitment to his career felt shaky, his commitment to following through with the Bowles investigation was not. He thought of calling Iain Mack, telling him about his extraordinary day, but decided against it. This was his last hand, and there would be plenty of time to recount his story after he had played his cards.

Eighteen

THE AFTERNOON POST the next day brought a registered letter from George Dearnley, informing Smailes officially of his paid suspension and the reasons for it. Smailes was reminded of the procedures and his right to representation at a disciplinary hearing. The letter was copied to the commander at headquarters who was in charge of internal affairs. The tone was cold and precise and Smailes felt sharply crestfallen when he read it. He knew how wounded and angry George must feel, and could not really blame him. Any defense sounded conceited and contemptuous, just as George had accused him of being. He dialed the union representative at the station, but hung up when the line was answered. He could not decide whether to just call it quits or to accept Lauren's strategy and throw himself on the mercy of his senior officers. It was the first time he had been in trouble after all. Officially anyway.

He spent the afternoon puttering about the flat in an agitated and uncharacteristic way. He cleaned his oven for the first time ever, and it made him shudder at the prospect of unemployment. He could just hear Yvonne, her outrage if he told her he was going to miss some child-support payments. His mother would be crushed too when she found out. He was glad when the light began to fail and it was time to meet with Gorham-Leach.

He walked briskly past St. Margaret's lodge with only a quick glance inside, and saw neither Beecroft nor Fenwick. Christ, if he met Lauren, he thought, what would he tell her? That he was going to see Allerton, to track down a photograph of Bowles, he decided quickly. He lived in Axton Court like G-L after all. He stopped at the foot of B staircase in the small dark courtyard and examined the elegant copperplate nameboard, the names white against the black background. He saw that in fact Allerton and Gorham-Leach shared the same staircase, and that G. Allerton was in B1 whereas M. P. Gorham-Leach was in B8, presumably the top floor. He found the lack of distinction in their listings quaint, an academic pretense of equality. He remembered again the story of Davies and the disputed nameboard, the origin of the bad blood between Hawken and the Welsh archaeologist. What had been the original name again, Forse-Davies? The name rang a bell with him, but the memory darted away like a minnow behind a rock and stayed hidden. He mounted two flights of stairs, made a right turn and knocked on the door of B8. Gorham-Leach opened it to him, beaming, and ushered him in.

The room was in considerably better array than G-L's study at his home, with merely a large number of books which seemed to fit adequately into the shelf space provided. There was a small red leather sofa facing the customary gas fire, and a matching wing chair that stood in a pool of light from a standing lamp. At the far end of the room was a desk cluttered with papers in another pool of light from a desk

281

lamp, opposite an open doorway that doubtless led to the bedroom. The atmosphere of the room was cordial and inviting, like Gorham-Leach himself. He solicitously helped Smailes remove his raincoat and poured two glasses of sherry from a bottle that he removed from a mahogany sideboard that stood to the left of the hearth. He waved at Smailes to sit down on the sofa and handed him the small fluted glass. Then he took up his position perched on the edge of the wing chair. He was wearing a neat light green tweed suit and a fawn cardigan. He held his head to one side in his odd, birdlike way and asked, "Now, Detective Sergeant, to what do I owe the pleasure of your company?" It was somehow typical that Gorham-Leach would be punctilious with Smailes's rank. He found himself smiling at G-L's exaggerated courtesy.

Smailes realized as he began his account that despite himself he did in fact believe Paul Beecroft's conjectures, both about the possible relationship between Hawken and Fenwick and about Simon Bowles somehow discovering it. He was aware also that this disappointed him, for it meant that Bowles's motive for taking his life was probably nothing more than jealous anguish. Notions of conspiracy, the theft of a file, were probably irrelevant. And while Nigel Hawken was still no doubt deeply compromised by these events, it was unlikely that anything further was involved in Bowles's death that could provide him with a trump card to play against the hand Dearnley was holding against him. But he could still take Hawken with him, he thought with some consolation as he gravely rehearsed for Gorham-Leach the circumstances of Alan Fenwick's interrogation, suspension and reinstatement. G-L listened with a rapt intentness, and then suddenly placed his sherry glass on the gray tile of the hearth.

"My word, you're suggesting that this man Fenwick has been reinstated in his position because of an improper relationship with the senior tutor of this college."

"No, I'm not. I'm just pointing out that it seems unusual. I would not even have known about it if I had not seen him when I visited the porters' lodge last night on a completely different matter. I managed to ask one of the other men on duty, confidentially, what had happened, and he told me that the college council ordered him reinstated at their meeting last Thursday. You don't happen to know if that's true, do you, sir?"

"Well, no, I haven't sat on the council for years. It's a committee of six fellows, you see, who do most of the administrative work. But we can jolly well find out. Ivor Davies will know."

Gorham-Leach got up and walked over to his desk and looked up a number in a small directory with the St. Margaret's crest on the front. "You probably know Dr. Davies, don't you?" he asked as he dialed. Smailes nodded. "He's on the council, you see, and well, we are old friends. He'll tell me what's going on."

Gorham-Leach paused and then Smailes heard the faint sound of a reply from the telephone receiver. "Ivor? Hello, it's G-L. . . . Oh, very well, thank you. Very busy, unfortunately. . . . No, not really. I want to ask you about something that might have come up at the last council meeting. About one of the junior porters."

Smailes listened as G-L discreetly outlined the case as he had understood it. He raised his eyebrows at the policeman as he repeated, "Oh, so that's the first you've heard of it, is it? Well, I'm sure there's some logical explanation. I say, Ivor, please don't say anything about this little chat for the time being, all right? . . . Yes, yes, I'll see you in hall." He hung up, and came slowly back to his chair, frowning.

"Well, you're right. The matter was never discussed, according to Ivor. It certainly does seem highly improper, doesn't it?"

"Yes, I suppose it does," said Smailes. "But you can understand that I did not want to go further with this matter until I had confirmed the information."

"Yes, quite," said G-L thoughtfully.

283

"And I guess now I need to ask your advice. What should I do about all this?"

"I thought you were going to ask that," said Gorham-Leach in the same tone.

"I should tell you also, sir, that I did speak with Dr. Hawken after our last meeting and inquired about any interviews he might have had with young Bowles before his death. I was quite careful not to reveal how I knew about the subject. And, well, he did confirm to me his intelligence role here and that he had had some kind of meeting with Bowles where Bowles had asked him about it. So I am informed about this matter, if you're concerned, sir."

"Yes, yes, I thought that might happen. Oh dear, this really is most troublesome."

"I believe that you've known Dr. Hawken for many years, haven't you, sir? Since before the war probably."

"Yes, indeed I have. Indeed I have." Gorham-Leach seemed on the point of confiding in him, and Smailes wanted to reinforce the impression of existing knowledge.

"And then I think you saw some wartime service together," he said.

Gorham-Leach seemed distracted and did not reply, then he exhaled quite loudly. "Candidly, Detective Sergeant, this does not surprise me. Only that it has taken so long for something like it to happen." He paused. "You see, I've been aware of Nigel Hawken's indiscretions, shall we say, for many years. Usually he has managed to confine his activities to outside the college, where he assumed no one knew of them. He was the same during the war. Always preferred fellows from the, well, lower classes, shall we say."

"You were both at Bletchley Park, I believe, sir."

"Yes, we were indeed," said Gorham-Leach without surprise. "That's what made his conduct when he first arrived here so infuriating, though I for one never protested, which I have sometimes regretted. Not that I didn't agree that some kind of thorough investigation was needed here, absolutely.

284

But the manner was quite reprehensible, and Hawken as an inquisitor was thoroughly discredited, I felt. I could have put a stop to it with a few discreet phone calls, I'm sure, but I was timid, concerned about my work. I assume you know why he was brought in here?"

"Yes, I do, sir. A security service appointment following the espionage scandals."

"Quite. Well, firstly, his academic credentials for the position were thin, and I think that has hurt the college's reputation over the years. Then the way he went about his work was quite unnecessary."

"How do you mean, sir?"

"Officer, you cannot imagine the witch hunt that was conducted within the walls of this university. I grant that there may have been some genuine security risks still in place, but their numbers were paltry compared with the dozens of entirely blameless men who were hounded from their positions into retirement or second-rate jobs because of someone they had once taken tea with or because of malicious gossip. And to see Hawken strutting through the whole procedure when he was an obvious security risk himself, well, I found the spectacle quite disgusting. But it was so typical of our security service in a way. Unable to present a proper response even at this late hour, because it was so stricken with the disease itself. And may well still be, for all I know. Please don't misunderstand me. I am quite in favor of positive vetting and undergo it regularly myself. Most important. But I have seen colleagues, worthy men, have their careers destroyed by our esteemed senior tutor on the flimsiest of grounds. And now it seems he has finally enmeshed himself in a scandal here at the college. Well, indeed . . ."

"There is, of course, the other matter, sir."

"What's that?"

"Whether this involvement had anything to do with how Simon Bowles died."

285

"Good Lord, I hadn't thought of that. Do you think perhaps he had discovered . . . ?"

"Sir, what does 'Who flagged the files from Bletchley?' mean?"

"I really don't know. What are you referring to?"

Smailes explained the note he had found in Bowles's wallet, his belief that it was directly related to his research, and his suspicions about a missing file on the same subject. He explained how he had learned of G-L's and Hawken's wartime service from Bowles's work and had researched the Bletchley institute from other sources. He considered his words carefully.

"You see, sir, I can't help wondering that the question has some ulterior mathematical significance. Young Bowles had done something similar with an investigation into the Kennedy assassination. That is, he decided the accepted version was mathematically impossible. Perhaps . . ."

"Yes, yes, I see what you mean," said G-L pensively. "Well, I'm really not sure, except it may refer to the belief that some have had that our work was compromised. 'Who flagged the files?' it said? Personally, I have always discounted those theories. Although . . ."

"Yes, sir?"

"Well, as I think I've explained, Hawken has always struck me as a security risk himself. He was military liaison to the War Office for the latter part of the Bletchley operation. And I've always distrusted zealots, you know. I suppose there's a possibility . . ."

". . . that Simon Bowles discovered Nigel Hawken was a traitor, sir?"

Gorham-Leach tugged at his lip in agitation. "No, I really can't believe that. But I know what you should do, Officer Smailes."

"Yes, sir?"

"You must report him to his superiors in London. It's the

only thing you can do. Any further investigation should be undertaken by them."

Gorham-Leach went to his desk and scribbled a name on a pad, tore off the sheet and handed it to Smailes. Smailes stood up to receive it. He saw the name Roger Standiforth and a London telephone number. "Standiforth is director 'D' at MI5, one of Hawken's superiors. He's head of 'D' Branch, the counterespionage branch. You must call him and tell him all you know."

Smailes stood looking at the paper for a moment, then folded it carefully and put it inside his wallet. He reached for his raincoat. Gorham-Leach said, "Please tell me what happens. I will say and do nothing until I hear from you."

Smailes was about to leave, but realized he had a further question for Gorham-Leach.

"Do you still hunt, sir?"

"What an extraordinary question. No, not since my undergraduate days. How on earth did you know I used to hunt?"

"Bowles's research, sir. Said you were a member of the Blenheim Hunt at Oxford."

"Quite right. Quite right. That young man really did have unusual abilities. And you too, Officer. I commend you on your thoroughness."

"Thank you, sir," Smailes said, and thought of saying something about calling him as a character witness at his upcoming hearing. "I'll be in touch."

Smailes hesitated outside Giles Allerton's door before knocking. Loud rock music was pulsating inside, and he realized how awkward this potential interview was. He just hoped he was not going to find Lauren in there. That would be extremely awkward.

"Come in," yelled Allerton's voice. Smailes stepped into the room and through a thick haze of smoke saw Allerton sitting on a chair facing a young woman who was lying slouched on the bed. She was not Lauren Greenwald. She was a skinny blond woman wearing a leather jacket and blue jeans. The music was deafening, and Smailes smelled the distinct sweet odor of marijuana. "Oh, Christ," said Allerton, getting up and switching off the record player. "Shit, what do you want?" He looked at Smailes with frightened, red-rimmed eyes.

"Just a word, Giles, if that's okay."

"Look, I don't sell the stuff, I only use it now and again, and Maggie here's got nothing to do with it, okay? Let her go, will you?"

"Sure," said Smailes. "Run along, miss."

The woman had realized quickly that Smailes was a policeman and had sat up nervously. She threw a questioning look at Allerton, who shook his head. She retreated unsteadily out of the room.

"Sit down, Giles. I'm off duty, and what you do with your private time is of no interest to me, all right? I just want to ask you a couple of favors."

Allerton sat down and looked at Smailes mistrustfully. Two fat roaches sat in the ashtray on the floor, and Smailes could see Allerton's drug kit on the desk top, the razor blade and silver paper partially wrapping a small black cake of cannabis. "I'm serious. I'm not here to arrest anyone for drugs, okay?"

"Are you telling the truth? If you tell Hawken, I'll get sent down. What do you want?"

"I want to visit your brother. How do I get in touch with him?"

"Hugh? Whatever for? You can call him at Merton College. He's studying to be a holy man."

"I just want to ask him some questions about Simon Bowles, that's all."

"Simon? Are you still looking into that? I was at the inquest, you know. I heard you all do your whitewash job."

"There's just a couple of things I want to clear up. You still believe it wasn't suicide?"

"Oh, I don't know," said Allerton petulantly. "I suppose

288

not. But I don't think you or the coroner found out why he died. I don't think you cared to."

"What's your theory?"

"We . . . I don't really have one, I suppose. But I thought it was weird that he wasn't wearing his glasses when you found him. I hear you didn't. I was going to come talk to you about it."

"No, I didn't, not particularly," said Smailes. "There's something else. Do you have a photograph of him?"

"Who? Simon?"

"Yes."

"I might. What do you want a photograph for?"

"To make some more inquiries."

"Just a minute."

Allerton turned round to his desk and thrust the drug kit clumsily into his jacket pocket. He opened the desk drawer and began pawing through its contents. Smailes moved over to stand beside him. Allerton produced a fat envelope of photographs and looked through them. He found one and handed it to Smailes.

"Here."

Smailes was unnerved to see Simon Bowles smiling weakly at the camera, seated on a bed next to a girl who had her arm draped affectionately around his neck. The girl was Lauren Greenwald. "Couldn't you have asked Lauren?" asked Allerton.

"She said she didn't have one," said Smailes. "When was this taken?"

"Last year, before Christmas, in Simon's room. I took it."

"Can I keep it for a few days?"

"All right," said Allerton uncertainly. Smailes looked down on the desk and saw scrawled notes in a script he did not recognize.

"What's that?" he asked.

"Russian translation. I've got Finals in less than a month. I've been trying to catch up."

"Yes, I noticed," said Smailes. "I'll send this back to you when I've finished with it."

On the drive home Smailes thought carefully about the advice Gorham-Leach had given him. He was glad to have an actual name to contact, but was not ready to put himself on the line yet with any accusations. He wanted to complete the trips to Oxford and London, to see if he could glean anything further about Bowles's activities during the last days of his life. He realized also that he could hardly call a senior official at MI5 without involving George, and he doubted George would look kindly on his unauthorized attempts to ensnare Nigel Hawken in a sex scandal. There was a further misgiving, he realized. Even if he could somehow call Standiforth privately and evade the subject of his suspension, he had read enough about the British security services by now to know of their dismal record with regard to traitors in their midst. He knew of nothing to suggest that their attitude of denial had really been supplanted. The information might get stuck, filed away somewhere, Hawken never even challenged about events. He might need G-L's help further, he reflected. This particular whistle might need to be blown by someone of his stature.

He was irritated to find on his return that the Post Office repair van was still parked by the manhole near his door, and he had to hunt around to park. He might even support the government's idea to sell off the outfit to private investors. It might make it run better.

Derek Smailes first noticed the odd-looking white Rover on the drive to Oxford. He had stopped for cigarettes and passed the car parked in a lay-by about quarter of a mile further up the A45. It caught his eye because the bonnet had been restyled as if to accommodate a custom engine job. Otherwise, it was a plain, late-model car. Only when he was driving away from Oxford on the motorway to London did he notice it again in his rearview mirror. So I'm being followed, he thought to himself, with more a sense of intrigue than alarm.

The meeting with Allerton Senior had been interesting, finally. The young man could hardly have been more different in appearance and behavior from his younger brother. He received Smailes in a small sitting room that he shared with another graduate student at the college. The other student, a mousy chap with a prominent Adam's apple, was sitting there studying when the detective had arrived, but beat a tactful retreat as soon as Smailes entered. Hugh Allerton was soberly dressed in a sports jacket, white shirt and tie, and was reading a book titled *Concepts of Grace,* which he put down to shake Smailes's hand. If he recognized Smailes from the Cambridge crematorium, he did not show it. He expressed surprise once more at the message to call the CID detective in Cambridge, and could not imagine why anyone would have questions about Simon at this stage. Smailes explained again that they were informal inquiries that he was conducting for CID. Much more informal than you would ever guess, Smailes thought to himself.

Allerton spoke candidly of his long friendship with Simon Bowles and the terrible impact his suicide had had upon him. He had felt himself sharply depressed since the event and still could not reconcile himself to it. He had no idea Simon was in a difficult state of mind. No idea at all.

Smailes allowed Allerton to describe Bowles's occasional visits to Merton College since he had begun his latest research project. Bowles had talked to Allerton about it at some length, but Allerton felt it was a wild-goose chase and was not a particularly sympathetic listener. He knew that Bowles's technique was to delve into contemporary records from the thirties at the Bodleian Library. Allerton had helped him get reader's privileges. At some point they had ceased to discuss the details any longer. They had many other subjects to talk about.

Simon Bowles's habit was to arrive in Oxford on the evening bus from Cambridge, stay the night on the sofa in Allerton's study, then spend a full day at the library, catching the evening bus back to Cambridge, usually without seeing Allerton again. On the Thursday before his death, Bowles had arrived as usual around nine-thirty and the two men had stayed up late talking, as was their habit. Bowles had told him he might stay two days, which was unusual, and had arranged to telephone him at the porters' lodge in the late afternoon to tell him of his plans. The last time Allerton had seen Simon Bowles was on the Friday morning, when he left for a lecture. Simon was just waking up and had told him sleepily that he would talk to him later. As arranged, Allerton had gone down to the lodge to take a call from Bowles at around five-thirty, and was told by Bowles that he had decided to head back to Cambridge after all. They made vague plans to see each other in a month or so.

"And during the visit, there was nothing in his conduct that suggested he might have been undergoing, well, a personal crisis of some sort?" Smailes had asked.

"Absolutely not. He was his old self, as far as I could see. Argumentative, a little mischievous. That's the way he always was with me."

"And you didn't know of any developments in his personal life that might have been troubling him?"

Allerton had wanted to know what Smailes meant, and the detective tried to ask delicately whether the two men ever discussed personal or romantic affairs. Allerton said that generally they had not, they were more intellectual partners. He had long suspected that Simon might be homosexual, but it was not a subject that naturally came up between them.

"And why did you think that?" Smailes had asked.

"Oh, some things when we were at school, things he would let slip unknowingly. I think it was a difficult subject for him, and I for one would never have brought it up," Allerton had explained. Smailes considered asking him his opinion of his younger brother's activities, but thought better of it. It would be difficult to defend the relevance of the subject.

Smailes had almost decided to leave when he asked casually whether the two men had talked on the telephone about what Bowles might have been working on that day, why he had changed his mind about staying an extra day.

"Not really," Allerton had said. "But wait a minute. I think he did say something about a skiing accident. Yes, before he rang off, he said he had found out about an interesting skiing accident."

"When?"

"Oh, he didn't say, and I didn't attach any significance to the remark. In fact, I'd forgotten all about it, until you just asked."

Smailes said nothing, and took no notes. He thanked Hugh Allerton again for seeing him, and left.

Smailes had decided to repeat Bowles's last trips in the order Bowles had taken them, and as he gathered speed on the motorway to London, he thought again and again of Allerton's last remark. Of course, he thought of Hawken, the withered, useless arm, and the explanation of the skiing accident in Bavaria while a student. Was this the interesting skiing accident Bowles had investigated? Had it led to further disclosures about Hawken's career? Smailes had to think that it had, and the information seemed to strengthen the likelihood that Bowles's increasing knowledge of Nigel Hawken's activities had been somehow involved in his death. But how? Hawken was hardly much of a physical threat with his disability, and it was difficult to imagine Hawken and Fenwick together somehow forcibly killing Bowles and then staging a suicide. Difficult, but not impossible, Smailes reflected, and it was then that he saw the white Rover again.

Smailes had to concede that whoever was tailing him was a pro. A light rain had been falling and Smailes had turned his wipers up to high in overtaking a trailer truck. He adjusted the wipers again as he moved back to the center lane and kept the truck in his rearview as he accelerated away. Just as the big machine was about to disappear behind a bend, he saw the Rover, distinguished by its flared engine cowling, overtake also. Smailes kept up his speed so as not to alert the driver that he had been noticed, and in fact only caught sight of the Rover twice again as he wove through the heavy lunchtime traffic of West London toward Fleet Street and Somerset House. No matter, thought Smailes to himself. He would contrive a way to get the number plate on the way back to Cambridge. He was sure his unexpected guest would accompany him back there.

It was awkward finding parking near the Aldwych at lunchtime, but Smailes eventually found a meter near Charing Cross Station and walked down to the Victoria Embankment, looking for the entrance to the huge Neo-Gothic building of Somerset House. Everyone in England knew that this building was the depository for all the records of births, marriages, deaths and census statistics in Britain since formal record-keeping had begun. There was apparently quite a thriving industry in the archives, drawing up genealogical records for curious Americans. Smailes climbed the steps beside Waterloo Bridge to Waterloo Bridge Road, where ornate metal gates guarded a circular driveway to what seemed to be the building's side entrance. He walked through a revolving door and confronted a government security guard seated on a stool at a wooden podium. He produced his police badge and asked if he was in the right place for researching births, marriages and deaths.

"No, guv'nor, you're not. Mostly Inland Revenue in this building now. A few wills kept in the Family Division Court, that's all. What are you looking for?"

"I'm not sure. I'm trying to find out whether a young man visited here last month." He produced the photograph of Bowles and said, "This is where the Public Record Office is, isn't it?"

"No, sir, different building entirely. Chancery Lane, off

Fleet Street. But if you want information on births, marriages and deaths, you'll have to go to St. Catherine's House on Kingsway. They're both just a few minutes' walk. Which is it you're wanting?"

"I guess the Public Record Office. The young man had a Reader's Ticket for it."

"That's right, then," said the guard, handing back the photograph. "You don't need a ticket at St. Catherine's. Just go up the Aldwych, right on Fleet Street, left on Chancery Lane. Can't miss it."

Smailes was fairly sure that the driver of the white Rover was close by, following him as he strolled with the afternoon crowds along Fleet Street, past the Temple Bar monument, which marked the official boundary between the City of London and the City of Westminster. He was not concerned to try to identify him, or to suggest in any way with his behavior that he knew of his presence. He walked past the ornate architecture of the Royal Courts of Justice and turned into Chancery Lane. In a few minutes he was standing in the inquiries office of the British Public Record Office.

"Yes, can I help you?" asked a small bald man mildly. He had emerged from an office and was standing behind a stout oak counter, in a room that was not unlike St. Margaret's porters' lodge. Smailes produced his identification again, and the civil servant invited him into the office and seated him beside his desk. Smailes produced the photograph and asked whether the man remembered meeting Simon Bowles the previous month.

"No, I'm afraid not," he said, frowning at the picture. "But then we get so many applicants for Reader's Tickets every day. But if you have a name, we should have a record of the application. Last month, you say?"

Without any difficulty the man produced for Smailes from a filing cabinet behind him the very application that Simon Bowles had completed barely a month ago. Every two months or so, the physical documents were copied onto microfilm, then destroyed, he explained. On the application Bowles had had to declare what type of record he was researching and for what purpose. Bowles had written: "Changes of name, 1930s," and under purpose: "Thesis."

"So he was here to research changes of name, was he?" asked Smailes rhetorically. "Do we know what he found out?"

"Well, we can go down to the Long Room and see," said the man. "Come with me."

Smailes was led down a long gallery in which massive iron-and-leather storage chests from an earlier era stood at intervals. They entered a large, airy reading room and approached a librarian's desk. A woman was seated in front of a computer screen and turned to smile at them as they approached. She was Indian and wore a brilliant turquoise sari.

"Ah, Mrs. Dutta, this is a gentleman from the Cambridge police. He wonders whether we have information on any records requested by a young man who was here in March. What was his name, Officer, Bolling?"

"Bowles."

"Right, Bowles. There is a photograph also. His application said he was here to inspect records of changes of name in the nineteen thirties. I was thinking, it might have been the one doing the book research. Do you remember?"

The woman took the photograph and looked at it closely. "Yes, I remember him, I think. He wanted the enrollment books of deed-poll records from the thirties. I think I remember him finding something that excited him too, because he came to ask for the court records after four o'clock, and I told him he'd have to wait until the following day." She had the lilt of Urdu in her voice, and her English was formal and precise.

"I'm sorry," said Smailes carefully. "Can you explain?"

"Well, yes. The Long Room contains the enrollment books for deed-poll records of changes of name since the late nineteenth century. You see, anyone changing their name by deed

296

poll after 1914 had to advertise the change in the *London Gazette* and also register the change with the enrollment clerk of the Supreme Court. The change would then be enrolled in the enrollment books. They are big ledger books, written by hand until quite recently."

"Can I see one?" asked Smailes.

"Well, certainly." The librarian walked over to a shelf and pulled down a fat, dusty ledger. She spread it open in front of Smailes and showed him pages of entries in elegant copperplate handwriting. "This book is from 1928. See, it gives the new name, then the former name and a date. Then there is a file reference to the actual court documents, which can be retrieved if requested."

"And you remember this man last month asking you for court records?"

"I think so," she said thoughtfully. "I have a good memory for faces, and it certainly looks like the same fellow. He wanted all the books from a certain date onward, I think perhaps 1933, and after a good few hours came over to my desk here, pointing out an entry and asking if he could obtain the court records. Well, of course, it takes some time and our rule is that after four o'clock, the person must come back the following day. We hold the documents here at the desk until they pick them up. Of course, nothing is allowed to be removed from the Long Room, or photocopied. Many of the records are far too fragile for that."

"And how did he react? Do you remember?"

"Well, he seemed quite excited and said it didn't matter. He couldn't come back the next day, but it wasn't important for him to see the actual record. I think he said he'd found what he was looking for."

"So you don't know what record it was that he had found?"

"No. If he had asked for the court papers, then of course there would be a record. But he didn't. He just put the ledger back and left, I think."

Smailes looked at the rows and rows of ledgers that

stretched up toward a fifteen-foot ceiling, and all the way down the reading room, which had to be sixty feet long. It was hopeless to try to duplicate Bowles's search, even if he knew what he was looking for.

"You're quite sure that this is the same man, are you? About five foot seven, slim build, about nine, ten stone?"

"Well, of course, I can't be *completely* sure, Officer, but it looks like the same young man. Don't you remember him, Arnold?"

The civil servant shook his head. "No, I don't. As I said, I wondered that it might be that chap who was doing the book. *Jews of Britain,* or something, wasn't it? Wasn't that the same period?"

"Yes, it was, but that was last year, and he was a very big man, I remember distinctly, and he was here for at least a week or two. This young man was much more recent, and he was very small, quite small. I remember him because it was toward the end of the day, the beginning of a week, I think, and he was really quite excited. Has something happened to him?"

"Yes, he's dead, I'm afraid," said Smailes.

"Oh, I'm sorry," said Mrs. Dutta, smiling sadly.

Smailes was deep in thought as he walked slowly back to his car. So it was changes of name Bowles had been interested in, not genealogy or other records. And he had found out something significant, he obviously believed. So whatever he had discovered in the Oxford library had led him to the Public Record Office. What was it he had told his sister? He had to visit Somerset House and needed to do a lot of research before he went. He had probably made the same mistake as he had that day, and been directed over to the Public Record Office from Somerset House. He had searched for hours through enrollment books and then requested court documents, but was too late to see them that day. It had not been important, and he had left, probably to take the train back to Cambridge. And the next night he had killed himself, Smailes reflected. Or been murdered. He reflected also on the precision of the librarian's memories. It heartened him that British society was beginning to give a little at the seams, regional accents on the BBC, immigrant faces in the civil service, things you would never have seen until recently.

Smailes unlocked the car and adjusted his position behind the wheel. Before turning the ignition, he reached over to the passenger side, lowered the visor, and removed the small vanity mirror from its vinyl sleeve. He tucked it inside his wallet and drove off.

He thought he saw the white Rover once on the laborious drive out to Tottenham and the A10, but he couldn't be sure. His plan called for the longer route rather than the quicker M11. As he was approaching Royston, he pulled into a filling station to buy petrol, and leaning on the roof of the car, pulled out his wallet. He adjusted the angle so the mirror showed him exactly where the traffic accelerated slowly away from the bend just before the turn into the petrol station. He pretended to riffle through the notes in the wallet, and then he saw the white Rover emerge slowly into view, then accelerate away. The letters and numbers were reversed in the mirror, but Smailes was able to read them easily. He sat back in the car and wrote them in his notebook. Tomorrow he would call Swansea and get the registration records. Then he might have something to tell George.

He saw no white Rovers when he pulled into his street, and he was relieved he could finally park outside his front door again. He called Lauren when he had taken off his coat, but she wasn't home. He didn't leave a message.

Nineteen

"IT'S REGISTERED to a Michael Fowler, Precision Motors, Ely," she said. "Does that help you?"

"It surely does, Susan," said Smailes. Over the years, Smailes had got to know by name most of the women who worked in the inquiries office at the Vehicle Registration Centre in Swansea. Predictably, the computers had been down when he had called at the beginning of business hours, and Smailes's query had to join the pile from around the country waiting to be punched in. It was midafternoon by the time he was called back. Susan hadn't asked why she needed to call him back at his home number. He thanked her and rang off.

So the white Rover was registered to Mick Fowler, of all people. It probably meant it was a rental car, one of Fowler's little side businesses. Smailes walked over to his front window again and craned his neck to see whether there were any white saloon cars parked in his street, as he had done ten times that day. There weren't.

Everyone at Cambridge police knew Mick Fowler. He was one of the more unpleasant local criminals, a small-time crook who had worked his way out of the scrap business into secondhand cars, then into a custom garage that handled antique motors and special-order engine and body jobs. It had also been a front for a bustling chop shop and parts-fencing operation, Cambridge police had found out less than a year ago, when Fowler and three of his associates had been pulled in on theft and conspiracy charges. To Smailes's disgust, Fowler had had enough cash to hire some fancy barrister from London, who managed to knock his sentence down to two years suspended and five years probation, pleading lack of previous record and remorse at the error of his ways. It was hard for Smailes to believe that experienced judges still fell for such rubbish. Meanwhile, Fowler was back in business, and for all Smailes knew, up to his old tricks. He was no doubt more careful these days, but Smailes was convinced he was still as bent as a poodle's dick. If he had hired out a car to whoever was following him, it meant the underworld was interested in his Bowles investigation, that was for sure.

He drove out to Ely along clear roads and with an empty rearview mirror. He pulled into the lot beside the new prefabricated building that housed Fowler's showroom and garage. Behind a corrugated iron fence at the back of the site you could still see the remnants of the scrap business from which Fowler had graduated. As far as Smailes was concerned, it was where Fowler belonged, back among the refuse.

He pushed open the glass door of the showroom and saw Fowler in his office down at the end, talking on the phone. He walked slowly past a restored Jaguar sports car, and a couple of big old luxury cars that might have been Bentleys or Daimlers. Fowler had seen him and was wrapping up his

301

conversation. He came out of his office with a big false smile and held out his hand.

"Derek! Long time no see. How've you been?"

Smailes took the hand reluctantly and caught the noxious smell of the cologne that enveloped Fowler. It was if he had never erased the odor of the scrapyard and overcompensated with too much Chanel or Dior or whatever he bought. He was a fat little man in an ugly yellow polyester suit, his hair bunched at the sides and combed horizontally to hide his baldness. He wore a blue shirt with ruffles down the front and on the cuffs.

"Okay, Mick, okay. You got time to answer a few questions?"

"For Derek Smailes, anytime. You looking for a new motor maybe?"

"Not yet, Mick. Let's sit down." With the door to the office closed, the smell of Fowler's cologne was even more overpowering. "You rented out a white Rover recently, right? Some kind of custom engine job?"

"No, I don't think so, Derek. Don't rent cars out, as a rule. My business is rebuildin' 'em and sellin' 'em, you know that."

Smailes pulled out his notebook. "Yeah, well, there's a W-plate Rover registered to you that's been seen in some odd places lately, and I need to know who's driving it."

"No, there's got to be a mistake. I don't know nothing about white Rovers. I sold one a while back, mind you. Maybe the record's not up to date."

"Crap," said Smailes. "Tell me who rented it."

Fowler said nothing for a moment, then reached into his trouser pocket and produced a fat roll of ten-pound notes. He licked a thumb and began counting them.

"No, it's a mistake, I'm telling you, Derek. How's yer little girl? She must be in junior school now, right? Now, your father, I could always do business with him. He knew when Mick said something was a mistake, it was a mistake. You see . . ."

302

Smailes's rage exploded and he lunged across the metal desk and grabbed Fowler by the lapels of his ugly suit. He yanked him to his feet and pushed him heavily against the wall of the office. The bank notes spun out of his hand and cascaded to the floor. Smailes pushed his fists, still full of Fowler's jacket, into his neck and then bounced him against the wall again.

"Listen here, you greasy little hood, how about I make a mistake and rearrange your face a little, then pull you in right now. Resisting arrest, we'll call it. Then I'll get a warrant and toss this place, and trace every serial number on every engine block and you'd better have paperwork on every single one or you're going down, Mick. Probation violation, a suspended sentence is automatically instated, you know that." He was shaking with rage.

"Steady, Derek. I didn't mean nothing." Fowler was scared. "You can't arrest me or get no warrant. You got no grounds."

"Oh yeah? That fucking Rover is tailing me, that's what. You don't call that grounds? A magistrate will give me a warrant, like that. What's up, Mick? Scared to have the place searched?"

"Let me go," he whimpered. "I'll tell you."

Smailes released his grip and pushed Fowler back into the wall. He sat down awkwardly, rubbing his neck.

"No need to get nasty," he said.

"Who was it?"

"Dunno. Bloke from the government. Said he needed something plain-looking, with a bit of poke. I hired him this Rover we done, with a Pontiac engine. Thing'll do a hundred and forty. He paid cash."

"What do you mean, government?"

"Said he was Ministry of Defense. You know, ask no questions. Put a grand down on the car, said he wanted it for a few weeks, and if it worked out, well, could be the start of an account. We agreed three hundred a week. Would always be

303

cash, he said. What am I s'pose to say? It's a straight piece of business. I done nothin' wrong."

"Did he show you identification?"

"He flashed me something with a portrait of the Queen on it. Looked official enough to me."

"You do paperwork?"

"You think I'm stupid? Of course I done paperwork. That motor's worth four, five grand."

"Show me."

Fowler opened the file drawer in his desk and produced a standard car-rental form. The form was filled out in the name of Stanley Hicks, Ministry of Defense, Whitehall, London. There was a flashy signature. The rental rate was three hundred a week. It was dated ten days ago.

"You check this against his ID?"

"I seen his card all right. Looked official to me."

"What did he look like?"

"Tall, skinny, balding. Maybe thirty-five."

"He come alone?"

"There was another, older geezer hanging out by the showroom door the whole time. Didn't do no talkin', just the skinny bloke. I showed him the Rover, then we done the money and the paperwork and he drives it off. Somebody must've drove 'em out here, because five minutes later I seen their mate drive off from round back. Listen, I think it's got to be something hush-hush, you know, cash and all that and wanting a special motor. I know what's going on at Molesworth and them Yank bases. Who'm I to say no to a piece of business like that? I'm a patriotic bloke, you know."

"Fuck off, Mick. How'd he talk?"

"Whaddya mean?"

"What kind of accent, I mean."

"He talked like a gent, that's what. He's with the government, what do you expect?"

Smailes thought for a moment. "You got a xerox machine?"

"Yeah, next door."

304

Smailes handed him the rental contract. "Copy that for me." Fowler disappeared obediently. Smailes's anger at the reference to his father had cooled. He saw the money lying on the floor, and kicked it away from him. Someone from the government was tailing him? Did that mean the security service? Why would they be renting cars from a scumbag like Mick Fowler? It didn't add up.

Fowler came back and handed the photocopy to Smailes. "Sorry, Derek, gettin' you worked up like that. I was only tryin' to protect somethin' I thought was confidential like."

"Fuck off, Mick," said Smailes again.

On the drive back to town Smailes wondered whether to go straight to Dearnley with what he knew, but the pieces weren't in place. Who was having him followed? Hawken? George? And why? All he'd done was repeat a couple of trips Bowles had made in the last week of his life. The rental contract was ten days old. Had he been under surveillance since then? He thought of Lauren, and realized that whoever was tailing him must know about his relationship with her. Should he tell her? He kept glancing in the rearview, seeing nothing. One thing he had to do, he knew, was make a decision about his hearing. He should go to the station, see the union guy, get a referral. It was also a Friday, the day the biweekly expense claims had to be in, and Smailes had no reason to pass up the reimbursements he was legitimately owed. He'd omit the trips to Oxford and London. He doubted George would appreciate the joke.

There were two or three detectives in the CID room when he breezed in and he exchanged awkward greetings with them. Ted Swedenbank came over and eagerly told Smailes about a breakthrough they'd had tying the lorry theft to a group of Sikh businessmen in Felixstowe. They were expecting arrests any day. Smailes congratulated him wanly and Swedenbank lowered his voice to express his hope that Smailes would beat the discipline charge against him. They'd all been talking about it and agreed George had been too hard

305

on him. They should consider his record, what he'd done in his time on the force. But when Ted asked him why he'd done it, he could only shrug and say it was a long story. He felt uncomfortable in the detectives' room. He'd only been out a few days, but already he felt he hardly belonged there. Maybe he shouldn't fight it after all, just accept reality.

The number of working typewriters was down to two and Smailes had to wait in line to type up his expenses. The machine he used was on its last legs and jammed a couple of times. He had to free the key bars and got ink all over his fingers. He swore softly and tore the sheet angrily out of the machine. He stalked out of the room, saying nothing to the other men, and headed upstairs.

Gloria looked terrible when he handed in his form, as if she held herself responsible for his problems. He was touched, but tried not to show it.

"Come on, Gloria. It's not the end of the world. What kind of mood has he been in?"

"Lousy, Derek, ever since that day. I don't know if he's still angry with you or angry with himself. I wouldn't go in if I were you."

"I wasn't planning on it, believe me."

"What are you going to do?"

"Haven't decided. Got to talk to the union, I suppose. Take it from there."

But he didn't. He left Gloria's office and kept right on going down the stairs and out the back entrance to his car in the multilevel car park behind the station. He drove home and parked. Now the white Rover was back, parked also, about fifty yards down the street. He could see the outline of a man sitting behind the wheel. He thought about walking straight down the street and confronting him, and then thought again. He went into the flat, feeling scared.

His thoughts were racing as he fumbled with the wrapping of a loaf of bread. He was hungry, needed a sandwich or something. He took out two slices of white bread and then cursed loudly as he saw ink stains from his fingers spread all over them. Cheap fucking administration, couldn't even provide CID with modern electric typewriters, whereas every secretary in the place had one. He threw the bread in the rubbish angrily and ran the tap. Then a realization hit him so hard that he actually gasped. He wrenched off the tap and grabbed a towel. Holy Christ, he thought. Bowles had had an IBM Selectric, right? The type with the carbon ribbon, right? That meant no messy fingers, right? *Because the ribbon cut a neat carbon stencil of every character and was only used once, right? Which meant that whatever had been written on that machine was recorded on the ribbon! All he had to do to find out what Bowles had written the night he died was rewind the ribbon and read it! Right!*

He rushed to the telephone, found Alice Wentworth's number and dialed. A stranger's voice answered. He asked for Mrs. Wentworth, and it took several minutes before she came on the line.

"Hello?" she said, the cool voice sounding uncharacteristically anxious.

Smailes introduced himself hurriedly.

"Oh, Mr. Smailes, I'm sorry, but I'm with the police. We've had a burglary, I'm afraid. That was one of them that answered the phone. I'm sorry, I'm in a bit of a state."

Smailes felt his bowels turn to ice. "What was taken?" he asked slowly.

"Oh, you know, the television, the record player, the typewriter, what you'd expect."

"What about your jewelry?"

"No, they don't seem to have been upstairs." That clinched it. Even a second-rate house thief went for the jewelry first. The other stuff had been taken to cover for the theft of the typewriter, make it look like a routine burglary. He felt dizzy.

"When?" he asked.

"It must have been sometime this afternoon. I found it when I came home from work. I called the police right away.

307

They've just arrived. The house is such a mess. Oh, Sergeant Smailes, I can't tell you, this feels like such a violation. The children are very upset."

"Mrs. Wentworth, I know this may sound odd, but have you changed the ribbon in the typewriter lately?"

"Why, yes, I was typing the parish magazine with it on the weekend and the ribbon ran out. Peter went out and bought new ribbons and put one in for me. It's quite simple, and works so much better than . . ."

"What did you do with it? The old ribbon? Did you throw it out?"

"Well, yes, I suppose it's still in the wastepaper basket in the study. Really, what on earth does this have to do . . ."

"Will you go and check, please?"

"Check the ribbon?" she asked in disbelief.

"Check and see whether the old one is in the wastepaper basket."

It seemed like an age before Alice Wentworth came back to the phone. Smailes could hear the blood crashing in his ears.

"Yes, here it is, I've got it," she said brightly.

"Hold on to that, will you. I'll be there in an hour."

"Really? Well, Rickmansworth is a little bit longer drive than that, Officer."

"Just don't let it out of your possession. And let me speak to the policeman who answered the phone."

When the cop came back on the line Smailes told him under no circumstance to leave before he got there. He explained that he thought the burglary might have been aimed at the typewriter ribbon specifically and that the thieves might be back when they realized they hadn't got what they wanted. The man sounded puzzled, but compliant. Smailes rang off.

His heart was pumping as he went back to the front window and looked down the street at the white Rover. The car could do a hundred and forty, Fowler had said. His Allegro had a top speed of eighty-five, if he was lucky. He should call the station, get a squad car, but then he remembered he was suspended. Maybe he should call George, explain the whole thing, get an escort. He discounted that idea. Maybe he should act tough, walk down the street, try to arrest the guy. For what? he asked himself. Then he decided to make a run for it. He'd lay odds that he knew Cambridge better than the wise guy parked down the street.

He walked casually out to the car and pulled out slowly toward Mill Road. In the rearview, he saw the Rover pull out and edge slowly up the street. At the main road, Smailes fished inside the glove compartment for his magnetic police light and flicked it on. When he saw a gap in the traffic he reached out and slapped it on the roof, then let out the clutch and roared off toward town. He kept his foot down through the gears and hit the Mill Road roundabout doing about forty. He had a split second to assess the traffic and screeched round the two cars slowing for the turn and threw the wheel left. He felt the off-side tires thud against the curb of the roundabout as he straightened the car out down Gonville Place. Forty, fifty. He saw the Rover in the rearview make the same turn. The lights at Regent Street were changing, the traffic slowing down. He leaned on the horn and pulled out into the oncoming lane and said a prayer. He screamed through the red light at more than fifty, just in front of a double-decker bus that had started up and narrowly missing a middle-aged woman who was waiting astride her bicycle in the outside of the oncoming lane. He looked back quickly and knew the Rover would never get through that crossing until the lights changed again. He made the light at Trumpington Street on green and was well on his way to the motorway before he allowed his speed to slacken at all. He was clear, he thought, provided the white Rover didn't know where he was heading, in which case it would overhaul him easily.

He left the police light on the roof the entire way to Rick-mansworth, keeping his speed between seventy and eighty. He reached the outskirts of the town in about an hour and a

quarter and found Alice Wentworth's street without difficulty. He had not been followed. The Wentworth house was
large and detached and stood behind an enormous beech tree
next to the parish church. A police car was parked outside.

A uniformed constable answered the door. Smailes introduced himself and showed his identification. "What happened?" he asked, trying to sound calm.

"Came in through the French windows. Simple lock to
force. Might have been a one-man job, because what was
taken could have been carried by one man, one trip."

"Come in from the front?"

"No, there's an alley runs up the back. Neighbors said they
saw a Post Office van up there this afternoon. Probably
nicked. Bloke comes through the garden, then out through
the alley. Nobody sees him."

Smailes didn't hear the end of the statement. He was suddenly remembering the Post Office van that had been parked
outside his flat for days, doing repairs.

"Post Office van?"

"Yeah, neighbors thought nothing of it. You got the telephone wires back there, they think he's workin' on them."

"Thanks, Constable . . ."

"Bristow."

"Constable Bristow."

"You don't have to stay. Is Mrs. Wentworth here?"

"Yes, in the back, I think. All right, I'll be off, then. Can I
say what all this is about, then, when I write it up?"

"It might be nothing. I'll have to let you know, okay? Can I
call you at the station tomorrow?"

"Yes, I suppose. Something about the theft of a used typewriter ribbon, you say?"

"I may be wrong, okay? I'll let you know."

Bristow looked skeptical but said nothing further. He
turned and left noisily enough to express his irritation at taking orders from out-of-town CID.

Smailes found Alice Wentworth in the back of the house,

310

seated at a table in a large kitchen, eating dinner with her family. The upheaval did not seem to have affected Peter Wentworth's appetite. He was digging into a huge slab of quiche and got up clumsily from his chair when the detective entered, his mouth full. The two children were eating fish sticks with sullen expressions. When she saw Smailes, the girl pushed her brother and then smirked into her food. Alice Wentworth looked a little pale, but otherwise back in control.

"Hello, Officer," she said, getting up. "Do you want me to show you what's missing? It's so good of you to come. I'm sure it's just an ordinary burglary."

"I'm sorry to disturb you. I'm interested in the ribbon, if you have it. I think you said it had only been changed once since you brought your brother's typewriter from Cambridge."

"Yes, that's right. The parish magazine was really the first lengthy thing I'd used it for. Much better than our old portable. Yes, I'll show you. In the study."

She led Smailes back down the hallway to the front downstairs room, which was a large, airy study and music room. There was a piano, a desk, bookshelves and a filing cabinet, which Smailes recognized immediately. "Did they go into the files?" he asked.

"Simon's files? Good Lord, no. They took the record player from over there, the typewriter from off the desk and the television from next door. Why would they want files?"

"Yes, I'm sorry, that's silly," said Smailes. "Is the ribbon here?"

Alice Wentworth walked over to the desk and switched on a gooseneck lamp. "Yes, right here, although I can't think why . . ."

"And a copy of the parish magazine that you typed?"

"Why, of course, on the piano seat. I'm afraid the style is a little laborious, but I get very little help with it, you see . . ."

"You typed it in order, front to back?" asked Smailes, flipping through the four pages.

311

"Yes, of course," said Alice Wentworth, a little annoyed. "Is there anything else?"

"No. I'd like to stay a while, if I can, and study this. Is that all right? Can I use this pad here?"

"Why, of course. Would you like a cup of tea?"

"Love one," he said with a smile.

When Alice Wentworth came back with the tea, she said, "You can read the last things Simon wrote on there, can't you? Is there something I should know about? Is that why we were burgled?"

"I don't know," said Smailes. "I need to look."

Rewinding the ribbon cassette slowly, Smailes was able to reconstruct the last words that Alice Wentworth had typed, and then find them in the magazine. The letters flowed across three tiers on the ribbon, in waves, and he had to allow for strikeovers where the self-correcting key had been used for errors. It was awkward at first, but he got the hang of it. He rewound it about a foot and found it was much easier to read forward. Then he took a breath and rewound the ribbon slowly to the beginning. He began to transcribe and found notes he thought he recognized from Bowles's research into the Oxford archives. It was laborious work, and Smailes's stomach growled. He hadn't eaten since breakfast, he realized. The light was failing and he looked out into the street. There were no white cars in sight. He kept transcribing, slowly, hour after hour.

Then the text suddenly became more recent. Smailes read an account from the Oxford archives of an unusual skiing accident. A very unusual accident indeed, considering with whom Smailes had been speaking just the previous day. Then he read an account of a visit to the Public Record Office in London, and felt his throat go dry. Then there was a gap, and Bowles's typewriter had pecked out the letters *THE CAMBRIDGE THEOREM.* At that moment Alice Wentworth came back into the room and Smailes felt as if he leapt about a foot in the air. He was thankful she did not try to read over his shoulder.

"Mr. Smailes, it's half past ten and we're going to bed. Are you going to be much longer? It's all right, of course, but I could stay up if you think you're going to have something to tell me."

"No, I'm afraid I was wrong," he said. "Everything here I think I recognize from Simon's files. At least so far. I'm nearly finished. Probably another hour or so."

"Oh, well, that's what the police said. They said these big houses are vulnerable because of the French windows in the back. I suppose we should get a stronger lock, or something. I think the insurance will cover it. You know, I ought to tell you, since it was sort of your suggestion that made me think of it. I showed Simon's Kennedy manuscript to an old university friend of mine, who's a literary agent in London. She was impressed. She thinks she may be able to get it published."

"Really?"

"She said something about the last half needing heavy editing, but that, overall, the piece had merit. Peter and I are very pleased. It will be sort of Simon's testament. Well, you can let yourself out, I suppose. Will you tell me if you find anything unexpected?"

"Yes, I'll call," said Smailes.

When she left, he resumed the slow transcription of Bowles's final piece of detective work, the summary of all the research he had done in Oxford and Cambridge, the devastating conclusions he had been able to reach from his unique combination of doggedness and recklessness. The implications were extraordinary, and Bowles had spent the last night of his life carefully cataloguing the corrosive impact of the treachery. When he had finished, Smailes could feel the sweat standing on his face, could feel it sticking between his fingers. He was under no illusion about the nature of the document that lay in front of him. It could wreck careers, fracture alliances, even bring down a government. Smailes was haunted

313

by his sense of the dead student's brilliance, the lucid intellect speaking to him in this quiet suburban night from beyond death. A death which now could be seen as an obvious murder. And Bowles's killers had so nearly got away with it—a flawed destruction job, a botched burglary, elementary mistakes. When he reached for the telephone on the desk and told the operator to reverse the charges to George Dearnley's number, he felt quite calm. He looked at his watch and saw it was almost midnight.

He heard George hesitantly accept the charges and then growl angrily at him, "Derek, what the hell is this?" After Smailes had explained his activities since their last meeting, and taken the fifteen minutes or so to read him the transcript, George said, "Jesus Holy Christ," and then said nothing for a long time.

"You at the sister's, you said?" asked George eventually.

"Yes."

"They know what you found out?"

"No, I bluffed. Said there was nothing new."

"Come back. Come straight over here. Bring me the papers. I'll wait up."

"What are you going to do?"

"Call the commander of Special Branch in London. I've got a twenty-four-hour number somewhere. Take it from there."

"George, I've been tailed the last few days. Tried to follow me over here, but I threw him. A custom Rover registered to Mick Fowler. Said he hired it out to a bloke from the Ministry of Defense."

"Mick Fowler? Ministry of Defense? Jesus, Derek, why didn't you tell me?"

"George, I had nothing until half an hour ago, did I?"

Dearnley swore softly and there was another pause. "This Rover over there now? You want to get a squad car from the Rickmansworth station? I can call."

"No, I'm pretty sure I threw him. They'll know they've blown it by now. I doubt they're still around."

314

"Who's 'they'?"

"You tell me, George. You tell me. I'll be there in an hour. So long."

He thought he heard George tell him to be careful as he hung up the receiver.

Twenty

THE DRIVE to George's house took even less time than the drive in daylight. He was in a numb, dreamlike state the whole way. He was by no means convinced that their man was trapped. He knew the whole thing now would be taken out of his hands and felt frustrated. Would whoever George had shaken out of bed in London be able to catch the ball? Maybe the whole operation was on its way to an airfield or a port somewhere, in the white Rover. He kept pressing against the typewriter ribbon with his elbow to reassure himself. His seven-page transcript lay on the passenger seat beside him.

George came to the door in a long tartan dressing gown. The carriage lights at the side of the door were on, and the flesh of George's face looked gray, like overcooked meat. He handed him the transcript without comment. He didn't want to be invited in.

"What's going to happen?" he asked quietly.

"They're coming up from London. First thing. Be in my office, nine-fifteen."

"Our man flown the coop?"

"They don't think so. Got someone in place already, I think. We'll go in first thing in the morning."

"We, George? What about my suspension?"

"It's revoked," said George expressionlessly. Smailes said nothing. "Don't go home, Derek. Go to your mother's. Go to a hotel. Stay away from your flat tonight, okay? Whoever's been on you, they think it's first division stuff."

"KGB?"

"It's a good guess." Smailes could hardly believe he and George were having this conversation. George did not ask him for the ribbon, and Smailes would not have wanted to give it to him. "Nine-fifteen?" he said. "Okay."

At the end of George's street he stopped at the phone kiosk and dialed Lauren's number. He could hear the coin-box phone ringing on the upper landing, waking the whole house. He was thankful that Lauren got there first.

"Derek, my God, where are you? I've been trying to get you all night. Giles is missing, for Christ's sake, then I couldn't get you. Derek, I've been so scared. What's going on?"

"Lauren, go to your front window, okay. Look out into the street and tell me if there's a white Rover, W registration, parked in the street. Have you got that?"

"Derek, what the fuck is a Rover? What are you talking about?"

"It's a midsize car, okay? White, four-door. W is the last letter on the registration plate. Just do it, Lauren. Go and look."

There was a silence, and then Lauren came back on the line. "Derek, it's there. There are two men sitting in it. What's going on? I'm so scared."

"Just listen to me, okay? Get dressed. Get a toothbrush.

317

Come downstairs and wait inside the front door. When I shine my flashlight through the window in the door, come out quickly, and don't say anything. Get straight into my car."

"Derek, will you tell me what's going on?"

"Did you understand the directions?"

"Yes, I think so."

"Okay. I'll be there in ten minutes. Get ready."

After he hung up the phone on Lauren he dialed his sister Denise's house. It was almost one-thirty, but when her husband, Neil, picked up the phone, he sounded as if it was the middle of the afternoon. Neil always sounded like that; Smailes guessed that salesmen had to.

"Derek, long time. How've you been?"

"Pretty good, Neil. Is Denise there?"

"I think she's asleep. Just a minute. Denise. It's your brother."

Denise had come on the line with all her predictable resentment and ill will. "Derek, for bleedin' hell, what do you mean calling at this time of night?"

"Can I come out and stay in the box room tonight, Denise? It's important. Otherwise I wouldn't have called."

"Are you all right? Are you in trouble? Derek, what's going on?"

"I'll explain tomorrow, okay? There'll be two of us. Just throw a couple of blankets and sheets on the bed. We'll make it up."

"Aw, Derek. I'm layin' out a frock. You know I use it as a sewing room."

"Can't you move your stuff? It's just for one night."

"I suppose so, but you've got a nerve. It's not that American piece you're bringing over, is it? I still talk with Yvonne, you know."

"You'll meet Lauren tomorrow. She's not a piece. She's an engineer. Leave the front door on the latch, will you?" He rang off.

318

He kept trying alternatives for the two jokers in the Rover but still had no plan when he pulled into Lauren's street. He could see the Rover parked across the road, about twenty yards from Mrs. Bilton's gate. He pulled up outside with no attempt to disguise his arrival. This is where I wish the British police were armed, he said to himself. Still, he doubted the characters in the Rover knew, one way or the other. He reached inside the glove compartment and pulled out his heavy police flashlight. He shoved it into his raincoat pocket and got out of the car. He crossed the street with his hand on the flashlight, the butt raised and protruding through the fabric of his coat. Just like a gun, he hoped. He walked slowly toward the Rover, which was facing away from him. He saw the driver's neck jerk as he followed him in the rearview mirror. He was tall, balding. He seemed to say something to the figure next to him, who was shorter, older. Smailes was almost parallel with the rear bumper when the engine started and the car pulled away, slowly at first, then picking up speed. Smailes kept the butt of the flashlight pointed at them through his pocket until they were gone. Then he exhaled slowly. He walked quickly back to the house and flashed the light through the window. Lauren ran out and into his arms.

"Derek, I saw you drive up. Who was in that car? Did you speak to them?"

"No, they didn't seem to want to socialize."

"What were you pointing at them? A gun?"

"I wish." He grinned and held up the flashlight. "Let's go."

On the trip to his sister's house in Histon, Lauren told him falteringly about Giles Allerton's disappearance the previous night. He had not shown up to meet Maggie, his new girlfriend, his bed had not been slept in, and he hadn't been seen all day. Lauren had told the head porter at the end of the day when he still hadn't turned up, and then had tried to call Derek. She wanted to know where Derek had been.

"I'll be able to tell you soon, okay, Lauren? By tomorrow night, I hope."

"Is it about Simon? Was he murdered?"

"Looks like it."

She buried her face in her hands and sobbed a little. Then she looked at him. "Derek, this is so creepy. Who was in that car?"

"I don't know," he answered truthfully. Someone from the Ministry of Defense, he felt like saying.

"Where are we going?"

"To my sister's."

"Why?"

"We're invited."

"Derek, this isn't fucking funny."

"I know. I'll tell you everything tomorrow. I promise."

They let themselves into his sister's house quietly and climbed the stairs without switching on lights. They turned right on the landing and Smailes led her down the hall to the end room. He walked to the bed and turned on the lamp. There was a pile of sheets and blankets on the bed. On a folding table Denise had her sewing machine and a number of pieces of fabric with paper patterns pinned to them. There was a chair, but nothing else in the room.

"She has two boys," whispered Smailes. "They share a room."

They made up the bed wordlessly and then Smailes snapped out the light and they undressed quickly. The room had no curtains.

Smailes climbed into the small bed next to Lauren and she clung to him silently for several minutes. Then they made love fitfully, Smailes anxious that the bed would creak, distracted by the surroundings, but excited despite himself by Lauren's quick sexuality. She fell asleep immediately and he felt the soft rhythm of her breath against his shoulder. He lay on his back and dozed but knew he would not sleep. The hours passed slowly. As it grew light he stiffened with fear as the outline of a goat's head came slowly into perspective just a few feet from his face. He grinned ruefully when the gathering light revealed the shape as his sister's sewing machine.

He shook Lauren lightly. "Let's go," he said. "You can meet the family another time." They dressed, used the bathroom, and left before seven, before Denise or her boys were up. Smailes knew he would catch hell from his sister for his rudeness, the sheets, the unmade bed. He drove Lauren to the college in silence, and gave her her instructions for the day, promised he would find her that night. Then he made the decision to go home.

It was a mistake. The front door had been jimmied, and the inside door to the flat had been simply kicked off its hinges. The place had been destroyed. The furniture in the sitting room was slashed and broken, the books thrown over the floor. The bedroom was worse. The mattress had been disemboweled like a butchered animal, drawers upturned, the mirrors on the wardrobe doors and the dresser smashed. He walked back down the hallway to the bathroom and found the ultimate insult. Someone had taken his Tony Lamas, thrown them in the toilet pan, and pissed in them. They certainly had not been concerned about noise, but then their surveillance had told them the landlord was never there. There had been no danger. But at least they didn't have the ribbon, Smailes told himself. He could still feel that in the inside pocket of his jacket. The Bowles file was gone, of course, but that was no matter. That was not what they had been looking for.

He managed to change his clothes and shave, despite the wreckage. He wondered abstractly as he left for the station how he would explain the damage to Les, his landlord.

He had been lounging at his desk for forty-five minutes before the call from Dearnley came through. He was trying to read Ted's report on the Sikh lorry theft, but could not concentrate on it. It had a gloating tone that was irritating. Swedenbank had come in around nine and had obviously been surprised to find Smailes sitting at his desk reading the paperwork in his in tray. He had said something about the weather and Smailes had responded with a grunt. He let the phone ring three times before he picked it up, to show Swedenbank there was nothing unusual in his behavior.

"Smailes," he said.

"Could you come up, Sergeant Smailes?" said George's voice. It was obvious there was a stranger in his office. Smailes was never Sergeant Smailes except in front of strangers. He understood the gesture toward professionalism, however, and straightened his tie as he left the office. His palms felt sweaty on the rail as he mounted the two short flights to George's office. His eyes felt scratchy from lack of sleep. He wondered how much sleep George had had the night before. It had been something after one when he had handed him the transcript, the most extraordinary document George had ever handled in his long career, that was for sure. Two people had been murdered to suppress its contents, Smailes was fairly convinced.

Gloria kept her eyes down on her desk as Smailes walked past her into Dearnley's office. He wondered how much she knew. Enough to keep her head down, clearly.

He stepped into the office and closed the door behind him. George was seated behind his desk, and to his right sat a man of slender build, with fair hair brushed back from a high forehead. He had pale blue eyes and a pointed face like a whippet and gave the impression of complete relaxation. His long legs were crossed and his hands rested in his lap like birds. In front of him on the corner of Dearnley's desk were two file folders, one orange and one manila.

"Have a seat, Sergeant," said Dearnley. He swung his massive shoulders to his right. "This is Commander Standiforth of the Special Branch."

And I'm Broderick Crawford of the Highway Patrol, Smailes said to himself. Even if he had not already known Standiforth's agency and rank, he would not have mistaken him for a Special. The Specials were cops, after all, and this

322

guy had the dark pinstriped suit and manicured nails of the civil service. He bristled at the patronage. Who did they think he was? Standiforth made no movement to offer his hand, so Smailes took the vacant chair in front of Dearnley's desk.

"Are you all right, Sergeant?" asked George. "You look a bit shaken up. Did you stay with your mother?"

"I stayed with Denise." He had decided to leave all mention of Lauren Greenwald out of these proceedings.

"This fellow Allerton's missing."

"No kidding," said Smailes. He wondered whether George had known last night, whether that was why he had insisted he not go to his flat. "Probably on a binge somewhere. He's a lady's man. Likes the horses."

"Doubtful. He missed some meeting with a tutor day before yesterday and no one's seen him since. Family hasn't heard from him."

"Could be he was picked up by the same zombies did my place last night," he said offhandedly. Standiforth leaned forward slightly in his chair and clasped his hands around his knee.

"What do you mean?" asked George, a trace of alarm in his voice.

"After I left Denise's this morning I went home to change. The place had been taken apart. Maybe they were looking for the ribbon. They took the Cambridge files, that's all."

"What Cambridge files?" asked Standiforth in a voice that indicated he'd been to the right schools.

"Bowles's files on the links between Cambridge University and Soviet espionage. I lifted them from his room before his sister cleared out his things. At least I lifted what was still there. I think our man must've got back in there Wednesday night to remove what he thought was most incriminating. A file on Bletchley Park at least, maybe more."

George Dearnley looked winded and passed his hand in front of his face. He looked painfully at Standiforth and then said to Smailes, "How come I knew nothing of this?"

"Couldn't be sure, George. No physical inventory, see."

"It's a little irregular to go removing evidence like that, Sergeant," said George.

"I had the sister's permission," said Smailes. He turned to Standiforth. "Nothing much in there that wasn't already in the record. Some original stuff on activities in the thirties that he had dug out of the library here and at Oxford. Some interesting speculation."

"Such as?"

"He was asking himself, 'Who flagged the files from Bletchley?' I guess he solved that one, didn't he?"

Standiforth said nothing. Smailes reached into his inside pocket. "Whoever they are, these clowns have been tooling around in a custom Rover, rented out from a local wide boy." He produced the photocopy of Fowler's paperwork. "Says they're with the Ministry of Defense. I guess this is your department, Commander. Know any Stanley Hicks?"

"Let me see that," said Standiforth. He looked at the contract and made a little noise of disgust. "This is one of our friends' sour little jokes. So that if they're spotted and the car is traced, we might waste some time chasing our tails. No, the Ministry of Defense has no need to rent cars from garages in Ely, believe me. I hear a Post Office van was used also? That's fairly simple to explain. Some comrade in the postal union, a vehicle booked in for repairs, loaned out for a few weeks. Believe me, Officer, you were quite fortunate you were not at home. That was a KGB assassination team that visited your flat. In fact, they were more than that. They were a Sorge team, only the second group that has ever ventured onto British territory, to our knowledge.

"We were alerted that they had come in through Prestwick two weeks ago, but we lost the trail. You see, we do know a little about the cover they use."

"Sorge team?" said Smailes, trying to sound interested.

"The Sorge Institute is an elite facility outside Leningrad. Named for the Soviet Union's most famous spy. The agents trained there are the most skilled and dangerous the Soviets can deploy, and therefore the least often used." Standiforth pronounced the word "orfe-ten."

"Yes, I wondered when they came through that it might involve Conrad."

"Conrad?" interrupted Smailes. Dearnley's face was impassive.

"The cryptonym of a very high-ranking agent. We've known of his existence for many years. Except it seemed probable he was either dead or retired by now. And all the evidence pointed to Whitehall. The consensus was that Cambridge was clean.

"No doubt they were summoned because Conrad thought this man Bowles might get too close to his identity. They didn't kill him, however. They would never have made such a simple mistake as leaving a typewriter ribbon. In fact, they must have realized the oversight, which led to the break-in at the sister's. When they found they still did not have the original, they visited you. You were not home. Unfortunately this man Allerton was not so lucky. A friend of the dead man, I understand. Did he know anything?"

"I really doubt it," said Smailes. He thought of Lauren, and felt a sudden wave of fear. He was shocked at how expansive Standiforth was being. He felt flattered, a little unnerved.

"By the way, do you still have it?" he asked.

"I'm sorry?"

"The ribbon. Do you still have it?"

Smailes thought of bluffing, but the bulge in his jacket pocket was probably conspicuous. He handed it to Standiforth reluctantly. It was his last physical proof of Bowles's extraordinary discovery. Standiforth looked pensive and waved the ribbon cartridge at him.

"You know, Officer Smailes, when I first finished speaking with Chief Superintendent Dearnley last night, I was very angry with you. That you had not consulted higher authority much earlier in this investigation. I was planning to recommend an immediate suspension, in fact." Smailes did not look at Dearnley. "But I realize how unlikely this case must have seemed, why you chose to go it alone. And I must commend you on your excellent work."

Dearnley changed the subject. "Won't they have tried to spring their man after they came up empty at Derek's? I mean, at Sergeant Smailes's?"

"No. You see, they don't even know who he is. The KGB has never quite overcome its conspiratorial origins, and even its senior agents are told as little as possible. Conrad's identity has been such an unusually well-kept secret all these years, my guess is that no agent has ever learned his name and position unless it was absolutely necessary. These two have been briefed on whom to watch, whom to eliminate if necessary. But since they bungled the burglary, my guess is they're probably waiting for further orders. They're probably not even part of his escape team. Besides, our chaps tell us he's only been out once so far, to walk his dog. No phone calls."

Standiforth gestured toward the bookcase on his right, where a small two-way radio was resting. Smailes was relieved that unseen hands had taken over. He wished someone was watching Lauren.

"Why didn't we pick him up last night?" asked Smailes.

"Well, Officer, it was quite late when I finished speaking with the chief superintendent. Certain arrangements have had to be made. And our watchers were in place by five-thirty. Nigel Hawken knew the name of a neighbor, fortunately."

"Hawken?" said Smailes, stiffening.

"Yes, Mr. Smailes. I'll get the details from you later. I understand there are certain questions that need answers. No, if my theory is correct, our man doesn't even know he's blown."

Standiforth reached inside his suit and produced a silver cigarette case. He offered it to Dearnley and to Smailes, who took a cigarette and accepted a light from a matching lighter.

Standiforth flipped back the cap of the lighter and put it back in his pocket with a languid gesture.

"One more thing, Officer. Do you carry a weapon?"

Again, the stupid patronage. Of course he didn't carry a weapon. This was Cambridge, not the Bronx.

"No, but I'm an authorized shot. Take me five minutes to sign one out."

"Is your card current, Derek?" asked George. Police regulations required two days of training every eight weeks to keep the authorization current. There had been an embarrassing incident last year when George Dearnley had gone to book out a weapon during the hostage siege at Fen Ditton and had been sent away by the armorer because his card had expired.

"Yes, sir," said Smailes, keeping his face straight.

"I really don't anticipate anything untoward," said Standiforth, "but caution should prevail."

Smailes stood up, but found his irritation at Standiforth's deception had gotten the better of him.

"Look, if you're with the Specials, why don't you use your own men to make the arrest. They've got an office down the hall. They can't both be out at Molesworth singing 'We Shall Overcome.' "

Dearnley looked shocked, but Standiforth smiled and then stood and extended his hand.

"Mr. Smailes, I do apologize. I really did not think you had such slow wits. I'm just plain Roger Standiforth with MI5. Secrecy becomes an obsession with us; it's almost a vice. I wasn't sure how much you already knew and didn't want to complicate things.

"Of course, we have no powers of arrest, as I'm sure you know. Please get your weapon. We'll leave as soon as you're back."

Twenty-one

MARTIN GORHAM-LEACH answered the door slowly and peered out at them, looking amiable but puzzled. It was a Saturday, and he was dressed informally in an old blue cardigan and slippers. The two policemen were standing behind Standiforth, their coats turned up against the heavy rain that had begun falling.

"My word, Roger, this is a surprise. And Detective Sergeant Smailes. Well, do step in. It has turned quite nasty suddenly."

The three men followed the old scientist down the hall. Predictably, he turned into his study. The electric fire was turned on and Gorham-Leach went to stand in front of it, next to the old black Labrador, who was asleep on the hearth rug. He looked at the three men quizzically.

"Well, I suppose the detective sergeant must have taken my advice after all. It's a sorry business, I agree, but something

328

had to be done sooner or later. Roger, I could have said something earlier, I admit."

Dearnley cleared his throat and spoke. "I'm Chief Superintendent George Dearnley of Cambridge police. Martin Gorham-Leach, you are under arrest for multiple offenses against the Official Secrets Act. You are also under arrest for the murder of Simon Bowles and the suspected murder of Giles Allerton. You have the right to remain silent. If you do not remain silent, what you say may be taken down and used in evidence. Do you understand your rights?"

"Roger? There must be some mistake. What on earth is he talking about? You know my security record. Simon Bowles murdered? And who is Giles Allerton? Really, is this a prank?"

Standiforth produced the typewriter ribbon from his pocket and held it in front of Gorham-Leach. There was both weariness and malice in his voice. "Technology changes, Max. You got too old to spy. This is the ribbon you forgot to remove from Bowles's typewriter. It contains a complete transcript of what he wrote the night he was killed. He discovered who you really are, didn't he, Mr. Gottlieb?"

Gorham-Leach took two steps toward the window and turned to look out at Standiforth's black Jaguar and the sheets of rain that had begun to sweep across Jesus Green. He stood motionless for a long time. The minutes began to extend. Eventually, George Dearnley said, "Sir, if you'll come with us, we . . ."

"Superintendent," Gorham-Leach interrupted angrily, "I have lived a life of flawless dissimulation, only to find myself discovered by a spotty maths student and Mr. . . ." He turned to the three men, as if lost for a name. "Smailes here. Permit me my moment of gall." They resumed their wait. Then Gorham-Leach began to speak.

"It was a very simple plan, really. I suppose that is why it worked so well all these years. You see, I could hardly come back under my own name, could I? Given my background, no one would have believed my renunciation, would they?

"Max Gottlieb, Martin Gorham-Leach, it wasn't even such a big adjustment to make. There were plenty of people giving up their Jewish names for solid English names in the thirties, believe me.

"Of course, there was always the slight danger that the discrepancy in dates might be noticed. A three-year gap between undergraduate and graduate careers is a little unusual. Then there were the official court records of the deed poll somewhere. I must confess, I never thought that the fate of the original Martin Gorham-Leach would be unearthed. I met him once, you know, the year before he was killed in the Alps. Unspeakable young man. Always chasing young boys, or foxes, it seemed. Still, he had some loose interest in getting a science degree, so it provided the needed continuity when we finally got around to positive vetting. By that time, anyone who knew I had applied as Max Gottlieb but come up as Martin Gorham-Leach was long since dead. As far as my colleagues were concerned, I came from an upper-crust Surrey family. That I was actually born in the Baku oil fields and was a Soviet citizen would have sounded too farfetched to be conceivable.

"You see, there were some who took the long view, even back then. After I led the Oxford party to Moscow and decided to stay, I was gradually convinced that it might be more beneficial to Soviet science if I returned to Cambridge. Incognito, of course. You see, the Cavendish was always the prize. There never could have been an atomic bomb without the Cavendish. Some saw that the defeat of Hitler would only be a preliminary in the much longer struggle against capitalism, and that scientific knowledge would be crucial to the survival of our revolution. History has proved us right, wouldn't you say?"

Here Gorham-Leach moved slowly across the room toward the three men. He suddenly looked stooped and frail. He steadied himself against the back of one of the wing chairs, tossed some magazines onto the floor, and sat down heavily. He resumed his monologue without looking up.

"You know, the two institutions are really remarkably hermetic. I would occasionally meet someone who had known me at Oxford as Max Gottlieb, and would have to convince them they were mistaken, I was Martin Gorham-Leach. From time to time someone would ask me if I was related to the Gorham-Leach who had been killed at Chamonix, and I would say we were distant cousins. But it happened very rarely, and only at first. You see, everyone knew that Max Gottlieb had returned to the motherland. I think there's still some journeyman in the Academy of Sciences using my cover. They give him an award every now and then, to keep the name alive."

Smailes looked over at Dearnley and reached for his notebook. He was concerned that Gorham-Leach was singing so loud and nothing was being recorded. Dearnley shook his head discreetly, and Smailes wondered if somehow they had been able to wire the place, that somewhere recording tape was turning.

"I wondered actually, Roger. When Winston and I went out this morning, the young girl with the pram, I'd never seen her before. Of course, I'd sent for help, they could have been ours, I didn't know. But I still thought it was improbable that young Bowles's detective work would be duplicated. Simple mistake about the ribbon, really. I've always used the manual type myself, you see. Didn't think."

Gorham-Leach turned to look at Smailes. There was a look of slight amusement in his eyes.

"So he had asked himself about the files from Bletchley, who flagged them, eh? You know, it wasn't that difficult to discern, really. No great mathematical precepts involved. Simple arithmetic should have convinced anyone that Kim couldn't have done it alone, processed all those raw intercepts with the speed that was needed for the Eastern Front. But no one seemed to stop and think about the sheer volume of the Bletchley material by the end of the war. It was being delivered to SIS daily by handcart. But Simon Bowles obviously did, perhaps because he had the kind of mind that thought instinctively along physical, mathematical lines. I went back, of course, the next night, to look for his original file, after I reflected how his deductions must have proceeded.

"I signed off on everything as it was translated, you see. A simple numerical dating system was all that Kim needed. We always worked quite well together, he and I."

Here there was a sustained pause as Gorham-Leach was seized by a coughing fit. He eventually produced a large white handkerchief, wiped his face and mouth, and resumed slowly.

"I must admit you surprised me, Detective Sergeant, with the question about the Blenheim Hunt. No one had asked me that for years. Were you trying to catch me out?"

Smailes did not reply.

"Then, of course, the Cambridge Research Institute was founded. A great stroke of luck, since the Cavendish was always a little high-minded about military work. We became the research and development lab for the Ministry of Defense. Whatever was developed in the private sector would come to us for testing and approval. Oh yes, there's been quite a bit over the years. The diesel engine for the Centurion tank, the swing-wing fighter, the jump jet. British military science has always been the pioneer of the Western alliance. So I think I've been able to keep our development costs down considerably over the years. In fact, I would claim that I am more responsible than any man alive for the current military parity of the Soviet Union. When you think about it, you'll probably agree, Roger."

Gorham-Leach beamed at Standiforth, who was staring at him impassively.

"But the achievements of the past are pale compared with our current work. You see, that fool in the White House has

332

been listening to his German scientists again. We all got a few of the fascists at the end of the war, but I think the United States got the most foolhardy. Oh, it's not public yet, but I've no doubt it will be in the next year or so. He will put on his makeup, go on television, and declare that space-based weapons can render nuclear arsenals obsolete. A questionable assertion, I think, when you consider the simplicity of the countermeasures, but the physics are at least plausible, we have found. An orbiting laser could destroy an ICBM before reentry, conceivably. Oh, there will be plenty of ballyhoo about the militarization of space, and the arms race will escalate further, which is the whole point. You see, the point is not deployment. The point is that the bulletheads in the Pentagon want us to cripple ourselves in the research and development phase. They still believe that sufficient material deprivation will lead the Soviet people to revolt against their government. It really is quite galling. Gentlemen, do you know what percentage of the popular vote the party would win if free elections were held next week? Around ninety percent. Do you know how many citizens would vote to close the gulag, free the dissidents? Maybe twenty percent. You see, the Soviet people have never known anything but authoritarian government. They see this obscene squabble of life in the West and want no part of it. No part of it. And the military and political leaders in the West have never understood the capacity of the Soviet people for suffering and endurance. Mr. Smailes, do you know how many people died in the siege of Leningrad? One million people. More than all the casualties of all the Allies, civilian and military, combined. Do you know how many were lost in the whole Patriotic War? Twenty million. And yet these men in the Pentagon, who grow fat driving around in carts chasing a little white ball, think that lack of butter or meat or leather shoes will cause the Soviet people to rise up against their leaders. It's despicable."

Here G-L rose unsteadily to his feet. He seemed exhausted.

"Well, my friends, I have ensured that our hardships will not be too great. Our scientists now know the same physics that CRI does, or the Germans in California, for that matter. And there have been virtually no development costs."

Smailes could not understand why they hadn't taken the scientist away, why they were continuing to listen to his monologue. Standiforth seemed rooted to the spot, as if in a trance. He did not look over at the two policemen.

"Murder? I don't think so, gentlemen," continued Gorham-Leach. "Oh, I don't deny that it might have come to that, because he was a very bright chap. That's why I decided to supervise him when I learned from Ivor what his next research project was going to be. I don't believe he ever suspected me until the very end. I was particularly alarmed when I knew he was going down to London after visiting Oxford again. It was, I thought, probably a matter of time before he found something in the Alpine Society's minutes or something about Gorham-Leach's untimely demise. But I had a little trump card to play, you see, and it worked quite well. I knew of his, er, friendship with the new porter, and I also kept my ears open to see whether Nigel Hawken would be able to resist this latest piece of rough trade. He couldn't, of course, having made the decision to hire him himself. Roger, you will never learn about the extent of homosexuality in the service, will you?

"So after I knew he'd gone down to London, well, I placed a discreet note in Mr. Bowles's pigeonhole, explaining that his new friend was not, shall we say, the monogamous type. The next night, it led to a furious row between them. Fenwick tried to deny it, but then he demanded to know how Bowles had found out. You see, I know all this because he told me when he came over to my rooms after he found the body. You see, Bowles threatened to kill himself unless Fenwick promised to stop doing 'favors' for Hawken, and Fenwick got angry and refused. He left and was on his way home, he went as far as the marketplace before he got worried, changed his mind, and came back. Well, it seems our distraught little detective had not been bluffing after all. Fenwick found him dead, and panicked. He knew I was duty tutor and came to my rooms and woke me. We went back over to Bowles's room together. Around two. Well, I saw the scene and I saw that misleading suicide note and I saw his file sitting beside the typewriter. And so I made a little bargain with our unscrupulous Mr. Fenwick. I told him I would keep quiet about his involvement if he would keep quiet about mine, and he accepted eagerly. Then I told him to leave me alone.

"The file really was quite complete, wasn't it? He even went back over my whole career, to try to put together a damage assessment. If anything, I'd say it was a little conservative. Not even our talented young sleuth could know everything I've been involved with, could he, Roger?

"And then, if I had only thought to lift out that ribbon. But you see, I was flustered, I confess. Should have checked the filing cabinet then and there, removed the Bletchley file before anyone even knew it was there, shouldn't I, Mr. Smailes? Well, well, well. Perhaps you are right, Roger. I've grown too old to spy." Here he paused, and looked at each of the three men in turn.

"So, I suppose I should get ready. I suppose I'll have to undergo the tedium of debriefing. I don't think I'll ever see prison, though, do you, Roger? You see, Detective Sergeant Smailes, you are a little new to this business, but the most important thing now is to avoid a scandal. Particularly, to prevent the Americans finding out. That would be a disaster, wouldn't it, Roger? After all the assurances you've made that the files are clean, that the service is purged? I think we did rather a good job of making you think Conrad worked in Whitehall, don't you? Our own defectors even believed it. We had controlled even our own gossip, you see.

"No, Mr. Smailes. There will be some exhaustive questioning, no doubt. Damage reports will have to be written. But there will be no trials in camera, no garish publicity. A discreet exchange of important citizens perhaps, on the condition that no press conferences are held, a mutual condition. My colleagues will be given some plausible explanation for my sudden retirement, no doubt. Well, shall we?"

Gorham-Leach gestured to the door and the three men crowded into the dark hallway. Gorham-Leach gripped Smailes by the elbow to steady himself as he put on his heavy outdoor shoes. It was an oddly intimate gesture. The detective helped him as he struggled into a heavy raincoat.

"I don't think I shall enjoy the Moscow winters. They really are terribly harsh," he said. Then he turned to Dearnley.

"Is it all right if I use the bathroom, Superintendent, before we leave? I suddenly feel a little unwell."

Dearnley turned mutely to Standiforth, who gave a silent nod. Smailes was shocked. He had seen smaller fish than Gorham-Leach swim out of bathroom windows. Neither did he trust the tone Gorham-Leach had been using. He instinctively followed him down the hall and stood outside the bathroom door as he heard the latch fastened from the inside. He waited impatiently, then heard a cry and the sound of a body falling. Smailes took a pace back and kicked open the door, but he was too late. Gorham-Leach was on his knees, his face contorted in a rictus of terror. The sodium cyanide had already stopped the muscles of his heart. A small cabinet door over the sink stood open.

"Jesus, George, down here," he shouted, grabbing the dead man by the shoulders. As Dearnley crouched beside him he looked past him down the hallway. Standiforth had opened the door and was looking out across Jesus Green, where the rain still fell in sheets.

The interrogation of Fenwick was infuriating. He clung for a long time to his original story and maintained that he had not seen Bowles alive that night, had not argued with him, and had not spoken with Gorham-Leach. An enraged Dearnley let him know that his relationship with Hawken was discovered, that the police would make sure the college council at St. Margaret's was informed of his behavior after all. At first he had bluffed and denied the allegation, but finally acknowledged it. Standiforth had been in the room for the interrogation and made a disgusted gesture with his hands at Fenwick's confession. Eventually Fenwick told Dearnley that he was concealing only one thing from them, and tried to bargain with them. He would tell them if they brought no criminal charges against him. At this Dearnley almost went for the man's throat, and warned him they would make no deals, but that if he wanted to avoid being charged with everything they could think of, he had better tell the truth. Finally, Fenwick confessed that after the discovery of Bowles's body he had called Hawken at home in panic from the porters' lodge. They could check the phone records and find he was telling the truth. Hawken had said he would take care of the details and told him to take time off from work if he needed it. He had asked whether he thought anyone in the lodge knew of their association, and Fenwick had lied and said no. All other attempts to get Fenwick to change his story failed. He was adamant he had not spoken with Gorham-Leach or anyone else that night except Hawken. He had not argued with Bowles, who had not known of his liaison with Hawken. Dearnley ordered him kept in custody anyway.

Smailes glowered at the notes on his pad and fought the suspicion that hovered at the edge of his consciousness. He didn't know why he should believe Fenwick, but he did. He felt Gorham-Leach had been trying to protect someone with his swan song. Then there had been his forgetting Smailes's name and rank, an odd slip.

He pulled out a Cambridge University directory and found the name of the chairman of the Engineering Department, and called him at home. Then with some difficulty he obtained the weekend number of the FBI office at the American Embassy in London. He had to do some cajoling, but eventually the agent agreed to make some further calls for him. It was a weekend and might take some time, he warned him. Then Smailes thought for a long time. He pulled out the Bowles file and found Klammer's fingerprint report, and then thumped his forehead with the heel of his hand. It was late afternoon before Smailes's phone rang again, and he had to fight the knots in his stomach as he furiously scribbled notes. Then he called up to Dearnley.

"Standiforth still here?" asked Smailes.

"Yeah, we booked him into the Cambridge Arms. Be here at least a few days, he said. Derek, on the suspension, I'm drafting a memo to Hinchingbrooke, okay, dropping . . ."

"Get him over here," said Smailes. "I'm on my way up."

It was dark when he pulled up outside Lauren Greenwald's digs. He parked the Allegro at the gate and looked in the rearview as Standiforth's Jaguar pulled in a few houses down. "I'm going in," he said, before getting out of his car. He reached under the window box where Mrs. Bilton hid the spare key and let himself in quietly. He could hear Mrs. B. vacuuming in the back. Lauren's light had been on; he prayed he was not too late.

He moved silently up the stairs and across the landing to Lauren's door. She was wearing her blue Mets baseball jacket and was throwing clothes hurriedly into an open suitcase on the bed, her back to him. He stepped in and said quietly, "Where are you going, Lauren? A quick dash to Heathrow, or is there a Polish freighter moored at Grimsby maybe?"

She wheeled around and frowned at him. "Derek, you scared me. My Uncle Morrie has had a heart attack. My mother called this afternoon. I've got to go back for a while. I've been trying to call you. You weren't home."

She stepped toward him and reached to put her arms around his neck. He pushed her away angrily.

"Forget it, Lauren. You see, I made some calls after we went to arrest Gorham-Leach this morning. You knew that's where I was going, didn't you? Because you'd realized about the ribbon. Boy, that was a bad mistake. A really bad mistake.

338

Then the KGB botched the burglary at Simon's sister's, so you had them wait for me here. Hadn't you told them I didn't pack a piece, Lauren? I guess I'd really fallen for it, hadn't I? Just like Simon. Just like Giles. Why did you have to kill him, Lauren? Did he find you talking to one of the gorillas? Or did he finally demand to know the real reason why you'd had him lift the Bletchley file from Bowles's cabinet the afternoon I was interviewing the sister? Or did he find something lying around written in Russian? That was probably it. You forgot he spoke Russian, didn't you?"

"Derek, what on earth are you talking about?"

"First, I spoke with the chairman of the Engineering Department. He remembered you. You see, you already have a Ph.D., don't you? That's why he thought it was odd you wanted to do undergraduate course work. But, well, any recommendation of G-L's was good enough for him. There was no Fulbright scholarship, was there? Because you're twenty-eight years old and have already been working for two years for National Aeronautics, the defense contractor on Long Island. And their security procedures must really suck, if they hired you."

"Oh, why's that?"

"Because your parents were both members of the American Communist Party, that's why. Not that you showed any interest yourself through school and university. But your father's suicide must've really had a powerful effect, right? He took the Fifth at the McCarthy hearings and could never work in television or films again, could he? Must've broken his heart, teaching those sullen kids in the suburbs. That's why he killed himself, right? It was a bullet, not a stroke, that killed him, wasn't it? You might have an NRA in your FBI file, a Nothing Recorded Against, but your parents sure don't. Quite a little saga, in fact. You told me how devoted you were to him, remember? Must've made you feel like revenge, deep down, even though you'd shown no interest in his politics.

"So it was quite a smart move when Ivan approached you on the kibbutz, right? Must've been one of the Arab field offices, yeah? No Soviet diplomatic missions in Israel after all. They'd done their homework. Leaving out the ideology, it must've seemed like a chance to strike back at the system that killed Howard Greenwald. But I figure once you signed on, you really got into it. That second trip you took to the Middle East, the one after you were recruited, I bet it wasn't to Israel at all, was it? Did you learn the unarmed combat stuff at one of the Syrian camps in the Bekaa Valley, Lauren? Is that where you met Ari, the Jordanian, or should I say Palestinian? Is that when your commitment was really firmed up? Because you obviously decided you were going to be good, and you're fucking well determined, I'll say that. I must say, Agent Venditti had some even more interesting stuff on Momma Greenwald. Mimi Greenwald, formerly Sapora Levy, an agent runner for a pretty big cheese out in Turkey before she emigrated to the U.S. and married your father. Must have been his mistress too, since the file says she had a child by him. You never mentioned your half sister, Lauren, even though you have a pretty famous stepfather, I'd say."

"Oh yeah, who?"

"Philby," said Smailes.

He made no effort to stop her as she reached into the bottom of the suitcase and pulled out a small automatic pistol and pointed it at his chest. It looked like a Beretta.

"Shut up, shithead," she said coldly. "Put your hands on your head."

He complied, and as he did so, felt the tape that held the microphone against his chest stretch against his skin. "Put the gun down, Lauren. You're under arrest for the murder of Simon Bowles and Giles Allerton." He tried not to say the cue line too loudly. They had discussed the possibility that she might have a gun, but Standiforth had said he thought it unlikely. If she did, all he had to do was let her know about the backup in the street and she would probably fold. If she

340

didn't she would lose her concentration when they forced the door and he could jump her then. Smailes had gone along with the plan.

"Now, Lauren, you'll never get that through airport security, will you?" said Smailes. He was listening for the door, the sound of feet on the stairs.

"I said shut up, shithead," she repeated. "Did you drive?"

He nodded.

"Show me the keys. Slowly."

Smailes went into his right-hand coat pocket and held up his car keys.

"Let's go," she said. "You're driving."

Where the hell were they? Something had gone wrong, he thought with a flicker of panic. Christ, she had better not frisk me, he said to himself.

"Move," she said. Lauren slipped the automatic into the pocket of the baseball jacket as they left the room and walked down the stairs. He heard nothing except the vacuum cleaner. The street was dark and he did not look back for the Jaguar. He climbed into the car and Lauren got in the passenger side. She pulled out the gun again and kept it on him. "Drive," she said. "North. Huntingdon Road." He looked in the rearview and thought he saw a black car pull out before they turned the corner at the end of the street, but could not be sure.

He tried to keep his voice easy as he pulled out into Huntingdon Road and headed out of town past Fitzwilliam College. "You see, it seemed pretty obvious that Gorham-Leach —or should I call him Gottlieb?—was protecting someone with his little farewell speech. But he was angry and it made him trip. You see, he never forgot a title or a rank, and he almost called me Mr. Plod, which must have been your little joke about me, right? He did the honorable thing, you know. Fell on his sword. His story about Bowles killing himself after a fight with Fenwick just didn't jibe. It must have been the

341

most incredible night of Simon Bowles's life. He would hardly have been so upset about the supposed behavior of a boyfriend he'd only just met. And if the Fenwick story was a cover, how did he know about him? Then the cover story about the theft of the Bletchley file. Gorham-Leach didn't have a pass key, so how could he have pulled it off after we'd sealed the room? You see, I'd told him about the missing file earlier in the week, and he must have worked out that you were responsible. And I figure the only way you could have pulled it off was to con Allerton into taking it for you while he was over there alone with that deadbeat bookseller friend of his. What was the pretext, Lauren, that you were going to keep the investigation alive yourself? Is that the same line you gave him about the spectacles in the case, Lauren, why you had to go to me yourself? So you see, it all began to point to you, Lauren."

Smailes was desperate to get some kind of reaction out of her, to distract her from her terrible intent, but her face remained fixed and impassive, staring out onto the road and the night.

"Bowles certainly wasn't interested in seeing you, was he? But you had to go across there, preferably with Allerton as cover, because you knew he'd been to Oxford and then down to London and Gorham-Leach had warned you that that was the danger sign, hadn't he? So you showed up and managed to get a look at what was in the typewriter and it confirmed your worst fears, right? Gorham-Leach was blown and you could bet that Simon wasn't just going to sit on the information. You must have had quite some influence on him to get him to go out to the bar with you, given what he was in the middle of. Because the original plan had misfired, hadn't it? The idea was for you to show up as an innocent, displaced fellow scientist and get friendly with Bowles so you could keep tabs on him. But when you found out he was gay, you turned to Allerton as the closest alternative. Then me. It was safest to get me in your bed to monitor whether I could re-trace what Simon had done. That's why you jumped the gun when Giles got suspicious about the glasses in the pocket, right? Since Giles intended to speak to me anyway, you had to beat him to it. That was a really dumb mistake. Couldn't you just have put them back on the body?

"You see, you left Giles at his staircase and pretended to go get your bike at the front gate to go home. But you hung around until the bar closed and things got quiet, then you went back to Simon's place. He was certainly not interested in seeing you a second time, was he? Because he was almost finished typing up the theorem, and he didn't want anyone looking at it until he'd decided where to go with it, right? But, of course, he was unsuspecting. He maybe even appreci-ated it when you started to rub his shoulders. After all, he must have been feeling tense and he was pretty easy with you physically, right? I saw it in a photograph Giles took of both of you; you had your arm draped around him and he looked quite relaxed. Is it difficult to break someone's neck with your bare hands, Lauren? I guess with your strength, it's not that difficult, is it? You rupture the spinal column at the first and second vertebrae, which is the same injury that kills someone who is hanged, right?"

He looked across at her. Oncoming headlights streaked her face with light. She turned and looked at him expression-lessly, the dark orifice of the gun leveled at his heart. They were a mile or so out of town. "Right to Girton," she ordered.

Smailes swung the car off the main road toward Girton village. He could see no black Jaguars behind him, no flashing blue lights. Christ, had he been hung out to dry? Where were George and Standiforth? Why had they not come through the door on the cue line, or when they had heard her pull the gun? He was fighting a dreadful awareness, that Standiforth wanted him dead. *Secrecy becomes an obsession with us.* He had known Gorham-Leach was going to kill himself, and made no move to prevent it. And although the idea sickened him, he

343

thought George might even fall for it, the king and country stuff, expendability in the national interest. His tongue felt dry. Keep talking, he told himself.

"But then you started making mistakes, right? The glasses had flown off when you broke his neck, and you didn't think about them until later. You wanted to make it look like suicide, so you typed up that stupid note. Then you wiped the machine, and took Simon's hands and pressed the fingers on the keys. Except you pressed the thumbs flat on the space bar, Lauren. That's not how typists hit that key, is it? Think about it. They tap it with the sides of the thumb, don't they? You left the wrong print.

"That's when you went over to get Gorham-Leach. Must have been quite late by now. No one saw you. Was he expecting you? Had you already decided that tonight had to be the night? Probably, because he was duty tutor for only a week, right, and if you needed help to stage a suicide, you had to act fast. So you went back together and managed between you to get Bowles strung up by his belt on that hook. You were careful, wiping off the plant pot. Then you remembered the glasses, right? Lying there on the floor. You found the case, wiped them off, and stuck them in his pocket, never thinking that Allerton would find out and talk about coming to me with the story. He might even have blurted out his own role in removing the file. So you got to me first, and getting me in the sack was playing safe, wasn't it? Actually, maybe your acting was good so far, but I always thought your fucking was weak, Lauren. I was just too much of a gentleman to say so."

They had come to the T junction in Girton village and Lauren pointed to the right, the road to Oakington. Smailes's monologue was becoming more forced. He thought feverishly of the information Standiforth had given him that morning.

"I'm just surprised you fell for the whole thing from the start, Lauren. Didn't you realize you're a discard? No one has

344

learned about Gorham-Leach's identity over the years and lived to talk about it. You thought you were superior to those jokers from Leningrad? They didn't know who he was, right? Somewhere on the road to the airport tonight they would have turned off and blown your brains out, sweetheart. And you thought you were such a hotshot, such a major mission for your first outing, stepdaddy pulling strings in Moscow and all that. You've been dead for months, Lauren."

"Left," she said angrily.

Smailes drove down a side road, council houses on the right, bungalows on the left, giving way to hedges and open fields. The road dead-ended in a car park, and the headlights caught a sign: *Girton Golf Club.* "Left," she said again, and Smailes pulled into a small overspill car park. It was surrounded on all sides by a thick hawthorn hedge.

"Kill the lights. Out," she said.

Smailes stepped out onto the wet gravel and into the pitch-dark night. His legs felt shaky. Where the fuck were Dearnley and Standiforth? Why hadn't they taken them out on Huntingdon Road? Or had they just driven off as soon as Smailes disappeared into the house? Were he and Lauren both discards, in fact?

"Keep your hands out from your sides. Walk. Through the gap in the hedge."

He walked slowly toward a clearing in the hawthorn at the end of the car park, his feet splashing through pools of rainwater, his eyes adjusting to the darkness. His breathing was shallow and his chest felt tight. He was fighting panic, his thoughts careening. This must be where she had brought Allerton to kill him, he thought. He was on his own. Unless he did something soon, he was dead too. He walked through the clearing in the hedge and stumbled on a root. In the darkness he could see a drainage ditch to his left, a small thicket of young birch trees to his right. Half a mile away across a field the headlights of cars streamed silently north on Huntingdon

345

Road. Far away to his left were the lights of Girton village. There was a strong smell of wet earth and rotting vegetation.

The sound of his blood was pounding in his ears. In his desperation he thought of a goalkeeper's feint, inviting the shooter to fire away from the body, the natural shot. With his right hand he reached inside his jacket to the holster and slipped the safety catch off the revolver. "Hey, keep the hands . . ." she began. Smailes buckled his right knee and fell forward to his right, and in the same motion drew the gun and flung himself to his left onto his back, firing before he hit the ground. Two shots roared in the night and he felt a bullet smash into the earth at his left ear. Lauren pitched backward. He was winded but got to his feet and moved toward her, the gun drawn. In the darkness he could see that her throat had been torn away by his bullet. A dark lake of blood was widening under her hair. Her mouth moved noiselessly, like the mouth of a fish, and the blood in her throat bubbled quietly, with a frothing sound. Her body began convulsing, first the torso, then the legs. Her eyes were frozen behind the round lenses, terrified and dying. He moved aside to vomit.

Strong hands gripped his shoulders. "Derek, are you hit?" said Dearnley.

Smailes was still retching. "Where the *fuck* were you?" he said eventually.

"We couldn't hear nothing for the bleedin' vacuum cleaner, Derek. Just static. Then we see you come out and we know she's got a gun on you. We couldn't jump you on Huntingdon Road, she could've started shooting. Jesus, I'm sorry. This was close."

"Too fucking close, George." He looked over at Lauren's body, which was still. Standiforth was looking down at it with a pen-sized flashlight.

"She dead?" said Smailes.

"Yes, she certainly is," said Standiforth. He walked up to them, and shone the beam at Smailes. "Sorry about that," he

346

said evenly. "But well done. You were right, of course. You were right about everything. Glad you still had the gun on you. Seems you needed it. That was quite a shot, falling backwards like that."

Smailes wanted to go for his face. Dearnley was supporting him, and he was breathing in great heaves.

"Let me see your hands," ordered Standiforth. Smailes holstered the gun and held his hands out in front of him. Standiforth held the beam on them. They were steady.

"Okay, leave. Take a week. Get out into the country, the hills somewhere. Just let it work itself out of you. Don't fight it. Tonight, stop driving as soon as the shaking starts, you understand? Just stop, spend the night somewhere. Remember, stop driving when the shaking starts. We'll take care of everything here. Everything."

Dearnley and Smailes walked slowly back toward his car, the older man supporting him around his shoulders.

"Jesus, Derek, I'd no idea this was going to be so dangerous. I'd never have agreed to it . . ."

"George, you telling me the truth? You didn't know what was going on . . . ? The mike, you couldn't hear . . . ?"

"Derek, I swear. Just static. Then when you came out, I realized we had trouble. Not even any uniform backup. Standiforth had a pistol. I had nothing. God, you were nearly killed. Are you all right to drive?"

They had arrived back at the cars. Standiforth's Jaguar had been hurriedly parked, the doors flung open, the headlights plowing into the hawthorn trees. Smailes could still smell cordite, and underneath, sweet wet earth.

"Yeah, I think so." He stood away from Dearnley and felt his own weight, searching for his face in the darkness. "George, I've got to believe you."

"Derek," said Dearnley, pleading, holding up his hand and squeezing his shoulder firmly. "You can't believe this was deliberate. I'd never let one of my men . . . Look, do as he

347

says. Take a week. Take two. Just call in, tell me you're all right. You want me tell your mother you're gone? Your sister?"

"Don't do anything, George. I can take care of myself."

Twenty-two

HE FELT A STRONG SENSE of unreality as he drove back down Huntingdon Road, although he felt unnaturally calm. The streetlamps seemed unusually bright, and the note of the car engine was a soft and insistent purr. The familiar streets rose and fell. He parked and pushed open the broken door. The hall light was on. Pinned to his inner door was a note from his landlord. *What hapened here? Call me at work imediately. Les.*

Inside the wreckage of the flat he worked methodically. He pulled down a canvas bag from the top of the storage cupboard. He found his hiking boots at the bottom of the wardrobe and threw them in. Most of his clothes were on the floor. He stuffed a few handfuls into the bag. In the bathroom, he looked down at the cowboy boots in the toilet. He felt a little light-headed, and the boots looked a long way away. He packed a toilet bag. He hung his raincoat on the hook in the

349

hall and found his parka. Then he stepped over the broken furniture in the living room and was on his way again.

His sense of unreality was intensifying. As he stood at the cash machine, punching in the numbers, his hands looked miles away, detached from his body, as if he were staring down the wrong end of a telescope. He headed east out of Cambridge, toward the motorway. He lit a cigarette from the lighter in the dashboard. His hands were steady.

Someone just tried to kill you, he told himself. *But she failed, because you killed her. The first time you've fired a gun in ten years on the force and you blew her head off. Just like that.* He thought he would head north and west, take the advice, go to the Lake District for a few days. He needed to think. *Sorry about that. Well done. You were right about everything. Just static. Derek, you can't believe, I'd never let one of my men . . .*

He noticed he was driving very slowly. There were few cars on the road, but everything was overtaking him. God, he had fallen for everything, hadn't he? He should have known. Realistically, she could see nothing in him. But the sex? Was it just faked? He saw her face, rocking in the darkness above him. Then he saw his father's frown, an echoing voice. *You should think about the police, you know, in case you want to settle down.* Then Beecroft. *It's got to do with betrayal. It makes you angry somewhere, very deep down, and you need some kind of revenge, even if it goes against your grain.*

Suddenly, the shaking started. Mildly at first, and he started to pull over; then uncontrollably. There was a petrol station, and beyond, a motor inn. *Traveler's Lodge,* said a large white sign.

He parked and put his head on the wheel and wept. His arms and shoulders shook. His legs shook. He could not stop shaking, and he could not stop crying. His father, George, Lauren. He thought he might be sick again but there was nothing in his stomach.

After a long interval he climbed unsteadily out of the car and entered the lobby of the inn. The light was too bright.

Sickly music oozed from an overhead speaker. There was a large artificial plant standing by the registration counter, where a clerk in an ugly uniform greeted him with a large artificial smile. He said something to Smailes which he did not hear. He went into his wallet and found a credit card. "Room," he said. "One night."

He lay on the bed in the dark and the shaking began again. It's shock, he told himself. It's natural, you nearly got killed. At some point he thought of the white Rover and panicked. He got up and looked out the window, but there were no white Rovers in the car park. He took off his parka and tried to take off his shirt but the shirt was stuck. He realized he was still wearing the gun and shoulder holster. He took them off and threw them in a drawer. Then he opened the drawer and put the gun on the nightstand. When he took off his shirt he found the mike still taped to his chest and the battery pack clipped to his belt. He tore them off and threw them at the wall. Had they even bothered to listen? He lay down naked under the sheets, shivering, staring at the ceiling. Cars passed occasionally outside the window.

They were making love again, hungrily, he had his hand in the thick black curls, but when he looked down to kiss her, her mouth was making its dreadful noiseless movements and her throat was torn open. He woke up suddenly, terrified, a weak metallic light was pushing its way into the room. He got up heavily and showered. In the light he saw that his trousers and shoes were covered in mud. He put on jeans, boots. The inn had a restaurant. He needed coffee, food. He had survived.

It was a bright April Sunday morning and he felt an odd clarity as he accelerated up the ramp to the M1, Britain's jugular vein of steel and rubber, and pointed the car north. It had been Standiforth's plan, from the start. Both he and George had argued in favor of driving straight over there with uniformed backup and pulling her in on suspected murder. Standiforth had stood his ground. There was no evidence

351

against her in either of the murders. Bowles was officially a suicide, and Allerton's body had yet to be found. She was obviously an illegal of some sort, but which sort? He argued heatedly that unless they could trap her into some form of confession she could invoke the protection of her embassy and then God knows where they would end up. It would mean the Cousins would find out the wrong way. We need to control that briefing, he had said. And besides, he was concerned she was a double. Maybe the Cousins had been on to Gorham-Leach for years, had sent their own agent to confirm him, not trusting the British. Did anyone believe a major defense contractor would hire an engineer with a background like hers? He had argued for the remote mike and the receiver and cassette recorder in the car. They had had to call in the technical people to rig it all up. It was a Saturday, so it had taken hours. Smailes had argued angrily at first, saying that she was a killer and a spy and that they were wasting time, but eventually he had gone along with Standiforth's plan. He was quite prepared to confront her himself, and there seemed to be no undue danger. Smailes still had his weapon, Standiforth carried an automatic. George, whose gun permit was still expired, eventually deferred to Standiforth also. He had shaken his head in disbelief at first when Smailes told him about his affair with the American girl. We'll talk about this later, Sergeant, he had said.

But now Smailes was not sure the whole thing wasn't a fraud. They had known about Lauren. They must have. They let him stroke his chin and make the calls and think he had nailed her himself, so that they could send him in as point man, then hang him out to dry. *Certain arrangements have had to be made*—that had been Standiforth's line. You bet. He just didn't believe the story about the vacuum cleaner and the static. Modern electronics were better than that. And he wondered whether George wasn't part of some plot, despite his protests. He thought back over some of his strange moves, his insistence on closing the case, his acquiescence in the Fenwick business, the speed and venom with which he'd suspended him. As he thought about it, he was convinced that George would grab his forelock if the brass invoked his patriotism, particularly brass like Standiforth.

Anger had cleared his head. He drove into the Midlands and through the neat angular brick rows of the Birmingham suburbs. Men were out in their gardens, trying to turn the soil for the new planting season, as they had done for centuries. He felt oppressed by the senescence of his culture, by the earthbound race of the British, bowed beneath their leaden skies and ancient divisions. There was such determination to resist. *We need to control that briefing.* God forbid an accounting should be made.

North of Birmingham he joined the M6 and the land gave way to tamed contours of pasture and arable land. Plump sheep and placid cows rested in the mild afternoon. Electric pylons strode away toward the spires of distant churches. He had thought to turn off into the Lake District but was adrift in his thoughts and drove right past both turnings to the South Lakes and Kendal. He climbed Shap Fell and began the slow descent toward Carlisle and the border country.

He was well over the border into Scottish lowlands when he saw the petrol gauge almost empty and felt around with his finger in an empty packet of cigarettes. A sign pointed to Cormond, and Smailes turned off on a B road that soon gave way to granite bungalows and then the sandstone terraces of the dour little town. The green hillsides swept down into the town itself, punctuated with sheep and patterned with dry stone walls. He passed a gray Victorian hotel on his left, the cars of the Sunday drinkers parked neatly in front, then guesthouses, a baker's shop, a café and a stationery store, which looked open. He drove through to the town square, where the war memorial stood, an iron statue of Victory, brandishing a laurel wreath like a deck quoit above the names of the fallen. He circled around and drove back down the main street and parked outside the stationery store. Next to it

353

was a sign announcing *Sandie's B and B*. He stepped out onto the street. A man in a tweed jacket and flat hat was loading a tray of seedlings into the back of a Land-Rover. A young woman pushed twins toward him, in an animated discussion with her mother.

He entered the small shop abstractedly, feeling like an alien, a refugee from a world of lawlessness and treachery. He glanced at the headlines on the ranks of Sunday newspapers on the counter. *Showdown Looms in South Atlantic,* blared the tabloids. The young woman behind the counter beamed at him. "Yes, sir?" she asked with her lovely ancestral sibilance.

He ordered his cigarettes and commented on the weather, drawn to this first genuine human contact since the blur of night and death.

"Och, it's no bad the day, but it's been awful. It really has. Are ye going far?"

"I'm not sure. I'm on holiday."

"Oh, that's nice."

He noticed her blue nylon work coat, the same color as her eyes. He felt an urge to ask if she'd talk to him, listen to his terrible story.

"I'm thinking of doing some hiking."

"Aye, well, there's plenty of hiking paths around here. Of course, it's no the Highlands."

He left the shop and stood in the street, looking back toward the statue of Victory and the sandstone turrets of the town hall that stood behind it. Somewhere there was a link between this ugly dance he had made and the implacable decency of this Scottish town. He realized he had no desire to drive further. He turned and looked at the sign for *Sandie's B and B*, and pushed open the door.

Sandie Cook was a suspicious woman in her mid-thirties with thick, fair hair, broad shoulders and broad hips. She accepted his deposit and showed him into a small room next to the bathroom on the ground floor with a single bed, a sink, a dressing table and chair and a portrait of the Monarch of the Glen on the flowered wallpaper. She apologized for the lack of towels. She had not expected guests so early in the season.

That night Smailes strolled down to the Black Bull in the town square, which sold good beer and better whiskey. From the public telephone out by the men's toilet he put in a call to Iain Mack.

Iain listened intently as Smailes tried to give him a condensed version of what had happened since they had last met in Cambridge. He interrupted with the occasional "No shit?" or by asking him to repeat something, but largely he just listened. When Smailes recounted the events of the previous night his tone became more urgent and he found himself stopping to take pulls on his whiskey. He found the visual images still vivid and had difficulty explaining everything in order. Iain had him go back over the chronology, from the death of Gorham-Leach to the call to the FBI to the decision to set up Lauren and their final, terrifying drive to Girton village and the golf-course car park.

"Derek, are you telling me this bitch was about to shoot you and Dearnley and the other guy are nowhere?"

"Yeah."

"I don't believe it. Go on."

Smailes had difficulty with the final act and his voice actually broke as he described the bullet hitting the dirt two inches from his ear and the dreadful gurgling sound from Lauren's throat as her life expired.

There was a silence from the other end of the line, then Iain said, "Where did you say you are?"

"Cormond. Just over the border. Sandie's B and B."

"I'm coming, okay? I'll get off early Thursday, take the train, you can get me in Carlisle or somewhere, right?"

"Right, but . . ."

"No buts. I'm coming. Look, will you be okay this week on your own?"

355

"Yeah, I'm just shaken up. I'll do some hiking, some think-ing. Iain, you know what bothers me most?"

"Yeah, that Dearnley and this bloke from MI5 just wanted you and her to shoot it out, no witnesses, right?"

"It sounds like that to you too?"

"I don't know. I need to think about it too. I'll call you tomorrow with the time of the train. Get some rest."

"Sure. And, Iain?"

"Yeah?"

"Thanks."

The weather stayed clear for the next several days and Smailes spent long hours tramping over low moors and through isolated glens. All he saw were sheep and crows and the occasional farm building. Once, miles from any road, he came across a battered Land-Rover and a man who must have been in his seventies slowly repairing a collapsed section of dry stone wall. The wind was high and raw and Smailes had to shout his greeting. The man looked up calmly and nodded. "Isn't it lonely out here?" yelled Smailes. "Och, when you've got your work ye dinna notice," the man replied.

Another time he climbed through a stile into a wide field to find himself confronted by a bizarre long-haired animal which looked like an evil-tempered Highland cow with curly horns. The beast snorted and made a run at him and Smailes had to hurry to get back through the stile. He descended past the side of the field and down a track to a low farm building where brightly colored pennants flapped from long poles in the breeze. A stocky young man, who did not look like a native, stood outside the door wearing Wellington boots, an oilskin and a woolen hat. He was holding a large cabbage. Smailes greeted him and asked about the animal that had chased him.

"Oh, that's Angus the yak," he said in a distinct southern English accent. He had a flat, wind-reddened face and wiry ginger hair.

"Yak?"

"Yes, he was given to the Tibetan center up the road, but he's too bad-tempered to stay on the land. We're trying to find a safari park to take him. Is that where you're staying?"

"No, I didn't know it was there. What is it?"

"It's a Tibetan Buddhist meditation center. It was started by some lamas a few years back. We used to live there ourselves, until we found this place."

Smailes wanted to ask how they made a living, but the question seemed impolite.

"It's open to visitors, you know, if you want to visit. Walk down to the road, then turn right. About two miles," the young man said.

"Thanks," said Smailes. He had seen a documentary about Tibetan lamas on television some years back. All he remembered was some bloke with hair like a doormat sitting in a cave tooting on a human thigh bone like a clarinet. It was a measure of his peculiar state of mind that he even considered stopping in, finding out what went on. But he turned left at the road and began the long hike back to Cormond.

He felt his entire career was moot. If it was true that Dearnley and Standiforth had collaborated in a plan that would have eliminated both him and Lauren, it made a mockery of all his notions of service and duty. There was no way he could prove it, of course, and a big part of him wanted to believe George's protestations, despite the peculiarities of his behavior. But the very possibility that it might be true made it impossible for him to continue serving George Dearnley and the Cambridge CID.

He was less sure where to go with his knowledge. In the morning of his second day he had driven to Dumfries, where he took out a whole shelf of books from the public library on espionage and the British security services. He found he no longer had any impediment to his interest or concentration. And it was all there, everything Iain had warned him of. The shocking record of incompetence, the persistent security lapses, the pathological fear of the Americans, the determination to lie and conceal. In the evenings he would lie on his bed and read one account after another, drinking whiskey slowly and trying to fathom his experience. His judgment was that of an outsider, but it seemed to him that Gorham-Leach had to be the most damaging Soviet spy since Philby, possibly of all time. He knew Standiforth and Dearnley between them would come up with some cover about the suicide and the deaths of Lauren Greenwald and Giles Allerton. There would be few people who would learn the truth of Gorham-Leach's career, maybe not even the Prime Minister herself. Unless Smailes blew the whistle. What should he do? Go to the press with his outrageous story? Why should they believe him? And what would be his motive? To precipitate another scandal? To send the press baying for resignations? Yet should there not be some accounting? he asked himself. Wasn't it his duty to Simon Bowles to ensure it?

His mind was filled with these questions during the long daytime hikes and during the nights as he lay reading in his room. His landlady had warmed up to him a little, and even invited him to have dinner one night with her family. There was no one else staying at the guesthouse, and she seemed to welcome the company. She had two girls aged six and nine, and eating with them made Smailes think of Tracy and wonder whether anyone had told Yvonne he was away. Sandie Cook told him about her life in Cormond, where she had grown up. Work was scarce and her husband was away most of the year working on the oil platforms in the North Sea. The guesthouse had been her idea after he had started working there two years ago. Smailes felt able to relax with this good-natured woman, but was not inclined to tell her the real reason for his stay in Cormond. He told her that his friend Iain was coming to stay Thursday and they would leave together on Sunday.

He had spells in the evenings when he felt shaky and unnerved, but he seemed to be able to medicate himself with whiskey and slept well. He suspected that whoever Lauren's accomplices had been were now recalled, that Moscow too would want to limit repercussions, that his life was not in danger. The sharpest pain was when he thought of Dearnley's possible betrayal, more shocking even than his father's. He knew he could not work with him again.

Iain arrived on Thursday evening and they spent hours in the Black Bull, where Smailes rehearsed the whole story from his incipient doubts in the Bowles inquiry to the affair with Lauren and the discovery at the Wentworth house in Rickmansworth. The rest of the events had moved so fast, but Smailes was able to recount them now with more detachment. He also felt a certain bravado in the telling, which his friend was quick to detect.

"Well, you seem okay," said Iain.

"I suppose so," said Smailes.

Iain, of course, loved the whole thing. After the revelations about Blunt, the Mole at the Palace, the notion that Britain's top military scientist, a Nobel laureate, was also a Soviet agent made him simply exultant. He knew it would make a fabulous news story, and told Smailes he could make a fortune if he sold the piece to one of the Sundays. In fact, Mack could write it for him and they would both clean up. He braked his enthusiasm when he saw Smailes's face cloud.

"You thinking of sitting on this, going back to work at CID?" he asked.

"No, I'm not going back to CID. But I don't know if I want to blow the whistle. I don't want to just act out of revenge."

"Why not? Don't you deserve it after what those two tried to do to you?"

Smailes had to concede that he was still undecided about whether Standiforth had prior knowledge of Lauren's complicity, or had deliberately tried to have him killed. He also needed to believe that Dearnley, his mentor, had not set him up to be sacrificed. When pressed, Iain agreed that he thought it unlikely too. After all, the British invented cricket, he said.

359

That's why they were in so much trouble in the modern world.

"So what will you do?" asked Iain.

"Sit on my hands and make them sweat," said Smailes.

For the next two days the two men hiked for miles, against Iain's protests, and talked again and again of the extraordinary events that Smailes had witnessed.

"You know, it's too bad that Bowles's Cambridge Theorem will never be published," said Mack the following day as they hiked down a lane east of Cormond. "He's the one who deserves all the credit after all. If it were not for him, Gorham-Leach would have passed into quiet retirement and would never have been blown. And the record stands that he killed himself in some neurotic fit. It seems unfair. You going to tell the sister?"

"I don't think so. Not if they don't want me to," said Smailes, surprised at his own words. "But at least the Kennedy Theorem has a chance of being published. There ought to be something on record of his work."

On Friday he called Gloria and told her he would be in George's office at nine on Monday. She sounded cool and professional and Smailes wondered what the story was in Cambridge about his whereabouts.

On Saturday night Smailes had to drive over to Dumfries to return the books to the bin outside the library, and the two men stayed in town for dinner and drinks. Iain wanted to know Smailes's next move and he said he thought he might look for work in London. They agreed that he could stay at Iain's place in Highgate until he got fixed up.

"And what's the move?" asked Mack.

"Living death." Smailes grimaced. "Private security. What else can I do?" said Smailes, counting out bank notes for the dinner check. The two men were walking slowly out to the car park when Smailes found his keys missing.

"Hold on, Iain. Must've left them on the table," said Smailes, leaving Mack standing in the night. The keys were

indeed on the table, which the busboy had just begun clearing. He handed them to Smailes with a smile, and it was then
the detective saw the figure sitting over in the corner, reading
a paperback: a burly, red-haired man Smailes recognized in-
stantly, although he could not place the face. He thought at
first it might be the homesteader with the yak he had run into
earlier in the week, but that guy had had curly hair, he was
sure, whereas this man's hair was thick, red and short. He
shook his head in frustration as he joined Iain again at the car.

"What's up?" asked Iain, seeing his face.

"Saw someone I recognize. Can't place the face. Frustrating," said Smailes. They drove back to Cormond.

He felt there was only one task left before the drive south
the next day, and that was to write his resignation. He would
type it when he got to the office, but he wanted to get the
wording right. George would know anyway. He wanted others who would see it to wonder, if only to themselves.

He sat at the small dressing table and poured a finger of
scotch into the small plastic beaker he had been using to rinse
his teeth. As he reached across to the nightstand for his notepad, there was a tap on the door.

"Yeah, Iain," he said.

"It's no Iain," said a woman's voice quietly. "It's Sandie."

Smailes looked puzzled, and thought for a second. Did she
think they would try to leave without paying? Or perhaps
there was a phone message. Maybe Yvonne had tracked him
down, or his mother.

"Come in."

"I'm sorry to disturb you," she said as she stood in the
opening of the doorway. She seemed anxious. She was wearing a dark woolen skirt, a yellow blouse, slippers. Her hair
was drawn back from her broad face in a ponytail.

Smailes stayed seated at the dressing table. "Oh, that's
okay, Sandie. I was going to be up for a while longer. What's
up?"

"Are you away the morn, like you said? It's just, I have to

361

speak to the butcher about the week, you know, the meat order . . ."

The detective smiled to himself at his own suspiciousness.

"Yes, that's right. Back to work, you know. We thought we'd leave after breakfast, settle up then." Then the implausibility of her pretext struck him. Talk to the butcher, at ten-thirty on a Saturday night? Maybe she was checking up on him after all.

Sandie's eyes had scanned the room and had come to rest on his bottle of whiskey. "It's good taste you have, in your whiskey."

Smailes smiled. "Would you like a drop? There's another glass here somewhere," he said, getting up and moving toward the sink, where a second beaker stood sheathed in plastic.

"Well, I don't mind a wee one," she said to his back. He could hear the door close and the slight sigh of the springs as she sat on the edge of the bed. He cocked his head slightly and raised his eyebrows as he uncased the plastic cup, still facing away from her. Was this what he thought it was? With the kids upstairs?

He poured her a couple of fingers of whiskey and held it up. "Water?"

"No, not with whiskey this good." She took the glass from him and took a long sip, swallowing slowly.

He leaned back and wondered what to say. He looked from her face to her broad-fingered hands cradling the plastic cup, the nail tips white and pointed.

They both began speaking at the same time. Smailes was trying to say something like "Well, I've enjoyed my stay," but pulled up immediately. Sandie had said something about a woman.

"Sorry, what?" he said.

"Was it a woman?" she repeated. "Why you had to come away? It's no the time of year for a hiking holiday, and that's the truth."

362

"Yes, it was," he told her, without strategy.

"Well, if she's no mind to look after what she has, she doesna deserve it," she said forcefully, as if she had given the matter some thought.

"She's dead," said Smailes.

Sandie Cook looked at him with wide eyes and then finished her whiskey in one draft. "Oh, I'm awfully sorry. I have no business here bothering you." She set the glass down on the nightstand and seemed about to rise.

"It's okay, she deserves to be," said Smailes. He was surprised at how calm he felt speaking the words, and how sure he felt of what he should do next. Sandie looked a little alarmed. "It's okay," he told her again, and reached out to place his hand on hers. Then he sat down next to her on the bed, and looking into her large, bewildered eyes, kissed her softly on the mouth. Her eyes closed and she responded gently, running her hand inside his collar and resting it on his neck.

"Oh, Derek, I'm so sorry," she whispered to him, and he kept repeating, "It's okay," as he began unbuttoning the yellow blouse and they kissed again.

"What about the kids?" he asked as she rose and put out the light, and he heard the rustle of the lining of her skirt as she slid it to the floor.

"Fast asleep," she said, coming to him naked, her flesh warm and soft, her breath quickening.

He felt enormous desire for her, her body so different from Lauren's, the flat expanses, the small breasts, the hair as thick as straw, smelling like soap. He felt grateful for her kindness, her willingness to trust him, a stranger. But he thought of the last time he had made love, at his sister's house, and felt a wave of fear and resentment, and as he knelt in front of her and she arched to meet him, he felt himself go limp, and lowered his head to her chest in defeat.

Sandie said nothing, but pushed him onto his back, kneeling astride him and reaching up to release the band holding

363

back her hair. Then she lowered the thick mane until it draped across his belly. Slowly, she moved her head back and forth, her hair brushing across him, lower and lower. He was shocked by the pleasure and clenched his fists. He endured her unfamiliar caress as long as he could, which was not long. The rest of their lovemaking proceeded without obstacle.

"So when did you decide to try this little gambit?" he asked later. They were drinking more whiskey and Smailes had lit a cigarette. In the glow of the tip he saw for a moment her broad, flat face with its band of freckles, the small, conical breasts hanging away from her body as she held herself upright on an elbow.

"It wasna my idea, fella. I was thinking about the butcher." Then she laughed softly to herself. "I dunno. A few days ago, I suppose. You see, my Alec, he doesna even come home much anymore. Three weeks on, one week off, supposedly, but he and his mates are away to Edinburgh or Perth for three, four nights after they get paid. I pretend I dinna know what he's up to, but all the money has gone to his head. He's tired of us down here, and we both know it. You wait, soon he'll no be comin' home at all.

"So it gets lonely. I've been here my whole life. I've thought about it, you know. We get traveling salesmen comin' through, and they're always making suggestions.

"But you." She ran her fingers through his hair, then cupped his chin. "I could see you were hurtin' and I thought you had maybe left your wife or something. You seemed to need a wee bit of affection." That made him laugh. "This is the first time for me. I canna think why I've waited so long."

Later, when she was getting dressed, she asked him, "Was it your wife who died?"

"No, I'm divorced. Someone I met."

"Derek," she asked just before she left, "are you with the police?"

"Used to be. How'd you know?"

"Well, you have a pistol and a holster in your bag and I

364

couldna think you were a criminal. I thought maybe you were a cop or a spy or something."

He laughed. "You've been looking through my things? I should report you to the tourist board."

"Aye, that's for sure," she said, kissing him again.

They maintained a friendly politeness as Sandie served them an unhurried breakfast the next day. She caught his eye on a couple of occasions, and smiled. He and Iain wrote her separate checks as they stood in the narrow hallway, their bags at their feet. Sandie held out her hand to Iain, and shook it firmly. Then she held out her hand to Smailes, and when he took it, she stepped toward him and kissed him deliberately, and lovingly, on the mouth. She stepped back and looked him in the eye. "Mind you come back now," she said.

As they drove out of the town, Iain Mack looked at him with incredulity and indignation.

"You sneaky, bloody bastard," he said.

Smailes grinned and kept his eyes on the road.

Twenty-three

HE WAS NOT SURE what to expect at the flat. Les had probably fixed the front door, but he thought he might have to grab whatever spare clothes he could and stay with his mother until the place was straightened out.

He dropped Iain at the station and drove home. The front door was fixed all right, and he bent down to pick up his post and a week's worth of the *Cambridge Evening News*. The inner door had been replaced entirely, although his key still fit the lock. The flat itself was restored. The furniture had been righted and the broken pieces replaced. The lounger had been supplanted by a new black vinyl armchair. There was a new mattress and dresser, and all his clothes and possessions had been stowed away. Even the cowboy boots stood beside the wardrobe. He wondered if they were still wearable.

It had to be Standiforth's work. Les Howarth would not have laid out a penny, and he couldn't imagine the project originating at the Cambridge station. He felt pleased. It was the least MI5 could do for him after all.

He sat down in the kitchen and began to look through the post and the newspapers. Under the headline *Student Lovers Found Murdered*, the Monday edition led with the discovery by a greenskeeper of two bodies near a drainage ditch close to the Girton Golf Course. They had been identified as students from St. Margaret's College, Giles Allerton and an American girlfriend, Lauren Greenwald. The story mentioned that Allerton had been missing for two days, but the woman had disappeared only hours before her body was discovered. Allerton's car had been found abandoned in a multistory car park in Huntingdon. Cambridge police speculated that the two friends had been murdered by the same person. No doubt George would create the ballistics evidence to back that up, Smailes said to himself.

Smailes thought anxiously again of Lauren and had begun reading the story of Gorham-Leach's suicide on the first inside page when the identity of the diner in the Dumfries restaurant suddenly struck him. It was bloody Rob Roy, of course, the so-called graduate student who had shared Lauren's digs. Smailes would swear to it, despite the severity of the barber job that had removed all his hair. What the hell was he doing in a Dumfries restaurant with Derek Smailes and Iain Mack? Not just eating dinner, that was for sure. He was tailing them, which made him a bit more than a graduate student, didn't it? Which meant that he also had tabs on Lauren Greenwald in all likelihood. Smailes's mind worked rapidly through the implications, and he shook his head in disbelief.

"Paul Beecroft, of course," he said at first. Then, moments later, "No, Ivor Davies. Ivor bloody Furse-Davies," the connections in his memory finally meshing.

There was nothing he could do to confirm his suspicions at that hour, so he turned again to the newspaper account, a cold cynicism in his heart. He would start work first thing in

367

the morning, and try to get into Standiforth's office by afternoon.

Gorham-Leach's body had been discovered on Monday morning by his housekeeper, but evidence suggested he had been dead for at least a day. White powder found in a vial near the body had been sent away for analysis. There was no note. The story quoted an unnamed family spokesman who revealed that Gorham-Leach had recently been diagnosed with inoperable pancreatic cancer and had only months to live. Very neat, Smailes thought to himself. The accompanying obituary was a fulsome tribute to Cambridge's most illustrious scientist. The senior tutor of St. Margaret's College, Dr. Nigel Hawken, described his colleague's death as "an inestimable loss to science and to scholarship."

Follow-up stories on the double murder throughout the week were relegated to inside pages, since the Falklands crisis had pushed everything else off the front page. Continuing inquiries revealed no new evidence. Chief Superintendent George Dearnley, head of Cambridge CID, had taken personal charge of the case and vowed to bring the perpetrator of the brutal killings to justice. But as yet the police had neither motive nor suspects in their investigation. In the Friday edition, Smailes found a short notice that made him smile despite his mood. Dr. Nigel Hawken, senior tutor of St. Margaret's College since 1964, had announced his retirement, effective at the end of the academic year. St. Margaret's College Council had announced that Dr. Charles Poole, a professor of botany currently on sabbatical, would take his place. The front-page headline that day read: *Marines Retake South Georgia.* And just to reinforce Smailes's anger and dismay, the jingoistic tag line above it read: *Blunder by Argy Captain Lets Lads In.*

Before going to bed, he could not prevent himself from walking to his front window and craning his neck up and down the street. There were no white Rovers or Post Office vans that he could see.

368

He was up early and at Mick Fowler's garage not long after it opened at eight. Fowler spotted him from the far end of the showroom and waddled toward him.

"Derek! What a nice surprise. How've you been? Say, no hard feelings, okay?" he said unctuously, advancing in his cloud of cologne, grabbing his elbow and pumping his hand. "What can I do for you?"

Smailes pointed to the Allegro parked out front. "Find me the bug in that, will you, Mick? Those guys I told you about must've planted something in it. That's how they tailed me."

Mick's face broke into a sly grin and he walked to the door that led from the showroom to the shop.

"Malc! Come in here," he yelled, and walked back to Smailes, looking thoughtful.

"Bygones are bygones, right, Del?"

"Right, Mick."

Malc turned out to be a witless-looking teenager in grease-stiffened overalls with long, oily hair and a ripe boil high on his left cheekbone. Fowler told him conspiratorially to hoist up the detective's car and find the listening device that was planted on it. Malc looked puzzled but took the detective's keys anyway. Fowler led Smailes back toward the offices.

"So what's the caper? You can tell old Mick. Personal interest, you see, Derek. You gotta believe I wouldn't never have rented the motor if I knew they was crooks."

"I believe you, Mick. But sorry, I can't talk, not on this one."

"Too bad. Coffee, Derek? I think maybe Elsie has a doughnut."

"Thanks, Mick, I've eaten. Like to borrow an office and a telephone, though, if I can."

"No problema," said Fowler suavely. "In here."

Smailes sat down at a metal desk in a small dirty office with a girlie calendar on the wall. On the desk were magazines representing the breadth of Fowler's interests—*Penthouse*, *Classic Car* and *Scrap Age*. He waited until his watch said eight

369

thirty-five, then called the reference library. You were allowed three questions on the phone, and the librarian answered his cheerfully. The answers were confirmation. He was hardly surprised.

He wandered out into the showroom, where Fowler was showing off one his Bentleys to a young, sharply dressed West Indian, who was probably a crook if he could afford one of Fowler's restored vehicles. Malc reappeared from the shop and caught Fowler's eye with a shrug. The three men moved into Fowler's office.

"Nuffink," said Malc.

"What?" asked Fowler.

"Don't find nuffink. Done the engine, the whole chassis, back to front. Nuffink. Could start tearing into them door panels, if you like."

Fowler raised his eyebrows at Smailes, who shook his head. "Thanks anyway," said Smailes.

"Bring the motor round front, Malc," said Fowler, and the kid disappeared.

"Sorry, Derek. He's good, mind you."

"It's okay. You get that Rover back yet?"

"Not yet. It's got another few days on the deposit, I think," said Fowler, worried. He'd obviously been thinking. "I'm not going to get it back, am I? Give me a break, Derek."

"Yeah, you'll get it back, my guess. Ditched somewhere," said Smailes. "Listen, Mick, when they picked it up, the third guy drove away later, from around back, right?"

"Like I said," said Fowler, distracted. He was thinking about the Rover, his investment in it. Malc parked the Allegro out front and honked. Smailes wiped off the wheel with his handkerchief and headed back to Cambridge.

He had half expected Standiforth to be sitting there with George when he arrived at the office that morning, and he was. His mood had solidified into a cold anger, and he felt no need to be polite.

370

"What's he doing here?" he asked, not looking at Standiforth.

"Roger has one or two things to ask you, that's all, Derek. How are you feeling?"

"Fine. Save me the trip to town anyway." He handed George an envelope.

"What's this?"

"My resignation."

"Derek, I had hoped it wouldn't come to this. You don't still think that Roger and I . . ."

"It's nothing to do with that, George. I gave this a lot of thought. It's time to call it quits. I never fitted in here, you know that. No hard feelings." He hoped George noticed the sarcasm in his voice.

George put the envelope on the desk in front of him and shook his jowls at it slowly. "Roger?" he said.

Standiforth was watching him calmly. "Detective Sergeant Smailes, I hope you are rested. I asked the chief superintendent whether I could be here today for a number of reasons. First, I want to thank you for the extraordinary work you have done in helping solve this case. I deeply regret that you were exposed to any danger. I take full responsibility for that, and I apologize to you most sincerely. As soon as I knew we had no reception over the remote we should have come straight in behind you. But I delayed, and then it was too late. I am only thankful that your agility and skill have saved my conscience from a lifetime of discomfort."

"Fuck you, Roger," said Smailes icily. Dearnley actually flinched in his seat.

"Derek . . ." he began.

"Shut up, George. I don't have to listen to this crap. Like an idiot, I was inclined to believe you, and him. That was until I ran into Rob Roy in the restaurant in Dumfries. That made me do my thinking all over again."

"Who?" asked Dearnley.

"Rob Roy," said Smailes. "Roger knows who I mean.

371

Where'd you put the bug, Roger? Had my mechanic go over the car front to back this morning, couldn't find it. There's got to be one. How else could you trace me to Scotland?"

Dearnley looked completely baffled. Standiforth drew on his cigarette and put it out slowly in George's heavy glass ashtray.

"You remove the ashtray drawer and clip it to the steering column, down inside. Very hard to find," he said eventually.

"Yes, well, I suppose Malc would have found it sooner or later. George, don't tell me you don't know about all this. I was set up from the start, wasn't I? You knew Gorham-Leach's confession was being taped, right? Roger must've told you he was already blown, I suppose. And you knew about Lauren, Davies, the theft of the file, the whole ball of wax."

Here Standiforth interceded. "No. I told the chief superintendent that we already had the evidence on Gorham-Leach, I concede. But he knew nothing about the girl or the other surveillance operations. The botch of the arrest was a tragic accident, as I explained to you. I take full responsibility."

"You really think I'm fucking stupid, don't you, Roger? Give me a break. When I ran into Rob Roy and I recognized him from Lauren's digs, I worked backward through the whole thing. So Lauren was blown and you had her under surveillance, okay? So if Lauren is blown, that means Gorham-Leach is blown too. Boy, I was slow. The night I came back from Rickmansworth, George tells me you've already got people in place watching him. They'd been there for months, right? Yet I fell for the line that Hawken's buddies down the street had been turfed out in the middle of the night. Which one did you get first, Roger? G-L, I'll bet, because Rob Roy had been down to the Public Record Office last year, combing the same records Bowles eventually found. Said he was doing a book on Jews of Britain, right? Took him weeks to find the record. Boy, I'll bet it sent you all running for the crapper when you found out who he really was. What was it, the sudden return from retirement that alerted you, or did you feel it was finally time to backtrack Hawken's work, Roger? You knew all about him too, I would guess. That's why he was put out to pasture here in the first place, his unreliability, I'll bet. I'm surprised our burly historian didn't rip out the relevant page at the PRO, but you would never have guessed that Bowles would get there too, would you?

"So you've got Lauren and you've got Gorham-Leach and you're able to intercept his drops and eviscerate whatever he's sending back home. You know she's been sent to cover him because he's worried about Bowles. At first I think that logically you've got Hawken, which means Beecroft, policing Bowles so he doesn't get too close and screw up your operation, because the stakes have gotten really high, haven't they? You've got one of the most important Soviet agents of all time under surveillance, and neither he nor Moscow knows it. Maybe you can even make up for some of the damage he's done, burn his whole network. And it keeps getting juicier. You get these Sorge boys coming through, and you can watch them in action. My guess is, you knew they were on their way from your interception of his drops. So you sit on your hands and give your ports and airports system a field test, see if they can handle big-time illegals, a real landing. I bet heads are going to roll at Prestwick, right, Roger? But it didn't matter that you lost them. You knew where they were heading, that they were Lauren's backup. You had them tailed from the time they hit Cambridge, I would guess. You followed them to Fowler's garage anyway. There never were three of them, were there? Mick saw the two of them leave in the Rover, then a third party follow on in five minutes. Watchers, right?

"But then I realize that Hawken's just too difficult and conceited to use in this operation. You've finally uncovered the Fifth Man under his nose and you've got a young kid hot on the same trail, and all the time Hawken is smugly pronouncing the files closed and pursuing his fancy boys. Gorham-Leach tossed me the bone of Hawken's intelligence work for

373

the same reason he tossed it to Bowles—to try to convince us that there really was nothing left in the cupboard, because Hawken believed it so passionately. My guess is that you took him out of the loop entirely, Roger. He was a complete liability by then anyway, wasn't he?"

Standiforth avoided Smailes's eyes. He was pushing ash around in the big glass ashtray with the tip of a cigarette.

"So who was nursing Bowles? You couldn't let him trip the alarms, could you? Then I remembered G-L saying that Davies had told him of Bowles's research, whereas Davies flatly denied any knowledge of it to me. Then all that stupid business about his name back when he first got here. Furse-Davies, right? He must've been related by marriage to Aileen Furse, Philby's second wife, right? That was the origin of the bad blood between him and Hawken; the little bastard probably had him tagged him as a security risk. And the suspicious stuff about the money coming out of the blue for his next dig out in Syria, or Turkey, or wherever. British Academy, right? I found out from the library this morning that the director is a member of the same club as you, Roger. What a coincidence. Now, Davies is hardly your front-rank field agent, is he, but he would have sold his soul to get back to his ruins, wouldn't he? Not hard to bribe him with the promise of renewed funding. And it was so logical that Davies should insist on renewing the tutorial relationship with Simon Bowles, after what he had attempted. Not even Hawken thought it weird. And who would have a better excuse to snoop around his rooms when he was away than his tutor, if he should be caught?

"Of course, he had a pass key as a member of the council, and a skeleton for a commercial filing cabinet is probably standard MI5 issue, I would think. Not that he needed it when you sent him back in to get the Bletchley file, Roger. The cabinet was unlocked. But it must have been hard to get him to do it—he looked guilty as sin when I saw him the following day, although, at the time, I didn't know why. See,

I realized G-L's claim to have taken it himself was a phony, a cover, since he had no way into the room without incriminating himself, and I assumed that he was covering for Lauren, which he was, of course. Now, you weren't going to tell him you'd had the file removed yourself, were you, Roger? He had to continue to believe he'd been blown by my detective work, right? G-L and I both assumed Lauren had taken it, and I took it a step further and figured she'd used Allerton to lift it, the day he was in there with the sister. But it never sat right, and I didn't work it out properly until just this morning. Very cunning. Am I losing you, George?"

Smailes looked over at Dearnley, who was regarding him with a kind of wide-eyed bewilderment. Standiforth said nothing. Smailes stopped to light a cigarette, gathered himself, then resumed.

"My guess is Davies called you as soon as Bowles's body was found, Roger. Probably pretty upset, never knew there was any physical threat to Bowles, or I doubt he'd have signed on. But you prevailed upon him one last time, he was implicated too deeply by now, told him to get anything that might incriminate Gorham-Leach out of Bowles's files before the police got hold of it, right? Anything about Bletchley, you probably said, not realizing that Bowles had written G-L's bio elsewhere and that I'd found papers in Bowles's wallet that told me where his ideas were going. Of course, by now you've got George in your hip pocket, as a backup. Either he knew about this whole operation already or he called you right after I told him about Bowles's hobbies and you enrolled him in your little club, right? After all, where's George's career heading from the top of Cambridge CID? The Yard or the Specials, that's about it. He doesn't have the political connections to make chief constable, does he? You need to stay on the right side of men like Roger, don't you, George?"

Here Smailes swung around angrily at George Dearnley,

who made a guttural sound and tried to speak. Smailes waved him down.

"Now, the fact that Davies was an archaeologist meant he was careful with his hands, left no prints on the side of the case, or anywhere, jumpy though he must have been whenever he was over there. See, I knew all along he must've been over there: he fell for the oldest trick in the book as soon as I met him. Told him I'd seen a picture of a particular party in Bowles's room and he corrected me, when he claimed he hadn't been near the room in two years. G-L, well, he sidestepped the question perfectly, as you'd expect. I gave Davies the benefit of the doubt, which was my first big mistake. Almost as big as giving it to you, Roger.

"You see, I figure that Davies didn't realize that Bowles was on to Gorham-Leach in time to warn you. So after he was found hanged you must have figured what had happened and known that Lauren and Gorham-Leach between them had found out and killed him. Again, since you and George are in cahoots, George is instructed to close the investigation and let the coroner jump through his hoop. But you've got Rob Roy at Lauren's place, so you know I'm on the trail myself. The odds are still against my finding out, and there's a good chance Lauren or the Sorge goons will off me if I do. For some reason, you're still waiting on the big roundup. Or maybe Gorham-Leach is most valuable to you as is, still operative and thinking he's clear.

"Anyway, against the odds I find out what Bowles learned and your hand is forced. You have no alternative but to wind up the network. George must have known all of this, right, or he'd have had me scribbling away when G-L did his opera solo. So you go through the pantomime of arresting G-L and letting him do the Hermann Göring bit at the end. It's crucial that he think he's been blown by the Bowles-Smailes combo, right? Otherwise he'll know whatever he's sent home is useless. Now he knows that the Bletchley file was missing, because I told him so myself, and he assumes, like I did, that

376

Lauren had made a last attempt to neutralize Bowles's work. I bet they kept their contacts to a minimum, there's no way he can double-check. But you've still got a big problem with her. You can't make it seem she's already blown for the same reasons. So you let me do my arithmetic and come up with the inevitable. You were pretty convincing arguing for the wire, Roger. Maybe she's an illegal, but what type? No one can resist playing the spy, can they? Particularly a guy like me. And all the time, you and George, or maybe just you, I'm still not sure, are planning the Shoot-out at the OK Corral: a hail of bullets, no survivors, the Leningrad boys escaping by the skin of their teeth, telling the brass back home that Conrad and his backup are wiped out but the stupid cop who discovered them bought his too. Neat, eh? And I might have swallowed the whole thing, had I not seen our man Rob at the restaurant. He must've bugged the car one night when I was at Lauren's. There were enough of those. Why did you tail me, Roger? Afraid I'd meet with the Fleet Street fellas, sell my tale? Must've given you the shits when Iain showed up, with his background. I'd decided against that, until this morning, when I finally put it all together. Because either you explain pretty good, Roger, or I'm straight out of here down to Fleet Street. Don't believe I wouldn't do it."

George Dearnley had grown progressively more slack-jawed and defeated by Smailes's account. He had loosened his tie and was sitting well back from his desk, staring first at Standiforth, then at Smailes. He broke the silence.

"For Christ's sake, Roger. You've got to tell him or . . ."

Standiforth held up his hand and waved a freshly lit cigarette. "You're a very bright man, Mr. Smailes," he said eventually. "Yes, I owe you an explanation, I suppose, although you have most of it anyway. I suppose I owe the chief superintendent an explanation as well." He let out a long, theatrical sigh. "Well, I'll have to tell you the truth, much as it goes against my grain.

"First, I must stress that you have reached the wrong conclusions about Superintendent Dearnley's involvement. The first time I ever spoke with him was truthfully on the evening you transcribed Bowles's typewriter ribbon. He had, as you guessed, informed Special Branch when you first told him what you knew about Simon Bowles. Routine in any investigation involving national security, no matter how remotely. Special Branch had routinely informed me, although I already knew about Bowles's death, you are quite correct, from Ivor Davies. The message that was relayed through Special Branch was simply to treat Bowles's death as a routine suicide and let the coroner reach the obvious verdict. Nothing more. The chief superintendent was not told anything further, but I'm sure he assumed, correctly, that the security services knew all about Bowles's research. But it was not obvious to assume that Bowles had therefore been murdered, which I of course suspected. We try to avoid asking our senior policemen directly to suborn the judicial process, you may be surprised to hear.

"When I eventually came up to Cambridge, I had to inform him about our surveillance of Gorham-Leach, of course, which understandably offended him. I was not able to tell him about the full extent of our operation, for obvious reasons."

Standiforth did not look around at Dearnley during his account, and Smailes noticed that George's color was rising. By this time, Standiforth was chain-smoking, and there was a pause while he lit another cigarette.

"Second, you're wrong with the order of our discoveries. We had the girl first. Completely unexpectedly. Our station chief in Vienna had a tape cassette delivered anonymously to his home in the autumn of last year. Heavily accented English, giving the background on an agent to be infiltrated into England within the next three months. American, female, CP family background. And the destination—Cambridge. It was the crucial clue that led us to her when she enrolled at St. Margaret's. Why the tip? No idea, except my guess would be that with all the musical chairs at the Kremlin, the people at Yasyenevo, the KGB First Directorate, are fighting over turf. One section boss trying to torpedo another's operation is the likely explanation. Not that he could have known whom Lauren Greenwald was being sent to cover.

"Yes, it was puzzling when we found her admission had been encouraged by Gorham-Leach. He was a very well-known and trusted man. His background had been checked a dozen times at least. But we had to check again. The only real possibility was that he *wasn't* Gorham-Leach, wasn't it? Peter Raffles, your Rob Roy, Officer, eventually found the record in the PRO, and it all fell into place, unfortunately. Your description was a little colorful, but yes, it did cause consternation when we realized how he had eluded us. I couldn't blame Hawken directly. I've expected very little from him over the years, as you surmised.

"The rest of your construction is fairly accurate, except for one further point. I think you said we 'eviscerated' Gorham-Leach's intelligence. 'Adulterated' would be a better word. We quickly discovered the drop—less than a mile from his house—and found we had twenty-four hours before it was serviced. So since last autumn we have had two senior theoretical physicists from Oxford writing alternative material—I don't understand entirely, but the principle is that the physical findings they constructed were plausible but fundamentally flawed. That has been the real value of this operation, Officer. I don't know what you understood from what Gorham-Leach revealed before his death, but his current research represents the most important military discovery since atomic fission. Billions and billions will be spent on it in the next twenty years, on both sides of the Iron Curtain. It all sounds like science fiction to me, but it's to do with lasers, defensive shields against nuclear missiles, the implications of which should be obvious.

"So, yes, Gorham-Leach had been tremendously damaging during his secret career. But he might finally have been of

379

some use to us. I always thought it was too simple, you know, that there was a fifth spy still at Cambridge. I was wrong."

Here Standiforth paused to adjust an onyx cuff link and to pick a thread from his trouser leg. He resumed slowly.

"Well, as for Mr. Bowles. Yes, you have that right. Ivor Davies was a little reluctant at first, particularly in view of whom his aunt had married and the embarrassment it had caused him professionally, but as you guessed he overcame his scruples when I told him I thought we could lean on the British Academy for new research funds. It wasn't the best of arrangements, but in such an odd place as Cambridge, you work with what you have, I'm afraid. I'm surprised he did as well as it seems he did during your interrogation. Of course, I would never have sent him back into Bowles's room had I not known you'd already interviewed him, and he really did remonstrate quite fiercely. But I had to obviate the possibility of some CID detective trying to pursue an investigation of those persons Simon Bowles had been researching. Of course, we couldn't get it all, so I told Ivor to just take anything about Bletchley, which was a bit of a shot in the dark, I concede. It seems it missed. I was a little puzzled when Gorham-Leach said *he'd* taken it, of course, but that's now all explained. But then you never really suspected Davies, did you? You got sidetracked by this Hawken and Fenwick business. They've both finally gotten the heave-ho, if you didn't know.

"Indeed, it did seem likely Bowles was murdered, although hardly incontrovertible. I didn't really work it out until you did, until after we'd heard Gorham-Leach's rather ingenious story. Then it seemed clear that the girl had seen what you discovered, that Bowles had in fact worked the whole thing out. And I must concede, I was prepared to let her get away, Mr. Smailes. That was the sole reason for my fussiness, you see, messing about with microphones and the like. And I assure you, the superintendent knew only that we had Gorham-Leach. We've had his telephone wired for months—his confession is all on tape, as you suspect."

380

Standiforth's explanation had begun to placate Smailes, but there was one crucial aspect that he still needed to clarify.

"Obvious reasons, Roger. You said you couldn't tell George the full scope of your Cambridge operations for obvious reasons. What were they, please?" he asked.

"Really, Mr. Smailes. If I had told the chief superintendent about the girl, then it would have been clear she was involved in both Bowles's death and the disappearance of Allerton. I knew he was already a little uneasy about the inquest business, and I could not expect that he would allow me to let a double murderer escape. At least, not without an enormous fuss. Please don't believe that of him. But I had to let her go, you see, to preserve the viability of our work for the past year. I don't regret it, only that my plan went so badly wrong. I didn't want you endangered, Detective Sergeant—I already had other plans for you. It was almost a calamity, as you know, except in one crucial aspect it was a complete success. Our friends from Leningrad will escape with the right story—that Gorham-Leach was blown by the two of you, as you so aptly put it, and not any earlier. So you see, I really am indebted to you. And yes, I had to protect myself from your divulging your knowledge to any inappropriate sources, I concede. Peter watched you as best he could in Cormond, but it turns out you could be trusted. Now, I have some questions . . ."

At this point Dearnley could no longer contain himself. His color had returned to normal, and he interrupted with a cold venom. "You bastard. That's the last time I cooperate with any of you. I don't care what happens. You play me for an idiot, you risk my men, you throw the law down the toilet. You . . ." Words failed him and he leaned back in his chair with a gesture of disgust. A distended vein in his temple was throbbing.

Standiforth gave a nervous smile. "You see, Detective Smailes. Obvious reasons. Now, I have a question for you. Can you still be trusted? I need to know."

"Roger, you have a bloody nerve talking about trust," Smailes said with difficulty.

There was a long pause, and then Dearnley, with icy control, added, "I agree, Derek. A right bloody nerve."

The silence extended as Smailes sought for a reply. He looked hard at Standiforth. "This is a tough one for me, Roger. I can see you do unpleasant and dangerous work, it's probably necessary, and maybe the fewer that know, the better your chances. But the way you've manipulated everyone throughout this whole business is downright criminal. You would have told me nothing more, right, unless I'd guessed it?"

"Absolutely. I would have told neither of you any more," said Standiforth, stone-faced. "It's a bigger view, that's all, Mr. Smailes. You are a brave and intelligent man. I'm asking you to understand." There was a distinct appeal in Standiforth's eyes and a sudden vulnerability in his voice. Fine drops of sweat stood on his top lip.

"George?"

"It's not my business to give you advice, Derek. I owe you an apology. It's up to you," he said.

"It's a joke to ask whether I can believe you, Roger. But frankly, I just want to forget the whole business. It makes me sick. I've got nothing more to say. Period."

Standiforth relaxed visibly and could barely contain his relief. He reached for a handkerchief and wiped his face and mouth.

"I wasn't sure, but I thought I could count on you. Which brings up another topic I want to broach with you. Your resignation actually gives me some encouragement. Frankly, Mr. Smailes, I have been most impressed by your abilities. You are a simply superb investigator. I want to offer you a job. It so happens that protection of our diplomatic missions has recently become one of our major responsibilities, and we particularly need to strengthen our security at the UN Mission in New York. Bloody place has become a Third World country club, an espionage free-for-all. I can offer you the number two job with our office there. Of course, there would be training here in England first. Please think about it. No doubt, you have the typical view of our service, that it's manned by overprivileged and incompetent people who all went to the same schools. Well, perhaps that used to be the case, but times have changed. You wouldn't be the first recruit from a provincial police force. Of course, it's civil service pay, but there's a special living allowance for New York, which is quite necessary, I understand." Standiforth's figure was approximately double Smailes's current salary.

"Please take time to consider my offer. I'm interested to know your initial response, however."

"You're buying me off."

"Not at all. We desperately need men like you in our ranks, Mr. Smailes. Had you decided not to cooperate with our appeal for discretion, then, of course, there would be no offer. But my decision to recruit you was made long before this meeting. The superintendent knew it was one reason I wanted to see you today, although he was reluctant to see you leave CID."

Smailes looked across at Dearnley, who gave a grudging nod.

"It is you who would be doing us the favor, not the reverse."

"I appreciate the thought. But I don't think so."

"Why not? You acknowledge that our work is necessary. I can quite appreciate your anger, but please say you'll take a few days to think about it."

"It's not that. I don't think I've got the stomach for it."

"Detective Sergeant Smailes, you were exposed to more in one weekend than most officers experience in an entire career. Don't you realize that? And you dealt with it quite brilliantly. Not to mention your uncanny understanding of what transpired here. I'll be here until Wednesday afternoon. Will you call the Cambridge Arms and let me know your decision?

383

I'll also be available to discuss the position further, if you wish. Whatever your decision, I am immensely grateful for your contribution to this operation, for your courage and maturity. And as I said when you first came in, I too owe you a sincere apology. You are a credit to your country, Sergeant Smailes." Standiforth rose and shook his hand, which Smailes grasped weakly, suddenly embarrassed.

"Okay," he said meekly.

Smailes had risen to leave, but Dearnley stopped him. "You're still welcome here, Derek, if you want to reconsider." He looked at him searchingly, then added, "And, Derek, there was no reception over that bloody remote."

"I know it, George. Let me think about it."

He tried to keep his face straight as he left the office, walked past Gloria and out to his car. But as he entered the parking garage he let out a whoop and punched the air. Of course he knew they were buying him off. He also knew he had them, both of them. He could do anything he chose. New York!

He removed the ashtray from the dashboard and reached down across to the steering column and fished around for the alligator clip, which he released carefully with his thumb and forefinger. He retrieved the tiny transmitter slowly, tossed it in the air, caught it, and put it in his pocket.

Epilogue

KIM PHILBY steadied himself against the corner of his desk and sat down heavily in the swivel chair. He was already well over his self-imposed allowance, but whiskey was the only analgesic he trusted. He stared glassily at his rows of shelves, which comprised one of the largest private libraries in Moscow. Most of the books had been Guy's thoughtful bequest; God knows where he had got them all. Good old Burgess, dreamer and degenerate, had had the stoutest heart of them all.

He swiveled to face his desk and felt a sudden wave of nausea. The report on the two deaths lay in front of him, stark in the finality of its implications. The sketchy information from Veleshin about the first death had been confirmed by the report in *The Times*, although the laconic news item was undoubtedly a smoke screen thrown by London Centre. The terminal condition was an unquestioned fiction, a script

385

for the melodrama of the exit. The obituary had added nothing. The predictable salutes in *The Times*'s baleful understatement. Yet he had come so close.

Conrad's cover had undoubtedly been blown, which the intelligence of the second death only confirmed. It shook his faith in his old friend's infallibility. A graduate student and a provincial policeman, it seemed, had succeeded where a legion of professionals had been defied. It was cruelly ironic. The work, of course, was largely complete and the damage control would be nothing more than an exercise in rage and anguish. Would the Americans learn? For that matter, would the British cabinet?

He wondered about the settlement of Conrad's estate. He had once personally supervised considerable disbursements into a numbered account in Zurich. Wasn't there a married son somewhere, in South America? He considered a recommendation for action, then smiled grimly at the futility of his authorship of any further initiatives.

That the report had arrived from Veleshin was an eloquent statement of the disposition of the case. Suslov, the ideologue, had died in January and in the power struggle that had ensued Andropov had prevailed. Now in May he was poised to vault over Chernenko into the second secretary's office at the Central Committee. Physically, the distance between the Lubianka and Old Square was five hundred yards; politically and psychologically they were a continent apart. The chairman could shed the darkness of his KGB association and present himself as a party loyalist and statesman as Brezhnev's health sank further. No doubt deals had been cut with the military leadership that would ensure the succession, and the extinction of Conrad's intelligence would not weigh against the scale of his career achievement. The report from Veleshin was the chairman's farewell, his reminder that since Painter's mission had been his construction, the blame would rest with him. Reorganization would be deferred, it seemed, since Fedorchuk, the crusher of Ukrainian dissent, had been summoned to succeed Andropov, leaving Gryslov and all the others at First treading water. That Veleshin's career would also be eclipsed was cold comfort, since when the succession finally came, there would be no acclaimed return from retirement, no historic appointment of the first non-Russian head of the First Chief Directorate. But he had come so close.

The Moscow spring had been cold and the radiator was pouring out its customary suffocating heat. He raised himself with difficulty to crack the casement further and caught the reflection of his face in the dark panes. As he stared at the pale features he found himself reviewing the emotions he felt at the news of the second death.

She had been young and untried, and perhaps he was guilty of nostalgia, the affliction of age, for a response with such obvious risks. But he had known risks in the field as a young man in Austria and Spain, and nothing, nothing had ever matched the exultant thrill of the experience. He had offered an opportunity, that was all, which had failed. She would have died hereafter.

Remorse or grief? Contrition or pride? He eased himself slowly back into his chair and acknowledged that he was a stranger to all of these, except perhaps pride. He was after all the master spy of modern times, decorated and lauded, while Conrad had gone unsung to his grave, his secrets buried with him.

Above all, he felt a profound weariness. He was old now and tired, and knew he would not live to see the course of history fulfilled, a history that would vindicate him, that would vindicate them all.

He drained his whiskey in a single gulp and reached again for the bottle.

Britain's Prime Minister closed the report from Sir Keith Bowman and placed it carefully on her rosewood desk. Martin Gorham-Leach's unfortunate death now made it unlikely that the Cambridge team could consolidate its discoveries before its work was overtaken by the Americans. It was a tremendous disappointment, having come so close, but hopefully British industry would still share some of the spoils. There were recommendations for further posthumous honors for Gorham-Leach, which she saw no reason to refuse. Men of such commitment were an example to all others in his profession who continued to emigrate abroad in such profusion.

She was less concerned about the loss of expected prestige. Since the unforeseen opportunity had arisen over the Falklands her popularity had soared. It seemed the Argentine generals were now getting cold feet and were ready to settle; at least, that was what her Defense Secretary in Washington had told her. She was not interested in a settlement. She would sink that battleship at the first opportunity. The British people wanted victory, and she would stop at nothing less. Then she would call an election, in which she would be unbeatable. She was already being called the most resolute national leader since Churchill. And, by golly, she'd show the world she was.

About the Author

Tony Cape is a graduate of Cambridge University's Fitzwilliam College. He now lives outside New Haven, Connecticut, and is at work on his second novel.

BOOKMARK

The text of this book was composed in Janson type by Berryville Graphics Digital Composition, of Berryville, Virginia. The display type is a reverse image of Trump Mediaeval, composed by Zimmering Zinn & Madison, Inc., of New York. It was printed and bound by Berryville Graphics. The typography and binding design are by Paul Randall Mize.